About the author.

Ron McIntosh was
He emigrated to Ca
in 1967.
Retired in 1998 he spends his time writing short stories and poetry.
He and his wife live in Calgary, Alberta.

This is his first novel.

To my friend Gordon

Ron McIntosh

WHISKY DOLLIES

WHISKY DOLLIES

by

Ron McIntosh

CENTRAL PUBLISHING LIMITED
West Yorkshire

Paperback ISBN 1 903970 29 6

**Published
by**

Central Publishing Limited
Royd Street Offices
Milnsbridge
Huddersfield
West Yorkshire
HD3 4QY

www.centralpublishing.co.uk

This story is very loosely based on an actual occurrence.

Whisky Dollies

CHAPTER ONE

The house was full of people dressed in black and speaking in whispers. Rode sat in a corner of the room which served as a living room and kitchen, hoping they would all go home. It was nice of them to come to the house following her father's funeral, but she wished to be alone.

She rose from the old leather chair that had been her father's pride and joy. It smelled of him and seemed to have the contours of his body embedded in the seat and arms. She walked over to the tray with small cakes and sandwiches that old Marda had made, and went round the room offering them to the guests, hoping, that by doing so, they would decline and say it was late and that they should go. Some did, but a few stayed on, talking about the life that had been taken to the arms of the Almighty. Rode could not order them to go as they were villagers who had known her father longer than she had herself.

At last all the mourners left and Rode went through the routine of clearing up the food and dirty dishes, as she had done so many times before. Tonight her brain was not functioning too well, so the task was left unfinished and she went to bed.

Next day the house was very still. Some guests had returned, but just briefly, to see how she was coping. Rode was now alone in the dark and solemn house, a house that had never changed for as long as she could remember. It was a simple dwelling consisting of the main room and two tiny bedrooms. The furniture was sparse and, except for her father's chair, plain. The once ornate tiled floor had seen better days, as the tiles were chipped and those in front of the living room door well worn. All those years she had cared for him throughout his lengthy illnesses. He had contacted diabetes many years before, and, although encouraged by his daughter and friends, would not go to see a doctor.

Over the years his condition had worsened, while, unknown to everyone including himself, his heart suffered. He had had many strokes during the last few years of his life, but had steadfastly refused to have a doctor to attend him. All this time, Rode had patiently looked after him, suffered his many moods and insults and prayed with, and for, him while he was in pain.

Her mother had died giving birth to her and there were no other children. So Rode had never had anyone to turn to or love her. She was aware that her father cared for and loved her; however, he was unable to communicate his love.

Romance had never been a factor in her life either, although many boys had asked for dates. Caring for her father had robbed her of that part of growing up. Being an avid television watcher, especially of the American soaps, she was well aware of what was missing in her life.

Her favourite was General Hospital, which she watched every day if she could. The character she identified most with was Emily Quatermaine who, like herself, was quiet, kept things to herself and was motherless. Friends said she resembled Emily in some ways.

Now that her father was gone, she could do what she wanted, get on with her life. At twenty-two she was free. Free at last, but to do what? What did she want to do? Her father had left her a little bit of money and the house, but homes in their small Mexican village were never sold. They were left to next of kin. No one bought them so they had no value.

The next morning the hot Mexican sun was blotted out by dark thunderclouds threatening an impending storm. Rode awoke with more questions in her head than answers, yet determined to find out about her future. She would visit Father Acquilienta, her priest, and ask his advice. "Yes, that is what I will do," she heard herself say out loud as she dressed in her best clothes. She was free but she did not feel free as she put on the same sombre clothes that she always wore to Mass. In her head she could still hear her father from his bed: "Now Rode, you are going to the House of the Lord, so dress respectfully. The Lord God needs obedience in all things from all who visit His house."

She smiled at the memory, and yet tears came into her eyes as she remembered her Father's face. The tears multiplied until she could hold them back no longer. She flung herself on the bed and cried and cried. Cried for all the years of her own and her father's suffering, cried for all the parties missed, all the romances that had probably passed her by. She cried until it seemed that there was nothing left within her and that her body had been cleansed, dry and empty. Rode stayed indoors that day and watched the rain teem down in a typical Mexican storm. There was a lonely feeling in the pit of her stomach.

"Come in, Rode. Sit." Father Acquilienta smiled as he ushered her to a wooden stool in front of his kitchen fire. The fire was low, as it was not lit for heat but to put his visitors at ease. Glowing embers seemed to have a calming effect. It always worked as it did at this moment for Rode. Many hundreds before her had also stared at that fire.

"That was a good turn out for Senor Benetino's final farewell. He is now in God's safe hands and free from pain. So many people, he was much loved, as are you, Rode. Now then, what can I do for you?"

"Father, what will I do with my life?" Her heart started pounding against her breast as she spoke. "What is to become of me?"

Father Acquilienta listened but said nothing, as he settled into the only available chair.

Rode looked at the room. She had never been here before, although she had been coming to Mass at this church every day for as long as she could remember. It was very spartan and the furniture looked old and worn. So too did the priest. A cat sat on a small carpet square in a corner.

"Where am I to go? I have no relatives and I do not want to stay in the village, not with all the memories inside me. Yet I have nowhere to go." She sat in silence and stared at the fire.

Father Acquilienta said nothing. The only sound was his Grandfather clock in the alcove next to the fireplace. Its tick seemed to get louder as the silence between them lengthened. Rode looked at her priest. He seemed to be lost in prayer or asleep, so she carried on.

"My Father left me some money so I do not need help in that regard. Also I think I would like to travel and see other villages and towns. What do you think, Father? " She looked over at him again. His eyes were still closed. Had he fallen asleep, she wondered?

The priest was not asleep. He had discovered many years ago, having read it somewhere, that if he stayed silent and pretended prayer or sleep, then people in trouble would answer their own questions. All he had to do was wait.

"Do you think that is wise, Father, to travel?" Rode asked. "I cannot drive a car and I have never been outside this area. I know I should be frightened to go, but I'm not. Is that the right attitude to have? Perhaps it is. It is decided then. I will go to the city and see what happens."

There followed a pause as she thought things out in her mind. The priest said nothing.

"Where will I stay? I know no one in Cuernavaca." She went quiet again, listening to the tick of the clock.

Rode jumped and almost fell off the stool as Father Acquilienta suddenly said, "Rode, my child, it is God's will that you come to me today." Not noticing her start, he went on. "My sainted sister Rosita, who lives in Cuernavaca alone, has two days ago fallen and broken her leg. I'm sure I speak for the Lord when I tell you that you should journey to Cuernavaca and live with my sister until she is well enough to look after herself again. It will also give you time to contemplate your future."

Before travelling to the city of Cuernavaca by bus she sent her father's leather chair round to the priest with the message: "My father, I know, would approve of you having this. Please accept it for all the years of love you gave to him and me."

Rode knew that she would never return to the village, but what lay ahead?

CHAPTER TWO

"Time, gentlemen, please," the Publican of 'The Wee Dram' public house shouted the time-honoured phrase.

"Okay folks that's it, everybody out." He was getting just a little bit annoyed with the last of the evening crowd's reluctance to leave the premises.

Katie Docherty rose from the small round table, which was laden with empty glasses and dirty ashtrays, and tried to lift her companion Dougie with her. He was a big chap, heavily built with a strong handsome face. She liked to see that in the faces of the men she took to her bed, and Katie had taken quite a few.

"C'mon Dougie, we'll go to my place, eh?"

"Aye, aye, whatever you say, luv."

She linked her arm in his and they staggered out into the cold damp streets of Edinburgh. Her place, a small flat on South Street, was just a few minutes away. They swayed gently as they walked in silence through the old sombre streets of the city that she loved.

Her tenement building was on a quiet street just off one of the busy thoroughfares that had cinemas, theatres and shops. Her street could have been called 'Tenement Street' as every building was very nearly alike, dark grey from centuries of being covered in dirt and grime.

Amidst this background the doors of each building beckoned their respective families home to their comfort and peace, in a strange way. Their gleaming brass nameplates with bell-pulls for each name stood out like beacons lighting the way homeward.

Each tenant took turns to polish the plates and that morning it had been Katie's turn. As she and Dougie stepped inside the building, Katie rubbed the plate with her coat sleeve to remove a handprint.

They climbed the stairs in silence, their feet echoing up the stairwell. Dougie was not used to the steps which were worn from millions of feet, and in his condition slipped a few times. Katie held on tightly.

On the first landing a lamp flickered on and off, as it had done for several weeks. Not repaired yet, thought Katie as they passed and went on up to her flat on the second floor. Here there were two doors with more gleaming brass plates, letter slots and, in the top centre of each door, a large brass knocker. It seemed as if the tenants were in competition to see who could outdo the other with ornate knockers.

Arriving inside, Katie took off Dougie's coat, saying, "Away ye go to the loo, honey. Wash your hands and face. I don't want you falling asleep on me too soon, right?" and poked him in the side with her elbow. "You'll find a pair of pyjamas in there, put them on, there's a good lad."

Although she was only twenty-five years old, Katie seemed much older to all the men in her life. She acted like a mother hen to them. She did not like men that were much older than herself. In her opinion older men were impatient, usually fat and talked far too much about their wives and marriages. No, she did not like older men at all.

While Dougie was spluttering and muttering in the bathroom, Katie slowly got undressed and looked at her body admiringly. She was fairly tall at five foot seven inches, and had nice blonde hair which the guys said suited her fair complexion. Her breasts were the dominant feature of her body. It was her breasts the men liked the most, and it was the fondling of them that gave her the most pleasure. Katie loved the act of sex, thinking it was the most beautiful union between a man and a woman. Money was not the reason, yet most men were generous with their 'donations', as she liked to call them. It helped with the household expenses, however, as the student loan she had been granted was only just enough. But the sheer pleasure she derived from seeing the pleasure she gave to the men was more important. She got into bed naked and waited for Dougie to join her. The bathroom door opened and as he switched out the light he said, "I could only find the pyjama jacket, no pants."

Katie giggled, as it always puzzled her men folk. It gave her a small sense of power over them.

He jumped into bed clumsily, and started fondling her with his strong labourer's hands, all covered in cuts and scratches. Katie, for the first few minutes was in heaven. Slowly, however, she noticed a change come over him. His hands that had started off softly caressing were now getting stronger and starting to hurt her. He was taking her nipples in his hands and squeezing hard. So hard that she let out a cry. "Stop! You're hurting me."

"Shut up and let me do my thing," he growled.

"No, Dougie, please, you are being too rough with me."

At that he raised himself and punched her hard across the face. "Just shut up slut, and lie still."

She started to struggle and again he punched her, this time giving her a bleeding nose. She tried to get up, saying, "No, Dougie! I don't want violence so just do it and then get the hell out of here."

Katie then lay back and did not say another word. The night was a long one. Every time she tried to get out of bed he hit her and continued his rough and coarse treatment of her. Thankfully, daylight came and he got up and dressed.

"I'll be back tomorrow night. Be here," he said. "Or else."

Her face was a sorry sight as she peered groggily into her bathroom mirror. Her eyes had blue and green bruises where he had hit her. Her top lip was swollen and puffed over the bottom lip, giving an appearance of having no mouth at all. Blood had seeped from her nose and hardened, making breathing difficult.

She started the painful task of bathing the wounds and applying make up and powder around the eyes, making them appear half decent. Then she brushed her long golden hair. This gave her so much enjoyment, brushing her hair. It always calmed her, and made her reflect on the day that had passed, and the day ahead. Whenever troubles made her uneasy, she would pick up her hairbrush.

She looked at the clock. Ten thirty. Too late to go to the Business College where she was in her final year of a Business Administration Course. It had always been a dream, to run her own business. What kind of business, she did not know, but it would have to be a business where she could meet and talk to people. People seemed to like her and think she was fun to be around.

Breakfast was a farce as she was unable to eat anything or even find her mouth. It felt as if she had been to the dentist.

Katie had never been at home at this hour of the morning so the sounds outside her door were new to her. The young mother from upstairs was going out with her baby, who cried at every bump the carriage made on its way downstairs. What was the baby's name? Hamish. Such an old-fashioned name that had gone out of favour. Poor kid, she thought, going through life with that name.

Then silence again, until the old man from across the hall, Mr Prentice, coughed and hacked his smoker's cough all the way out of the front door.

I can't sit here and mope all day, she thought, so she dressed and went out shopping. Even with a scarf around her face she found people staring at her. Their looks seemed to say, 'Serves her right, all those men!' After last night's episode maybe they are right thought Katie. It had not occurred to her until now that because she enjoyed the sexual attentions of men that others would not see it the same way. The thought made her shiver.

She climbed the stairs back up to her flat with great difficulty as her body had now started aching. Delayed action no doubt, she guessed. Then she heard it. Her phone was ringing in the flat. She struggled to hurry, fumbling for her key, stumbled through the door, and picked up the phone sending the cradle crashing to the floor.

"Hellob." Her voice came painfully through closed lips. No answer. "Hellob, who's dere?"

"Me." The voice was low. "Remember our date tonight? You had better be nicer to me this time."

Katie's heart missed a beat. It was him again. What he had said to her this morning, she had taken no notice of, and had forgotten. She started to tremble as he had started speaking again, his voice now louder.

"If you're not nice to me, and you know what I mean, then you will never be able to look at another man again."

Her breath came out in gasps in time with her fast heartbeats. She was unable to speak.

"See you later, sweetie, be nice." He hung up.

Katie dropped the phone on the floor and sat, or at least fell into a chair. Was this happening? She shook her head trying to clear her thoughts. She had never believed he would come back until now. Now she was scared.

What do I do? Who can I ask for help? Should I call the police? No, that would not be a good idea with her previous track record. Don't panic, lass, think, be sensible. Maybe he's simply trying to scare you. If he is, he is succeeding, she thought. He's trying to get even for my non-compliance last night and has no intention of returning. No, I have had other men, she told herself, who had not been completely satisfied, but they had not done this; that is, threatened her. No, there was nothing to worry about.

Keeping busy was what she had seen people do in the movies, so she got up and busied herself around the flat, making the bed, doing dishes, making a late lunch. But however hard she tried she could not get his voice and threats out of her head. Over and over she heard him say: 'Be nice, remember'.

Picking up the phone, she called her friend Maisie, who lived in the flat next door. Katie had thought of asking Maisie, sometime in the future, to be a partner in any business venture.

"Hello, Maisie, Katie. Can I pop over for a cup of tea and chat if you're not too busy?"

"Sure thing. What happened to your voice?"

"I'll be there in a minute." She dabbed more powder around her eyes and went next door.

"Katie, whatever happened to you? Oh, my goodness, love, come on in and sit yourself down. I'll go and put the kettle on."

Maisie was a tall skinny redhead who ate practically nothing as she harboured ambitions to be a model.

"It's a long story, Maisie, and that cuppa will go down a treat."

Katie told her the story, remembering that Maisie did not know of her sexual activities. She told it as if it were an isolated incident.

"Why didn't you go to the polis, Katie? You should charge this bugger with assault, sexual assault maybe, or even rape. No, you cannae dae that, you invited him, didn't you?"

"Yes, yes, I did and I don't want to go to the police. All that fuss and bother, and in the end it will turn out that I am the guilty party. No, I want none of that."

"Nonsense." Maisie said indignantly, "It's done all the time. It's high time these slime, who think they're God's gift to women, get what they deserve. Oh shit, there's the phone, I'll no be a minute." She trotted through to the kitchen.

Katie heard her shout back, "It's Mum, shan't be long." The conversation, Katie was sure, was the story Maisie had just heard.

Their voices droned on in the next room. Maisie was right, of course, about the Police but Katie did not want Maisie to know her past. Her thoughts started to wander and she fell into a deep sleep.

It was six-thirty when she awoke in a now dark room. She got up slowly and walked toward the kitchen door. Voices could be heard from inside the kitchen. The moment she went to open the door and call out, she heard Maisie saying, "What is she like, this new girl friend of yours?"

"Och, I dinna ken too much about her yet," replied a man with a low gruff voice. Katie was poised with her arm in the air, transfixed by what she had heard. It was Dougie in there, in Maisie's kitchen.

"I only met her last night, Maisie," the man went on. Katie listened but the words were hard to hear for the beating of the blood in her head. "We slept together last night, but she was not very accommodating, I'm afraid."

Katie's brain was in turmoil. What was he doing here? Did he know Maisie?

" I don't wish to know your love life," Maisie answered. "Are you seeing her again?"

"Yes, I have a date tonight; in fact, in about an hour's time."

That was all Katie needed to hear, so with every part of her body trembling, she tiptoed across the room and, turning the outside door handle as noiselessly as she could, crept out into the hall.

Scampering back to her flat she did not put the light on but as quietly as possible collected her handbag and the tin box that held all her personal papers. Putting on her warmest coat she left the room, then remembered at the last minute to hurry back and get a scarf to cover her face. She took one last look at the place that had been home for the last three years, ever since she had left home in Falkirk to come to the college in Edinburgh. Her parents had died in a car crash about fourteen months ago. There were so many memories, in this flat. She shrugged and left.

Reaching the outside, Katie ran and ran until the tenement building was out of sight. Looking around, she found herself in a busy thoroughfare with bright neon signs, so she stepped into a doorway and draped the scarf around her face, as if returning from the dentist. Pulling her hat down over her eyes she surveyed herself in the shop window. Satisfied at last with her appearance she set out walking. While she had been running away, the decision had been made to leave Edinburgh and go to London. It had always been a desire of hers to see the big city and the bright lights. This was her chance. Now, having calmed down, she made her way to a bank machine to draw out some money. But the fears and thoughts came back and she started to cry. Did Maisie know about Dougie and her? Had she been aware of what had happened last night? Why, Maisie why? I thought you were my friend. Some friend, she thought, as the tears streamed down into the scarf.

She fumbled for her bank card and some jerk passing said, "I cry too, when I take out money, 'cause I ain't got none, ha!"

Six hundred pounds was all that there was. She decided to draw out three hundred for now. It was then she remembered that she was carrying the tin box, containing her birth certificate and insurance papers. Stuffing the papers into a coat pocket, she left the box beside the bank machine. Now there was nothing in her hands, making her reflect that she had left all her clothes behind. New ones would have to be bought as soon as she reached London.

Off to the railway station she went, asking herself, 'Am I over-reacting to what happened? Should I not stay and go to the Police? No, I might meet up with them in the future and then what? Yes, I am doing the right thing, leaving town.'

Having convinced herself, she set out for the station with a spring in her step.

Arriving there she purchased a one-way ticket; however, the train did not leave until eleven twenty that night. That left about three or four hours to pass. Most passers by kept staring at her face, so she dodged into a drug store and bought herself a pair of sunglasses.

There was a cinema inside the station that showed films twenty four hours every day, continuously, so she decided to go there. It smelled of popcorn and the floor was covered in the stuff and spilled coke, causing her shoes to stick with every step she took. She hobbled to a seat like a person with a limp. There were only two other people there. The movie was a typical British comedy, but she was in no mood for laughter. She did however, see the funny side of the situation. Here she was with two other patrons watching a comedy where all the stars were laughing their heads off. Yet there was complete silence in the theatre.

While she sat in the dark with her thoughts, she could not know that Maisie was kissing her brother, Walter, goodbye as he went off to meet his new girl friend, Lisa. Maisie was left wondering what had happened to Katie, as the teapot was still full, but stone cold.

The station was quiet and empty as Katie left the theatre, as if all the workers and the public had just abandoned it and gone elsewhere. Surprisingly, though, the train was quite busy. However, she did manage to get a window seat. She had nothing to read.

"Blast it," she thought. "It's going to be a long six-hour journey."

As the train hurtled through the darkness, taking her to her new life, she noticed a young man across the aisle. "Hmm," she thought. "He's nice. I wonder what his body is like?"

Katie would never have had such thoughts had she known that, at that precise moment, Dougie had kicked in her door and was trashing her flat yelling, "I'll get you for this, you little tramp. Just see if I don't"

Maisie was next door, huddled against the intervening wall calling the police.

CHAPTER THREE

Rode's bones ached as the little dust-smeared bus, with passengers crowded in like animals, creaked and bumped to a halt at the Estrella de Oro Bus Station on the Avenida Morelos. Where could everyone be going? Rode wondered. There seemed to be more people on the bus than were in her village back home. She smiled a wry smile. Home, where was home?

As the bus pulled up at the edge of the sidewalk, there was a line of people waiting to get on. There seemed to be as many outside as there were inside. She noticed old women with sacks, with who knew what inside. Little children were pulling at the skirts of the women. There at the back of the line up was a young couple who were obviously tourists. They wore shorts and their skins were pure white. Quite a number of youngsters who had been peddling their *C*hiclets and chewing gum were also there, tired after their long day of selling in the city streets.

The Priest had told her to look out for Manuel, a small, large-bellied man with a distinctive bushy beard, who would take her to his sister's place. Rode saw him as he craned his neck to see from behind the line of waiting passengers.

Although Rode had seen him, she decided to wait until all inside the bus had gone, as she knew that as soon as she disembarked a new life would begin. She was not sure why, but at that instant she wanted to hold on to the old life.

"Are you Rode Benetino?" the small man asked in a strange falsetto voice, belying his appearance, as he poked his head around the bus door.

"Yes, and you must be Manuel," she said, collecting her Portmanteau.

"Is that all the luggage you have?" he asked, eyeing her one suitcase.

She nodded, feeling rather sad. All the years of her life in one bag. Manuel read her thoughts, and his voice was full of compassion as he said, "I have a car around the corner, Miss, if you will follow me, please." He smiled and gently took her arm. Rode warmed to him immediately and wondered if she would meet him after getting settled in. "Senora Roha's house is about ten minutes drive from here"

Rode sat in the back seat, as she was not sure what to do. She was a single girl in a stranger's car. She watched through the window as he drove her north through the main square, which he informed her was called The Zocalo. The buildings were magnificent, like those she had seen on travel programs on television. Those had been her favourite shows.

"Have you been here before, Senorita? Manuel asked while driving, and before she could answer he went on, "Cuernavaca means ' Place at the edge of the Forest' but is more commonly known as the City of Eternal Spring."

"Why is that?"

"Because of the plentiful flowers and the gentle climate. Our most famous landmark is the Palacio de Cortes, built in the year fifteen hundred, or somewhere around that time."

" Will we pass it on our journey to Senora Roha's house?"

"No, but anyone can tell you where it is."

He drove her through a maze of streets, all the time honking the car horn which made her smile, as it sounded like a duck. All the other cars were honking as well, so the streets were full of noise.

It was now dark and the heat of the day had turned to the mellow warmth of the evening. It was a pleasant change, she thought, after that hot bus trip.

Suddenly, the car jerked to a halt and she was sure she heard Manuel curse under his breath as the engine seemed to die.

"We are here, Senorita. Wait until I open the door." He jumped out and came round her side to let her out. "Let me take the suitcase for you. Go on inside," he said pointing to a fairly large stuccoed house, which had a small plaza with a dried up fountain at the front. A circular driveway with cascades of flowers everywhere gave the house an appearance of being well cared for.

"Good," thought Rode. "We both seem to share the love of gardening." She was warming to Senora Roha already.

Rosita Roha had been a widow for about seven years. After having been married for forty-one years she missed her husband every day of her new life. It was how she came to break her leg, in fact. He had been a banker and while she was visiting his bank the other day she had been daydreaming about the times he must have climbed up and down those same stairs. She had been coming down them when she was jostled and fell about four or five steps.

It had made her feel quite foolish, for she had been coming here every month since her husband's death to collect her cheque from his estate, and had always negotiated them safely. If only her thoughts had not been elsewhere, then she would be fine today. However, at the age of sixty-six, her bones would not heal quickly and she had caught an infection from somewhere. So here she was in bed, her leg in a plaster cast. The doctor had warned her to stay in bed, and not to try to walk on the leg for at least four weeks, and then only sparingly.

Phoning her brother, the Priest, had not been much good. He could not come to see her, but said that this young girl, Rode Benetino, had lost her father recently and needed some solace. Rosita remembered her brother's words very clearly. "God, in his infinite wisdom, has found the means to bring you two together. If you know what I mean?"

Indeed she did. The inference was not lost on her.

Although married for a long time, she and her husband had had no children. A daughter had been lost through 'crib death' many years ago. Her name had been Carla.

Rosita was thinking of her brother's words as she turned to look at the Crucifix in the alcove on her bedroom wall that had lovingly been made by her husband when they had first come to this house. Silently she recited a prayer of thanks. Her brother, she thought, was very wise. He knew the power of prayer. One of his favourite phrases was: "God gave us the power of prayer. He hears our prayers. It just takes Him a while to answer, sometimes."

Rode and Rosita took to each other immediately. Rode had found the mother she had never known while Rosita had found the daughter that she had lost years before.

Both of them poured their unspoken love out to each other in having similar interests, especially the gardens. Rode was expert in growing and tending the vegetables, while Rosita's love was always the flowers.

Rosita had the cast removed from her leg after eight weeks and spent the next couple of months hobbling about with a cane. This cane, which Rode had bought for Rosita's birthday, was now a permanent fixture, as her leg would not heal properly.

Rosita's spirits were high, nevertheless, as Rode had brought a ray of sunshine into her lonely life. She was a joy to have around as everything in the house appeared new to her. She had never seen things like carpets or kitchen gadgets. Rosita was immersed in Rode's wonderment.

Although the new life that Rode now enjoyed was new and exciting, it was still a life of service. The main differences, of course, were the surroundings and the fact that she was very much appreciated.

'The Cottage', as Rosita and Manuel called it, had about an eighth of an acre of land nestling at the foot of some low-lying hills. It was a large house by the local standards, having three bedrooms, two bathrooms and a spacious farm-style kitchen. The name 'Cottage' was a complete misnomer now, but in the old days it had been a house on what was once a large estate owned by a Spanish nobleman. He had lost interest in it after the Revolution and returned to Spain, selling off the estate in lots.

Twice a month, Manuel would drive them both into the city where they would visit Rosita's bank. Afterwards all three would have lunch in one of the many restaurants that seemed to abound in Cuernavaca.

Rode was convinced that Manuel had a crush on Rosita. They were both about the same age, she deduced, and he jumped at her every request. He was a history fanatic and he loved his city with a passion. This made Rode a little jealous. To have such passion for anything, other than soap operas, was what she desired. Quite often he took Rosita, who had been born in Mexico City, and her, to the beauty spots and famous landmarks of the 'City of Eternal Spring'.

The Palacio de Cortes was the first place he took them. This medieval-style fortress which stands in the Plaza de Armas was a home to Cortes when he was known as the Marquis del Valle de Oaxaca. Also on Manuel's itinerary were the ruined pyramids outside the city and famous homes of the Mexico City gentry.

One morning, at breakfast, Rode seemed nervous and ill at ease.

"What is the matter, my dear Rode? You look troubled. Can I help at all?"

"It is nothing, Mamacita," said Rode, using the loving term only brought out on certain occasions. "I will work it out."

"Work it out? Sounds serious. Please tell me what worries you so."

"I do not want to hurt you, Rosita. I love you too much for that."

"Now that does seem grave." Rosita smiled, but inwardly dreaded the news she knew was coming. "Out with it then, or it will fester inside your brain, and we will all be the worse for it."

"I have been thinking, Mamacita. I cannot live here with you and not contribute some money toward the household expenses. I should really get a job, but I made a promise to your brother that I would take care of you."

"Yes, you did," answered Rosita, "but also it is fitting that a girl of your age would want to go out in the world."

Rode opened her mouth to speak but Rosita held up her hand for quiet.

"No, let me finish. I can look after myself now. It is time for you to have your own life. Have you given any thought as to what you might do, or where you would go?"

Rode sat quietly for a moment before saying, "I was not meaning to leave you here alone. I meant that I would like to continue living here, but get a job, here in Cuernavaca. Is that all right with you?"

The old lady wanted to jump for joy, but speaking in as calm a voice as she could, answered, "Yes, that's fine with me. What can you do? Do you have any special talents? You are a very beautiful young lady, but is that going to help you, I wonder?"

"My favourite TV programs, as you know, are travel shows. Perhaps I could get a job in a Travel Agency."

"What a splendid idea, Rode. We will start looking tomorrow."

So it was that Rode did indeed find a position with a Travel Agency. With her looks, her Christian attitudes, and her charm, she quickly graduated to looking after the travel arrangements for the influential businessmen who were part of the Agency's clientele. At night, after work, she studied hard to learn English. A few months later she graduated, very high in her class. With the permission of Rosita, she was transferred to the Mexico City main office and was given the most influential clients.

As the firm's profits increased due to her business acumen, so, too, did her income until she was one of the highest paid agents. She did not think of herself as a travel agent, however, but more as a personal travel secretary. Her clientele included the top businessmen in Mexico City, some government officials and officials of the church. She rented a fashionable condo in the heart of the city. Weekends and holidays were spent at the house in Cuernavaca with Rosita. Life for Rode was good.

During the next year or so, she was able to travel extensively throughout North and South America seeking out the best hotels and restaurants for her clients. At last she was fulfilling her dreams of travel and on more than one occasion she was able to take Rosita with her. This gave them both the greatest joy.

Rode had one client who used the Agency more than any other, Senor Julio de Valaras Santiago. He was a member of one of Mexico's premier families and his patronage brought great esteem to both the Agency and Rode. He travelled to the most unusual and exciting places, using her expertise and knowledge. She once asked him what he did for a living and he had replied, “Oh, I have a finger in a lot of pies, my dear, most of which you would not want to know about.”

It was Senior Santiago who, while arranging a special trip for himself and some of his business colleagues, had asked Rode to go ahead and check out the hotel at which he intended to stay. As neither he nor Rode had been to this city before, she willingly agreed. After all, her expenses were paid by the Agency.

Before she left, he took her aside and asked her a strange question. Could she check out the nightlife, especially places and phone numbers where men on a business trip could obtain suitable female companionship? She knew what he meant, and flatly refused. After he threatened to take his business elsewhere, she told him that she did not approve of that sort of behaviour. He explained that it was because of her behaviour and her being a good Catholic girl that he was asking. He went on to say that if he was to send one of his own men, they would be told of places that would probably turn out to be squalid little joints. But she would be told of places with more class as befitted his important clients. Places that they were already used to. When she hesitated further, he told her that all she had to do was speak to cab drivers, head waiters and hotel clerks, get a phone number or a name, that was all. She finally relented.

The city that she flew to was Boston, a city in which she felt at home. There were old buildings seeped in history all around, as in Mexico City. The weather, though, was not similar at all. Torrential rain was falling when she arrived and continued during her entire stay. The local Bostonians, however, seemed to take it all in their stride.

Having obtained a room in a very fashionable hotel, close to Back Bay, she approached the hotel desk clerk to ask the question she was dreading, but another customer came to the desk at the same time, so she backed off and waited for the desk area to be clear. Finally the guest departed and the desk clerk disappeared into a back room, and a female clerk came out. Rode became flustered and as she was near the desk, the clerk asked, “Can I help you, Madam?”

“Yes, well, err, I wished to speak with the young man who was just here. Is that possible?”

“Well, he is on a break at the moment. Is it important?”

Rode was about to say “No,” and leave, when the young man appeared.

“I heard the conversation, I will look after the lady, thank you, Trudy. Yes, ma’am, how may I help you?”

Rode took a deep breath, looked around to see if the coast was clear and said in a whisper, "If I was a man. . ."

"Yes, ma'am, if you were a man," he repeated parrot fashion, staring back blankly at her. To him it was just another strange encounter. His life here was full of them.

Rode was now most uncomfortable, but continued, "Where would I find, err, some ladies. I mean... ladies...of the night, so to speak."

"Ladies of the night?" he repeated, rather too loudly for Rode's liking. She looked around anxiously. "Well now," he went on in his monotone voice. "If I understand you properly, you mean women of ill repute," and his voice dropped to a whisper. "Prostitutes, yes?"

Relieved that she was finally getting somewhere, she whispered back, "Yes that's exactly what I mean, but not the street types."

"Ah, now," he said reverting back to his loud monotone. "You should speak with Clancy, the cab driver. You will find him at the cabstand on the corner of sixty-eighth and Mission. I may say, Madam, that I have had many strange requests while at this position, but for someone like yourself to want, well, we will not say what, it does seem very strange indeed. Could you tell me why you require this knowledge?'

At that moment a guest came up to her side and Rode blushed and started to get flustered again, then blurted out, "Another time, perhaps. I will give it to you when we are alone."

Both the desk clerk and the guest exchanged glances, while Rode excused herself and almost ran to the safety of the ladies' room. She sat in the cubicle and tried to calm down, and as the excitement of the encounter subsided, the tears came rolling out. "Oh, forgive me Father, forgive me Mamacita, forgive me Papa." She held the crucifix around her neck, as tight as she could, and vowed never to go through that ordeal again.

A few weeks later, she was preparing to close down for the day. The tickets that her clients would need were all ready for the courier to pick up and deliver in the morning. The phone rang and stifling a yawn she answered, "Hello, this is Rode."

"Miss Benetino, this is Maria, Senor Santiago's secretary."

"Hello, Maria, how are you today, and how are your twins? I always admire the way you keep your very busy position with Senor Santiago and yet manage to run your household as well."

"You admire me, Rode? You are the one to be admired with all the influential people you have at your fingertips. Speaking of that, Senor Santiago, as you know, is leaving the day after tomorrow for London."

"Yes, that's correct."

"Well he wondered, if it is not too much trouble, if you could deliver the tickets to his hotel room this evening. He has a meeting at the *Hotel Krystal* and will stay there tonight and tomorrow night before flying out."

"I don't see why not," said Rode. "Any particular time I should be there?"

"Any time after six o'clock, he said."

"Okay, Maria. Give my love to your husband and family. Buenas noches. "

"Buenas noches, Rode."

CHAPTER FOUR

Niklos Andreas was bored. He had flown into Mexico City from Los Angeles where he had completed the deal for his father. It was his first visit here and he liked what he saw. He lay at the side of the hotel pool, soaking up the sun. Taking off his sunglasses he closed his eyes tight letting the sun pound his eyelids. The searing heat seemed to enter his body and go right to the depths of his soul. It felt good and relaxed him.

Lying on his chaise he recalled playing, as a child, the 'eyes shut' game as he and his pals had called it. He had not tried this for several years so why not now, he thought.

He opened his eyes briefly then closing them tightly he waited until he saw colours emerge in his brain. Concentrating on one colour, normally blue, he would try to create different shapes, circles and squares, then try to enlarge the shape then diminish it. After a few minutes it would disappear altogether and the game would be over.

The Mariachi band playing behind him in the gazebo started to play one of his favourites; the theme from 'Beauty and the Beast' and he opened his eyes. The sharpness of the sunlight hurt as he scrambled to replace his sunglasses. He looked around, feeling rather foolish at playing a game from his childhood. No one seemed to notice his embarrassment. They were all either sleeping or engrossed in their novels. Nikki could never understand why people took books on holiday with them. When he went on vacation, it was to do things differently from 'back home'.

His tall thin body was already quite bronzed. He was pleasant looking, although not what you would call handsome. His most striking feature was his eyes; small and piercing, and when he looked at someone, it was as if he was staring right through them. Most people who knew him tried to avoid looking into those eyes during conversations; they said his stare could penetrate one's soul.

This business he had just concluded for his father had been routine. One of the Los Angeles Mob syndicates combining to deal in ivory smuggling with the Greek 'Company', run by Cicero Andreas, Nikki's father.

It was a mystery to Nikki, this particular brand of the ivory trade that his father dealt in. The 'Company' would send someone to Africa, usually Kenya, to oversee the slaughter of elephants for their tusks. The tusks would then be flown out by helicopter to a deserted

World War II airfield, long since reclaimed by Mother Nature, thence by private plane to Greece.

Once there, the tusks would be covered by alabaster in the form of garden statuary, to look like Gods of Greek Mythology. They were then shipped as works of Greek art to the United States, in this case, Los Angeles, and sold to collectors.

Nikki recognised these 'hiding places' as works of art in their own right, and thought it sad that they would be smashed open for the tusk inside.

These collectors were the same ones that bought stolen paintings and lodged them in vaults and secret rooms, in their expensive mansions. It all seemed silly to him, but those people paid enormous sums for their 'Trophies'.

Anyone could have done the negotiations, he knew, but it had been a sort of punishment, or banishment, inflicted by his father. When it had been completed, Nikki had phoned home to Nicosia and was told that his father was still upset about the 'incident' and that Nikki was to cool his heels for a few weeks.

The 'incident', as his father had named it, had happened about two months earlier. Nikki reflected on the past couple of months.

It had all started in Athens. Nikki had just finished a course of computer programming at a local college and was kicking his heels for a few days before returning home to Cyprus.

His father did not want him to enter the family business of ivory trading, racketeering and gambling, among other things, just yet. That suited Nikki just fine. He did not care too much for Cyprus, but preferred to live in Greece, which he loved.

That particular evening he was sitting in a bar that he usually gravitated to when in Athens. He knew the owner/bartender, Angela, quite well and enjoyed her company and conversation.

About an hour before closing time, Angela asked him to come to the end of the bar as she wished to speak privately with him.

"Yes, Angela, what is it?" he asked.

"Sorry to ask this of you, Nikki, but do you see that heavy-set man at the bar? He's at the fourth seat from us."

"You mean the guy with the felt hat?"

"Yes, him. Well, he has told me that he wants very badly to see me at closing time. I do not know him so I refused. He told me that if I did not agree, he would start a ruckus and destroy my place. I'm so scared, Nikki."

"What would you like me to do, Angela throw the guy out right now?"

"No, no, not that, but perhaps you could stay here until the last, then if he sees you here, he will go away and forget it all. I don't particularly want you to get in a fight, but, well, knowing your background and everything, I thought you might know what to do."

"If I can be of help, Angela, then I will. You have been a good friend to me." Nikki tried to sound brave and confident. However, he looked again at the man she had pointed out. He was six feet four and very heavily built. Much too big for Nikki. He became a little scared.

He looked at the clock; about forty-five minutes to closing. He decided to get some courage inside him so he ordered a few more drinks, which Angela gladly gave him 'on the house'. He asked for the beer to be put in a metal tankard, and not a glass. The tankard, he thought, might make a handy weapon if needed.

As the clock inched towards eleven o'clock, closing time, the room emptied except for Nikki, the big guy and an old man drunk and asleep in a corner.

Nikki walked over to the big guy and said in a voice that he thought was menacing, giving his patent stare, "Are you leaving ,sir? The lady wants to close up and go home."

"Piss off, kid, I'm not going anywhere. Beat it or else."

"Or else what?" asked Nikki grasping the tankard tightly behind his back.

The big guy laughed and stood up. He was slightly taller than Nikki, but much more muscled. "I doubt you want a fight, kid. I'm waiting here to take the lady home. Isn't that right, Angela?"

Angela smile a wan smile, but said nothing. She looked anxiously at Nikki and moved her eyes towards the front door. Nikki got the message.

"I'm waiting for the lady, too," said Nikki, "so we have a stalemate, don't we?"

"What's that?" asked the big guy. "You calling me names, kid? Do you want to settle it here or outside?"

Nikki remembered Angela's eyes darting towards the exit and said, "Outside, I think, I don't want Angela seeing you all bloodied."

"Oh, Nikki, be careful," Angela said, tears welling up in her eyes. "Just forget what I said, go home. What will your father say, if he finds out?"

"Ah, a Daddy's boy," laughed the big guy. "Can't do anything without Daddy?" and as if to encourage Nikki, who seemed to be in doubt about what to do, lunged forward and slapped him hard across the mouth. "Does that do anything, Daddy's boy?"

"Outside, now!" hissed Nikki, ushering the guy to precede him. He did not want him to see the tankard. The big guy went ahead towards the door laughing as he did so.

Now Nikki had been in fights before but they were of the schoolboy-cum-boxer type of fights. This was not what was needed now, he thought, so he tried to recall what his father's thugs did to other thugs. He had seen them fight often, unknown to his family.

The big guy turned and faced Nikki as soon as they were outside. Nikki was not quite ready and he took a heavy left hook to the side of the head which dropped him to the ground. Dazed he started to get to his feet, but as he did, he took the big guy's foot full in the back of his head, once more knocking him to the ground. Nikki lay there with his eyes closed trying to clear his head. The big guy thought that Nikki was unconscious and came over to stand above his victim. Nikki heard his deep breathing and, gripping the tankard as tightly as he could, he leapt to his feet and aimed the beer mug directly at the face with as much force as he could muster. It hit the big guy right between the eyes. He let out a yell and as the blood spurted from his head he slumped to the ground unconscious.

Nikki's heart was pounding with exhilaration. He had never had this feeling before, and, to his surprise, he enjoyed it. He looked down at the man to see if he was still alive. Sure that he was, Nikki said slowly and deliberately, "Anyone who messes with my lady friends, messes with me, and nobody better mess with me."

He turned, as he heard a sound coming from the shadows.

"Who's there?" My mind is playing tricks with me, he thought, hearing things that are not there. He listened for a few more minutes, but there was nothing. He left.

A few days later it was his thirtieth birthday. In the morning the phone in his bedroom rang. It was his father summoning him downstairs to the study. His father had a way of speaking, that when he asked you to do something, it sounded like a command that just had to be obeyed. Even the simplest request had an authoritative ring to it. He did not mean to be harsh, although it sounded that way. Many years of ruling over servants, employees and even family had given Cicero Andreas this authoritative air.

"No doubt he wants to give me my birthday present," thought Nikki. The previous year his father had handed him the keys to a brand-new Maserati.

"Ah, there you are, Niklos. Come in, sit yourself down. No, here beside me," he said patting the leather chair next to the large mahogany desk that Nikki thought his father loved more than his family. He spent the bulk of his time behind it.

Nikki sat and looked around the room. There was his mother, and others he knew that worked for the 'Company'.

"Has everyone got a glass? Mama, get a glass for Nikki, good, thank you. Now, Nikki, you have reached the age of thirty. Quite an age, huh? Another decade under your belt, so to speak." So saying he laughed, as he thought he had said something funny. As nobody else was laughing, he stared at the group. As if on cue they all started to titter, Nikki included.

"Niklos, stand up please. I wish to give you, your present." Nikki stood. "What did I give you last year, son? Oh, yes, I recall now, it was the car, right?" Nikki nodded, he was not enjoying this one bit, but he was anxious to know what the gift was. His father might not be the most thoughtful parent, but he was the most generous.

"Well, this year I am giving you an unusual gift and it is in this envelope, here, take it, son, with your Mama's and my blessing." He took a quick look at his wife, saw her expression and turned back to Nikki.

Everyone was smiling, benignly as Nikki took the envelope from his father. "May I open it now, Papa?"

"Certainly, son, go ahead."

Nikki removed from the envelope a bundle of papers. On closer look they appeared to be airline passes, but of a kind that he had never seen before. Also, there were some credit cards, new and shiny. He looked at them and as his brow began to crease in question, his father laughed again and said, "He does not know what he has in his hands. Do you, son?" He paused, as Nikki let his gaze go round the room. They were all beaming at him. They apparently knew.

"What you have in your hand, Niklos, is a set of round the world airline tickets that will enable you to fly anywhere you wish to go. There is also a set of credit cards, each with a maximum amount, enough for even your extravagant spending."

They all applauded, and Nikki smiled. It was a genuine smile as now he understood the generosity of his father. He gave his father a big hug and said his thanks.

Cicero Andreas now cleared his throat and asked all assembled to leave the room. As he did so, he said quietly, "Stay with me please, Nikki. I wish to talk with you."

When they were alone Cicero came over to his son's chair and sitting on the arm said in a deliberate voice, "I understand you had an incident recently, in Athens. Am I right?"

"What do you mean, Papa, an incident?"

"You know perfectly well. You got into a fight with a man in a bar. Now there's nothing wrong in that. I have been in many bar fights myself. This particular man, however, belonged to a group of individuals who would like nothing better than to see me out of business, so to speak. You follow my drift?"

Nikki did indeed! His father, being so powerful, had many enemies, apart from the authorities who were always trying to pin something on him.

"How do you know of the fight? It was such a simple situation."

"You were observed, but that does not matter now. What matters is that the bosses of the man you fought do not know yet who was responsible. It will not take them long to figure it out. That's why I have given you the tickets and credit cards. I want you to take a holiday."

"But I don't need a holiday. What I need is a job. Something to do, to occupy my time."

"You know my wishes are that you should take over from me, but," and here he hesitated, "not just yet. Still, there is something you could do for me." He rubbed his chin, as if thinking. "You could attend a meeting in Los Angeles for me, next month." He then went on to explain the details and Nikki listened fascinated. It was the first time in his life that he had been privy to his father's business.

When Nikki left the Study, Cicero Andreas picked up the phone. "Ask Vlascis to come and see me, it's urgent."

All that had happened two months ago. Why was his father still upset after all this time, and who had observed the fight? Was it the old man in the corner of the bar? . Had it been him? Nikki never asked.

The sun was setting rather earlier than he was used to, so he packed up his white hotel towel and returned to his room. As he was walking down the hallway towards his suite, a door opened beside him and a young lady ran out and bumped right into him. "Perdon, no fue intentsional mente," she uttered, as she fell to the floor. Her handbag and its contents went scattering. She just sat there crying, then, noticing Nikki, said in a quiet voice, "Perdoneme."

"Not at all," noticing as he helped her to her feet, that her blouse was torn, showing a bra partly ripped. Her hair was dishevelled and her makeup was smeared across her face. Tears were streaming from her eyes which were red, as if she had been crying for some time.

"Can I help?" he asked, "You look like you are in trouble."

"No, it is quite all right, thank you, sir. I can manage from here," she replied in English. She touched her hair as if trying to fix it and started to leave, saying, "Thank you again, you . . . " she fainted and fell.

Nikki picked her up and as his room was three doors away, he took her there and laid her on his bed, placing the coverlet over her, to save embarrassment when she woke up. "Boy but she is beautiful," he thought. "What was that language she spoke, Spanish?" He then went into the bathroom and filled the wash hand basin with warm water. Soaking a face cloth and taking a hand towel, he returned to the side of the bed and started to wash her face gently. She awoke and started to shout in Spanish, then changed to English. "No, please, leave me alone, you brute, stop or I'll . . . " She then noticed it was Nikki and sat up and said, "Sorry for that outburst, I thought it was him again."

Nikki left the cloth and towel beside the bed saying, "I am going through to the living room. Feel free to use the bathroom to wash up. There is a dressing gown of mine in the closet, should you wish to put it on." He went away and called room service. "Could you please send coffee and cakes for two to room 1139? Thank you."

Rode lay on the bed motionless. She could not get Senor Santiago out of her brain. As a young girl, whenever she wanted to erase bad thoughts from her mind, she would think of something that she enjoyed.

She now recalled the time her father took her to see Julie Andrews in the *Sound of Music*. When the song '*Raindrops on roses, whiskers on kittens*' was sung she turned to her father and said excitedly, "That's what I do, Papa." He had told her to hush, but was smiling as he said it. At that time in her life, she used to go to bed, close her eyes tight and think about skipping with a rope. She loved to skip, so it was natural to use that as her escape from nasty thoughts.

Now, lying in this stranger's bed, she closed her eyes, very deliberately and thought once more of skipping in the street outside her old home. It would work for a few seconds, but then the scene would change to Senor Santiago's leering face, bulging eyes and his voice, although quiet, rasping. She opened her eyes and jumped out of the bed.

What had the stranger said? Something about a dressing gown. She looked at her blouse, it was beyond repair. Rode opened the bedroom closet, and there squashed between male suits and shirts was a lilac coloured speckled robe. After putting on the robe she washed her face and tidied her hair. Opening the bedroom door she had the feeling that this man must be wealthy to afford to stay in a suite like this. He stood up as she entered.

As Nikki saw her standing there in his dressing gown, he knew at once that she was someone special. She was so beautiful, with her shiny black hair and dark eyes. Small, shy and vulnerable; he wanted to pick her up and squeeze her saying, "Don't worry, I will look after you." Instead he said, "There you are, good. I have taken the liberty of ordering coffee for us. Here, come and sit beside the trolley. Do you take sugar?"

"Thank you," she broke in, "I will help myself. You are so kind."

"Not at all. By the way, allow me to introduce myself. Niklos Andreas, Nikki to my friends."

How formal he was, and kind. Her thoughts strayed to her father, who also had been so polite. He would have liked this young man.

"And you are?" Nikki was asking.

Rode shook her head and said, "What? So sorry, my mind was wandering." She looked at him. "My name is Rode, Rode Benetino. How do you do?"

He inclined his head in a small deferential bow. Her voice sounded like a gentle stream lapping over small stones, rippling and clear. He was mesmerized.

'Why does he stare at me like that? Such a piercing look. Can he see through my clothes?' It seemed as if he could. She started to feel herself blush. 'Stop it,' she told herself. 'You're acting like a silly schoolgirl.' She picked up her coffee cup which had a lovely rose pattern, and seemed to be very expensive china. Refusing the cake he offered she stammered, "No thanks, the coffee is fine." She drunk it down fast and said demurely "May I have another one, please?"

"You like your coffee, don't you? Rode. That's a beautiful name. How do you spell it?"

"R-O-D-E, pronounced Roday," she said, placing sugar and cream into her cup.

"Rode, is that a Mexican name? I am from Greece, well, Cyprus actually."

"Yes, it is Mexican and you are from Cyprus?"

'Am I really talking like this? This is an inane conversation,' she thought.

'This is stupid,' he said to himself, 'I am acting like a young lad who's afraid of girls.' "When you woke up, a few minutes ago, you thought I was someone else. A brute, I think you called me," he smiled.

"I called you that, really?" She returned his smile.

"Well no, not me exactly, but I assume the person or persons you seemed to be running from. I do not know the 'who' but I can guess the 'why' from your appearance. Would you like to talk about it? Some people say it helps. Better than keeping it inside the head, they say."

"I'm not sure," she hesitated.

"While you think it over, why don't we get you home."

" I cannot go like this."

Nikki viewed with dismay, the remnants of her blouse. "Hmm, no not a good idea. Tell you what, I will go down to the lobby and see if I can get something for you to wear." He got up and as he did so she put her hand on his arm.

"No, please. I cannot allow you to spend money on me. I will ring for a cab and go home and change. Please, Mr Andreas."

"Nonsense! How do you propose to get out of the hotel looking like that? No, leave it to me. I will get you something to hide your blouse." With that he hurriedly left the room and left her staring into space, small tears starting to come into the corners of her eyes. His kindness touched her. They had only known each other for a short time, yet here he was, acting as if he had known her longer.

Outside the room he stopped and hearing nothing from inside, turned towards the staircase down to the lobby. He hesitated, turned around and retraced his steps past his door to the suite that Rode had run out off. Suite number 1141. Yes, that was it. That was the room. He turned and went downstairs.

Reaching the lobby, he went straight to the desk and enquired where he could find the hotel dress shop.

"I am sorry, sir" said the clerk, "the shop is closed for the evening."

"Oh, dear." Nikki replied, "now what?"

"May I help you with your problem, sir?"

"No, that's O.K. But yes, maybe you can. Can you tell me the name of the occupant of suite number 1141?"

The clerk punched the suite number into the computer on the desk. "Yes, that is occupied by Senor Julio de Valaras Santiago. Will that be all, sir?"

"Yes, thank you."

Nikki started towards the stairs wondering what he was going to do about Rode. As he passed a beautiful wine-coloured sofa, he removed the magazine that was there and said, "That will do. I think." Returning to the room, he saw that Rode had brushed her hair and tried to make herself presentable. He thought again how beautiful she was. He vowed that this girl would not get away from him. He would have to see her again and get to know her better. He had heard that love came in the most curious of circumstances. Was this one of those times? He didn't know, but at least he knew he felt peculiar.

He explained about the dress shop and said, "Place this magazine across your chest to hide your blouse. Yes, like that, good. That should be fine. Is that comfortable for you, Rode?"

"I think so. It is not that far to the front of the hotel. I'll manage."

Before leaving the room Nikki picked up the phone and asked for his car to be brought round to the front of the hotel. Then the two of them made their way down to the lobby.

The lobby was very elaborate. It had a white marble floor and the walls and ceiling were entirely mirrored. It was not too busy, as most of the guests would be at dinner. Some excellent jazz music could be heard from one of the bars adjoining the main lobby.

Rode and Nikki made their way slowly, as they did not want to draw attention to themselves. Once outside Nikki looked for his car and saw it approaching the main entrance. Tipping the driver, he whispered to Rode, "Get in the back. There's a blanket on the seat. Wrap it around you."

Rode did as she was told, and then wondered why she accepted orders from this man without hesitation. It had been her intention to go home by cab, now it appeared that he was taking her there. She seemed to like the idea, but thought it very strange behaviour on her part.

"Where to?" he asked her as the car sped away from the hotel.

"Just keep driving and I will direct you when necessary. It is about seven minutes away."

Both their hearts were beating faster than normal; his because he was still with this girl that he found irresistible. He had not wanted her to go home without knowing where she lived. After two months of having a boring holiday and travelling all over, he at last had found not only a place that he liked, but a companion that he could share it with. At least, he hoped he had.

Rode was excited also. For the last couple of years she had been an independent woman, making decisions for not only herself, but also for Rosita. Now this young man had come into her life by accident and had not only taken control of the situation, but also of her. 'What is happening, and what happens when we get to my place?' She had never been in love with a man nor had she ever been on a date. Her life to now had been entirely taken up with her career, and in service to others. This was a new and strange experience.

They both sat silently, and every now and then they would lock eyes in the rear view mirror and hurriedly turn away. Rode gave him directions and they pulled into an underground garage. Nikki got out and opened the rear door. As Rode stepped out Nikki caught a glimpse of delicate pale skin which had become uncovered. She noticed his look and hurriedly pulled at her blouse.

Her flat, which was comfortable without being ostentatious, had many small paintings around the walls, which she told him came form the local Mexico City markets. It had started with a couple, but now it had become a collection.

"I will go into the bedroom and change. I'm sorry but I do not have anything to drink. Can I take you out to one of my favourite restaurants? It will be my treat. It is the least I can do for your kindness."

His mind was not reacting properly. Kindness, she called it, but to him it was falling in love with this beautiful girl. Having admitted it to himself he wanted to blurt it out to her, but instead he calmly said, "I would like that very much." She disappeared into the bedroom and his heart said, 'Go in after her, you dope,' but his mind instead made him shout after her, "You can introduce me to your Mexican cuisine. Since being in Mexico I have dined mainly on things I know and feel comfortable with."

"What kind of food would that be?" she called back from the bedroom.

"Fish mainly, and the good old American Hamburger."

She came out from the bedroom and he whistled as he saw her. She blushed and hurriedly said, "Let's go. You're embarrassing me."

"I mean to, you look very beautiful, Rode. Now let's go eat."

They drove just a few blocks from her flat to a restaurant on the Avenida Madero. The tables were in the courtyard of an old sixteenth century Pueblo tiled house. She ordered a vegetarian plate consisting of ejotes, calabacitas chicharos and chayote, which are string beans, squash/marrow, peas and chayote fruit. He said he would prefer a meat dish, so she ordered pozole, which is hominy and meat stew.

Throughout the meal, which they ate in silence, they stared at each other, both of them wrapped up in their own feelings. Or so they thought. In fact both of them had similar feelings, of a love newly formed and found, but as yet unspoken; a very exciting time for each of them.

After a time he interrupted the spell which had been cast on them by asking, "Do you wish to tell me what happened in the suite next door? Remember you were about to, back in my room."

"Yes, I was, but I don't know if I should." She smiled at him and he put his hand over her hand as it lay on the table, and his eyes said, "Please".

"Well, all right. I am a travel agent with the largest agency in Mexico City, and am responsible for the business travel arrangements for an influential clientele. The best customer I have is Senor Julio. . ." She stopped. "I had better not say his name. So anyway, he asked me to bring his airline tickets for London to his hotel suite, which I did not even remotely think was a strange request. He offered me coffee which I accepted and when we had finished I got up to go. He started telling me that for a few months now he had been crazy for me. Yes, those were his exact words."

"Did you know about this, Rode?"

"No. I knew nothing about it. He had never said or done anything to suggest it."

"Go on," said Nikki, "what happened next?"

"He flung me down onto the couch and started tearing at my blouse, all the time professing his love for me and how much he wanted my body. When I started to wrestle his hands away from my breasts, he switched his hands to my legs and tried to reach up my skirt. At that, I slapped him hard across the face."

"Good girl! Then what?"

"I kicked out at his legs, but I missed, so I ended up pushing him backwards, and as he toppled, I ran out of the room."

"Good for you. I loathe men like that - men who mess about, and force their attentions on women. I have never done it and I hope that I never will."

"Tell me about yourself, Nikki."

"Not much to tell, really. I arrived here from Los Angeles where

I was doing some business for my father. The pace of the place was too hectic for me, I'm used to the slower life in Nicosia. So I decided to go wandering, and here I am."

She smiled and looked at him, and he caught her eyes and said, "I'll pay the bill, Rode. Yes, I know what you said, but let me, please. The age of chivalry is not dead yet."

They drove back to her flat, in silence, both of them knowing that they were in love for the first time in their lives. When they arrived, he went round and opened the door for her, while saying, "Good night, my dear Rode. You must be tired. I know I am, so I'll say goodnight here." He then bent down and kissed her lightly on the cheek.

She was taken by surprise. She had felt sure he was going to invite himself up to her flat; in fact, that was what she wanted more than anything at that moment. She felt cheated a little and could only say lamely, "Yes, I am a bit tired. Thank you and goodnight, Nikki."

One last wave before he sped off into the darkness. 'Would she see him again,' she wondered?

Once in bed her thoughts were only of Nikki. She tossed and turned, patted her pillows about a dozen times and could not get him or her romantic fantasies out of her head. She got up and made herself some hot chocolate, dropping in a couple of Aspirins to help her sleep. Still she could not stop thinking about him. What was he doing now? Was he thinking about her?

Senor Julio de Valeras Santiago was asleep between the pure silk sheets, dreaming of women fawning over him as if in a harem. He awoke with a start as a gloved hand was pressed over his mouth, hard. It was also at that moment that a sense of panic came over him mixed with nausea. He felt something cold and sharp touch his not very large penis. The voice of the gloved hand said very slowly and quietly, "Listen scum, if you mess with young ladies again, you will never be able to have another lady friend. Understand, Senor?"

Senor Santiago nodded his head erratically and he could feel his hot urine trickling onto the sheets below. The sharp thing was rubbing against his manhood smoothly and deliberately, then he felt a scratch. His body went rigid with fear. A cry from a parched mouth was trapped, unuttered, in his throat. Mercifully darkness descended....

CHAPTER FIVE

Rode awoke to the sunlight streaming in through her open window. The curtains were swirling lightly in the warm gentle breeze that is so much a part of the attraction of Mexico. The fragrant smell of flowers filled her nostrils as her brain slowly awakened.

Images of last night and Nikki entered her head immediately. She knew now that she was in love.

Arching her back and stretching in bed, she once again sensed the aroma of flowers. She got up and went to the window. There was nothing there except the quiet little side street that was so familiar to her. No flowers there, then what do I smell? She walked around the flat and saw the torn blouse still on the floor where she had dropped it hurriedly last night.

Still sniffing, she opened the front door and there, blocking the whole doorway, was the largest bouquet she had ever seen. There were over fifty red roses nestling in a large white basket-type vase. The whole ensemble measured four feet from top to bottom.

Clasping her hands together, as a schoolgirl would on receiving a piece of candy, she said out loud, "Whoever?" then, putting her hands to her cheeks as if it had dawned on her said, "Nikki, my sweet, was it you?"

Carrying the bouquet into her flat, she set it down on the floor whilst retrieving the card which nestled in the flowers.

To the girl who has captured my heart.

Must see you again, will call later today

N.

She took a single rose from the vase and caressed it across her cheek, and a tear of joy rolled down into the flower, and glistened there like a raindrop.

The telephone interrupted her thoughts and jarred her back to normality. She ran to the phone. It must be Nikki telling her of the flowers. "Yes, I will see you again," she said as the receiver was lifted.

"Hello, Miss Benetino, Rode?" a man's voice asked, a voice she could not identify.

"Yes, this is Miss Benetino. Who is calling, please?"

"Father Acquilienta. Rode, how are you? I hope you are well."

"Yes, Father, I am very well. How may I help you today?"

"I bring sad news, my dear. My sainted sister, Rosita, passed away yesterday afternoon."

Rode felt the blood drain from her face. "Oh, Father! Rosita! It cannot be."

"Yes, my child. It was not unexpected, though. You know as well as I do that the poison in her leg was getting worse, and her heart was heavy. Is it possible that you can come down here to the house? The funeral will be on Monday."

"Of course, Father, I will come. I need to go into my office and clear up a few things. Then I will drive out this afternoon and be there sometime late this evening. Oh, Father, whatever will we do without her?"

"Pray for her and have faith in the Almighty. Goodbye, Rode."

"Goodbye, Father. See you tonight."

She showered and dressed, then threw some clothes and things into a small suitcase, checked around the flat and left for the Agency.

The travel agency 'Total Travel' was situated in the heart of Mexico City. The staff did not like the location for many reasons, the least of which was the traffic noise, which gave a constant hum all day. The noise was interrupted daily with the blare of sirens and klaxons as the ambulances and police went careering along this avenue.

The inside was half-moon shaped with the receptionist and typists in the centre, and the travel agents in separate offices around the perimeter. Rode had one of these offices and as she entered there was the usual round of 'hellos' and 'good mornings'.

A colleague, Rosanna, came into Rode's office and asked what Rode was doing. Rode explained about Rosita's death and the funeral and told Rosanna that she was taking a few days off and going to Cuernavaca.

Rosanna saw the single rose sniffed it appreciatively, and asked where it had come from. Rode then told her about this man in her life that she had just met. How charming he had been. The telephone rang.

"Hello, Miss Benetino." It was Nikki. "Did you get my message this morning?"

"Yes I did." Without thinking she picked up the rose and held it to her cheek as before. Rosanna touched Rode on the arm, pointed to the phone, then the rose and raised her eyebrows in question. Rode blushed even more and nodded. Rosanna gave a knowing wink and left.

"Rode, are you there?"

"Yes Nikki, I'm here, at least for a little while. I have to leave town today." She heard a gasp from Nikki.

"Why, Rode? I want to be with you."

She went on to explain about Rosita and that she had to go, and today.

"I will drive you," said Nikki in the voice of authority that Rode was getting used to hearing from him. She was, however, still taken aback by his insistent tone.

"Where's your Agency." He was given directions. "I'll pick you up in thirty minutes, but remember I can't park outside. You'll be ready?"

"Yes," she heard herself saying demurely.

He hung up.

He was fed up of waiting. This was his second day watching the house, and nothing had happened. There was nothing to do up here on the hill behind the house, but listen to the birds singing and watch the cattle off to the north gently feeding, then trotting off when the gate opened to let them out. It was also hot. Not the heat that he was accustomed to, but a humid heat that made his clothes cling to his body. Yes, he was fed up.

They had given him a small motor home to stay in, parked down the hill, away from the house and not visible. He was pretending to look like a tourist who was also a bird watcher. That explained the heavy binoculars around his neck.

He was ordered to stay here until either the man or the woman arrived. They may be together, he was told, and if so he was to concentrate on the man.

Thinking of his family back home kept his spirits up. The thought of all the money he was to get for this job had sustained him up to now. He would buy his wife a new coat and his little daughter Magda some shoes and toys. Perhaps the money might give them all a little holiday. If he got the man, yes, as he was promised more for him than the woman.

A car drove up and he lifted the high-powered rifle to his shoulder and looked down the sights. It was a small black car, the kind, he thought, that every Mexican seemed to own. His heart quickened at the thought of the kill. This was what he was born for. The excitement of the kill. His father had been renowned for his prowess with the gun. Before that his grandfather also had been a sharp shooter. All of them hiring out their services.

As he lay on the hot ground, he was proud of his family. Already he had made a name for himself, having already killed several people for the cause, thereby perpetuating the family tradition.

The car stopped and his hand went to the trigger and lovingly caressed it. He gave out a sigh as he saw a priest step out of the car and enter the house. His gaze went to the windows, which were all draped. Back home that meant there had been a death in the house. Was it the same here, he wondered? Is that what the priest is doing here? He had seen no one around, either inside or out. Was that what had happened here, perhaps?

The day wore on and nothing more happened at the house. He was parched dry as in the hot sun he had drunk the day's supply of water. There was enough in the trailer for many days, but he hoped it would not be necessary to use it all. The shadows of evening began around the house and lengthened as the sun sank in the sky, a great orange ball that seemed to be dropping out of sight. He had not been long in this part of the country, but he had witnessed the early sunsets before. Much earlier than at home.

He rolled over to get some feeling in his aching body and then he heard the car approaching. In the gloom he saw that it was a red sports car. This was more promising, he thought. It was the type of car the young man would drive. He raised the gun again and looked down the barrel to see if there was enough light for the kill. Yes, plenty of light. Good, at last I may get out of here tonight.

His fingers went to the trigger and rested ever so gently against the metal. His heart again began beating faster. This was exhilarating. He saw a man and a woman get out of the car. Great! It was them! Careful now, concentrate on the man. The telescopic sights roamed past the woman and came to rest on the man's forehead. He appeared to be asking the woman questions, as his arms were gesticulating. The finger gently rested against the trigger.

The last thought, as his head was blown apart, was of the money and his family. Pieces of his brain went shooting in all directions, while the green leaves of the nearby bush instantly became a glossy autumn red. His body lay in the same position, but was now cold and lifeless.

CHAPTER SIX

"What a lovely place this is Rode. And the setting! The setting is beautiful. A beautiful vista of the river basin and nestled in these rolling hills." He was pointing in all directions as he admired everything around.

"Yes, I fell in love with this cottage as soon as I saw it," whispered Rode. It seemed fitting to whisper, to preserve the ambience of love that enveloped the house and garden.

Nikki wandered off through the paths surrounded with flowers and vegetables of all kinds that Rode and Rosita had planted. Rode recalled the laughter of Rosita, on her knees planting the herbs, flowers and vegetables. After a while she would be unable to stand up, and would start laughing. Rode would then start giggling and together they would try and raise Rosita to her feet. More often than not, it would result in both of them toppling over giggling like little girls. Happy memories indeed! How she would miss her dear friend!

Nikki was excitedly shouting something but she couldn't hear. It was special having him here now although she was not yet sure of her feelings for him.

Rode recalled the time when she had been watching an evening soap opera program on TV, and the young lady in the story was professing her love to a young man. Rosita had scoffed and said that what she should have been professing was her infatuation. Asked to explain, Rosita went on to say that there are certain stages of love.

The first or early stage was infatuation, and not necessarily only between young people. Older people went through the same stages. Infatuation was when, at the first few meetings, desire was the main attraction; not just sexual desire but also the wish to touch, hold or simply stare at one another.

The second stage, Rosita told her, was romance. This was when couples liked being together, enjoying each other's company, learning about one another and doing favours to please and make each other happy. This stage usually lasted, Rosita said, for several years and developed into true lasting love.

This love was strengthened through raising a family or enduring troubled times, but mostly by being together. It became a melding of minds, she had said, a total commitment to each other's needs.

"This is why," Rosita had told her, "that we had the courtship before marriage. If we just got married straight away, then that kind of commitment would not have time to strengthen."

"But what about love at first sight?" Rode had asked.

"Oh, yes," Rosita had answered, "it can happen. But don't call it 'love at first sight' but more like 'Attraction at first sight'. Not a romantic expression you will agree. Love," Rosita went on, "does not need to be two-way. I love my husband Raoul still, even though he is dead, and I know that Manuel next door has loved me for many years. We both are very happy with our love, each in our different ways.

"However, the best kind of love is not only love of total commitment, but a love that includes all of the stages. If you love someone for many years and still find joy in touching and looking, and doing special things to please, then in my opinion that is pure love."

Rode's thoughts came back to the present. "I hope I can find that kind of love," Rode said softly to herself and looked over at Nikki.

Nikki felt wonderful. Here he was in a garden full of beautiful trees and flowers, on a beautiful day with a beautiful woman, who he felt sure he loved, watching him.

This place was Rode. It had her beauty, tranquillity, and her neatness. All the qualities that he loved about her. Indeed, she lived in a world that was completely alien to him, but one in which he wanted to live.

He now knew for certain that he was in love. Every moment near her he wanted to hold her in his arms and tell her his most innermost thoughts and feelings.

He turned back to look at her, standing motionless and obviously deep in thought. What was she thinking? Could she be thinking the same thoughts? More likely she was thinking or reminiscing about Rosita.

"Oh God," he muttered under his breath. "I do love her so, but what does the future hold for us? Our lives are so different." He shuddered and erased those thoughts from his mind. What will happen will happen.

"Nikki, let's go inside," she called.

He waved and started back towards the cottage.

Father Acquilienta greeted them as they entered the cool and shady cottage. The blinds on all the windows had been drawn but thin shafts of sunlight fought their way through cracks to get into the room, like the shafts of light in a dark forest. It created a surreal effect, and whispering in that atmosphere came easily.

Rode knelt before the Priest and he laid his hand on her head.

Nikki was also Catholic but had not been to Mass or church for many years. Not since Sunday school, in fact. However, he too knelt as Father Acquilienta said a short prayer.

On finishing, the Priest helped Rode to her feet saying, "How are you Rode? It is a long time, too long a time, since we last saw each other."

"Yes," replied Rode. "I am well, thank you. Father, I am so sorry about Rosita."

"Hush now, my dear," he said still holding her arm. "You will miss her as much as I will, perhaps even more. You two, I know, were very close. God answered my prayers, you know," as he gave her his mischievous smile.

"I know. He did. Where is Rosita?"

"In her bedroom. Do you wish to see her?"

"Yes, please," whispered Rode. "Nikki? Oh I'm sorry Father, this is Nikki - I mean Niklos...err.. Andreas."

"Nikki, please, " interjected Nikki holding out his hand which the Priest took and held firmly for several seconds, as if questioning.

Rode then left them and disappeared into the bedroom.

Father Acquilienta then motioned to Nikki to be seated on one of the chintz-covered chairs, and they both sat.

"I pride myself on having the knack of knowing where people come from, but unless you say something soon I will never begin to guess. How long have you known Rode?"

"Not long. I met her in my hotel in Mexico City a few days ago."

The Priest listened intently but with a furrowed brow said, "Even after hearing you I am a little confused. I can see from your skin that you are from the Mediterranean area but where escapes me."

"Greece originally, but now my home is in Cyprus."

"Of course, how silly of me. With a name like Andreas I should have known."

Nikki inclined his head slightly, in deference.

"It was nice of you to drive Rode out here after such a short acquaintance. How do you find it here? I mean in Mexico. Is it much different from Greece?"

"I wanted to bring her out here." As he said those words, the Priest noticed the imperceptible glint in the young man's eyes; the same shine that he had seen in Rode's when they had entered. "As for the difference," Nikki was saying, "the main one that I can see is that Greece is more dry and arid and Mexico is so rich and fertile."

Just then Rode came back into the room. Her eyes were red and puffy from tears. Both men rose as she entered and stood there awkwardly, on seeing her distress.

The Priest broke the spell of the moment. " I have prepared a cold meal for us if you would care to partake." So saying he preceded them into the kitchen and they followed.

During the meal Father Acquilienta told them of the funeral arrangements for Monday, two days away, and of the meeting on Tuesday at the office of Rosita's lawyer in the centre of Cuernavaca.

He could not fail to notice the tiny glances that Rode and Nikki gave each other when they thought that each of them was not looking. The Priest once more smiled that impish smile of his. He rose from the table and excused himself, saying, "I have to go to Father Louis where I will stay the night. He will be assisting me at the funeral service." He was greeted with a stony silence, which he expected. He did not expect them to rush and offer him a bed here. He bade them goodnight and left with a happy heart and a new jaunt in his step. As he stepped outside, he muttered to himself that phrase from the Bible: 'When God closes a window, He opens another one somewhere.' Shaking his head, knowing full well that he had misquoted, he walked briskly away with a gentle smile on his face.

Rode cleared the table and crossed to the sinks and started washing the dishes. Nikki remained at the table watching her. She was small, had a narrow waist, and her long black hair was all dishevelled after the days events. Her legs were thin but shapely and were accentuated by the slim black skirt. She was dressed for the occasion in black. The sight of her being domesticated made him yearn for her even more. In Mexico City she had been dressed for work with almost designer-like clothes with her hair and make-up all in place.

He came up behind her and he could see her body stiffen a little knowing he was there, but not knowing what was happening. As he stood behind her, he smelled her hair for a fraction of a second, before saying, "Can I help you with those?"

"Here," she said and tossed a drying cloth to him.

His standing there close to her was what she wanted. Seeing his apparent discomfort in drying the dishes, which judging by his actions he had never done before, she smiled. She knew he had been watching her and her skin had been crawling, all the nerve ends crying out to be touched. There had been moments during this day that she had felt his hand or arm touch her and it had given her a tingling feeling. At those times she had decided that she was acting like a lovesick schoolgirl. But now when he was so near and she was alone in the house with him, she realised her vulnerability. She was no longer a girl but a young innocent woman whose needs and desires were beginning to take over her mind and body.

As he stood slightly behind her, he saw a pulse that throbbed softly in her graceful tanned neck, just below the ear. Small beads of perspiration were forming on her neck.

He could stand it no longer. He put down the cloth and cup that he had been drying, and placed his hands on her shoulders. "Rode," he said as he gently turned her around to face him.

She came willingly and he placed both his hands on her cheeks and bent down to kiss her ever so softly on the lips, which were warm and moist and very inviting.

Nobody had ever kissed her like this before. Her desire now taking hold and the depression which she had felt when she had seen Rosita lying in the bedroom all came together in that long delicate kiss which neither of them seemed to want to end.

He then took her in his arms and held her. Not too tightly, but with caring. She could feel his passion enter her body through his strong arms and enfold her. Her body seemed to be transported. As she seemed to fly, looking upward, she thought she saw a face. It was Rosita and she was smiling.

Their bodies separated and he very quietly and tenderly said, almost in a whisper, "Rode, I'm sorry. That was completely uncalled for. I could not help myself, because I have wanted to hold you ever since I met you. But here, in this place, at this time ..." He nodded toward the bedroom wherein lay Rosita.

Rode placed a finger on his lips and started to cry.

"You're crying. I am so sorry."

"Stop, silly. I'm not crying for Rosita. I'm crying because you have no idea how I wanted you to do that. Kiss me, I mean." She then pulled his head down and kissed him again.

" Leave the dishes, Rode, tomorrow . . . "

"No," she interrupted him. "There's only a few left. You go and sit down and I'll finish them. Pour some more of that nice table wine that we had earlier."

He did as she asked and sat on the couch, his breathing becoming faster every minute, as his mind raced ahead.

Rode finished the dishes and joined Nikki on the couch. She nestled into his body as he draped an arm around her shoulders. He handed her the glass of wine.

"To the future," he said raising his glass.

"I hope there is a future for us, Nikki. However, you live half way around the world in a life I know nothing about."

"Hush, Rode, let's not spoil the moment." He kissed her hair and then her ear then lowered his lips until they were resting gently on her upturned inviting mouth.

Rode had seen too many soap operas not to know what Nikki expected of her this night. However, never having had a mother to talk to nor a father in whom she could confide, her mind was in turmoil. Of course she had a desire for him but her religious upbringing and her own shyness stopped her. She also sensed, just by the way he conducted himself in her company, that he had been with many women before her.

'She seems scared,' thought Nikki. Judging by her body language, this was all new to her. Although he had been through this before, he felt that he had to let her dictate what happened.

What should he do? He felt sure he loved this beautiful young lady and he knew somehow that he had to spend the rest of his life with her at his side. She obviously had similar feelings toward him, otherwise they would not be kissing like this.

Rode slid further down into his arms and his body was slowly straddling hers. The kisses were now becoming more intense.

The telephone rang, sounding like a fire alarm in the solitude of the moment.

"Who, who could be calling at this time of night?" Rode asked, clumsily freeing herself from Nikki's arms.

Nikki watched her cross the room to the telephone and had to smile. Typical of a woman, he thought, there she was straightening her clothes and tidying her hair to speak on the phone. Who was going to see her?

"Hello?" Rode looked over at Nikki, her forehead creased in question. "Hello, who's there? Is anyone there?"

Nikki walked over to her. "No one there?"

"No," said Rode handing him the phone. "You listen."

He listened then said in a loud voice, "Hello, who is this please?" Silence; then he heard the tone go at the other end so he put down the receiver. "Somebody playing a joke, one that is in bad taste," he said angrily.

Rode nodded in agreement and glanced at the clock on the mantel. "Oh dear, it's late. I will make up the bed in the spare room for you. It is a single bed but very comfortable." She gave him a winsome smile, knowing full well what his thoughts were.

"That will be fine." He gave her the saddest looking face he could muster at that moment. She saw it but turned away and went into the bedroom.

Both fell asleep that night alone with their thoughts and both regretting that telephone call.

During the funeral service Rode was very calm, wondering why she could not cry. Rosita had been very close to her.

Just a handful of people showed up at the church, a few cousins and a woman who appeared to be extremely old as her face was wrinkled beyond any recognition. This was a grandmother, Rode had been told.

As they left the church at the end of the service, Father Acquilienta handed her a sealed mauve-coloured envelope. Written on it was simply: 'To my Daughter'.

"This is for you Rode. Read it when you are rested and at peace."

"Thank you, Father." Barely glancing at the envelope, she asked, "Are you coming home with us, Father? Nikki, Manuel and I are going to have a simple meal at the cottage."

"No thank you, my dear. You three go on without me. I will see you, of course, at the lawyer's office sharp at nine thirty tomorrow, yes?"

"Yes, I'll be there."

The Priest hurried off with the wind billowing his black cassock behind him.

"Poor man," said Manuel. "He not a happy man. Try not to show it but he very sad. More sad than he talks."

The three of them drove back in silence.

Rode excused herself and went into Rosita's bedroom and sat down on the bed. Looking around the room, everything was familiar to her, the religious pictures on the walls, the brushes and hand mirror on the dressing table. Each night when Rosita had not felt in good spirits, Rode would come into the room and brush Rosita's hair. This had the effect of calming both of them. These had been precious moments, but had become fewer since Rode had moved to Mexico City.

Remembering now those special times when Rode and Rosita had shared their thoughts and feelings, a tear came trickled from her eye, and like a raindrop on a windowpane, eased itself slowly down her cheek.

"I'm so sorry to have left you here alone, Mamacita," sobbed Rode, the tears coming freely now. "I should never have left you. I knew the condition of your leg. Please forgive me, Mamacita."

A gentle breath of warm wind entered the room through the open window and disturbed the mauve envelope that she had placed beside her on the bed. Picking it off the floor she wiped her tears and opened it.

My Dear Carla,

You will read this when I am gone and hopefully before you and my brother Pedro go to the lawyer. I have told him tohand it to you personally. Hopefully he will respect my wishes.

The reason I am writing in this manner is to ask a favour of you. Would you give Manuel the Crucifix on my wall? Your father made it when first we came to live here.I know that Manuel has loved me for many years and I am sure that your father would not object. He and Manuel were dear friends.

A Crucifix should belong to a person with love in theirheart and Manuel certainly has that. Tell him what I saidbut do not show him this letter.

Since you came into my life I have been happier than Icould ever have expected. Do not grieve for me. You knowthat I am happy to be joining my dear husband at last.

As for you, there is the rest of your life ahead, and youhave so much love to give. Find yourself a life partnerand bestow on him all the love within you, and which was privileged to receive when we were together.

I love you, my daughter.

Mamacita, Rosita.

Rode put down the letter and sat for a long time thinking about the words of love she had read. Had she indeed found her 'life partner'?

There was a knock on the door and Nikki poked his head round and looked in. "Can I come in?"

"Yes, please." She wiped her eyes and went over to the dressing table to brush her hair.

"Manuel has gone home. He said he was not in the mood for company."

"Neither am I," whispered Rode. "Rosita has written me a letter and she must have been quite ill as she seems confused as to who she is writing to. She seems to think I was her daughter Carla who died as an infant."

"Come through, Rode and tell me about this person Rosita. You never have told me much about her."

They both went and sat on the couch and without thinking took up the same positions as on the previous night, she cradled in his arms.

Rode told Nikki how she came to live here in the cottage, and of her life with Rosita. It was getting dark as she finished. She then asked Nikki to tell her of his life which he was reluctant to do. However, without going into too much detail he told her of his life as a student in Athens and about his family in Cyprus. He was having a holiday in Mexico after being at meetings in Los Angeles. He omitted to tell her of his father's business except to say that it was regarding imports into the United States. He knew when he said it that it was corny but at that moment it was all he could think of.

As she lay in his arms, he could see that she was getting sleepy, so he gingerly rose so as not to disturb her and made his way to the spare bedroom. He heard a noise behind him and turning saw Rode come to him and lay her hand on his arm.

"Don't turn the light on," she whispered.

They stood in the middle of the bedroom floor, locked in an embrace. His hands wandered feverishly over her body, as he tried to take her clothes off. Although his hands were rough and clumsy, they did not hurt her.

As he finished his hands touched her bare skin. Her back arched and her lower body swayed toward him. She lifted her mouth to his.

His kiss was a kiss of asking, longing, even demanding as he excitedly started to undress. When finished he got into the bed and stared at her in admiration.

The curtain at the window stirred noiselessly with the evening breeze, causing little shafts of soft Mexican moonlight to dance across her body.

Standing there she became self-conscious and covered her little firm breasts with her arms, and shyly looked at Nikki as he sat up in bed. His body was strong yet supple with his chest a mass of dark hair. He looked lean and hard and his masculinity made her tremble. "Nikki, I don't think I'm going to be very good at this." Her throaty whisper was barely audible.

"Come," he ordered her gently.

She slid in beside him backwards. Putting his hands, which were now soft and tender, on her shoulders he turned her toward him, so that their bodies were facing and touching. He took her in his arms and she responded with a grip of his body so tight, it said: 'I will never let you go'.

CHAPTER SEVEN

Nikki did not go into the Lawyers' office with Father Acquilienta and Rode. Instead he left them at the main entrance to the building and strolled over to the square opposite. He sat on a bench and soaked up the sights and sounds of Mexico. This was his first glimpse of the Mexican people and the lives they led.

As he sat there, birds wandered at his feet pecking at every bit of food available. As this appeared to be a favourite place for tourists and for lunchtime office workers, the birds' efforts were well rewarded.

All around was the hustle and bustle of life in a Mexican city. Stalls were set up over to his left, covered several feet high in T-shirts. Tourists were sifting through them, haggling over prices.

Little children, dressed neatly, wandered past him many times, offering for sale such diverse items as Chiclets, straps for wristwatches and beaded necklaces.

Behind him on the roadway, traffic was practically at a standstill. A policeman dressed in a white hat, a white shirt and white shorts was frantically blowing his whistle trying to direct the mass of cars and buses which drove past at racing car speed. Nikki smiled. The policeman blew his whistle every few seconds, yet he seemed to be losing the battle.

Even though it was not yet mid-morning the city heat was stifling, a marked change from the pleasant heat of the countryside.

CRACK!!! Nikki jumped as he heard the noise and felt a draft pass by his right ear. The birds rose noisily in unison and flew to the safety of the trees. People started running in all directions. Not knowing what had transpired they nevertheless ran out of fear. The policeman's whistle was now issuing forth a constant blast.

CRACK!! CRACK!! Nikki turned as two more shots rang out. He saw a car pull away from the side of another car parked at the edge of the kerb. As it sped off, he thought the face of the driver was familiar.

He rushed over to the parked car and arrived there at the same time as the traffic policeman.

"What happened?" shouted Nikki trying to be heard over the screeching of tyres and shouts of the people.

"Do not know, Senor, but we will ask this driver . . . " He stopped abruptly as they both saw the man slumped over the open window. Blood poured from two bullet holes in his back. A gun was still in his hand which swayed back and forth, fingers twitching as the life slowly drained from the body.

The eyes were looking upward, staring directly at Nikki. He turned away feeling great discomfort and fear. He looked back at the body. The eyes were now half closed, the eyelids dropping as death finally overcame him.

Nikki shivered. He had never seen a dead body before, let alone watched a person die before his eyes.

The square was now in an uproar with police descending from all points of the city. The traffic policeman was trying to keep control but folks were milling around trying to view the car and body. He was fighting a losing battle. In all the disturbance Nikki turned toward the lawyer's building still trying to grasp what had happened. He went over every detail in his mind, the first shot, when the birds had taken flight, the rush of air near his head. Had that been a bullet? He tried to recall who was near his position at the time, but no faces came to him, except the face of the man in the car that sped away. Where had he seen that face before?

Something was not right and it bothered him. Had he remembered the driver of that car, he would have been worried even more.

He entered the building and was confronted by a mob of people pouring out of the doorway who had heard the shots and seen the crowds in the square.

"Nikki, over here," Rode called out as she saw Nikki enter the doorway a few feet from her. He was staring straight ahead and did not hear her. She said to Father Acquilienta, "He does not hear me, Father, can you reach him?"

"I'll try." The priest slowly inched his way through the crowd that was now being held up at the front of the building. This created a jam of people in the foyer. "Excuse, please. Excuse, thank you. Excuse, oh, sorry sir." Father Acquilienta was pushing and shoving. He shouted Nikki's name every few seconds until finally Nikki turned and saw the priest struggling toward him. The two of them finally met and embraced.

"Oh, Father, I have seen something awful happen. A man dead, gun shots, blood all over the place. Oh, Father, it was terrible."

"Come now, try to calm down, Rode is over there. Do you see her?" Nikki nodded. "Rode," the priest shouted at her, "make for the back door and we will meet you there."

"What did you say?" shouted Rode who could not hear over the crowd noise.

Father Acquilienta shouted back while pointing to his right. "The back door, through there."

Rode at last understood and turned against the throng and proceeded to the back of the crush.

They finally met up, and Rode literally jumped into Nikki's arms. "What happened out there? Did you see anything? I heard gunfire or something."

The priest said, "Not now, Rode, let's get out of here. We will talk of this later. Nikki is in no frame of mind, at the moment, to discuss what happened."

"Why?" asked Rode. "Was Nikki involved? Oh, Nikki," and she clung to him as closely as she could.

The back door led out onto a side street that led to away from the town centre to the Cathedral.

Rode said she knew a small restaurant in the next street where they could relax and have coffee while they waited for the crowds and police to disperse.

The three of them hurried along the narrow street, each alone with their thoughts.

Father Acquilienta was distressed by his sister Rosita's Will. He had loved his sister very much and since her husband's death had taken care of her and tried to help in any way he could. He had visited her in the cottage many times over the years and had made no secret of the fact that he loved the house and gardens as much as Rosita had. He had hoped that he could settle down with her, in retirement, at the house. So when she died he thought that at last he could leave the Church, retire, and spend his twilight years in the comfort and solitude that the cottage offered.

For the last forty-eight hours, though, he had wrestled with the problem of 'coveting'. He wanted to retire, and had hoped that Rosita had left the cottage to him. He had prayed for guidance and humility in this matter, but his desires of this life were strong and would not leave him. He had been disappointed this morning, when the lawyer had read Rosita's Last Will and Testament. Oh yes, she had left him a sum of money in the form of an Annuity for life. Also a very generous contribution to his Church, but the cottage she had left to Rode.

Hurrying on, the bell of the Cathedral of our Mary of Guadalupe pealed out and cut into his thoughts like a knife. He stopped suddenly in the middle of the street while Nikki and Rode looked at him.

"What is wrong, Father?"

"Nothing, my dear Rode. Please excuse me, I have to go to Mass.

The Cathedral is back about a hundred yards or so. You two go on ahead. Goodbye." At that he turned and hurried away.

"Strange," muttered Nikki.

Father Acquilienta did not see himself as strange, but as one who had been sent for. He must not doubt the will of God. He went to make his peace.

Nikki's thoughts were of the dead man. He had never seen a person die before. He reminded himself of the newsreels that told of so-and-so's death. Or the battle and murder scenes in movies, where death was something remote and unreal, something that happened to others and therefore not personal. No longer would he think that way. This death had been personal to him. He felt it for sure, when he recalled the man's eyes staring into his soul. Who was he? Why the gun, was he shooting at someone? Had he left a wife and family behind? Should he grieve for him, say a prayer or something? He heard the bell of the church close by. Should he do it now?

Rode's mind was in turmoil and heaven at the same time. She had been overcome when told by the lawyer about the cottage. Nor could she be mistaken by Father Acquilienta's apparent disappointment at the news. He had visibly shrunk in his chair. Rode had wanted to blurt out there and then, "Take the cottage, I don't want it." But she did want it. It had not only given her the happiest times in her life but now it was the place where she had discovered Love. That night with Nikki had surprised her. She had not thought herself capable of doing the things she did. The love that she had shared with Nikki, and she was convinced it was returned, was nothing like that in the soaps. They had it all wrong. They had never shown her the love that she now felt for Nikki.

The Cathedral bell rang out the half hour, so she quietly said a prayer. '*Thank you God, for sending me Rosita, and thank Rosita for sending me Nikki.*'

Over coffee Nikki described to Rode what had happened in the square. He went over every detail hoping that by doing so, he himself could make sense of it.

Rode was very understanding, yet when she innocently said, "You don't think he was shooting at you, do you?" He could feel a cold sweat come on his forehead.

Nikki froze, as the thought had never occurred to him. How could he have been so stupid? Had the man actually been staring at HIM? Had he been the target? No, that life was back in Cyprus and Greece, not here in sunny Mexico in a town like Cuernavaca. But yet, what was it his father had said to him? "A group of people who wanted to see me out of business," and that because of the incident in Athens Nikki had to go.

That man from the bar that he had left. Had he been unconscious or.. . .had he killed him? Nikki's face went white and his cup rattled in the saucer when he picked it up.

"What's the matter? You look awful, Tell me, has that man's death upset you that much?"

"Man. . which? Yes indeed it has. Let's go away somewhere, to the cottage, perhaps."

"That fine by me, darling." It sounded funny, but yet nice calling him that. He did not seem to hear her but leaned forward and kissed her.

"I do love you, Rode. Now let's go to the tranquil peace of the cottage."

"But first to my work place. I cannot walk out without telling them where I am."

"Okay, to the agency." As they left the restaurant, neither of them noticed the car parked at the end of the street, with a lone driver watching them.

Total Travel Agency was busy when they entered. Rosanna, Rode's friend and confidante excused herself from a client and followed them into Rode's office. "Is this the young man who sent the flowers?"

"Yes. Rosanna, meet Nikki."

"How do you do, Nikki? Oh Rode, did you hear about Senor Santiago?"

"No, I've been away, what about him?"

"Well they found him dead in his hotel room, the night you delivered those papers to him. Was he all right when you saw him?"

Rode looked at Nikki before replying in a shaken voice. "Yes, I think so. He had been drinking, that's all."

"Well," went on Rosanna, delighted to at last have some news that Rode had not heard first. Rode was always the first to hear any tittle tattle gossip. Breathless she blurted out, " They say he died of fright. They found him in bed with his eyes wide open, staring. He had no pyjama bottoms on. Isn't that something?" Rosanna stood tall, as she was proud of the way she had told her story. Nikki turned away.

"Poor man," was all that Rode could say. "Rosanna, Nikki and I are going to the cottage for a few days. We will phone you when we are coming back. Give my regrets to my clients, tell them I will be in touch soon. Thanks."

As they stood outside, in the now blazing sunshine, the noise of the downtown traffic jarred on their ears. After two days in the quiet of the country it was a shock to their system.

"I had better go to my hotel, Rode. My room is still booked under my name, also all my clothes and luggage are there. Have you anything to do now?" Rode shrugged. "Well then, why don't you come with me and help. Better still," he said, putting his arm around her waist and touching the bottom of a breast, "why don't you come and give me some comforting. After the events of this morning, you must admit that I do need comforting."

She laughed, and noticing his faked hangdog expression, pressed her arm against the hand on her breast and led him off.

They made love in the cool comfort of the hotel room. It started with giggles and teases, and murmurs of love and devotion, then suddenly it became charged with an intensity that neither of them thought they were capable of achieving. "I love you," she cried at the end, a cry that came from the very depths of her being.

It took them a while to again become two separate people. The place they had been had taught them that never again would they be completely separated. They had experienced a deeper union than that of their two bodies. It gave them each an inner strength that they did not have to voice.

"Do you feel comforted enough?" she asked as they lay in the giant bed with its satin sheets caressing their bodies. They were on their sides, he nestled in her back with the contours of their bodies fitting perfectly. His hand was gently caressing her breast, playing with the nipple. In response he kissed the nape of her neck and whispered ever so softly, "I suppose so.. . .For now, anyway."

They fell asleep with their bodies pressing closely.

Two hours later Rode left the hotel to return to her flat to gather up some clothes. Nikki was to meet up with her there.

Minutes after she left, there was a knock on the door. He opened it expecting to see Rode. Instead, he was met with the full force of a heavy body charging into him and knocking him to the floor. While falling he felt a hand clamp a cold moist cloth against his mouth and nose. It really hurt, and as he opened his mouth to cry out from the pain he could feel moisture on his teeth. He tried to struggle as he instinctively knew he was being chloroformed, but the men were too powerful and his resistance was getting weak because of the drug. There seemed to be two of them, as one was kneeling on his arms, pinning him while administering the chloroform while the other held his legs and lower body. Not a word had been spoken so he could not tell who they were. His vision was becoming blurred and his last thought before he blacked out was, *it's useless to fight, it won't do any good.* The needle went deep into the side of his neck.

CHAPTER EIGHT

Cicero Andreas put the phone down as his wife Kasta entered the study. She heard her husband say, "Thank you, Vlascis, I will contact him."

Kasta rushed to his side hoping to get a chance to speak on the phone, but he replaced the receiver.

"Was that about Nikki?" she demanded tugging at her husband's arm.

"No, Kasta," he said dislodging himself from her grasp.

"You lie, Cicero. I know when you are lying. All those years, I know you too well. Tell me, what news of Nikki?"

"He is in trouble, Mama." So saying he took his wife in his arms. "I sent Vlascis to look after Nikki and there have been two attempts on Nikki's life."

"Oh, Holy Mother of God!" shrieked Kasta, tears bursting forth as if from a tap inside her head. Her hands went to the sides of her cheeks then to Cicero's chest where she started beating as hard as she could. "Tell me, damn you. Tell me, is he dead?"

"No, he is fine. He knows nothing about the attempts on his life."

Kasta turned away, wringing her hands in a sign of grief, then wheeled around with hatred in her eyes. Such a look as Cicero had never seen before. "You knew when you sent him abroad, he could be in trouble. Didn't you?" He was silent. "You bastard," she hissed at him. "I love you, Cicero, but there are times." She did not finish the sentence, but kept quiet. He could see her brain working overtime behind the terrible look in her eyes. Calmly she spoke again. "You knew, yet you sent my son on this so-called business trip. Why? What had he done?"

Cicero turned away from his wife as he did not want her to see the shame which had appeared on his face. His thoughts were of Nikki. What have I done to you, my boy, my baby? He very softly said, "He's my son too, you know."

He was dragged around to face her. "Your son too," she mimicked. Then mustering as calm a voice as she could, but speaking deliberately so as there would be no mistake about the meaning, she said, "Get him home, you hear, before something does happen. Should he die, I swear before God, Cicero, husband or not, love or not, I will kill you."

Cicero Andreas' face went white. All his life he had given orders.

EFX LEASING

ENERFLEX LEASING LTD.

Never once in the illegal activities and the killings, had he ever been threatened with death. He knew Kasta too well, this was no idle threat. She meant it.

"I'll try to contact him, Kasta. You do not know, however, that he has met a Mexican girl, quite a pretty thing I understand, and that they have spent a lot of time together. She works in a travel agency in Mexico City. No doubt I can contact him there."

Kasta's face softened on hearing this. "We will move to the house in Athens, as soon as possible. I wish to be there when" - at this word she glared at him - "he flies home." Muttering under her breath she said, "I've never been happy in this house." Then again raising her voice she uttered, "See to the arrangements right away!"

She walked over toward the door and on reaching it she turned and said without emotion, " Remember, I swear before God." She crossed herself and left the room.

Cicero picked up the phone and reverting to his position as head of the family business, started barking out orders.

The rain teemed down and pattered on the roof of the large aircraft hanger. Two men waited at the side of the coffin which had been placed on a hospital gurney. They idly watched the open doorway where there was a waterfall of rain dripping from overhead. The humidity inside the hangar was becoming unbearable to both men as they wore heavy black overcoats and sedate black hats. They had been waiting for half an hour and with no seats available were getting rather irritable with the delay.

A door opened, then closed with a loud crash which reverberated around the hollow interior of the building. Two men entered, one dressed in airline uniform carrying a clipboard while the other was wearing a white hospital coat.

They approached the two Overcoats beside the coffin. "Open up," said the White Coat. The lid of the coffin was prised open with the help of a screwdriver, and laid on the ground. The White Coat peered at the body inside, which was dressed in a suit and had heavy make-up on its face. He placed a hand on the chest and waited. Then he bent down with his head on the chest and waited. He took from his pocket a small piece of shiny metal about two inches long and one inch wide. It looked like aluminium. This he held below the nostrils of the body. He turned to the airline man and nodded.

The Airline official looked down at his clipboard and turning to the two Overcoats said, "Is this the body being shipped?" The smaller of the two Overcoats nodded.

Airline Uniform then looked again at the clipboard, signed his name on the paper and handed it to the small Overcoat, saying, "The body of Niklos Papandropolous Andreas is free to travel."

CHAPTER NINE

A week after arriving from Edinburgh, Katie Docherty had still not found a job, yet she had applied and been accepted for evening classes at the London School of Business Administration. Jobs, she discovered, were hard to come by, especially for someone who had only been full time at College since leaving school. Many positions were offered that only paid the minimum wage, but to her this was not acceptable as she needed tuition fees for the evening course.

A small flat in a run-down area not far from Kings Cross station, where she had landed after her train ride from Scotland, was her home for the present. It had just one room and a toilet. After buying clothes and other necessities, the money was running out fast.

In the evenings she pored over the jobs available in the newspapers, and the next morning would start the process of phoning to try to obtain an appointment. She wished for something in the clerical line as the work experience would be helpful in her course. The only things available were for waitress and barmaid jobs, both work for the evenings.

After being in London for two weeks her evening course commenced and she found it much more difficult than she had imagined. Many attempts at obtaining grants had fallen through. She managed to stick it out for three because of a lack of funds.

In desperation she answered an ad for work as a waitress-cum-bartender in a small club in a back street, just off the theatre district in the West End. She presented herself one lunchtime at the club and was introduced to a middle aged man called Marty.

"What experience have you had, young lady, in this line of work?"

"None, sir, but I need the money, and I'm willing to work hard."

Marty looked her over with a keen eye for beauty. Her eyes had a cheeky, impish look that seemed to be asking a question all the time, and she had a warm, genuine smile.

Liking what he saw he said, "Can you start this evening? I will give you a trial."

"Yes, thank you, sir. What time should I be here and do I wear a uniform?"

"Yes, you will be fitted out when you arrive at seven. The hours are from seven thirty until two in the morning. Also the name is Marty."

"Fine, thank you, Marty."

"Ok, 'til seven then."

Katie got dressed for the new job at the Club Aladdin. "What should I wear? I don't want to appear like a prostitute, wearing a short skirt and revealing blouse. Neither do I want to look like a prig."

She opened the large heavy wooden doors of a wardrobe that filled an entire wall. It was covered in knotholes and had names scratched all over from previous tenants of this 'flea bag' of a flat.

Laughing a little about worrying over her appearance she opened the wardrobe. Hanging inside was one pair of slacks, one dress and two blouses, neither of which were the least bit revealing. Below was a pair of sneakers, and a pair of flat shoes.

The brown blouse and slacks she had worn earlier in the day, so they were out. The dress it had to be.

When she had washed and dressed, she sat on the end of the bed. "What am I doing going for a job as a waitress in a club? Some club, more likely it will be a 'dive'. I have a good education, have almost completed a Business Administration Course, so I deserve something better. But I have to eat and pay rent," she thought, "so beggars cannot be choosers. I need the money."

Putting her raincoat over her arm, she left the room in a disconsolate mood. As it was still the supper hour, the underground train to Leicester Square was packed. She found herself hemmed up against the sliding doors. She had acquaintances who travelled to work this way every morning and evening. How they coped doing this, she could never understand.

The train lurched to a squealing halt and the sliding doors disgorged its mass of humanity. The wind from down the tunnel to her right blew her skirt around her thighs, and there were whistles and catcalls from a group of orange and blue haired punks. She recalled seeing one of them inside the train. He was over six feet tall and had one of those spiked hairstyles. It was so high that the spikes hit the roof of the compartment and the ends bent flat.

Not being in a rush, as she had left early for the appointment, she let the crowds get ahead of her, and when she reached the escalator she had it to herself. Idly glancing at the advertisements on the wall as the staircase moved her upward, doubts started to enter her head. "Still not too late to back out, old girl," she heard herself say.

As the escalator deposited her at the top, her heart beat a little faster. Ever since she had come to London, the highlights had been her frequent trips to the 'West End' as the Londoners called the area around Piccadilly Circus and Leicester Square.

She emerged from the station and, leaning against a shop front, looked around in awe. The neon lights of the huge cinemas and theatres flickered on and off and covered the whole of the fronts of the buildings. All the new films were shown here first. When it was time for the Queen to attend a Command Performance, it was to these theatres she came. No matter how often Katie had seen this sight, it always gave her goose bumps.

She walked slowly along in the hot muggy air that seemed to hang over London all year round. People from around the world passed her by and nobody took a second glance. There were Arabs dressed in flowing white robes, nuns and priests in their flowing black outfits, Africans with their colourful clothes and little pill box hats that were so appealing, Yanks with their cowboy hats and boots.

Katie soaked it all up like a sponge. She loved being part of this huge 'Stage of Wonderland'. That was the name she had given this part of London. To be in London, in the centre of the West End, was to her like being at the centre of the Universe. To a young woman from Scotland this was the pinnacle of her life to date. Or, as the Americans would say, 'This is as good as it gets'.

Turning a corner into a shadowy and narrow side street that led to the Club Aladdin, she had forgotten her misgivings. She was going to work in this wonderland! Life was not so bad after all.

The Club Aladdin in Firth Street was not what Katie had expected. It was a fabulous looking place beautifully decorated on the outside in a deep red and gold. There were four alcoves along the front set between Byzantine-looking arches and into these alcoves were set four stained glass windows. Nestling in front of each window was a small statue, replicas of the British and American Oscars and the American and British television awards. Being close to the theatre district of London the Club Aladdin attracted many stars of stage and screen.

Inside, the decor continued this tasteful appearance with plush leather seating and heavy pile carpet. Four large chandeliers gave off subdued lighting. At one end of the room, which was not too large, there was a stage, which was home to the 'Lamplighters', a four-piece combo with a female singer.

When Katie entered, the stage was empty, so too was the main room. Two girls were working at the bar. She walked up smartly, anxious to make a good impression.

"Excuse me," she called to a barmaid who was washing glasses in the sink below the counter.

"Yes?" came back the reply in a low, husky but cultured voice. "What can I do for you?"

"I'm here to start work this evening. Is Marty around by chance?"

"I think so. Go through that door over there, down the corridor to a door marked 'office'. He should be there at this time. May I ask your name?" So saying she extended a wet hand. "I'm Rose. Rose Wilson."

"Katie Docherty. Pleased to meet you, Rose," she returned the handshake.

Following Rose's instructions she found the door marked 'office' and knocked.

"Come in." She entered. "Ah, the new girl. Come in sit down. Your name again, sweetheart?" Marty asked.

"Katie, sir," she replied, sitting down. She noticed that Marty was now dressed in a fine tuxedo, and better looking than she remembered from this afternoon.

"Now, now, none of that 'sir' talk. My name is Marty, got that? Katie … ah yes, the one with no experience, right? Never mind that, with a body like yours and your looks it will not matter. I know it sounds like sexual harassment, my dear, especially these days, but our customers like to see someone worth looking at. You will fit in nicely, I'm sure. I'll get Rose to take you in hand."

"I 've met Rose," blurted out Katie trying to show that she was not timid, but could hold her own in a conversation. "She seemed very nice."

"Yes, she is," Marty said as he looked at her critically. "I don't wish to appear rude, Katie but have you got anything nicer to wear than that dress? You will, of course, be fitted out with your own uniform, but I do like my girls to be neatly turned out at all times." He flashed her his big generous smile.

"Well, err, I mean … " stuttered Katie, all the earlier confidence shattered.

"No money, eh?" He took out a fat wallet from his back pocket and extracted a few notes. Handing them to her, he said in a kinder voice, "I've been there Katie, I understand. Here take this, get yourself a nice outfit and new hairdo before you come in tomorrow night. There's a good girl."

Katie was overcome by this act of kindness. "I'm sorry, but I cannot take this . . . I can't repay you.."

He held up his hand to silence her. "No need, it's a gift, not a loan. Now run away and see Rose."

Katie was stunned. Her new boss had just given her about four hundred pounds. She left the office as in a trance, and went out to the bar.

"What's the matter, Katie? You look like you're in shock."

"Maybe I am, look." She held out a hand with the bills in it. "That's what Marty gave me to buy clothes and things."

"How much?"

"Don't know, haven't counted it yet, but close to four hundred pounds, I should think."

"Wow! I knew he was a generous person, but that much! He must have taken a liking to you, Katie. Now, did he say that I was to help you?"

"Yes, please. I am rather new at this type of work. Always having been on the other side of the bar. By the way, is that our uniform?" Katie pointed to what Rose was wearing.

"Yes. Not much is it?"

"Not much is right," laughed Katie. Rose was wearing a bra, what looked like skimpy boxer shorts and high-heeled sandals, nothing else. The bra and pants continued the dark red with a gold trim motif of the rest of the establishment.

Katie noticed that Rose only just fitted into the bra, her bust was aptly named. Unlike herself who was small yet fully developed, Rose was a large-boned woman with broad shoulders.

"Do the customers, ever, well you know, touch you?"

"Very few, but they like to look at your breasts and it is expected that you show them off, and not be self conscious about it. Our clientele is from the stage and screen. They come here after being either at the movies or from appearing on stage. They come in for a quiet drink and some anonymity." Katie raised her eyebrows. "Yes," Rose went on, "we may get Sean Connery or Michael Caine in here and what they do not want is to see someone gawk at them, whisper and be silly. They like us to respect their privacy. So remember, no whispering when a so-called 'star' comes in."

"Does it happen often? That a star comes in, I mean."

"Not so much at weekends, as you can appreciate, but on weeknights, yes quite often. As a barmaid your job is to take an order, relay that order to the Bartender and then deliver the drinks to the table. Most of our customers run a tab, and pay either on leaving or at a later date. That decision is for Joey, the Head Bartender, or Marty. After a while you may be asked to tend the bar. If they pay cash, that's fine, then you deal with it, but check with me, Joey or Marty. One or all of us are at the bar at all times. The main thing to remember is that this a very select club, so therefore it commands respect for the customers. Smile, wiggle if you want, but always be courteous and polite."

"I'll remember, Rose, but I'm just a shy wee Scots lassie." As Katie said it, she turned her body, lowered her head and cowered before Rose. They both burst out laughing.

"Come, let me introduce you to Angela, the other waitress working your shift. Then we'll get you a uniform. I mean, an outfit."

Next day, Katie spent most of the money on new clothes, shoes and a new hairdo. Then, with what was left over, much needed groceries to keep her going.

Katie settled into this new life and enjoyed every minute. The pay was good and the tips fabulous. So much so, it was not long before she moved into a brand new flat. This had a bathroom with a shower which was heaven on earth as far as she was concerned. Her expenses were minimal. When not at work she was asleep during the day, so saving money came quite easily. A car was the first thing on her want list. Not one of those old bangers, but one she could drive to the club without embarrassment.

One evening while she was having a break in the staff room Marty walked in. Katie was a bit agitated. Why was the boss there? She had noticed him watching her some evenings, but could not make out why from his expression. She liked her job, her co-workers and Marty as well. He was kind to the staff and not a bad looking fella. She put his age at between forty and forty-five. Short in stature, he nevertheless was broad shouldered and muscular.

"Hi, Katie."

"Hello, Marty. Can I help with anything?"

"Yes, I think so. I know you have been aware of me watching you lately, right?" Katie lowered her eyes. "Well, I have and the reason is that tomorrow night there is a special party coming to the club. It is mainly MP's and their, er … guests. They will be occupying the private dining room and require special treatment."

"Special treatment?" she asked. "Do you mean what I think you mean, Marty?"

"No no, nothing like that, my dear." Taking her hand as if to comfort her, "No, just one waitress to serve them, as long as they wish to stay. Your services in the main room will be covered. I'm sorry to have scared you Katie, I didn't mean … "

"You didn't," smiled Katie. "I wouldn't have minded, anyway." She again smiled at him but with a seductive look in her eyes.

"But Katie, I ... I don't think I understand what you mean."

"I mean, dear Marty, that I have been with men before and as long as they are clean and respectable I don't mind. Not too old either," she added. "I can't stand old men."

Marty stood with his mouth open, not knowing what to say.

"Do I shock you?"

"No, well maybe, er, no ... I don't quite know." He stammered incoherently. Then trying to become once more the master of the situation said, "So tomorrow night's OK with you?" Katie nodded. "Good, thank you." He started to walk backwards toward the door. He got to the door and as he turned the handle sidled out muttering, "Thank you, Katie, thank you." When he left, she smiled and shook her head.

Katie had surprised herself, talking the way she had, especially to the boss. However, it had been almost a year since her last time with a man, that guy in Edinburgh who was rough and had punched her. She tried, but could not remember his name.

The next evening Marty waited in his office. It was now past closing time of 2.00 am.. The special party had not yet ended. He wondered if Katie would drop a few hints about the time, and her need to get home. He would make sure she got a nice bonus in her next pay cheque.

Katie had been the only girl that he had approached for this extra work, although she was new and inexperienced. Rose or Angela should have been his first choice, but there was something about Katie that he thought distinctive. Something that he liked very much, but could not pinpoint.

He tried hard to do some paperwork that had got out of hand, but he could not concentrate. Was Katie safe in there? All those men with her only. He became rather edgy when there was a knock on the door. Looking at his watch. - 3.05 am. - he got up and went to the door.

"Katie, thank goodness, come on in. Have they all gone, then?"

"Yes, finally. I thought they were there for the night."

"Sit down, luv, you look tired. How about a small drink to relax you?"

"No thanks, Marty, but I could murder a cup of coffee. Do you have any around somewhere?"

"Yes. I have a coffee pot in my flat upstairs." He noticed a surprised expression come over her face. "Sorry, I did not mean to insinuate … "

"No, it's not that. I didn't know you had a place here in the club."

"Yes. I need to use it when I work late, it saves a long trip home to Wimbledon."

"Let's go then," she said eagerly, anxious to see this pad of his. She did indeed want a cup of coffee. However, since the other night when she had admitted her past, strong feelings were forming for him. They were alone in the club and she felt sure he had the same feelings for her. She knew that he had been watching her for a few weeks, and felt sure it had nothing to do with this special event tonight. Men had been interested in her before, and the signs were obvious.

"Through that door over there," he pointed. "There is a spiral staircase which leads to the flat. You go on up, the door is open. I must clear up here and check that the club is locked up for the night. I'll join you shortly."

"OK Marty. Do you want coffee, too?"

"Yes, fine, OK."

He cleared his desk of the papers he should have attended to but had not. He then walked through the darkened club and checked all the doors. Smiling to himself, he went up to the flat.

Katie already had the coffee on and was sitting, relaxed looking, in one of the armchairs wearing his dressing gown.

"I made myself at home. I hope you don't mind?"

"Not at all." He removed his tie and jacket and slumped down in the other chair. "That was unfair of those men to stay that long. What were they doing all this time?"

"It was supposed to be a Committee meeting, at least that's what it started out as. But after many drinks, oh, by the way, you're out of cognac and soda, they resorted to telling stories from their past and finally ended up telling dirty jokes. By the time they had finished a few of them had passed out."

She got up and went and poured a cup of coffee and, placing it in a saucer, brought it over to his chair. On leaning over him to place it on the adjoining table, he caught a glimpse of a breast. Realising that she had nothing on underneath, he looked away fast.

Katie saw the look though and recognised it for what it was. "Do you really want a cup of coffee?" she said glancing toward the bedroom door.

"Not really." He rose and grabbed her in his arms and kissed her. She led him to the bedroom.

That night Marty got a lesson in the depth of a woman's desire. In all the previous affairs he had been the aggressor. Now here in this bed he was surprised by the fury and power within that tiny frame. A beautiful young woman with a body that defied description, but with a profound sense of passion that he thought only existed in jungle animals. She devoured him and left him battered and bruised. Then she would start over again. Her appetite for his body was voracious and seemed never to abate.

At last, utterly exhausted, he lay on the bed beside her and looked at her. She smiled. He felt he had to say something but could not think of anything.

She answered for him. Clasping her hands above her head and stretching that lithe voluptuous body: "Boy that was good, eh Marty?"

He did not answer, but telling himself that he loved this girl with the raw passion, this desire for total absorption in the act of sex. She was like no other he had known. He got up and sat on the edge of the bed. Turning his back on her he said quietly, "Katie, I think I'm falling in love with you."

She rose on her knees and clasping her body into his back, hugged him. "I know, Marty. I've known for a while."

"You have? I never said … "

"No need to. The way you have been watching me the past week or two."

"You mean it was that obvious?"

"To a woman, yes; at least to me." Katie turned his head and kissed him, her mouth open in anticipation.

"Oh, Katie, I know it sounds like a line from a young buck with tight jeans, but I have never felt like this. I never knew that one could."

She pulled him back on the bed and where passion and lust had ruled their bodies, love now took over. With their love came tenderness, caring and the joy of savouring each other, touching, kissing, delighting in the wonderment that each sensation gave to them.

The night ended with the blending of not only their bodies but their minds. A melding so beautiful that it was magnificent. The way a woman and man were meant to have union.

Daylight came, with them still locked in an embrace that neither wanted to end. However, reality slowly took over their senses and reluctantly they got out of bed.

"Before I drive you home, let me give you a key to this place. Feel free to come whenever you wish." Taking the key from him, she held it up to her lips and kissed it.

Life changed dramatically for both of them. Marty would work nights to be close to Katie, causing rumblings and questions among the staff. They would sleep in the morning and in the afternoons they would go for drives in the countryside around London. Once outside the city they would abandon the car for long walks through the green English fields and forests. When finished, they would stop for a meal at one of the small public houses that seemed to spring up everywhere they travelled. Quite often they would rent a room for an hour or two, registering as Mr. and Mrs. The sight of the local people looking down their noses in disgust when they heard not only Mr. and Mrs. Smith but that the room was only required for two hours, would send them laughing to their room.

Both of them now experienced some of the delights of being in love: the asking of questions of each other; the telling of stories from childhood; their planning of the days ahead, and discussing their hopes and dreams for the future - all essences of the making of two people into one, and the discovery of what real love was all about.

Over the next week or two Rose noticed the change in Katie. At a convenient time she asked Katie if everything was fine with her life. She seemed somehow different and the other members of the staff had noticed it too. Rose had not said anything, but they had their suspicions.

"Yes, Rose, I am different. So beautifully different. I'm in love." She then danced round the bar singing, "I'm in love with a wonderful guy."

"Great, do I know this lucky fellow?"

"Yes, yes, you do. It's Marty."

"Marty, our Marty? Oh, I didn't know." She feigned surprise.

"Well, we have kept it a secret, but, what the hell, it's out now."

"How nice," said Rose and walked away.

Katie thought her actions a bit strange, maybe she was jealous or maybe it was the fact that it was the boss and all that.

Later that same evening the main room was not busy, almost empty in fact, when Rose suggested a coffee break in the staff room. Katie agreed. Over coffee Rose took a deep breath and said in a serious tone "Katie, you know that I'm your friend. Don't you?"

"Yes I know that, Rose. Why do you ask?"

"Well, as a friend and for no other reason." She hesitated. "You do know that Marty is married?"

A punch in the stomach would have been better than the jolt that

Katie got. It was as if she had been suddenly exposed to an electric current. Her body started shaking and the nerves at her fingertips and toes were tingling crazily.

"Oh Katie, my dear, I am so sorry. I did not mean to hurt you like this." She took Katie's hands in hers then held her close. "I thought you would have known."

Katie shook her head and as the tremors of her body calmed down, the tears started to flow. How could she have been so stupid? It had never occurred to her to ask. Why had he not told her? Questions that started to burn holes in her brain. Why had he kept it from her? Through a tear-stained mist, she saw Rose leave the room.

She really did love the man. Maybe not at first, he was just a means to have her sexual desires met. But later she had come to love him as no other.

After composing herself she went out to the bar. "Rose, cover for me for half an hour, please." Not waiting for an answer she marched to the back, up the spiral staircase, and using the key for the first time, entered the flat. She stood in the middle of the floor, not certain where to start looking. She tried the bedroom first, glaring at the bed. She again started to cry as she recalled the heat of love that had been shared there. Shaking herself as if to discard the mantle of love from around her, she opened the drawers of the cabinets. There were books, tissues, some handkerchiefs and some hand towels. Hand towels? What were they doing there? She took them out, and placed in between two towels was a framed photograph.

Her knees buckled and she slumped to the floor with the picture grasped tightly in her hand. It was of a pleasant looking woman, quite handsome in a way, with black hair showing tinges of grey. She was smiling. Katie's tears were dropping onto the glass as she rose, and without a backward glance marched downstairs into the main room, and thrusting the photograph into Rose's face demanded, "Is this her?"

Rose stepped back a pace. "Yes that's Mrs Charles, Theresa, his wife."

Katie's resolute manner was leaving her rapidly as she timidly asked, "How long have they been … ?"

"Seventeen years, and before you ask, no children."

Katie fell into Rose's arms. "Oh Rose, how could he? We made so many plans, even talked of getting married." Pulling herself away she spoke slowly. "I'm not the only one, am I?"

"No, there have been others."

CHAPTER TEN

For eight days the sun had scorched the country, raising the temperature to a searing 110 degrees. Now today, the cloud cover had enveloped the city so that the humidity rose to unbearable levels. Forecasters had warned of severe thunderstorms for the entire area.

The overcast and sticky conditions had not deterred the hundred or so people who had arrived in long black limousines. A few had ventured here in sports cars, which caused glances of disgust from the band of chauffeurs who stood in groups beside their cars. The long line of cars twisted through the Cemetery like a snake, with the few sporty models at the rear giving it a very colourful tail.

There was no respite from the heat as the mourners stood at the graveside. The few trees that were there had not fully grown and offered little shade.

The men there stood with sweaty armpits and crotches in their three-piece suits. Hats in hand, the mostly balding heads were covered in perspiration.

The women wore long dresses and hats, both of which had to be anchored by a hand, as the wind started. It did not make for a very graceful stance at a burial scene. The wind got stronger heralding, no doubt, the impending storm.

One person who did not look uncomfortable was the priest. Without a pause and in almost parrot fashion he intoned the burial service. Only a handful were in fact listening. The others were no doubt hoping that this interminably long service would come to an end, so that they could get home and enjoy the comfort of their swimming pools.

"Ashes to ashes … Our dear departed son, Niklos Andreas." The priest went on in his monotone voice.

A mournful cry shattered the hot sultry silence. The foot shuffling stopped while all eyes turned to stare at Kasta Andreas, the mother, who was now sobbing hysterically. Cicero, her husband, laid a large gnarled hand on the small of her back and patted it gently.

Everyone stood uneasily, as the priest had apparently stopped chanting. Now all eyes turned to the priest, who was motioning Cicero Andreas to the side of the coffin. The father seemed to hesitate, not quite certain what to do, so the priest again said, "Ashes to ashes." This time in a loud insistent voice.

Just then there was an almighty bang from the sky and all the mourners jumped in fright as if on cue. The thunder reverberated around the sky, the claps getting more distant. At last the rain came. Everyone looked up at the sky. It seemed as if they did not know from whence it had come, or what it was. Their faces were greeted with a torrent of hard rain which soaked them through within seconds.

Cicero looked at the priest who nodded and in the voice used only in sermons shouted, "Amen." This triggered a stampede for the cars where the chauffeurs had started the engines, reminiscent of Indianapolis.

Meanwhile, ladies in their high heels were getting bogged down in the mud surrounding the burial plot. Husbands were frantically trying to extricate them, but under their breath, cursing the delay.

Within six minutes all was quiet once more by the coffin of Nikki Andreas. The rain stopped and a watery sun emerged from behind the clouds.

A small van drew up at the bottom of the hill and two men with ropes and spades got out and walked up to the coffin. They started to prepare the coffin for burial in the ground.

Five hundred yards out of the cemetery, Kasta's misery showed in the darkness around her eyes. Alone in the car with her husband, whom she thought she had known until this day. He sat silently, staring out of the window. Neither had spoken a word since they had left the burial site. The rain had finally lost its battle with the sun and the warmth made the roads steam, giving the cemetery an even stranger appearance.

Kasta and Cicero had met thirty years before. They were at University, she studying Mediaeval Arts and he studying Law.

As soon as he graduated, they married and it was decided that she would leave University after only two years of her four-year course.

He started his law practice in Piraeus, and in the first few months their income was extremely scant. He was a good lawyer but there were many young lawyers just starting out. The competition for clients was fierce, and young Cicero was forced to sit for hour after hour in the local police station waiting for any clients in need of a lawyer. Kasta, meanwhile, took mostly baby-sitting jobs to help eke out the family budget.

While sitting in the waiting room of the police station, which was only a few streets from the docks, Cicero was summoned to the front desk by the officer on duty.

"We have a case of attempted smuggling, an African, name of…

Mata … something … whatever. Do you want it?"

"Does he have any money?" asked Cicero. "Or is he a vagrant?"

"I doubt he has money, but he needs a lawyer. The court will probably pay your expenses."

Matakeema Attabeele was from Botswana and had been seen down near the harbour carrying a small twelve-inch statue. When stopped by the harbour patrol Attabeele had panicked and run. The harbour police had finally caught up with him and asked him for proof of ownership of the statue, or alternatively a customs clearance form.

Having neither, they took him to the station and charged him with possession of stolen goods and smuggling illegally into Greece.

Mattabeele could speak a few words of English but did not understand Greek, so thinking he was hiding something the police had decided to charge him, especially as he had run from the harbour patrol, thereby proving his guilt.

Cicero was led into the interview room to meet his new client, and asked to be left alone with Mattabeele for a few minutes.

Speaking English, Cicero discovered that Mattabeele had brought the statue off a ship that evening and was to deliver it to an address in Athens. When arrested he had quite a sum of money on him, no doubt for travel expenses.

He would not tell Cicero why he had to deliver the statue or to whom. All he would say was that it belonged to his mother, and that he had to give it to a woman in Athens. As the statue was of an African woman and child in a Madonna-like pose, it sounded plausible.

At the hearing before the Magistrate the next morning Cicero argued that Mattabeele had run away when stopped only because he was afraid of anyone in a uniform. Not speaking Greek, he knew he would be arrested, and he had come a long way to give the statue to one of his mother's friends in Athens.

As the police could not prove that it had been smuggled or stolen, the case was dismissed and Matakeema Attabeele was discharged. Cicero never saw him again.

A few days later Cicero had a visitor to his small office situated in a run down area of Piraeus. This stranger was well dressed and said he had been recommended to Cicero by the local magistrate. Cicero, who had never got along with this magistrate and had several run-ins with him, did not believe this stranger, but listened to what he had to say.

When the stranger left, Cicero had his first genuine legal brief. A case involving a disputed amount of alimony. The fee was very handsome and that night he celebrated by taking Kasta out to a restaurant in the centre of the city.

The stranger, whose name was Ari, brought Cicero many cases over the months that followed. Cicero by this time had figured out that Ari belonged to the local crime syndicate and the 'clients' were indeed members of that organization. Kasta was worried and told Cicero to refuse the next time, but Cicero pointed out that the money was coming in regularly and in fairly large sums. Their standard of living had increased to the point where they had enough for a down payment on a modest house.

Kasta tried to argue, but she too knew that until this connection with the syndicate they had struggled to make ends meet. Now their life was completely changed around. She felt uncomfortable with what Cicero was doing but her common sense told her that it was legal, and indeed as Cicero had said, the money was good, so she went along with it.

Through the years Cicero moved up through the hierarchy of the Organization until, shortly after Nikki had been born, he had complete control.

Not long after the stranger's first visit Cicero learned that Mattabeele had indeed been a courier for the Organization, and that evening had come ashore to make a delivery to a client in Athens.

The statue, when broken open, contained a three-and-a-quarter by two-inch briefke, those special papers folded a certain way to form a container for gemstones. This briefke had contained six pink diamonds worth about ten thousand US dollars.

Mattabeele had been in the Organization as a courier for several years, and was highly regarded for his ability to feign innocence when cornered by the police. He had pulled this trick often on his deliveries throughout Europe.

As they left the cemetery, Cicero noticed a car entering the park. As the two cars passed Cicero looked at the driver, and as he recognised him, said with a tremor in his voice, "Janus' driver." It had darkened windows so he could not see the occupants.

This car stopped below the site where the workmen were preparing the burial. A rear window opened noiselessly, a voice shouted up the hill. "Whose grave is that, please?"

One of the workmen fished a piece of paper out of his pocket, and reading from it, shouted, "Niklos Papandropoulous Andreas, father Cicero, mother Kasta Andreas. Anything else?'

The car window closed and the car drove off without a sound.

CHAPTER ELEVEN

Theresa Charles put down the morning newspaper that she always read at breakfast, and glanced up at her husband Marty as he entered the Solarium.

She always felt a quiver of excitement when he was dressed ready for work. He was indeed a handsome man.

Years ago she had gone with a few friends to a restaurant that everyone was talking about. It was called 'Tolleys' after the owner Karl Tolleffson. And was situated in a basement of an old factory building.

As people were seated, a strolling accordion player would approach and play an appropriate piece of music for the female guests.

Theresa seated herself and on cue the accordion player stood behind her chair and played 'Pretty Woman', the Roy Orbison hit. She blushed as everyone in the restaurant turned to look.

It was at that moment Marty appeared. He smiled and hunched his shoulders, as if to say, "Sorry about that."

As her party gave their orders she could not take her eyes off Marty. He was very dashing in his tuxedo, but when he spoke it was with a hard north country accent, which seemed incongruous with his handsome appearance.

She fell for him there and then and knew that he was the man she wanted to marry.

Over the ensuing weeks she discovered that Marty was a born restauranteur, brimming with ideas on how to take a small restaurant and make it a success financially.

Their courtship was short as they had come to terms. If he married her then she would supply the money and use his 'know how' and open up their own restaurant.

She loved to eat here in the solarium, especially in the spring and summer months, the quietness and aromas from the flowers and plants made a meal an event instead of something to get over with as soon as possible.

Marty looked tired and worn and his shoulders were sagging. His whole appearance was of a man who seemed to have given up on life, which was how he felt at that moment. Seeing the wife he liked a little, but did not love, did nothing to alleviate his demeanour.

"The Steinbecks have invited us to make a four at Bridge, this evening. I told them we would be there, all right?"

He hunched his shoulders in a non-caring fashion and sat down to eat. A maid appeared as if from nowhere and laid a plate of cereal in front of him. He nodded and smiled and her.

"Oh dear, are we going to have another one of those silent periods? I suppose you have found a floosie. Another one to add to your extensive list. What's her name this time? Do I know her? Does she work at the club?"

He snarled at her, "Questions, always questions. I never ask about your fairly lengthy list of suitors. God knows what they see in you, it must be your money. Do you lavish your extensive funds on them in return for favours?"

"Calm down, Marty. What's got into you?"

"I want a divorce, Theresa." She sat and stared at him, but said nothing. "Did you hear me?"

"Of course, I heard you, stupid. But you know my feelings on the matter. I will not divorce you."

"Why not? You and I have never loved each other. I have fallen in love with someone. Someone special, and for the first time in my life. You knew that I only liked you when we married, didn't you?"

The maid returned and silence fell over them as the maid took away the dishes and placed a plate of eggs and bacon before him.

'Yes,' Theresa thought, 'he did not love me then, nor now, but I have always loved Marty and still do.'

"Yes I knew that, but you also know my feelings for you."

"Feelings? How can you have feelings when you screw around with every Tom, Dick or Harry that comes along? If you had any feelings for me, Theresa, then you would be faithful."

"I screw around, as you like to call it, because if you can go off and leave me time after time to satisfy your lustful urges with all the large-breasted girls that you employ, then I can have some fun as well. You always came back to me, Marty, and I was always here waiting. I love you, even though I know you are a sonofabitch. I will not divorce you."

"You don't need me now. The club is doing well and I will relinquish my share over to you as part of any settlement. You needed me in the early days. Your money, I know, paid for the club, but with the hours I have worked to build it up to where it is today, well, you know I have paid my dues, so to speak, in spades!"

"Does this girl know you are married? Have you told her, yet?" He nodded sadly. "Ah, I see. She found out and you have had a bust up with her, right?"

He sat at the table, the food now quite cold. The maid kept hovering nearby but on hearing them argue, retreated out of sight.

"No doubt she has threatened to leave, and you, always the gallant knight, said, 'I'll get a divorce'. Is that what happened? Well, you can go back and tell your floosie that there will be no divorce from me."

"She's not a floosie. Not like the others. She's different."

"Different! They have all been different. To you they are just an easy lay. What's her name and does she work at the club?"

"Is that your final word? Because if it is then I will not need a divorce, Theresa. I will simply get out of your life and live with her some place else." So saying he rose from the table and left the Solarium.

Theresa sat for a minute or two. The maid returned to take the food and dishes away, but her mistress waved her hand to say, "Leave me alone."

She opened her purse and took out a wallet. From the wallet she extracted a business card and with the card in her hand went into the house and picked up the phone.

"Joseph, is that you? Good. Theresa here. Meet me for lunch today at, say, one o'clock. The usual place. Thank you." She replaced the phone.

"Hello, Miss Docherty?"

"Yes, speaking."

"Miss Docherty, may I call you Katie? My name is Joseph."

"Yes, Joseph, what can I do for you?"

"Well, Katie, I would like to meet with you to discuss a proposal that would be very beneficial to you financially. May I meet you today at five o'clock?"

Katie was on her guard immediately she heard this man say 'beneficial to you financially.'

"What do you mean, beneficial? You mean that I have inherited some money or something?" She laughed, but it was a nervous laugh. "I do not know you, Joseph, and I have heard that strange things go on this big city of ours. And when you mention money it makes me all the more nervous."

"No need to be, Katie, I assure you. This is nothing underhand, illegal or, and as I know your reputation, sexual. If you like I will meet you in a very public place of your choice. Our meeting will only take a few minutes."

"If you can assure me, Joseph, that I will come to no harm, then I agree."

"You have my solemn promise that you will not come to harm at our meeting."

"So be it. Then I will meet you at five tonight in the foyer of The Royal Opera House, Covent Garden. How will I know you?"

"See you then, Katie."

Katie was perplexed. She dialled the club and asked if Marty was in. No one had seen him today. He had phoned to say that he would be out of town for a few days, seeing to the opening of a new club in Manchester. She phoned his home in Wimbledon and asked for either Marty or Mr. Charles , and was told that both parties were out, but also that Mr. Charles was out of town on business.

Since that eventful day when she had discovered the photograph, Marty had tried to explain to her about his marriage and how he would ask his wife for a divorce. It had taken a lot of pleading on his part, and soul-searching on hers, but eventually she had succumbed to a nervous truce, telling him that she wanted some time to herself and that she would get in touch with him when she was ready. The first contact had to come from her.

But now there was this Joseph fellow, and his weird phone call. She had a feeling it had to do with Marty, but what? She looked at her alarm clock by the side of the bed, four o'clock. Just time for her to get herself dressed and get across town to Covent Garden.

Promptly at five minutes after five o'clock, Katie entered the foyer of the Royal Opera House. It was a woman's prerogative to be a tad late, was it not? She looked around the beautiful ornate entrance hall where Kings and Queens and many Heads of State had entered before her. She had never been here before but it was the only public place she could think of near the club.

"Katie?" She jumped at the sound of her name and turned round to see a pleasant looking man dressed in a pinstripe suit. He looked like a lawyer. Suddenly it dawned on her! A lawyer! Surely she must have come into an inheritance.

"Excuse me, Katie, I am Joseph." He held out his gloved hand with a black umbrella in the crook of his arm. He then doffed his hat and bowed slightly. Katie was very impressed, and taken aback at his polite manners.

"I'm so sorry, I thought you would look quite different."

Taking her arm in his, he led her to an enormous couch which could seat about six people. It was covered in pink brocade and looked as if it had never been sat upon.

"Now to business. I won't keep you very long. I have been empowered by a Mrs. Theresa Charles to offer you a substantial amount of money."

Katie gasped. "What do you mean . . offered money?"

"Just what I said, an amount of cash, but please listen as I will say this to you one time only, understood?"

As she nodded her head, her mouth fell open in disbelief at the sharp serious tone of his voice. No longer the perfect gentleman.

"Good girl, Katie. Now listen. As I have said, I have been asked by Mrs. Charles to offer you a sum of money. A large sum, I may add, but it comes with certain conditions. The sum I am prepared to offer you is five thousand pounds."

Katie whimpered and then placed her hand over her mouth to keep it shut. "This amount will be paid into a bank account of your choice immediately, on the understanding that you will leave town, or better still, the country, within one week. On no account must you communicate with Mr. Charles or with any friends or acquaintances of either, or both of you. Should you decide not to take this offer," and here he smiled a smile that sent a shiver down her spine, "I cannot be responsible for the consequences."

"Consequences, what do you mean?"

"I mean, dear Katie, that I think you would be a wise girl to take the offer. I expect an answer from you by this time the day after tomorrow. Five o'clock on Wednesday. If you agree the money will be in your bank the next morning." With that he got up bowed slightly and left her sitting there speechless. Katie walked home with very mixed emotions. Why Mrs. Charles had offered her such a sum of money was easy to understand. She must love Marty very much. But then, if she loves him like that, a divorce would be out of the question. Five thousand pounds to Katie was a fortune. She could do many things with a sum like that.

What she could not understand, though, was the apparent threat that he had made. 'It would not be wise,' he had said, meaning that if she did not accept … then what? Would she be beaten up, threatened or what? No, things like that only happened in the movies. Did Marty know of this, she wondered?

When she arrived at her flat, she called the club and asked for Rose. "Hi, Rose, Katie. Have you seen Marty around?"

"No, Katie. He has not been around for a couple of days."

"Fine, thanks Rose. See you soon, I hope."

Katie then called the Charles' house, and a cultured voice answered. Could this be Mrs. Charles? "Is Marty Charles home, please?"

"No, I'm sorry, he has left town on business."

"When do you expect him back, please?"

"In about ten days or so. Is there any message you wish to leave?"

"No, but thank you."

She had just replaced the phone, when it rang, startling her. "Hello?"

"Katie, Rose here. I was wondering when you were coming back to work. Angela is very sick and should be at home in bed."

"All right, Rose, do you need me tonight? If so, I can come in at the usual time."

"Yes, please, Katie. I'll tell Angela. She will be ever so grateful. See you in an hour then."

Angela left as soon as Katie came through the door. Both she and Rose then flung themselves into their work, now doing that of three people.

Although Katie had so many questions to ask of Rose, there was no time that evening. Katie went home none the wiser.

The following evening Angela was still off sick so once more Rose and Katie found themselves shorthanded and busy.

Later that evening, when things had quietened down somewhat, Katie asked Rose to join her in the staff room while asking Joe the bartender to cover for them.

"Rose, what kind of woman is Mrs. Charles? How well do you know her?"

"Not too well. She's been in the club a few times and Marty has spoken about her. It would appear that their marriage has not been too happy. It's an old familiar story. A wife has money, marries an ambitious man, sets him up in business. You know the story." Katie nodded solemnly. Rose went on, "But look at this place." She waved her arm around. "Marty's doing. When it comes to business, Marty is the best! Rumour among the staff is that she loves him very much, and is very jealous if he looks at another woman. Also his success takes him away from home a lot, like now for instance, so the marriage has been on shaky ground. I'm sorry to go on like this. Why do you want to know?"

"No, that's fine, I simply wondered about his private life. Marty asked me to marry him as soon as he can divorce his wife."

"What, Marty and you? When did he pop the question? "

"A couple of days ago, why?"

"Well, when Mrs. Charles phoned to say that Marty had gone out of town we all thought it a bit sudden."

Joey, the bartender burst into the room as Katie was about to tell Rose of her encounter with Joseph. "Get the lead out girls, we've got work to do."

They hurriedly followed him to the bar. Sure enough a large group had arrived and Katie recognised a blonde lady, well known for her roles in the American soaps. She apparently was the main attraction tonight.

The next day was Wednesday and Katie was no further forward with regard to her decision. She had until five tonight when no doubt she would receive another phone call from Joseph. Who was he anyway? A lawyer, stockbroker, banker or what? He certainly dressed like those professions.

She awoke at noon, had a meal and when finished, had reached a decision. Katie phoned. "Hello, is Mrs. Charles at home, please?"

"No, I am sorry" answered the same voice as before, the voice Katie guessed to be Theresa Charles. "Is there any message?"

"No thanks." Then on an impulse she blurted out "Is Joseph there by any chance?"

"Joseph who?" asked the lady.

"Sorry I must be mistaken," Katie was now all flustered and hurriedly replaced the receiver.

Theresa Charles held onto the phone and thought that was definitely her. It had been the previous time also. The asking for Joseph and not Joe had given her away and proved it beyond doubt. She could not be looking for Marty. She smiled to herself. That had been a nice touch of hers, sending Marty away. It made her feel good when she recalled telling him: "I will think about a divorce, Marty, but in the meantime there is a club for sale in Manchester. Could you go up there and check it out? Do a complete inventory and come up with a total. They are asking five hundred thousand, and I need to know if we are getting a good deal." Yes, Theresa Charles was very proud of herself.

Katie had decided that when Joseph phoned, she would ask for more time.

He called at five. "Hello, Miss Docherty. Joseph."

"Yes, Joseph. You are very prompt."

"In my business it pays to be."

"What do you do for a living?"

"No need for you to know that, my dear. Have you decided to take the offer?"

"Not yet. I would like a bit more time, please, say a week. It is my future after all that we are discussing." She produced a nervous laugh.

"I will be in touch," was all he said and hung up.

'How rude of him,' she thought. There were no answers to her questions, and nobody to help her. Marty, dear Marty, not around and heaven knows where. Five thousand sounded nice indeed, but what of Marty? Had he asked his wife for a divorce and had she refused? Was that why the money? She had to know before deciding. Surely Joseph realised that, or even Mrs. Charles.

She glanced at the clock, nearly time to go to work. The flat needed to be tidied before she could go and she had to take out the rubbish. While tidying around, a section of the newspaper fell to the floor. She noticed it was the Classified Section. Sitting down, she thought about the money. "If I took it where would I go, what would I do?" She decided to give her mind a treat and look for the most exotic jobs available, by glancing down the overseas posts. Oil workers for the Sudan. Railway Clerks in South Africa. Nurses in Chile and Kuwait. Nothing for her, obviously, but then she saw:

Large fashionable night club in Mediterranean
requires Hostess / Asst. Mgr. Experience of business
and admin. an advantage. Interviews held at
Plaza Court Hotel between 11.00 am and 4.00 pm
Room 602. Call 998-5555 for appt.

'Interesting,' she thought. 'Now that's something I could do.' She then crumpled up the paper and flung it into the garbage bag.

She went to work that evening with thoughts of palm trees and sandy beaches.

Clack-Clack. The sound of the outside door knocker was quiet yet insistent. The clock by the bed showed 4.20 am.

She awoke with a start yet lay still, letting her eyes become accustomed to the dark of the bedroom. Had she heard something?

Clack-Clack. There it was again, but this time a bit louder.

Katie rose and sat on the edge of the bed. Who could be … ? Marty, it must be Marty. She stumbled, in her drowsiness and haste, to get to the door. *Clack-Clack*. "I'm coming, Marty, wait!" She fumbled in the dark with the special lock that she had installed to repel burglars, and finally yanked the door open. Before she could offer a word of welcome two large apparitions forced their way in and one of them hit her with a hard right hook across her chin. She spun around, slipped on the mat at the door, fell heavily into the edge of the door then crumpled in a heap. She cried out in pain and tried to get up, but then her hair was grabbed and tugged so tightly that she screamed out in pain. The guy who was holding her hair then dragged her across the floor toward the bedroom. For a fleeting instant she had a curious picture of Fred Flintstone pulling Wilma, his wife, the same way. The other man by this time had closed the outside door and had gone from her sight.

'Hair Puller' then lifted her bodily by her hair and she felt the strands breaking and falling over her eyes which were filled with tears from the pain being inflicted.

"Stop, please, let go you're hurting me." The words came out between her sobs and her mouth was becoming filled with strands of her hair. She was then flung onto the bed, face down and her hands tied crudely, with what felt like macrame cord. Turning her over on to her back, the other guy then sat on her legs to pin them. He was very fat and must have weighed over eighteen stones. His body was pressing her toes back flat. She yelled at him "For f---'s sake don't sit on my toes." He moved his position slightly. "What the hell are you doing?"

'Hair puller' was standing at the side of her head and he muttered in a sort of foreign accent, "Shut the f--- up, bitch."

Katie did as she was told. Although she had been to bed with many men, she had never before been raped. It had been rough sometimes but she had never had it done against her will, or had more than one man. She was sure that this was what was going to happen here and now, realising that in her flimsy nightgown, which by now was revealing a lot of her body, she presented herself as easy pickings.

'Hair Puller' now crossed a leg over her chest and sat astride her, sitting on her stomach. He then grabbed her hair again and by pulling it down behind her back, made her head and neck arch backwards. She yelled once more as the pain shot through her head and then into her eyes which were now being stretched as well. She imagined her eyeballs were being uprooted from their sockets. She could not see anything as the water flooded into her eye sockets, before cascading down her face.

'Hair Puller' moved his face close to hers and whispered, "You were asked to take the offer of money, but you thought you would be clever, didn't you?"

"No, no no, please don't pull any more. I can't think straight."

'Hair Puller' then released his grip a little, then taking a knife from 'Leg Sitter', touched the point of the blade to her stretched-out throat.

Katie heard a gasp from across the room. Startled, Katie twisted her eyes to see into the darkness. The sound she had heard , a light gasp as if from a woman, made Katie say loudly, "Is there someone there? If so, for God's sake help me." Silence greeted her outburst.

She was brought back to reality by the knife being pushed closer to her throat. "This is to let you know, you f------in' bitch that next time we won't be so nice to you. If you refuse again and have not gone within 24 hours, then I will personally enjoy f---in' you, before I kill you. You're lucky that I can't do it now." He then let the blade run down her neck into her cleavage, and he massaged an exposed breast with the cold steel blade.

'Leg Sitter' touched him on the back, and 'Hair Puller' turned around and looked into the shadows. Nodding, he got off Katie, tipped her over, and released her numb hands. As they left the room Katie peered into the shadows near the door and saw a third figure turn to go out. The way the figure moved Katie could have sworn it was a woman. Her earlier suspicions had been correct, then?

The outside door closed and she was left on the bed, still smarting from the treatment she had suffered. Her head was pounding hard as the blood which had been drained from it started to pulse life back into her brain.

Had that been Mrs. Charles watching? This thought above all worried Katie. This game was now deadly serious and if Katie wanted to spare her life and get rid of Mrs. Charles, Joseph and the rest of them, plus make five thousand pounds, then she must leave as soon as possible. She rose from the bed and went into the outer room, putting on the light.

There, sitting behind the front door looking forlorn, was the large black rubbish bag that she had forgotten to take out when she had left earlier.

The advertisement, of course! It was in the rubbish bag. Opening the bag she rummaged around and finally found the part of the newspaper she had been reading earlier.

She went to the kitchen and put on a kettle for a cup of tea. It reminded her of the British movies. Every time something dreadful happened, it was almost always smoothed over by a cup of tea.

Why would Mrs. Charles want to witness her pain? Out of revenge? Curiosity perhaps? Or downright pleasure at seeing her suffer? Whatever, Katie had made up her mind to call the Charles residence and tell whoever answered to place the money in her bank, as she would leave town as soon as she got hold of the money.

The Plaza Court Hotel was one of the select private hotels that are found throughout the centre of London.

The foyer was straight out of a Charles Dickens' story. Brown panelling on the walls, quiet refined wallpaper and carpeting, and off somewhere could be heard the playing of chamber music by a string quartet, or similar ensemble. The whole atmosphere was of an age long since passed.

Katie approached the uniformed old gentleman seated behind the desk. "Room 602, please. I have an appointment."

The old man, hardly noticing her, pointed a limp arm over her shoulder. Turning she saw the elevator, which happened to be the type with two grill gates that one operates oneself by means of levers and arrows pointing to floor numbers. 'Mr. Otis would love this,' she laughingly thought.

As the elevator ascended out of his view, the clerk looked approvingly at Katie's disappearing legs. Best he'd seen all day, he mused, before the crossword puzzle again took his attention.

When she knocked on door 602, a woman's voice called out, "Come in, please."

Katie found herself in a square shaped lobby or vestibule. There was a desk and against the wall several chairs. Seated behind the desk was an elderly lady looking very prim and proper, her greying hair done up in a bun - an old-fashioned style that seemed to blend in with the decor downstairs.

"I'm here for an interview."

"Take a seat, please."

Katie sat next to a young lady who seemed to be the same age as herself. The two of them looked shyly at each other. When seated, Katie did as the other girl was doing, and stared at a set of double doors opposite. It was a full hour before Katie was ushered behind those doors.

Inside, the transformation was unbelievable. Whereas downstairs had been eighteenth century, here it was strictly twenty- first century. Mirrored walls, with surrealistic paintings of who knows what; floor lamps that bent into the most unusual shapes; metal chairs that had no visible means of support. The floor appeared to be marble with scatter rugs with the same hideous patterns as the paintings. There was a large antique-looking coffee table around three sides of which were the plushest and silkiest sofas that Katie had ever seen. Enormous cushions seemed to be everywhere, allowing no space for seating.

Katie was ushered to sit at one of the sofas by the smaller of the two men already seated.

"I am Kouros, George Kouros." The small man offered his hand which she shook gingerly. "And this is Demetrius Thermopolous, May I take your coat?"

As he helped Katie remove her coat, she had to struggle a bit, noticing that the big man, Demetrius, was ogling her bust. She took a dislike to this man, although to have men staring at her breasts was normal for Katie.

As the big man coughed and changed his position on the sofa he said excitedly, "Please sit, Miss Docherty. Did I speak it correctly? You will please excuse my English, it is not as good as I would like."

She nodded and smiled demurely. Then followed a silence which gave her time to study both of them.

Kouros, the smaller, was thin and had a sallow complexion. His face was covered in acne and moles from which small tufts of hair protruded. The only redeeming feature was that he had a really genuine smile which he had lavished heavily on Katie since she entered the room.

Demetruis was the exact opposite, large, fat, and bald headed. But he also had a cheery smile under a very tanned face.

Both men wore immaculate suits with the largest cuff links that Katie had ever seen. Their clothes and appearance seemed to suggest lots of money. Katie was encouraged by that thought.

As she sat on the sofa opposite this odd couple, Katie crossed her legs, which, with the deep plush of the seat, made this task a little onerous. Demetrius noticed a quick expanse of slip and white thigh, and his eyes could not hide his delight. Katie had noticed his look.

"Well, Miss Docherty," said Kouros, "Do you feel that you have the necessary qualifications for the position we are offering?"

"Yes, indeed I do." Katie then went on to elaborate on her present position at the Club Aladdin as well as her education in Business Administration.

Demetrius sat and listened, all the while staring at her and tapping a pen against his crossed leg. Nice body, nice legs and extremely good looking. He switched his gaze from her figure to her face. She was talking about her ability to speak French quite well. He noticed that while she talked she stared back at him. What was that look behind those eyes of hers, he wondered? Aggressiveness, even defiance? She knew how to convey thoughts by her eyes.

Katie had not liked this Demetrius fellow from the start. All the time she had been carefully stating her credentials, he had been drooling over her body. He had no other interest in her. Well, she would show him that his staring would not deter her in any way.

Demetrius came to a conclusion. Not only was this girl the most attractive that they had interviewed, but that defiance he had seen in her eyes was the quality that he was looking for. Someone who in an uncomfortable position could still hold her own.

Kouros was yapping on and on so Demetrius interrupted. "Miss Docherty, you appear to be exactly what we were looking for. If you wish the position then it is yours."

The smaller man turned and stared at him, questions forming in his furrowed forehead.

"Yes, thank you, sir," said Katie with a lilt in her voice.

Kouros saw the look in Demetrius' eyes and turned to Katie. "Two things, er, Katie. May I call you Katie?" She nodded and gave him a beaming smile. "Our club is in Nicosia in Cyprus. Now, when can you start?"

She was startled by the idea of Cyprus, not being quite sure where it was, but muttered anyway, "Good, I can start as soon as you like."

Demetrius stood up offering his hand. "Miss Docherty, nice to have you with us. See you in Nicosia." With that he strode out of the room.

Kouros explained about salary, air fares, flights etc. Did she have a passport? "Good, then we will see you in a few days, Katie."

Before leaving the hotel, Katie used the public telephone, to call Mrs. Charles. As she was not home Katie left a message to say that Miss Docherty would be leaving the country in forty-eight hours and would Mrs. Charles have the money paid into her bank account at the earliest opportunity.

CHAPTER TWELVE

When Nikki awoke, the first thing he saw was the nurse.

"He's coming around, Doctor," whispered the nurse in Greek. Her face then disappeared and a bearded man with a white hospital cap leaned over him. "How are you, Nikki? Welcome back."

Nikki heard his name as from inside a metal tube. The bearded man slowly vanished in a mist. Once again Nikki's eyes fell into darkness.

"He will be fine now, Nurse. Monitor him well and summon me the moment he wakes completely."

The doctor then left the room and walked along a short corridor, then entered a tiny office.

"Hello, hello, is that … ? Oh, good." He paused, listening. "Yes, just a few minutes ago." Another pause. "Yes, I have left instructions to that effect … certainly … goodbye."

As Cicero sat in his study, the place he loved more than anywhere else, the shadows were lengthening creating little pockets of shadow on the desk and the few papers that were there.

When he was a young man, he had always dreamed of being rich and famous and having 'A Study'. He wanted people family and friends to say: ' He is in his study' To Cicero, it was the epitome of luxury.

As a teenager he had seen a British whodunit movie where the body was discovered in the study of an old country manor house. From that movie he had created a mental image of what his room would look like if ever he had the funds or the house.

Not too many years later when he and Kasta purchased this home he told her of his boyhood dream. Thinking him a little crazy she laughed and told him to go ahead.

They went on holiday to England and while there, in London, he went to one of those superior furniture shops found there, in Bond Street, to try to find some chairs. He had gone through many rooms and floors without seeing anything that remotely matched his dreams.

An assistant, surprisingly elegant in morning coat and tails, had been watching Cicero for some time. When he saw the disappointment on the customer's face, he asked what he had been looking for.

"I'm looking for matching leather chairs and couch for my study, but have been unable to find something suitable."

The assistant looked at him carefully as if sizing him up. Was this gentleman old money or new money? He decided wrongly that Cicero was old money and said, "If you follow me, sir, I have in the basement a set of chairs that was brought in for re-upholstering. Unfortunately the gentleman owner died shortly after, intestate, I'm afraid, so it is still here untouched."

He led Cicero down a very wobbly-looking wooden staircase that looked as if it had been made only yesterday and by the owner's son. It was made of plain wood, unfinished, and the nails had not been hammered in correctly, they were bent over.

"The furniture has lain down here for several months." The assistant said and, noticing Cicero's disgust at the staircase, added, "We don't use this much. We usually use the loading dock to get in and out. Mind your head at the bottom."

They arrived at the foot of the stair and the assistant fiddled behind a faded tapestry and found the light switch.

"Now where was it?" he said absent-mindedly. "Ah, the next room, I think. Follow me and watch your clothes, the stuff down here is quite dirty."

Cicero noticed that on saying the last sentence the assistant's posh accent tended to revert to what Cicero thought would be his way of speaking - a heavy accent heard around London. Cicero smiled. Shop assistants were the same, the world over.

"Yes, this should be them," he said as he threw off some dustsheets.

Cicero stood transfixed. This was it! Here were his dream chairs. His heart began pounding. There were three chairs, a three-seater couch and a two-seater or love seat. Two of the armchairs were large with high backs which he liked best. The modern furniture seemed to consist of low backs which did not allow one's head to rest. The third armchair was smaller but was also a 'rocker'. Cicero decided then and there, that was the chair to sit behind his desk.

The furniture was in dark green leather and all the pieces had indentations on the seats and arms. They had a 'lived in' look but still the leather was in fine condition.

With a stammer in his voice he asked, "Are they for sale?"

"I don't know, sir, but I will make a phone call and find out. You're interested, then?"

Cicero could only nod as the realization that he might own this furniture seemed like a dream. No doubt he would soon wake up and find himself on the hotel bed next to Kasta.

They retraced their steps back up the makeshift steps to the main showroom. While the assistant went into the office to make his phone call, Cicero slumped onto the nearest chair, completely breathless. Not from the climb back upstairs, which had been difficult, but from the sheer excitement at finding such a beautiful suite of furniture. The fact that it had been well used suited him, as when installed in his study, it would not appear to be new.

The assistant stood at the door and called out, "Sir Thomas Faversham, the owner of this establishment." At this he waved an arm as if he was warding off a fly. " Would like you to confirm your interest?" He handed over the phone as Cicero approached.

Cicero smiled as he took the phone. The assistant had reverted to his 'posh voice'. "Hello, is this Sir Thomas?"

"Yes, and your name, sir?"

"Cicero. Cicero Andreas from Athens."

"Well, Mr. Andreas my assistant tells me you're interested in that suite of green leather in the storeroom that belonged to Mr. Davidson. Is that correct?"

"Yes, it is, sir" replied Cicero warily.

"Well then, Mr. Andreas, it is your lucky day. It's yours. "

"Really!" blurted out Cicero, interrupting Sir Thomas. Then recovering his posture asked as nonchalantly as he could, "And the asking price?"

"Nothing, Mr. Andreas, just the cost of getting it out of my shop."

"Are you sure?"

"Yes, by all means and tell ... what's his name ... Rodney, I think, tell him, no need for paperwork. Thank you, Mr. Andreas and good day to you."

"Thank you very much ... " Before he could finish the sentence Sir Thomas had hung up.

As he sat in the 'rocker' amidst the deepening gloom of the study recalling the incident, his eyes wandered around the room. He could recall where and when every item in it had been obtained. The desk he sat at had come from a sale at the Army base that was closing down. The government in its infinite wisdom of cost-cutting, had closed the base and thrown hundreds of civilians out of work. The desk, made of fine dark rosewood, had graced the officers' mess. It was really too large for Cicero but size to Cicero was impressive, and over the years it had been much admired. Also, on his visit to London, he had acquired the velvety smooth Wilton carpet at a price that staggered Kasta, but as the chairs were free, they did not mind the cost.

On either side of the fireplace, which had artificial logs in a sterling silver grate, were two busts. One was Philip II of Macedon and the other Alexander his son, two great Greek heroes of the past. He did not believe they were the actual faces of these great men, but as there was no one who knew what they looked like it didn't matter.

Above the fireplace was a striking portrait of Kasta, done by a local Athenian painter. He had captured both her strength and her tenderness magnificently.

The rest of the walls had single bookcases full of volumes, none of which he had read. Between the books were paintings of Greece and the Greek islands. The whole tone of the room was of quiet elegance, mirroring Cicero's own demeanour.

Sitting there, with his head bowed as if in prayer, it had seemed like years since that day on Nikki's birthday. That had been the last time that he had seen his son.

He went through the ritual of tidying his desk and locking the drawers. A ritual he performed every night.

Closing the study door softly, he made his way up the wide semicircular staircase. He was rehearsing the words in his head.

He tapped on the door of the upstairs drawing room which Kasta used as a sewing room. He also had occasion to use it when sleep was hard to find. Lately he had used it often.

Kasta was there, sitting by the fireplace which had a small fire burning. No heat was emanating from the fire, but the flickering of the tiny flames created an ambience of comfort and tranquillity which permeated the entire room.

He approached his wife and kissed her hair. He loved the smell of her hair. Loved it because it was a smell peculiar to her, and which no other person in the world could smell. The smell confirmed his love for her. "You know that I love you very much, don't you?"

"Yes, Cicero, I know."

"I have good news. Nikki has awakened, or 'come to' or whatever they call it."

"Oh, Cicero, thank God." She said it as if sighing. "I did not show it, but I had a nagging feeling that maybe, just maybe, he wouldn't pull through."

"I had that same feeling. I simply wish that it had not been necessary to go through this charade."

"Yes, well, you know my feelings on that. Can I go and see him?"

"No, better not. The doctor told me there may be a touch of amnesia when he finally becomes awake."

"Oh, my God. You mean … "

"No, it will not last long. The effects of the drug will wear off shortly. We will have to make do with progress reports for now."

"Cicero, do you think this will end Janus' interest in Nikki?"

"Can't say. Time will tell."

Later that evening, in bed he turned and cuddled against her back. "Would you really have killed me, Kasta?"

"I cannot tell. What I can tell is that I was very annoyed that you had not told me the real reason you sent Nikki away. Angry that I had to drag it out of you and furious that you would not treat me as a person, an equal. We are supposed to be a partnership."

"I'm sorry. Yes, I did wrong in not bringing you into the decision making. But I had to act fast when I learned that it was Janus' son that had died outside the bar, that night, here in Athens. Thankfully, Nikki did not know him."

"Tell me dear, why has Janus hated you all these years, even before the death of his son?"

"You ask why? You, of course. He loved you as much as I did, but mercifully you chose me instead of him." At this he wrapped an arm around her and his hand started to wander.

"You men," she scoffed. "At your age. Are you not past it yet?"

"Not yet, my love."

As he opened his eyes, the headache started, a steady pain above the right eye. He closed them again, blinked a few times, but still the pain would not go away.

Raising himself by his elbows, Nikki discovered he was in a large double bed, which was situated at one end of a large wide room. On one side of the room were three large double door windows hung with heavy drapes in beautiful folds, which enhanced the windows greatly. The windows, he thought, no doubt led to a terrace or veranda.

The other wall consisted entirely of bookshelves on which were hundreds of ancient-looking books. He could see no covers that were modern or any paperbacks. They looked old, dry and no doubt were dusty as well. He smiled to himself at his use of that old worn phrase.

At the far end on the wall, opposite his own, was a large ornate fireplace made of what looked like marble. It was fully ten feet wide and the grate was about three feet wide alone. In front of the fireplace were two plush armchairs and two sofas. Various tables and chairs were scattered around the centre of the room.

The bed he lay in obviously did not belong in this room as it appeared to be a drawing room or library.

Gingerly he rose and sat on the edge of the bed. Although his head was aching, he tried to walk to the nearest window. On the second step he fell to the floor and lay there dazed.

What had happened? He tried to get to his feet, but he could not feel them. He could see both lying there, but he was unable to move them. Rolling over onto his stomach he put his hands out to push himself up, but his hands felt soft and mushy and could not support his weight. He fell down on his face.

What on earth was happening here? Try the knees. He pushed one knee into the floor hard. Good, he felt that. Now the other knee, even better. Now he raised his upper legs. Groaning under the exertion, he at last was on his knees with his head still face down on the ground. He pushed with his head and elbows. Sweating and panting with his head still aching, he managed to raise himself, animal-like, on his knees and elbows.

Now what? He raised his body erect and sat back on his heels. It felt as though he were sitting on a cushion. At least he was somewhat upright. But with no use of his hands or feet how was he to stand up? He started to laugh out loud. "Toulouse Lautrec, reincarnated."

While in this position, tears streaming from his eyes, half laughing and sobbing, the door opened behind him and a doctor and nurse entered. They stood for a moment looking at this pathetic figure on the floor, wondering what he was doing in that weird position.

They moved toward him and the nurse in her best bedside voice asked "What's so funny, Nikki?"

"What's so funny? Me, I'm so funny, look at me. Doomed for the rest of my life to live and walk on my knees and elbows." The tears started again as he sank ever so slowly, as if in slow motion, back to the floor in a heap.

They went to his aid and half carried and dragged him back to the bed.

The nurse poured a glass of water and gave it to Nikki with a pill. "Take this, it will help you sleep. Sleep is what you need."

As they left the room with their patient all tucked in like a baby, the doctor said, "Sleep well, Nikki."

Nikki's heartbeat dropped, his temperature went down and as the brain went into a semi-comatose state before slumber, it projected a series of jumbled images from his subconscious.

A flock of birds flew overhead chattering in a language he could not understand. He was sitting in a park with a bed next to him. In the bed lay a dead body. The body was speaking to the birds. The birds then dived toward him and started spitting what seemed to be pellets at his head. They missed him but struck a passing car. The driver of the car leaned out and waved to the birds, with a mug in his hands.

For two days he hovered between deep sleep and incoherent consciousness. His body temperature worried the doctor as it was dropping at an alarming rate.

The bed was moved to the other side of the room close to the fireplace. The fire was lit and kept going with huge logs brought in from the grounds. Hot water bottles were placed around Nikki's body and to keep them in place they lightly strapped him to the bed.

Shifts were set up for the doctor and nurse to take turns sitting by the bedside on constant vigil. While they sat at the bedside, although the patient remained cold, they had to strip down and almost sit in their underwear as the area around the fireplace was so sweltering.

No contact was made with the outside while Nikki's life hung in the balance.

Nikki rolled around in the bed and was muttering and coughing. 'What images was he seeing in his head?' the doctor wondered.

The doctor dozed off one night and was awakened by an inner sense. Gloom hung over the room as the fire had diminished to a few glowing embers. He looked at his watch. It was 4.20 am. There was no movement from the patient. Rising, the doctor went to the bed. Nikki was deathly pale, and very cold. The doctor laid his hand on Nikki's chest, no heartbeat. He took the stethoscope from around his neck and applied it to the heart, nothing.

"Nurse, come quickly," he shouted. No answer. He hurried over to the anteroom where she lay sleeping, and bursting open the door awoke her with a start. "Nurse, get the trolley quick. His heart has stopped."

The nurse was instantly alert and left the anteroom.

The doctor returned to the bed, pulled aside the bedclothes and tore open Nikki's pyjama top, as the nurse entered the room at a run with the defibrillator trolley.

"Quickly now," the doctor advised her. "I don't know how long he's been in this condition."

"You were asleep, right?"

"Yes. I dozed off."

"You know what will happen if he dies, don't you?"

While she was getting the equipment ready, he was applying rhythmic compressions to the sternum area. He stood aside as the nurse was ready and applied the gel, handing the paddles to the doctor.

"Stand back." He laid the two paddles onto Nikki's chest and with his eyes on the monitor, nodded his head. The nurse pressed the switch and ZAP! The body arched in an uncontrolled spasm and fell back to the bed. The graph on the monitor still showed a thin horizontal line.

ZAP! Again the body convulsed. The graph showed a little flicker. "Again!" the nurse shouted. "There is life there."

"Better not, this defibrillator could kill him also." The doctor placed his stethoscope on Nikki and listened while he watched the monitor. "A faint beat," he whispered, applying his hands in rhythmic unison to Nikki's heart and chest. The graph started to show the beats getting stronger.

"He's out of danger," the doctor said wearily. By this time the graph was undulating in regular patterns.

"Well done, doctor." She gave him a hug and they both clung to each other for comfort. Neither had performed this task before.

They made Nikki comfortable, stoked up the fire and replenished the hot water bottles. When they had finished their tasks they both sat quietly by the bedside alone with their own thoughts, together with thoughts about the young man lying there. Would he ever know that he had died twice? Once when he was injected in Mexico and now here in this room, but this time it had been for real.

Nikki's sleep was now deep, with the pain erased from his face. A calm repose once more settled not only on the patient, but over the room, the nurse and doctor, and the house.

The doctor, next morning made a telephone call.

CHAPTER THIRTEEN

At precisely ten o'clock at the St. John's Wood branch of the London and South East Bank, Joseph arrived.

Katie had been there for a few minutes mingling with the scattering of people awaiting the bank's opening.

"Good morning, Miss Docherty. All set then. I heard you have obtained a position overseas."

"Yes, Joseph, it is with … "

"No, Katie, don't tell me. The less I know the better for both of us."

The doors were opened by a bank employee and the small group of customers filed in.

"Over here, Katie." Joseph ushered her to one of the tables scattered around the walls. He opened his briefcase and brought out a plain folder. Sifting through the papers, he extracted three pieces of paper.

"Now, Katie, I have here a certified cheque for five thousand pounds as agreed. It is made payable to you." He looked closely at Katie and he could see the nervousness in her face. Her hands were moving all the time. "Now these two papers are both the same. One is a copy of the other. Please read it through and tell me you understand the contents."

Katie took the sheet of paper and as she read, it shook in her hand. Joseph smiled. A little feeling of pity entered his head. She was such a nice girl, a n innocent, caught up circumstances over which she had not much control. It struck him that she was far more innocent than the others he had dealt with.

"I have read it. Do you wish me to sign it? "

"Yes, please. Sign here to say that you agree to the terms and sign down there to say that you have received the money." He watched her sign her name. It was obvious from the way she laboriously wrote out her full name that she was not used to signing documents. Once more a smile filtered across his face.

"Now do the same on this other copy - the one which I will keep. Good, now I will witness your signatures, here and here. There, now we are finished. Go and deposit your cheque and to your future, 'Bonne Chance'." He rose, and bowing slightly from the neck left the bank.

Katie sat and reread the agreement. It stated that on receipt of the money she was to have no contact whatever with Marty or any mutual acquaintances, especially those employed by the Club Aladdin. There were other pages of legal jargon but the message of the agreement was clear.

PART TWO

CHAPTER FOURTEEN

Katie had seen and heard about Cyprus from newspapers and television; how the United Nations had troops stationed there to help keep the peace between the Greeks and Turkish populace on the island.

Although she was aware of the situation from the media, it had been of no interest to her until now. The fact that she was flying to Cyprus made her cast her mind back to those same news items. She tried to recall what she had heard but to no avail, and wished that she had paid more attention.

On entering the Cyprus Airlines plane the strange situation on Cyprus was brought home to her immediately. She asked the Flight Attendant what time the flight landed at Nicosia, the capital.

"Sorry, ma'am, but we do not land at Nicosia, but land at Larnaca, 16.00 hrs local time."

"Larnaca?" queried Katie. "Where is that, and why there?"

"It is a city on the south side of Cyprus. We fly there because as you rightly say the capital, Nicosia, is a divided city. Divided between the Greek and Turkish Cypriots."

"Oh my, I didn't realise."

"Not to worry. The distance between the two cities is only about 20 or 30 miles, not far."

"Thank you . . . er . . . Lori," smiled Katie noticing the name tag on the uniform.

As the plane approached its destination, the pilot announced that the temperature at Larnaca was 97 degrees. Katie's heart skipped a beat. She could not recall ever experiencing such heat.

The plane touched down and there were the usual waits, first to get off the aircraft, then in line for the luggage, then lastly going through Customs. Finally she made it to the main concourse.

Here she was caught up in the bustle of the crowds. Not only that, but the strange Greek language and signs that she could not understand seemed to emphasise the chaotic atmosphere of the place.

Finding herself a seat in the centre of the hall, she waited. Someone was supposed to meet her. Tired, excited and extremely nervous, the thought of not knowing the language had never entered her head in her haste to leave the country. Now she was having second thoughts.

The concourse was gradually emptying as she watched the passengers from her plane being met by friends or relatives with hugs, kisses and tears.

Luggage was collected, arms linked in love and children were rounded up crying - all the sights and sounds witnessed in every airport around the world.

Almost imperceptibly the concourse was closing down. Cleaners were crossing the floor with their large wide brooms in systematic sweeps. Car rental companies were being locked up and the shutters on the counters closed - a strange sight to see at an air terminal, but with only a few flights per day, Katie thought, and the time now five o'clock, not really surprising.

Cleaning ladies, all chattering at one another, were dropping off at the washrooms with their cleaning carts. Occasionally there would be a burst of raucous laughter as if a rude joke had just been told. Katie smiled wanly when they looked over her way, as if she too had enjoyed the joke, although not understanding a word that was spoken.

Katie now had that abandoned feeling that comes to everyone when confronted with a late meeting. Should she go outside or wait here?

Rising from her seat, as she now felt rather conspicuous sitting there, she crossed the polished floor, avoiding the sweeping brushes, toward the signs that showed buses. It was the only sign that she could identify.

The sunlight from outside leapt into her eyes and the heat hit her as if she had opened an oven door. After the cool of the air-conditioned inside, the change was enough to stop her in her tracks.

She groped in her purse for the sunglasses she had bought especially for the trip, while the sun was piercing through to her brain, numbing her thoughts and actions. Finding her sunglasses and putting them on, she found instant blessed relief.

There was no relief however, from the heat which rose from the roadway through her soft shoes. Her summer dress was beginning to cling to her body. She thought to herself that she must look an awful sight; a typical tourist, in fact.

"God, Katie," she murmured to herself, "what have you gotten yourself into?"

"Miss Docherty?" Her name was being called. She saw a man staring at her. They both smiled shyly as he approached, carrying a small hand sign that said 'Club Britannia' "Miss Docherty, yes?"

"Yes. Are you from the Club in Nicosia?"

"Oui, oui, I mean yes, I am. My name is Pierre. I am French." He sounded almost apologetic. "So sorry for the delay in arriving. You must have been terribly worried."

"No, not at all," lied Katie unconvincingly. He smiled at her good manners. A little furrow crept onto his forehead and his eyes were raised in question. The moment passed.

"Come, give me one of your bags. Follow me, the van is in the parking area."

Blindly, as all visitors to a strange place, she followed at his heels, not noticing anything that she passed.

Shortly they were at the van; a beige coloured van with 'Club Britannia' emblazoned on its side panels. There were phone numbers and the name Nicosia as well. Katie felt a little comforted on seeing the name. Journey's end was getting nearer.

"Jump in, Miss Docherty."

"Katie please, Pierre."

Inside was cool and comfortable. It had seating for about eight with sliding doors on either side.

"How long until we get there?"

"About half an hour depending on the traffic. I will take it a little bit slower than I usually do." He turned and smiled at her. "You will be able to see some of the sights of our island."

She turned her head and looked at him as he was pulling out of the parking area. She was warming to this man from France. He was extremely tanned, his face and arms a dark mahogany colour. He was short and muscular, giving him an almost apelike appearance. He reminded her of some of the bouncers that she had met over the years. Her mind flashed the thought that clubs and bars had been a big part of her life up to now.

"How come a Frenchman is working here in Cyprus?"

"Oh, my dear Katie, that's a long story. Suffice to say that I was in the Army and was stationed here as an UN soldier. When it came time for me to leave the military, I came back here to live and work."

"Is it beautiful here, then?"

"No. Not really beautiful, as in countryside and views, that sort of thing. But beautiful because it is warm all year round, peaceful, and if you stay out of trouble with the locals, a safe place to spend one's days. A haven, so to speak. The beaches are plentiful, the seas warm and the bathing relatively safe."

"Sounds beautiful to me." Katie was relaxing with every moment of this conversation and the doubts and fears were fast dissipating. "Tell me about the Greek and Turkish troubles?"

"Well, it goes back a long way." Pierre skilfully drove the van away from the narrow streets around the Airport and merged onto the main freeway- style road leading to Nicosia.

"How long?" interrupted Katie.

"I can't tell you in years, but it goes back to when the island got its independence from Britain. It was thought that the independence would stop the age-old strife between the Greek and Turkish residents here. The Greeks wanted the island to be part of Greece and the Turkish Cypriots wanted to be separated. The friction between the two factions escalated, resulting in killings and bombings. The United Nations was called in to keep the peace, and that brought about the partition of the island. I may not have told it right but that, in a nutshell as you English say, is the story."

"Oh look," shouted Katie, pointing to a grove of orange trees, "oranges, hundreds of them."

"Yes, they are all over the place. You'll get used to them."

" Sorry for the interruption, Pierre. Please go on."

"Where was I? Yes, the division of the island. The Turks are in the north and the Greeks are here in the south, the larger part. In between is, what is called 'The Green Line' or 'Green Zone', the border. It is not a line drawn on the roads, but more a name for the area. It is heavily patrolled by the UN forces."

"Only British troops?"

"At the moment, yes, mainly British. Prior to them we had the Canadians. They were the best as they had more experience in this sort of situation. The Club where you will be working is called the Club Britannia, right?"

"Yes, so what?"

" Well, up to a few months ago it was called 'The Canuck Club' because of the Canadians here. Now that the Brits are here, voila! The name change."

They had left the fertile coastal plain with its orange trees and palm trees and vineyards. They were now climbing up toward the mountains. Here amid the foothills, the trees were now pine and fir and there were many sheep dotted on the rocky hillsides. Snow could be seen on the higher elevations to the west and north.

"What's the Club like?"

"It is big, très magnifique, and makes lots of money."

Katie was not quite so worried now. The talk of beaches, fresh fruit and the Club being prosperous had settled her nerves.

They continued their journey in silence, both lost in their thoughts. Pierre's were of the questioning kind. This young girl beside him was out of place, he was sure. Why had she taken on this job? He shrugged; not his place to worry about her. Nevertheless he had taken to this young miss from Scotland and could not help worrying. He vowed that if ever she needed help he would be there for her.

On the road ahead of them they could see flashing lights as if from police cars.

"Must be a police check point. Let me do the talking." He laughed at himself for what he said. "I mean, I know you don't speak Greek, but even if he speaks in English, just smile and say nothing. Have your passport and work permit handy, just in case." He smiled kindly at her as he could see the fear in her eyes. "There's nothing to worry about, strictly routine."

They pulled up behind three or four other cars all waiting to go through. Katie could see two police cars and several policemen.

"Which police are they, Greek or Turkish?"

"Greek, this is not a border crossing, simply a spot check on travellers. They do this frequently."

"Good evening," a tall handsome policeman said in Greek.

Pierre answered him in Greek. "Good evening officer - Palus, isn't it?"

"Why, yes. Oh hello, Pierre. I did not realise it was you. Who have you got with you?"

"A young lady from Scotland, but please keep talking in Greek, Palus."

"Ah ha! I see you have a new Whisky Dolly and she does not know that yet." At that he started to laugh heartily.

Katie was very anxious as she could not understand what was being said but she had heard 'Scotland' and knew they were discussing her. The laughter, however; what did that mean?

Palus held out his hand for her papers. Katie was about to shake it when Pierre whispered, "He wants your papers."

Katie held the document out with shaky hands. Palus noticed the shake and said to Pierre, "Nervous little thing isn't she? Very nice though, very nice indeed." He thumbed through the two documents and when handing them back to her, smiled and said in perfect English, "Welcome to Cyprus, Miss Docherty. Enjoy your stay here. Good day."

"Thank you, Officer."

Pierre waved and drove away.

"What were you two laughing at? It was about me, wasn't it?"

"Nothing, dear Katie, just two men discussing your physical merits, that's all."

Katie knew he was lying, but said nothing.

The Club Britannia was an austere, three storied, flat roofed building looking more like a warehouse than a night club. It was a dull sandstone colour. The main entrance had a gaily coloured awning from which hung the club name in flashing lights.

" Not much from the outside, is it? " Pierre was beginning to read this young lady's thoughts. "The inside, though, is very nice."

As she viewed this grand building Katie's apprehension came back. The place looked much larger than she had imagined. The picture she had in her head was of one of those little night clubs that are dotted around the Soho district of London; small and intimate, not like this, large and very intimidating. It appeared to her like one of those large hotels in Las Vegas, but without all the glitz and glamour.

Pierre drove the van past the front entrance, which stood a good one hundred yards from the city street. The whole area was taken up by a parking lot. Taking her around the back, he drove up to a door with a small illuminated sign in Greek.

"I suppose I should learn a bit of the language, if I'm going to work here, eh Pierre?"

"If you want to. It's not really necessary as most people use English if they are addressed that way. The majority of the customers are British anyway. Grab a bag and I'll take the other."

"Why, Pierre, am I staying here; living in?"

"Yes, I will take you to your room."

While she followed him through a maze of corridors and up staircases, he explained that the building at one time had been an hotel. It had been converted to a club about twenty years ago. Some of the old hotel rooms on the top floors had been retained as staff quarters.

The room he led her to was extremely comfortable, and, as Pierre had said, it certainly looked like a hotel room even down to the shower and bathroom attached.

"I'll leave you now, Katie, but will come back for you tomorrow morning at about eight o'clock. Get yourself settled in. You must be tired after your journey."

"Yes, I am. I did not realise until now. Thank you, Pierre." On an impulse she went over, gave him a hug and placed a soft gentle kiss on his cheek.

He coughed slightly, shuffled his feet and mumbled, "Until tomorrow, then."

An hour or so later, after unpacking, she heard the faint sound of music and singing coming from downstairs. The desire to go and investigate was strong but so was her body's desire for sleep.

True to his word Pierre knocked on her door at eight o'clock. "Good, you're ready. I'll take you to meet Demetrius, he's one of the owners. Got your papers etc.?"

"Yes, here in my purse. I think I met him in London. Is he a big man, bald and always smiling?"

"That's him. A word of advice. Don't cross him, he is an influential man on the island. Some say … " He stopped, having said too much.

"Some say what, Pierre?"

"Nothing, just rumours. I have no proof."

"Proof of what?"

"You ask too many questions, Katie." He smiled nervously, wishing that he had kept his mouth shut.

They both went down a flight of stairs to the second floor, along a corridor that was brightly lit and through a door at the end.

The decor changed drastically from plainness to opulence. The lighting here was subdued, the carpeting lush. Where the walls had been bare, they were now covered in murals, paintings and tapestries, each with their own individual lighting. Katie was no expert, but even to her eye they looked like expensive works of art.

"This is the business side of the club. Just a few more doors," he whispered to her. His whisper did not seem out of place here as the whole effect of the corridor was ethereal.

He stopped at a rosewood door with very ornate panelling and knocked.

"Come in," said a voice.

They entered a fairly large, conventional office. Off to one side of the room were several chairs, which Katie imagined were for holding meetings.

"Ah, Miss Docherty, good to see you again, please sit down. Thank you, Pierre, that will be all."

Pierre bowed, turned, and smiled a comforting smile at Katie.

She looked him in the eye, and he could see the friendship there.

Demetrius noticed the exchange. "He is nice, isn't he?"

She turned from the door and faced him. "Yes, he's been very kind to me, Mr. Demetrius."

"Demetrius, Katie, just plain Demetrius."

She was reassured by his apparent friendliness.

"Do you have your passport and work permit with you?"

"Yes, I have, sir … I mean Demetrius." She fumbled in her large purse which seemed to contain all her worldly possessions. As she rummaged through, he noticed a piece of a comb, a part of a newspaper with a crossword puzzle on it, scissors, a change purse, tissues and a man's photograph.

"Here it is," she shouted as if she had found the winning lottery ticket. She held them up like a prize.

Demetrius held out his hand and taking them from her, flicked through the passport and unfolded the permit. "Good, all seems to be in order."

Rising, he went over to a large cast iron safe standing on the floor in a corner of the room. Turning his back to Katie, he said, "I'll put them in here for now." He opened the safe and deposited them in a small metal box.

Returning to his desk, he noticed Katie's expression. "I need them to show the Department of Labour, here in Nicosia. All visitors or workers have to register with the Department. When they have finished with them, you will have them returned to you."

Katie relaxed. "When would you like me to start and where? I am anxious to see the office where I will be working."

"Office? Oh yes, as assistant to the Manager. Katie, may I speak frankly to you?"

"Certainly."

"Good, very good. I knew I could. This is your first job, except for the position in the London club. Am I right?"

She nodded. What was he getting at?

"The position you applied for was as hostess and Assistant Manager. Well, as you have no experience in a night club of this kind, I would like you to start at the bottom, so to speak … "

"What do you mean, at the bottom? I came here on the understanding that I was to be the Assistant Manager, and … "

"So you will be," he interrupted her, "but not for a month or two. Of course, I want you in that position, I feel that you have great potential with this club. But not yet, Katie. Learn the ways of the club.

See how it is run, don't you agree ?" He had this spiel down pat and was very pleased with his presentation. Using the same speech many times over the years had made it sound almost plausible.

"I think so," hesitated Katie. "But what do you mean, at the bottom, though? You mean, as a hostess?"

"Yes, exactly. A hostess to our patrons."

"I have been around long enough to know what the word hostess means."

He raised his eyebrows.

"You mean," went on Katie, not noticing his feigned ignorant expression, "That you want me to go to bed with those patrons." She sat forward in her chair and raised her back. "And take their money for doing so. I could have done that back home. You don't want an assistant, you want a prostitute!"

"No, Katie, I didn't mean that at all, at least not the way you put it."

"Then how, how do you wish to put it, Demetrius?" She rasped out his name.

"Calm down Katie, dear, and listen. Can I get you anything, a drink perhaps, a glass of water?" Katie shook her head. "What I said before about learning the business is true. It is also true that the name Hostess can sometimes mean what you say. But if you do not wish to go to bed with our customers you don't have to. We are not running a prostitution racket here, I assure you."

"No?" shouted Katie angrily.

"No. What we would like you to do is to be a guest of the customer, a confidante. Talk to them and listen. They are mainly soldiers away from home, lonely for female company, businessmen on trips or just plain Greek locals who are lonely and have no place to go."

"No hanky-panky then?"

"Hanky-panky? What is this expression? I do not know … "

"Dirty stuff, sex, that kind of thing."

"Well, some of the girls do allow the customers to touch or fondle them a bit. However, if you don't want that, all you have to do is call one of my men. At your request they will ask the customer to stop and if the customer persists then he is thrown out."

"Oh, sure," scoffed Katie.

"I mean it. Speak to the other girls yourself. Don't take my word."

Katie sat silently, her head lowered as if in deep thought. After a moment she stood up. “I’m sorry, Demetrius, but I cannot do this. I came here to start a new life, a career if possible. I must be naive to think that you would want me in a managerial capacity. You never wanted my brain, just my body. Give me my passport back and I will leave this place.”

“I would not lie to you. I really do need an assistant. But I’m right in saying you know nothing about this business. Give me a month. Be a hostess, in whatever way you wish, listen, learn how the club functions. At the end of a month, if you still feel you want out, then I will return your passport.”

“One month?”

“One month.”

“Okay, Demetrius, if you want a hostess for a month, you’re going to get the best bloody hostess you have ever seen. Now show me where to go.”

Demetrius was surprised at her sudden attitude. As he waved his arm for her to precede him out of the office, he could not help smiling. He had been better than usual, he thought. How convincing he had been. He was proud of himself.

Katie was not too concerned about being a hostess and having men ogle and paw her. That had been a part of most of her adult life. Her indignation was somewhat feigned as she did not want to give the impression that she was a ‘pushover’. It also strengthened her bargaining power for later in the month.

She wanted the career that had been spoken of so badly that for the next few weeks she would be an exemplary employee. Demetrius would be compelled to promote her as his assistant. She also felt proud of herself.

He led her downstairs for her first glimpse of the main room. They called it The Lounge and it took her breath away.

It was a huge circular room about fifty yards across. A semicircular revolving stage where live shows were performed each evening took up a quarter of the large circle. Restaurant style dining tables completed the remainder of the floor area.

But what took her breath were the walls. Around the entire wall area were cubicles of varying sizes. Each space was adorned with heavy silk drapes folded in different styles. Between each cubicle was a marble pillar, each one exquisitely carved, with cornices and connecting arches. The whole thing was like something out of the Arabian nights. It was an interior Roman or Greek Coliseum. Twelve chandeliers cast a honey glow, giving the room an almost sensual ambience.

He then escorted her to two rooms behind the stage area. The first one was the gaming room, where Baccarat, Vingt-et-un and other high class games were played.

"This is a replica of the main room of the Casino in Monte Carlo. Smaller, I grant you, but exact in every detail."

The second room was small and cosy, and consisted of sofas and armchairs.

"This also is a replica, or as near as I can come. I was in London when I was younger and invited to one of your Gentlemen's Clubs. I was so impressed I tried to duplicate it here. I'm not sure I succeeded."

"I wouldn't know either," mused Katie.

Katie had only just heard his last remark as her mind was going back to what Demetrius had told her about learning the business. He had been right. She knew nothing of this style of business. It overwhelmed her in its scope. It had to be a multi million-pound enterprise. She was out of her depth and knew it. It only toughened her resolve to succeed.

"I have to leave you now. I will have Pierre paged and he can continue the tour. Be down here at seven tonight to start, and good luck to you."

Katie and Pierre sat having a cold lunch in a small bistro type cafe two blocks from the club.

She explained what had happened in the office. Pierre sat and listened in silence.

"So I am to be a hostess," she concluded.

"A Whisky Dolly," he said quietly.

"What's that?"

"That is what they call the hostesses here. Whisky Dollies."

"Why?"

"Because when a soldier, say, asks for company, you go with him to either a table or one of the cubicles. There you order whisky for both of you. Watered down, of course."

"Naturally, what other kind is there?" she laughed.

Pierre continued, "The drink for him is priced about three pounds or six American dollars, but your drink costs about ten pounds. As long as he keeps buying, he is entitled to certain privileges."

"Privileges?" Katie knew only too well what the answer would be.

"You want me to spell it out for you, don't you?"

"You are not shy, surely Pierre. Did you never avail yourself of a Whisky Dolly?"

"Well, yes, um, yes." Even under the deep tan Katie could see him blush.

"Demetrius said something about his men. Does he mean bouncers?"

"Right. If you don't mind the … er … privileges, so be it. If you do not mind and want privacy then you draw the drapes. If you do mind or the customer gets a bit, shall we say, carried away, then underneath each table there is a rubber ring. This runs all the way around the underside edge. No matter where you sit, just press the rubber ring and an alarm bell sounds in another area. Help is at hand within minutes."

"Neat idea. I hope I never have to press the rubber. Maybe if you were being privileged, Pierre, then I might have to use it, eh? Ha! Ha!"

Pierre looked away, completely embarrassed.

Katie regretted it as soon as she opened her mouth. She saw the longing and starved look in his face. He cares, she thought, which made her even feel even lower. "Sorry. That was uncalled for."

That night Katie became a Whisky Dolly and throughout the following weeks worked, listened and studied. True to her word, she became the top Dolly in the club.

CHAPTER FIFTEEN

"May I speak with Mr. Andreas, please?"

"I'm sorry, Mr. Andreas is not available right now," a female voice answered. "Would you care to leave a message, name or number?"

"My name is Giannakos. He knows my number. Please tell him it's urgent."

"I will, thank you."

"Thank you." Dr. Giannakos hung up.

A few minutes later his phone rang.

"Hello."

"That you, Giannakos?"

"Yes sir. Thank you for calling back so promptly. Can I speak freely on this phone?"

"Yes, go ahead. You recognise my voice, eh? How is my son?"

"That's what I'm calling about. Are you able to come to the house?"

"If it's necessary, yes I can. But it had better be really necessary."

"Your son, sir, has not regained his memory. I - and the nurse with me - are quite worried. The time for the drug to wear off has passed. We need to discuss what to do."

"Give me two hours." Cicero Andreas put the phone down slowly and deliberately. Should he tell his wife, Kasta? She did worry so much, but then, in light of past events, he knew he should.

Kasta was in the next room when he called out to her.

"Just a minute dear," she shouted back.

She entered his study out of breath as if she had been running. "What were you doing?" He then noticed her leotard. "Exercising. I might have guessed."

"It would not do you any harm to exercise." She sat in a chair and started mopping her face and arms with a towel. "What did you want?"

"News of Nikki."

"Oh good. Has he come out of that damn drug yet?"

"No, not according to the doctor. He just called. He wants me to go to the house and discuss what to do next."

"Oh Cicero, not another setback. First the heart attack, then this. You have to go, and as soon as possible."

"I'm leaving as soon as I can get ready. I'll take my own car so as not to arouse suspicion. If I get a chance, I will ring you on this number."

"Give him my love, Cicero."

"Where is he?"

"Follow me," said the doctor as he led Cicero Andreas to the large library that served as Nikki's hospital ward.

"Why in here?"

"We felt that the large room was better as it allowed him freedom to move around. The books, we thought, would encourage his recovery process. We guessed right, as the fire was very helpful, as you know when … "

"Yes, yes, I understand. Hello Nikki, how are you feeling son?"

"Pretty good. You are my father, right?"

Cicero turned to the doctor and said, "I thought you said he had not … "

"No, he has not. He simply remembers you were called that the last time you were here. Isn't that so, Nikki?"

"Don't you have any recollection of your past, son? By the way, your mother sends her love."

"Thank you, Father, or did I call you Papa?"

"Papa, that's right! You called me that." He turned away, not wanting his son to see the anguish in his eyes.

The doctor suggested that they leave Nikki to rest and get some sleep. The more questions, the more the brain is taxed.

Nikki lay still after they had left the room. His father seemed to be a nice man, as was the doctor. "Oh, God," he whispered as in prayer, "where is my memory, why can't I remember who I am?" A lump began to form in his throat.

In the next room Cicero Andreas asked the question he had dreaded. "What do we do now doctor?"

"I asked you here tonight for a reason, a reason I did not want to discuss over the telephone.

"As I told you, the effects of the drug Thermabellicin should have worn off days ago. So one of two things could have happened.

"It could be that the drug has not cleared his system and is still active, although I'm not sure why this should be. He is young, strong and was very healthy when the drug was administered. So I think it may not have washed through completely."

"You are beginning to worry me doctor."

"I'm sorry, but when using experimental drugs, anything can happen."

"What do you mean, anything?"

"Well, as I told you three weeks ago, the drug could possibly do some inner damage. To the brain, I mean."

"You mean that Nikki could have permanent brain damage from all this?"

"It's a possibility."

"What's your gut feeling doctor? I want the truth, sir."

"My gut feeling, as you put it, is that the drug for some reason has been retained in the blood stream and will not go away. I don't believe that there is any brain damage, but we have to find out."

"What do we do?"

"I suggest that he be removed from here to a place where we can take CAT scans and do a thorough examination. Judging by the secrecy that you have maintained in this matter, I would recommend a small sanatorium or nursing home."

"Do you know of such a place? I don't care what it costs."

"Yes, I do. There is a place, a sanatorium, at Vouliagmeni, down the coast. Also I suggest that we retain the services of a neurologist and a psychiatrist."

Cicero Andreas walked away from the doctor, apparently lost in deep thought. He stood some feet away and earnestly stared at the floor.

"Mr Andreas, sir?"

"Sorry doctor." He walked back to the doctor's side. "The mention of those two professions, made me … "

"I know. I'm sure there is nothing to worry about," he said in as reassuring voice as he could muster. "I'm simply being over-cautious. If there is no damage internally, then the neurologist will not be required and be dismissed. The psychiatrist will then help in recovering lost memories, through hypnosis and other means."

"Do what you have to do, but I wish to be at Nikki's side through all this. His mother, also."

"Certainly. I will make arrangements to have Nikki transported by limousine tomorrow evening, after the supper hour. We should arrive at the sanatorium just when darkness falls. I will jot down the address and phone number. Meet us there tomorrow night around eight or nine o'clock."

He handed the slip of paper to Cicero Andreas. "Until tomorrow, then."

Kasta Andreas sat beside her husband in the car, not noticing the beautiful drive down the 'Apollo Coast'. They had told the staff that they were taking a few days off by themselves and were travelling north, although they did not know where they would end up.

The car passed the lovely beaches of Glifada where she had enjoyed many a sunny afternoon as a child. However the ice cream shops, the bistro cafes and the modern marina, had not been there in her day. This did not deter the Athenians from coming at every opportunity.

The car sped on as the evening shadows lengthened into darkness toward the small town of Vouliagmeni. This was not quite as popular a spot as it was a little bit ritzier. Here the restaurants were more expensive.

"Do you know how to get there? It is getting quite dark."

"Yes, he not only gave me the address, but explained how to find the place. It is set in its own grounds on the south side of the town. We have a room set aside for our own use."

A few minutes later he said, "Watch out for a large white house with a gravel driveway. It's somewhere on this side road."

"Could this be it?" Kasta asked. "I'll get out and see what the plate on the wall says."

Cicero felt sure it was the right place and turned the car into the driveway.

"This is it," she said through the car window. "Follow me up to the front door."

As the car approached the front entrance a light above the doorway went on, and the door opened to reveal the doctor.

"Ah, good, you found it all right. Come in, leave the car, we'll have it put in the garages around the back."

"May I see Nikki please doctor?" asked Kasta.

"He is asleep. But I have no objection, as long as you are quiet and do not disturb him."

Kasta tiptoed into the room where a small night light at the side of the bed cast an eerie glow in the darkness. She sat in the small wooden chair next to the bed and stared at her son. Closing her eyes and putting her hands in prayer position, she quietly asked God to save her son and to send him back to her. She laid her head on the bedclothes as silent tears slid down her cheeks.

Nikki opened his eyes, tuned his head and saw a woman sobbing at his side. As his eyes once more closed in sleep, a deep sense of relief swept over him, and he felt very relaxed.

The next morning the phone rang in their room. It was the doctor inviting them to breakfast.

Breakfast was served in an atrium at the rear of the sanatorium overlooking a walled garden which seemed to contain every species of flower.

As they arrived, the doctor and a small weed of a woman rose to greet them.

"Good morning," the doctor said. "May I introduce Dr. Athena Anntiodes, our neurologist?"

"You seem surprised, sir. Is it a surprise to have a female neurologist?"

"No, I mean, well … er … yes, it is."

"Doctor Anntiodes is one of the foremost brain surgeons in the country."

Kasta sat down at the breakfast table and the others followed her example. Laying her napkin very deliberately on her lap, she said, "May I assume, Doctor Giannakos, that as the surgeon is still here that there is a need for her services?"

"I was going to let us have breakfast before going into that, Madame, but as you have brought it up, the answer is yes."

There was just a hint of a gasp from Kasta as she looked despairingly over at Cicero.

"May I see you alone inside, Dr. Giannakos?" asked Cicero rising from the table. "Please excuse us for a moment, ladies."

Out of hearing of the ladies Cicero turned to the doctor and placing his mouth close to the doctor's ear whispered, "Does this woman surgeon know who we are? Our names and the name of her patient?"

"No, she does not. All she has been asked to do is to examine a patient and inform the parents of the result. She did ask me but as a large amount of cash was offered, it quenched her curiosity. She will, I assure you, be very discreet. So will the psychiatrist if we should need one."

"You don't know the result then of the CAT scans?"

"No. I will let her tell you herself. Now we should join the ladies. Also, I'm hungry."

Kasta greeted the return of the men with: "Cicero, Madame Anntiodes was telling me that they have done a CAT scan on Nikki and that she has something to tell us."

Just then a maid entered and asked if they would like breakfast served straight away. They all started looking at each other, and nodding assent. The maid left.

"Go ahead doctor," said Cicero.

"I examined the patient, last night and again this morning. Has your son received a severe blow to the head, in say, the last six months or a year?"

Both of them shook their heads.

"Because I believe your son has a subdural haematoma."

"Oh no," gasped Kasta and gripped her husband's arm. She was near fainting as the doctor went on, "Don't be alarmed. It is not as bad as it sounds. Subdural means the area below the dura mater, a membrane that covers the brain and the spinal cord. Haematoma means blood. So we have a clot of blood pressing on this area of the brain. This has resulted in not only the lack of coordination of his limbs that you know about, but also the extended loss of memory. May I say here and now that God may have intervened in this."

"How do you mean, God?" asked Kasta.

"Had it not been for this memory loss we might never have known about the blood clot. It is providential, I can tell you."

"So what do we do about this clot?" asked Cicero seeing that his wife was too distressed to ask.

"It is a simple enough operation. Do you wish me to go into details?" Getting no response, she continued, "We anaesthetise your son and drill a small hole in the side of the skull. I then place a tube into the brain area and drain out the blood. Very simple, although it sounds rather complicated."

"How long will the operation last?" asked Cicero. "And will he be well again when it is done?"

"You have my word on that, sir. The operation will take about half an hour, and it should clear up his memory loss, with no ill effects."

"Will we be able to see him?" asked Kasta.

"Oh yes, but remember he will have his head heavily bandaged. It will look a lot worse than it really is."

"When can he be removed from the sanatorium?" Cicero asked, a little fear lurking in his brain. The longer Nikki was out of the 'safe house' the more he fretted.

"When do you think, Athena?"

"I'll know better tomorrow, when I can examine him. Provided he is under strict supervision, maybe a few days."

"In the meantime," the doctor said, linking arms with Cicero and Kasta, "feel free to use the amenities of the sanatorium."

The following day the neurologist came to them and told them that Nikki was awake. In her opinion he was fully recovered and his amnesia gone.

Arriving at the bedside Nikki moved his eyes sideways and seeing them both, said in a hoarse and cracked voice, "Hello Mama, hello Papa. Where am I, and what are you doing in Mexico?"

Cicero placed his hand on Nikki's arm and tried not to show the elation he was feeling. Kasta, meanwhile, fumbled in a pocket for a handkerchief, and turned away so that Nikki would not see her tears. She walked over to Dr. Anntiodes and taking her hands in her own said simply, "Thank you for giving us back our son." The neurologist, taken aback, hurriedly left the room.

"You are not in Mexico, lad. You have been ill and you are in Greece, in Athens."

"Why Father, what happened?"

"Not now son, there will be time later for explanations. Come, mother, our boy needs sleep."

Kasta took Nikki's hand and raised it and brushed it against her cheek. "Sleep well, Nikki. I love you."

"I love you too, Mama."

Nikki was worried. This bandage on his head must have been from the attack in his hotel room in Mexico City. Where was Rode? Did she know he was back in Greece? Questions, questions, and no answers. His father had said all in good time, but when?

He had been moved from the sanatorium and now found himself in a large room with a fireplace at the far end. One wall was lined with books.

He was perfectly able to walk around. His head had a plaster at the side, but it was still a little painful. He had tried the door and windows but all were locked. Was he a prisoner?

The doctor entered and immediately Nikki blurted out, "I need to speak with my father right away. Can you arrange it? My head is full of questions."

"Yes, I can and will, Nikki. I think you are ready now. Now let's look at that 'full of questions' head of yours."

Cicero stood outside Nikki's door, hesitating. He had looked forward to this for some weeks now, but dreaded the implications. How would he take the news? Would he blame him? He went inside.

"Hello papa."

"Hello son. Feeling better?"

"Yes, but I have a lot of questions that need answering."

"Sit down. I have a story to tell you. When I have finished, your questions, I am sure, will have been answered."

"Go ahead papa."

"You will recall, no doubt, that fight you had outside a bar in Athens, about four months ago?"

"Yes, I do, that big guy. You said the fight was important."

"Yes, I did, and it was. When you left him, he was alive, yes?"

"But unconscious. Why?"

"Well, he was Janus' son Michael, and he died shortly after."

"You mean … I killed him?"

"I don't know, but anyway, that's why I sent you on that world trip. I also sent Vlascis, you know Vlascis?" Nikki nodded. "Well I sent him to follow you and take care of you."

"You what?"

"As I said, I was concerned for your safety, so Vlascis was sent to be your bodyguard, so to speak."

"But I never saw him." He stopped, remembering the car racing away from the square. Had that been Vlascis? The face had seemed familiar. "Go on papa. Sorry for the interruption."

"No, you never saw him, but he knew every move you made. I'm glad that he did, as there were two attempts on your life … "

"Two attempts on my life?"

"Yes, listen. The first was at a home in the country. You were with a young lady."

"Yes, that's Rode. By the way, where is she?" His father glowered at him. "Sorry. Please continue."

"The second attempt was in the centre of Cuernavaca. There was a parked car, I believe."

Nikki opened his mouth to say something, but thought better of it.

"After that attempt I knew it was just a matter of time that Janus' men would get either one or both of you. That's when I decided to act. I had you attacked in your hotel room and put to sleep. While under the anaesthetic we administered an experimental drug … "

"You did what?"

"Yes. Sorry, but we all felt it was necessary."

"What kind of drug?"

"This drug seemingly attacks the nervous system, then the brain. Don't ask for details because I don't know too much. I don't really understand all that it does. Suffice to say it induces a death-like trance. Anyone checking would think you were dead. The symptoms of death last about forty-six hours."

"You mean I died for two days?"

"In a manner of speaking, yes. To continue, we brought you back to Athens in a coffin and buried you at the St. Christos Cemetery."

"Phew! I hope everyone turned up," he said with a glint in his eye.

"You would have been proud. Afterwards we brought you here to this house."

"Oh, yes father. Where and what is this place, this prison of mine?"

"Don't son. It hurts to think what I had to do. This house, very grand isn't it? It belongs to a Turkish friend of mine who's away on an extended holiday."

Nikki raised his eyes in disbelief.

Cicero continued. "Yes, a Turk. It seemed the perfect answer to our problem. No one, we thought, would ever think of looking here."

"What problem - or shouldn't I ask?"

"We wanted to keep you out of circulation - you are dead, remember - until we could decide what to do. Only a few people know the truth."

"That's quite a story, but why the bandages?"

"One of the after effects of this drug we used was temporary amnesia. You had that, but as you did not regain your memory in the time the doctor thought you should, we took you to a sanatorium for some tests. The medical people there discovered a blood clot against your brain. That, seemingly, was the cause of the memory problem. The clot was removed, and not only do you not have amnesia any more, but a possible real death situation was averted."

"It was that serious, then."

His father nodded. "It could have been, had we not caught it in time."

Nikki was quiet and Cicero knew that his mind must be doing cartwheels with all that it had absorbed in the last few minutes. He felt very sorry, yet very proud of his son at that moment.

"I only have one more question. What happened to Rode?"

"Rode, who is … You mean the girl in Mexico?"

"Yes papa, I am in love with her."

Cicero saw the sincerity in his son's face. "I don't know son."

"I will have to phone her, and let her know I'm … "

"No, sorry. I cannot allow you to phone." This was the moment he had dreaded. Vlascis had told Kasta and him of this girl but they had thought it was simply a holiday romance. "I wish you to stay here, undercover, for the time being. So, please, have no contact with the outside world. For all we know, Janus may be having Rode watched. We do not want to chance anything yet. If Janus got to know that you … "

"But I love her and I'm sure she loves me. She probably thinks I'm dead … Oh dear, what have I said? I mean she does not know what happened. When she left the hotel to pack, we were to meet in about an hour. Then poof! " He raised his arms. "I don't come back."

"I sympathize, as you well know, but perhaps, in a few weeks time … "

CHAPTER SIXTEEN

Teresa, a cleaning lady at the Britannia Club, was one of three women who were vacuuming the main room. Last night's crowd had been particularly messy.

She did not really enjoy her job. Being Italian and not speaking English made her a bit of a loner. The other girls, although Greek, spoke English well.

Teresa felt a tug on her sleeve. Looking up she saw a young black haired woman carrying a small suitcase. She was saying something.

Switching her vacuum off she said, "Si?"

"Do you speak English?"

When Teresa shook her head, the young woman walked away in apparent distress. Teresa continued her cleaning.

Rode then crossed the floor to the other cleaning ladies. "Do either of you speak English? " She had to shout over the noise of the vacuums.

"Yes," one of them answered, switching her machine off. "Can I help you, Miss?"

"Yes, please. I'm looking for a friend of mine, a young man. Niklos Andreas. Do you know him?"

"No, I don't, but wait. Maria, do you know a Niklos Andreas? This girl is looking for him." The cleaner shrugged and continued working.

"Sorry, Miss."

Rode slumped into a chair, tears welling up in her eyes. During the past few days she had seemed to do nothing else but cry. Her eyes were sore and red from the constant rubbing.

The cleaning lady went off through a door. A few seconds later she emerged with a security guard.

"Miss, I understand you are looking for a friend, a gentleman. I do not know this friend of yours but I will take you to see Demetrius. He is the owner of this place and he may know your friend."

"So sorry to be a nuisance."

The guard shook his head and led her up some stairs.

"Yes, George, what is it?"

"This young lady needs your help, sir." Rode appeared from behind the guard.

"Fine, Thank you, George. That will be all. Come in please, sit down. What can I do for you?"

"Thank you." Rode sat in a chair opposite the large one behind the desk. "I'm not sure if you can." At that the wet handkerchief again came out as the tears started appearing.

"Don't cry, Miss," he said handing her a tissue. "Calm down and tell me what troubles you"

"You are so kind."

Demetrius had been called many things in his lifetime, but never kind. He puffed out his chest and resumed his position behind the desk.

Rode dabbed her nose while trying to compose herself. Since arriving in Cyprus last night, she must have asked the same question about twenty times. No one seemed to know of Nikki. She had lost count of the number of times she had burst into tears. "I'm terribly sorry to go to pieces."

"Not at all. Perhaps we could start again. My name is Demetrius. And you are?"

"Rode, Rode Benetino."

"Benetino. That's a strange name. Where are you from?"

"Mexico City. Well, at least a town outside, Cuernavaca. I don't wish to appear rude, but it is quite a common name in Mexico." She smiled, making them both laugh. The tension in the room seemed to lessen.

"So, Rode," he faltered, smiling, "how may I help? And how is it you are so far from home?"

"I came here looking for a friend. His name is Niklos Andreas. Do you know him, perhaps?"

The innocent question was like a blow to his fat stomach. He opened a pack of cigarettes which he had been trying to ignore for the past few weeks and offered it to Rode. She declined. He had to answer, but how?

Without thinking he said, "Yes I do. How do you know him?"

"Oh, finally! Thank you so much. I thought I was going crazy. The thought had even entered my head that he had lied to me about Cyprus. I met him in Mexico. I thought that we had fallen in love."

"Thought you had?"

"Yes. It was never actually spoken of but his actions … Well, you know?"

"Mm, yes. I think I understand."

"Could you tell me where I could find him? Is he here in Cyprus, in Nicosia?"

'What do I tell her? She obviously does not know. The son of my partner Cicero. What do I do?' he wondered.

Rode waited patiently, wondering what the delay was.

"How long have you been here? In Cyprus, I mean?"

"I arrived last night. Why?"

"Well, Miss, I'm sorry to have to tell you, but I'm afraid that Mr Andreas is dead."

The tears once more started to flow. Demetrius got up from his seat and said, "I will get you a brandy."

As she sat waiting for him to bring the drink, she lived again the few times they had been together. Why had this happened? All those years she had been alone. At last she had found someone to love and someone who loved her in return; a love that she had thought would last forever - and now, this.

The hot tears rolled down her cheeks. She bent her head down to her knees and let the grief take over.

Returning with the brandy Demetrius saw her bent double, her shoulders shaking so hard that he thought she would fall to the ground.

No need of a drink just yet, better to let her heartache subside first, he reasoned.

He placed the glass on the desk and knelt down beside her. He felt genuinely sorry for this young girl. He put an arm round her shoulders and stayed there for a few minutes.

She raised her head and as she did he released his arm and handed her the drink. "Take this. It will help."

Taking the glass, she sipped tentatively at the brandy.

"No, not that way," he said. "Take it in one gulp. Trust me, it will settle you."

She shuddered as the drink was taken in one. "That's strong stuff."

"It's made locally."

" Mr. Demetrius, can you tell me how and where Nikki … ?"

"It was in Los Angeles, I understand. A hit and run. Very sudden and very tragic."

"I have to contact the family. Can you help?"

Demetrius hesitated. He did not want to get involved. "No, the parents, I believe, moved back to Athens afterwards but I do not know to where."

As if talking to herself, she said quietly, "What am I to do?"

"If I were you, I would go back home, home to Mexico."

"I can't. I have no money. I was hoping that when I met up with

Nikki … well, you know." She stood up and straightened her clothes and patted her hair. "Thank you, sir, I will not take up any more of your time."

Demetrius all this time had been admiring this young lady; very beautiful, lovely black hair, and her breasts, from under the blouse she wore, looked not bad. Her English accent was one of her most charming features.

"Before you go, Miss Benetino. You have no money for the flight home, is that right?"

"Yes, well, not enough, that is."

"Nor a place to stay either, I suppose?"

"No, why?"

"Would you like a job here, at this club? For a little while, perhaps a month. You would be able to save enough in that time to get you home. You could live here at the club, as most of my employees do."

"What kind of job? My experiences of this kind of place are very limited, I assure you."

"As a hostess, part-time bartender, or any other situation that may arise. My clients, mainly British soldiers and visiting businessmen, seek female company while they are here. All you have to do is sit with them, talk to them and listen to their troubles. They are lonely, being far away from home."

"I'm not sure I could do that."

"Of course you can. It's all strictly honourable and it would only be for about a month. You will get assistance from the girls already working here. What do you say?"

"Why not?"

"Good, that's settled then. Oh, one more thing. Do you have your passport with you?"

"Yes, in my case here." She opened the suitcase and started rummaging through its contents.

While she looked for the passport Demetrius explained. "I need it to present to the Department of Labour. All foreigners working in Cyprus are required to submit their passports. It will be returned to you, in due course."

Demetrius took the passport from Rode, and as before with all the girls, placed it in the safe, making sure that Rode could not see inside.

This girl had been too easy. The easiest one yet, in fact. Falling into his lap, so to speak. Most of the others he had to cajole and promise all sorts of things. But Katie, and now Rode, so easy. He was feeling good, thinking about the money they would bring in.

He returned to the desk and picked up his phone. "Is Katie around?" He waited a moment. "Good. Could you send her up please?" Turning to Rode, he said, "Katie will look after you for this evening and tomorrow. She will show you around."

There was a knock on the door.

"Oh Katie, this is Rode Benetino, from Mexico. She is going to join us for a short time. Could you please show her around? We'll put her to work tomorrow night. You and she may take the rest of this evening off."

"Okay, Demetrius. I'll look after her."

When the girls left Demetrius sat and pondered. Should he contact Cicero and tell him about this girl Rode? Do they know of her? Did they realise that Nikki had apparently fallen for this girl while he was in Mexico?

Perhaps this Rode was not telling the truth about Nikki's feelings. If he had been in love like she said, why wasn't she there when he died?

No, she might have been in love with him; after all he had been handsome and quite a ladies' man. But he in love with her? He doubted it. Nikki had been a well travelled, sophisticated person, while Rode, well, Rode was a shy young thing.

If Cicero knew of her then surely she would know them, but she did not. No, Kasta and Cicero, he fathomed, knew nothing of this girl. He was not going to be the one to tell them, either. He wanted some money out of her before that happened.

Anyway, relationships between himself and Cicero were a bit strained at the moment. Cicero was getting soft in his old age. Not like the old days when he would take chance after chance; now it seemed that their positions had reversed. It was he who took the chances. Look at what he had achieved at the club - the club he thought should be his. The place was a gold mine, all because he took chances.

He had the knack of conning the girls into working for him. The passport game was sheer genius. Holding them maintained his power over the girls. They did not like what they had to do to make a living, but he did pay well.

He stifled a yawn. Time for a nap before the evening festivities began.

He decided not to phone Cicero, but the next time he was speaking to his friend Tselios, in Athens, he would seek his advice.

Putting his feet up on his desk, taking the phone off the hook, he drifted into sleep.

Katie took Rode up to her room. The room contained two single beds, two large wardrobes, a walk-in closet for storage and an adjoining bathroom with a shower. There were the usual table, chairs and dressers found in the normal hotel room. The whole place was very tastefully decorated and very comfortable.

"You can share this room with me, Rode. It will be nice to have a companion to talk to."

Rode sat on the bed allotted to her and kicked off her shoes. Lying down on the bed, she looked up at the ceiling and lay there deep in thought.

Slowly a teardrop appeared in the corner of an eye as her body and mind finally started to relax after the hectic journey. She turned over onto her stomach, while Katie came over to her and asked, "What's the matter, Rode? Are you ill or something?"

Rode shook her head from side to side while it was buried in the bedclothes. She started to cry very softly, but as the hurt took over the sobbing became louder and louder even although the sound was muffled by the bed.

Katie did not know what to do, except to let whatever it was that was troubling Rode find its own way out of her system. Katie had cried herself like this, and knew that to be left alone was the best thing at this moment.

Lying down on her own bed, Katie was very pleased that she had been given the night off. Since starting at the club she had at first resisted the work, as it was not what she had hoped. It was the usual pawing of the men, not that she minded that too much, but she wanted to further her career. Stupidly, she had harboured the notion that Demetrius would eventually give her some office duties to perform or even some work in an advisory capacity.

Rode turned over and the cries became a bit louder. She murmured, "Sorry," and turned once more onto her stomach.

Katie knew that she had been tricked into coming here. The only reason she was here, she knew, was because of her body. Why couldn't someone think of her as a person and not just as a plaything for men? She was getting older and still no closer to a real career.

Demetrius had deceived her, she knew, and through speaking to Pierre she knew about the passport scam. If she could not get that back, then she would have to remain here until … who knew?

Her thoughts strayed back to Marty. What was he doing? Did he ever think about her? Was he upset at her taking the money, or did he think she had done the right thing? Those had been happy times with Marty and she still had a notion that she loved him. If only his damned wife would give him a divorce, then Marty could come and whisk her away. She smiled to herself. Marty did not look like any knight in shining armour.

She turned to look at Rode. What was causing all this grief? Rising from the bed she went over to Rode and sat on the edge of her bed. Laying a hand on her back, she asked, "Can I do anything to help, Rode?"

The sobbing died down and Rode turned over onto her back, trying valiantly to smile through the flushed face. She shook her head and sat up.

Katie said, "The bathroom is over there."

Rode went in and a few minutes later emerged looking almost respectable.

"I feel I owe you an explanation, Katie."

"Not if you don't want to."

Rode sat down beside Katie. "You see, I came all the way here to find a man I was in love with, and who I thought loved me also."

"And he does not love you now?"

"No, not that. Demetrius informed me that the man, Niklos Andreas, died a week or so back in Los Angeles."

"I'm so sorry to hear that, Rode. No wonder you are in the state you are. What happened, do you know?"

"A hit and run, I was told. What makes it even more devastating was that the last time I saw him, in Mexico City, I left to go and pack some bags. He and I were going to a country house that I own for a few days. We didn't even say goodbye."

"He did not contact you after that? Not even a phone call or anything?"

"No not quite. He left a note at the hotel desk, where he had been staying." She went over and got her purse. Handing it to Katie, "That's all I know, until I arrived here."

Have received word that my father is ill and
in Los Angeles. Am flying out with some friends.
Will call you as soon as I can

N.

"Was his father ill?"

"I don't know. He never did call. I waited the next day for a call from him. Going back to his hotel I was handed the note by the hotel clerk. Good, I thought, at least I know where he is."

"What did you do then?" Katie was getting wrapped up in this story.

"I waited for his call. I never left my flat all day. The next day I waited in for a short time then went to my place of work to see if he had contacted them. No one had heard a thing."

"By this time you must have been frantic."

"I was. The thought occurred to me that maybe I was no more than a one night stand and did not mean anything to him. Later that day I went out of town to my cottage and asked around of the neighbours and friends, nothing. I went back to Mexico City and phoned the Greek Consulate to find out something, anything, anything that would help me. After much pleading with many different voices, I discovered that a private plane had indeed taken off that first night, with a Niklos Andreas on board."

"What a relief that must have been."

"Yes, indeed. While I was talking to the secretary at the Consulate I asked him if he could give me the phone number of the family in Cyprus."

"Good thinking, Rode."

"That's what I thought. Do you know how many Andreas there are in both Cyprus and Athens? As I did not know the father's name or address it was a lost cause. That's when I decided to fly over here. In Mexico City I am a travel agent and can get cheaper fares so the cost was not too great."

"How long did it take to fly here?"

"About three days, at such short notice and there being no charters. I had to fly to London first and wait overnight for a plane to here."

"Yes, there's only one flight a day out of London. That's quite a story, Rode. That would make a good TV movie. Oops, sorry. I did not mean to be flippant. So now why are you starting work in this place? I nearly said 'dump', but it is anything but. This place is beautiful. I will show it to you tomorrow."

"I'm here because although I have a little bit of money with me, there is not enough to get me home. I thought that when I met up with Nikki or his parents I would not need - well, I hoped, anyway - that it would not be necessary."

"I see. Well let's get some 'shut eye'. I know you must be tired after your ordeal."

"Yes. I did not realise until I lay down here how tired I am."

The two girls retired for the night.

Katie could not help wondering about Rode. She was not the usual run-of-the-mill hostess type. She was too refined, and obviously came from a well-to-do family. Country cottage and all. Katie was impressed. Was there no one back home who could send her the money?

Rode was glad that she had found a friend in Katie. Glad also that her story had finally been told, and was no longer bottled up inside her. As she went to sleep, the turmoil of the day's events again took hold of her emotions and she turned away from Katie and cried. The sorrow of the present and the fear of the future poured out in silent tears. Oh dear God, she prayed in her mind, please let this month go fast so that I may return to the comfort of people and places I know.

The following evening Pierre sat in his customary corner of the main room, and watched eagerly as Katie and Rode entered.

He wondered who the new girl with Katie was, but was not too concerned. His eyes seldom strayed from Katie.

Since her arrival, his life had changed dramatically. He was in love, he knew, for the first time. A love that was not shared. Oh, she was friendly toward him and used him as her confidant, but as for extending that friendship to love, no; not from her perspective anyway.

As long as he could be near her, talk to her and watch her, he was content.

He came to this seat in the corner most nights and she would wave to him and smile. His heart was always uplifted by her smile. But then he would sit and watch as men touched and pawed her, above and below the table, and it would sicken him. If he stayed the whole evening, which was very rare, she would wave and smile a cheery goodnight.

He knew that what the customers did had no meaning for her. It only served to make him love her more.

This particular evening he was aware that what lay on the table before him could affect her future and ultimately his own; knowing that if he showed it to her he was liable to lose her. He did not have a great hold on her, but the little he had he was anxious to keep, however small and distant.

If only he could express his love to her. If she knew of that love, perhaps?

Taking the object from the table, and placing it in his pocket, he decided to wait a while before showing it to her.

Katie and Rode entered the main room and immediately Katie saw Pierre in the corner and waved a friendly hello.

The band had just started and was playing some ineffectual tunes which nobody could recognise. The stage show was not due until 8.30 when most of the crowds would arrive.

Katie introduced Rode to the other girls, about ten of them, who were on duty that night.

She told Rode to stay in the background and watch how the others dealt with the customers.

As Rode was privately sipping a fruit drink, a small strongly-built man approached. For a man with large shoulders and muscular arms he had a pleasant quiet voice.

"You're new here," he said politely, coming up close beside her. His breath smelled of beer and his eyes were a bit glassy. He obviously had been drinking before arriving here.

"Yes, this is my first night, sir."

"Don't call me sir, call me Les."

Katie had noticed the exchange between them and inched along the edge of the bar. As she came close, she heard him ask, "You a Whisky Dolly?"

Rode became nervous. What was a Whisky Dolly? She looked down the bar at Katie. Katie hunched her shoulders as if she did not know. Then, spotting Demetrius entering the room, nodded furiously.

"Yes, I am."

"Let me buy you a drink then … " He hesitated and inclined his head in question.

"Rode," she answered.

"Rode, that's a strange name. From where, Rode?"

"Mexico."

"Wow, you are a long way from home. Old Demetrius sure gets around, trying to give us our money's worth." He looked her up and down. "He has good taste, I can tell you."

Then noticing Demetrius across the floor, he shouted in a voice that was no longer smooth and gentle. "Hey, big D. Things are looking up. You know your stuff." And nodded toward Rode.

Demetrius waved back. He could not hear what was said but the tone and actions clearly meant he was impressed with Rode. So was he. Her first night, and already engaged with a customer.

Demetrius was pleased with himself and wrung his hands in glee. He walked around the room noticing that all the girls were occupied, so to speak. The place was filling up and even the band had a new lease of life which had been lacking earlier.

He decided to phone his pal Tselios.

Nikki had accepted his father's story and much to Cicero's relief had not applied any blame.

He had agreed to stay in this Turkish house, as he called it, for a week or so, but gave his father an ultimatum. Either he could come out of hiding and resume his life here in Greece, or he was shipped out undercover back to Mexico where he would marry Rode, and settle down over there.

Cicero was now convinced that Nikki was serious about this Mexican girl. However, before he made a decision one way or another, he had to know Janus' reaction to Nikki's death and the subsequent consequences.

He would contrive to meet Janus at lunch one day and test the waters. He was nervous at the prospect, but it had to be done.

Nikki, meanwhile, spent his days exercising in the splendid room set aside for this purpose. There was every conceivable piece of equipment at his disposal.

He was always accompanied by one or both of his two bodyguards, or wardens, as he thought of them. They were Vlascis and Tselios.

A good deal of time had been spent talking with Vlascis about the days in Mexico. Vlascis was, however, reluctant to discuss the killings, but Nikki could tell that he looked upon killing as a job that he was very well paid for. There was no emotion in his voice, even when pressed for details.

A good deal of Nikki's time was spent in the garden getting fit and strong under the hot Grecian sun. His young body had missed the warmth and inner strength that comes from sunbathing.

He was free to wander around the house at will, but not free to venture outside the front gate.

Although he never saw either Vlascis or Tselios he knew that wherever he went one of them was following. They seemed to have the knack of knowing where he was. They would ask him if he had enjoyed his visit to the kitchen, library or wherever. He would answer, wondering how in the world they knew.

He appreciated now why his father had hand-picked them for this duty. He was under constant surveillance yet had all the freedom he desired.

One evening he had left them in their 'Guard Room' while he said goodnight. As he closed the door the phone rang. Curious, as this was the first call he could remember during his stay here, he loitered at the door and listened.

He could hear Tselios speaking. There were the usual pleasantries, then silence. Nikki thought the conversation had ended and was about to leave when he heard Tselios shout. "What girl? What's her name?" Silence again. "No way," Tselios said in a deadly serious tone. "They don't need to know, stupid." Again there was a silence. "Do as I say or there will be trouble, big trouble." Tselios slammed the phone down

Nikki heard a chair scrape, as if being pushed back. He jumped to the side of the door so as not to be seen if it opened. No one came out, so he resumed his listening position. Tselios was explaining something to Vlascis.

"Yes, the Mexican kid, Rode, or whatever her name is."

"Rode Benetino, the girl friend?"

"Yeah, I suppose. She's looking for Nikki boy. Demetrius gave her a job as a Whisky Dolly. He wants to tell Mr. Andreas, senior."

"Does she know Nikki's dead?"

"Can't say. I forgot to ask. Guess she does. Demetrius does."

Nikki felt the blood rush from his face, leaving a cold moisture on his skin. His knees were weak and he was on the brink of fainting. He leaned against the wall, while his breath came out in short sharp gasps.

Rode … Demetrius … Cyprus ... the club. Visions rushed through his brain.

He stumbled back to his room and fell on the bed.

"Get a hold of yourself, stupid," he said out loud.

Had he heard right? Rode was in Cyprus at Demetrius' club working as a Whisky Dolly. How dare they, the bastards!

His strength was returning as the hate was growing. His Rode, a Dolly. The slime would pay.

"Oh my God," he uttered. "I'm dead. Demetrius has probably told her. He didn't know I'm … Rode, oh my love, what have we done?

You poor thing."

Of course she had not heard, so naturally she would go to Cyprus to find him. Then when she got there. … "Oh Rode, what must you be feeling? I love you so much. You must love me also which is why you came. Oh my darling, my darling, Rode. You sweet innocent girl. What must you be going through? What have they done to you that you would accept that horrible job? Those girls, they are no more than prostitutes."

His anger swelled up in him as he paced around the room, muttering to himself, and shouting curses upon all. He stopped as there was a knock on his door and it opened.

Vlacis stepped inside and asked if everything was fine. All the time his eyes were darting around the room seeking answers to the noises he had heard. Seeing nothing amiss he quietly said, "Okay, Nikki. Goodnight. See you in the morning."

"Yes, goodnight, Vlascis."

In that short period of calm when Vlascis was looking about the room, Nikki had come to a decision. He had to get out and go to Rode.

To hell with Janus, his father and all the rest of them, he had to escape from this place. But how?

CHAPTER SEVENTEEN

Katie watched nervously as Rode and Les, who was a Sergeant Major in the British forces, walked to one of the private booths.

They sat at the table and immediately a waiter appeared and said simply, "Yes?"

"A beer for me, and for you?" he looked at Rode.

While Rode hesitated the waiter said, "The lady drinks whisky, sir."

"Oh really! Is that right, Rode?"

Rode, now completely confused, looked the waiter in the eye, saw his glare and mumbled, "Yes, please, Les." The waiter retired.

"So, Rode, how do you like being a Dolly?"

Rode stared blankly at him. What was she to say? Not knowing what a Dolly was, she was scared to give the wrong answer. Deciding to try to be off-hand and non-committal she answered, "It's all right, I suppose."

"Good." He smiled moving his chair closer to hers. "That's what I like to hear."

She relaxed a bit, obviously having said the right words.

Les took her hands in his. "You seem nervous, lass. Do I make you nervous?"

"No, not really, Les."

"Even better," he said, as an arm went round her waist and a hand touched the bottom of her breast. She flinched a little but did not resist. Having watched lots of television she knew about being a hostess. They had to allow men a little latitude. After all, the guys were buying the drinks. Did not Demetrius say that the men here were starved of female company?

"Your breasts are nice."

She smiled as he moved closer and his hand engulfed her breast and started squeezing. He leaned toward her and kissed her on the neck.

What was she to do? He stank of booze. How far am I supposed to allow him?

He turned her chair round so that they were facing each other. The waiter appeared. "Another drink, sir?"

"What? Oh yes. Yes please, and one for the lady."

The waiter already had the two drinks on the tray and as he placed them on the table, he gave Rode a little smile. Rode took the smile to mean, 'it's quite all right, you are among friends.' She felt comforted by that simple smile.

The waiter hovered and looked at Les.

"Oh, of course." Les reached into a pocket and withdrew a ten-pound note, and placed it on the tray. The waiter did not move, but instead raised his eyebrows.

"Oh, really? Well, well, well." Les looked across at Rode, his eyes straying to her bosom. "What the hell!" He fished into his wallet this time and extracted another ten-pound note, and tossed it beside the first one. The waiter retired.

Les placed one hand on her breast again and kneaded it as if he was kneading dough. Breathing heavily he asked, "This OK. for you, honey?"

Rode was too scared to answer.

"You're very nice kid, but you don't say a helluva lot. The quiet type, eh? Cat got your tongue?" He laughed and Rode faked a laugh, wondering what a cat's tongue was all about.

He slugged down his drink in a couple of large swallows. "Drink your whisky, kiddo."

In her nervousness Rode took a large gulp of the drink. It tasted no better than the first one. This is definitely not good whisky, she thought, much too watery.

As they finished their drinks, the waiter appeared out of thin air, with two more drinks.

Les, obviously upset at the interruption, groped in his wallet lying on the table and took out a twenty. "Will this buy two more, and get rid of you?"

The waiter nodded and retired as noiselessly as he had appeared.

Les now turned his attention to Rode. "Where were we, doll?" His voice was becoming more slurred. 'Hopefully,' thought Rode, 'he will get drunk soon and pass out.'

Once more his hand went to her bosom, but this time he grasped her blouse and tried to rip it open. She brushed his hand away saying, "Naughty boy, Les."

Again he reached out for her blouse but this time when he tried to grab hold of it she slapped his hand rather hard. "No, please Les, don't do that."

"Bitch, I'm paying dearly for this little game." So saying his hand went straight between her legs and he clenched a large fist over her crotch. "Gotcha!" he declared in triumph.

Rode screamed. "Stop! Stop it!" and tried to stand up.

"No, you don't, bitch. What kind of Dolly are you, anyway?"

Her thoughts flashed to Nikki. Oh, how tender he had been when they had made love. She remembered how his hand had been so tender down there. Not like this ape. "Oh Nikki, where are you? I need you?"

Those thoughts were rudely shattered when she felt his other hand lifting up her skirt.

"No don't!" she shouted in panic. "Stop, leave me alone!" She screamed at the top of her voice, "Katie, where are you?"

In the struggle they had both tumbled to the ground, Les' hand still engulfed between her legs. The pain was excruciating for Rode who was now crying and sobbing hysterically.

His breath was coming faster and he was oblivious to his surroundings. He did not hear her cry out. All he could think of was this little desirable creature that he wanted. Wanted so badly. She had turned him on as no other dolly had, and he had to have her. As they lay wrestling on the ground, her fists pounding against his chest in powder puff fashion, Pierre heard the screams and gave out a loud whistle.

Two waiters started toward the booth. Pierre followed behind. The first waiter got to the two on the floor and gave Les a swift kick in the small of his back. Les groaned and released his hold on Rode. As he tottered to his feet, the waiter again aimed a kick. This time however, Les was waiting for it. He grabbed the waiter's leg in mid kick and twisted. There was a sharp crack of breaking bone and the waiter fell on the floor screaming, "My leg, my leg."

Rode got up and stood against the wall. As the waiter went down, she sidled along the wall of the booth and hurriedly went to her right and fell into Katie's arms, sobbing out of control. "Oh Katie, how could he?"

Katie cursed through clenched teeth. "I'll get the sod, Rode, you mark my words," she said, thinking Rode was speaking of Demetrius.

Meanwhile the second waiter arrived on the scene, having stayed back watching his friend take on Les. He stepped over his friend who was comatose and groaning in pain, his right leg lying in an unusual angle to the rest of his body.

He approached Les cautiously, and when he was within a few feet lunged forward. Les had anticipated such a move and side-stepped the lunge. As the waiter went past, Les gave him a severe punch right in the front of the throat on the Adam's apple. He fell at Les' feet gasping for breath. A few seconds later there was a sound like air escaping out of a balloon, rasping and whistling. Les looked down disdainfully and noticed moisture oozing from the mouth.

The room was full of military personnel who stood doing nothing. Sergeant Major Les Goulding was notorious on the island as a scrapper. No one had the courage to step forward.

Les stood in front of the booth looking almost like King Kong, his arms dangling at his side. He had not noticed that he had rendered useless two of the club's best bouncers.

He picked up a chair as if it was a pen and holding it aloft like a spear in salute, shouted. "Anyone else want to have a go? C'mon you arseholes, I enjoy this."

Pierre stepped forward, keeping a safe distance between himself and Les. Making sure the entire room heard him he shouted, "Come on, Les. You've had your fun. Time to go home."

"Shut up you fucking frog. I ain't going nowhere." With that he hurled the chair at Pierre. Pierre saw it coming and ducked. However, it hit him a glancing blow that was hard enough to make him fall on the floor where he cracked his head and lost consciousness.

Katie shouted, "Pierre! Pierre!" but was too frightened to run to his aid.

The room remained silent during this little skirmish. Then a voice from the shadows at the side of the room echoed through the silence: "How about me, asshole?"

Into the light at the booth walked a tall burly Canadian soldier with a large bushy moustache. "Will I do, punk?"

There were a few shouts of, "Go get him, Yukon" and "Atta boy, Yukon."

Les turned his body ever so slowly toward this intrusion. No one had ever dared face him like this before. Les was mystified. As he rotated around to face this 'person' a full bottle of beer was hurled out of the shadows. Les did not see it coming until it came into the light at the edge of the booth. It hit him full on the temple. As the blood spurted from the wound, he pole-axed to the ground, out cold. The Canadians in the crowd all applauded.

The quiet of the room suddenly exploded, as the British soldiers made for the Canadians. A few Swedish soldiers that were there, not wanting to be left out of the fun, joined in on the Canadian's side.

A full-scale brawl ensued with bodies toppling over tables and chairs being hurled in every direction.

The band, which had stopped playing when Pierre whistled, began to clear away their instruments. But with bodies being punched and kicked right on the stage, they bade a hasty retreat. Sounds of bones being crushed and fists hitting flesh were interspersed with chords from the piano and guitar strings being plucked as bodies smashed into the instruments.

Katie told Rode to go to the bedroom. She then made her way, crawling on the floor, toward Pierre, who was only now stirring. She had to avoid falling bodies, kicking legs, and bodies that lay motionless on the floor. Strange, she thought, some of them had smiles on their faces.

Reaching Pierre, who was just coming too, she cradled him in her arms. "Can you stand up?"

"I think so."

"Let's get out of here, quick."

Just then a large Canadian and a bare-chested Brit fell beside them. Both were pummelling away at each other, completely unaware that Katie and Pierre were there.

As Katie lifted Pierre to his feet, something fell out of his pocket. It appeared to be a cutting from a newspaper. It was obviously important to Pierre so Katie stuffed it into her blouse and half-carried, half-dragged Pierre to the safety of the stairs leading to the rooms upstairs.

Katie helped Pierre to his room and laid him on the bed.

"You okay now, Pierre? I'd better go and see to Rode."

"Yes, off you go. Poor girl. Didn't she know what was expected of her?"

"No. Demetrius didn't tell her. But I'll get him for this. I swore to Rode I would get even."

Leaving Pierre comfortable, she walked along the corridor toward her own room. Rode was at the dressing table fixing her face, which was red from tears.

As Katie entered she said, "Look at my face. Ever since I got here I have done nothing but cry."

"And you are not doing it any more, Rode. At least, not here in Cyprus. You're going home as soon as we can get you on a plane."

Rode started to speak but Katie held up her hand. "I know, you have no money, but I have. I will pay your fare."

"No Katie, no. I … "

"Rode, quiet. I've made up my mind. I want to get even with that swine Demetrius, and this is one way. You can send me the money from Mexico if you want, but I'm telling you it is not necessary. Tomorrow I want you to pack your things. I'll take you to a hotel in town until it's time for your flight."

"That's very good of you. I do not deserve this."

"Ssh, my mind's made up."

"Katie I do not have my … "

"What did I say Rode? No questions please."

"No it is not that. It is my passport."

At the mention of the word passport Katie wheeled around fast, yet spoke slowly and deliberately, as if dreading the answer, "What about your passport?"

"Demetrius has it. He's sending it to the Ministry of something or other."

"Bullshit he is, Rode. That's what he tells us, but I'm sure they're in his safe."

"But why?"

"Because he wants to have a hold over us, in case we want to do a bunk, … er, … I mean, get out of here just like now. He's a sleaze ball, Rode, of the first magnitude."

"What are we going to do?"

"Get it back of course." Saying it with great bravado was one thing, Katie knew, but doing it was another. She had no idea at this moment how to achieve their objective. How do you open a safe?

Rode was about to speak when Katie said, "Ssh, I'm thinking. Hang on here. I'm going to see Pierre. See if he can help. He might know how to get your passport back."

"What about you? Don't you want to leave too?"

"No, I kinda like it here. The island I mean. The weather, the coast the beaches. The work at the club? It's all right, I suppose. I'm used to this kind of life. I have nothing to go home for. Stay here. I won't be long."

As she walked along the corridor, she heard a rustling sound. She stopped and listened. What was it? Again she started walking and again she heard that sound. It suddenly dawned on her. Reaching into her blouse, she extracted the piece of newspaper she had picked up off the floor in the main room that had apparently fallen out of Pierre's pocket. Taking it out she made for one of the dim lights in the hallway. As she read, Katie went faint and had to lean heavily against the wall. It was a page from the English newspaper, The Daily Express, and was dated about a week earlier.

LONDON SOCIALITE FOUND DEAD!

In the early hours of Tuesday morning, a taxi driver came upon a car parked up on the pavement in Sloane Street WC.1., containing the body of

Theresa Charles, wife of Martin (Marty) Charles. A Police spokesperson said that foul play is suspected owing to the shady company Mrs. Charles had recently been seen with at London's swankiest parties. Martin Charles is at this moment helping the Police with their investigations.

There was a picture of Mrs. Charles taken at a recent West End party, together with details of her life.

Katie stood stunned. So someone had got to her? Good riddance! But Marty, had he killed her? She could not believe that of him. No, he could not have done it, she was sure. Yet the police must suspect him, otherwise why ... ?

Also why did Pierre have this clipping? He knew of Marty, of course, Katie had told him. But, was Pierre going to tell her? Perhaps not. She suspected that Pierre was sweet on her, so maybe he had not been going to say anything.

She stuffed it back inside her blouse and continued to Pierre's room.

"Pierre? It's Katie."

"Come in, Katie."

As she entered he emerged from the bathroom with his head in a towel. He had obviously been cleaning the wound.

"How's the head?"

"Fine, just a scratch. That chair, it hit my bald patch. Of all the places to hit me, it would be there."

"Listen Pierre, I need your help. Rode and I are getting out. Rode should never have been allowed to - well, you know. As for me, I've had enough of this place. That guy Demetrius could get us all killed."

"Not that he would care," cut in Pierre. "All he's interested in is money. As much as he can lay his hands on." He tried to sound upbeat and excited, but inside he was shivering with fear. Katie had said she wanted out. That surprised him somewhat.

"Why do you need my help?"

"We need our passports before we can go anywhere. I know he keeps them in that safe in his office. Is there anyway you know to get them out of there?"

"Me? Why me? What do I know of opening safes? No, leave me out of this Katie. I work here remember, this is my living."

"You don't have to do it yourself, stupid old dear. I thought perhaps you might know somebody. You are known to lots of people who I'm sure are just a tad suspect. If you get my meaning?"

Pierre was silent. Katie thought that he was thinking of names, but instead he was thinking of her. Of course he knew people who were capable of opening the safe. But did he want to tell her? If he told her then he would lose her. Why had she changed her mind? He always figured she was happy working here. She had loved the days off, when he had taken her to the beaches, or when walking through Nicosia they had picked fresh oranges straight from the trees by the roadside.

"Why do you want to leave Cyprus? I thought you liked it here? You seemed very happy. I know the club thing is not all that good, but you seemed to cope."

It was Katie's turn to be silent. Should she tell him? It would probably hurt him, and she was too fond of him to do that. Did she love him? She didn't know. It was not the same as what she had felt for Marty. Which feeling was love? She did not really know the answer to that.

"Yes it's very nice here, sure. But I have a chance to get out. I may not get another. Who knows what the future holds?"

"You are determined then?"

"Determined? I think so. I can always come back if I get lonely or homesick. Not for this dump, no, but for the island. The island that I know you love so much."

"So be it, Katie. Then here's what I want you to do. Go to bed, but be prepared to leave at a moments notice. You and Rode, that is. I am going to find a guy I know who can probably do the job. If he agrees then we will tackle the safe tonight when everyone is asleep. I will bring the two passports to your room. Try to get some sleep."

"Sleep! How the hell could we sleep knowing that you are … No, Pierre I want to be there when you … " She smiled wickedly. "When you do the dirty deed."

"I cannot allow you … "

"Nonsense, I'm coming and that's that. I want to have a look in that safe. Maybe there's some money we could steal, eh?"

"No, passports are one thing, but stealing money? I cannot allow you … "

"You silly old thing! I wouldn't do that. But it is tempting, you must admit. Seriously, though, I am coming with you. Where will we meet?"

"We will meet in your room at, let's say, 3.30. Wear clothes just in case we have to make a run for it outside. Whatever you do, don't bring Rode. She is too emotional, as far as I can see."

"No, I won't bring her, but I will have to tell her what we're doing. Thank you, Pierre," she said, giving him a tender kiss on the mouth. "You are a dear. See you at 3.30." She left.

"What the hell have I got into?" he thought. "I must be crazy. I am. Crazy in love. Whatever it is she wants to go back for, perhaps it will not work out, then she can return here to me. Oh my God! The newspaper cutting. I forgot to tell her." He went to his jacket pocket. It wasn't there. Where the hell was it? He fumbled though all his pockets, but to no avail. It had gone. Perhaps it was for the best, she should not know about that Marty guy.

The streets were dimly lit from the street lamps. The roads were glistening from the soft shower of rain that was falling. The big grey building of the Club Britannia was dark and empty-looking.

A car drove noiselessly past the front entrance and turned down the side street next to the club. It travelled very slowly like a bird looking for a nesting place. It hovered at certain spots, but finally stopped at a door at the rear.

As the car came to a halt, the door opened. The driver of the car got out and approached the door. Some whispered words were spoken and the door closed as mysteriously as it had opened.

The streets returned to their nightly loneliness, only interrupted by the occasional bell from a distant church, the bark of a dog or the patter of the rain as it fell on puddles, which now showed the reflections of the street lamps keeping their lonely night vigil.

Inside the club it was silent, as rooms and corridors usually bustling with life now stood empty and listless, bathed in shadows, as though wishing for the daylight to come.

Staircases were dark as lights had been turned off. An occasional cigarette butt or scrap of paper could be seen. No lights came from under the bedroom doors as the two figures crept along those same dark passageways. Turning a corner, there appeared, half way down on the right-hand side, a strip of light from under a door.

Inside this room Katie and Rode sat huddled together on one bed, Rode in a nightie with a dressing gown on top, Katie in jeans and black T-shirt. Neither spoke a word but stared at the alarm clock on the table between the beds. It showed 3.40 am.

"Where are they?" whispered Katie, breaking the stillness of the moment. "They should have been here … " There was a tiny tap, tap on the door.

Rode jumped with a start then rushed to the door. The two men glanced right and left down the hallway before entering swiftly. Rode held a finger to her lips, telling the men to lower their voices when they spoke.

"Good," said Pierre in a low voice. "You are ready, Katie. Sorry we are a bit late but we had to make sure there was no one about downstairs." He turned to the man beside him. "This is the safe expert. No names are necessary, nor introductions."

The girls nodded in unison.

"Put on a coat," he said to Katie. "It's raining outside, and you never know, we might have to go outside."

Katie nodded and got a light jacket from the back of a chair and put it on. "Ready," she whispered, her voice sounding scared.

Rode gave Katie a hug, saying, "Good luck, don't take chances."

Katie opened the door and peered outside. She then beckoned the two men to follow her.

The door was closed as quietly as possible, as there were other girls in the rooms next door and all along the corridor.

Pierre led the way with Katie behind him and the stranger following at the rear. Down the corridor, away from the direction in which the two men had approached, the three of them crept. They reached a back staircase which was made of metal. As they descended, their shoes made a noise on the metal treads. Pierre stopped and putting his mouth to Katie's ear whispered, "Take your shoes off and put them in a pocket. Tell it to our friend as well."

Katie tapped the man on the arm, and bending down removed her shoes. As she placed them in her pockets, the man removed his shoes but instead of placing them in his pockets tied the laces and placed them round his neck. Pierre meanwhile had done the same.

They continued down the staircase. Half way down, Katie glanced out the window. She saw the beam of a strong flashlight approaching. The beam was moving from side to side probing and searching the darkness of the building.

Katie tapped Pierre on the shoulder and pointed. "Security, get down."

They all dropped and lay there as flat as possible on the cold metal.

The light approached and shone on the window below them. Then as if an explosion had occurred, it burst through their window and lit up the entire area around. Katie saw Pierre's hair illuminated for a fraction of a second, then it was terrifyingly dark once more, as the deadly beam continued its nightly search.

They continued their slow descent of the stairs until they reached the first floor where a fire door blocked their way.

Katie whispered to Pierre, “Will it open?”

“I hope so. Let us also hope the security is not so good around here.” He tried the handle, turning it slowly. He held his breath as he pulled. It was extremely heavy and Katie had to help him. The safe cracker came forward to help but they got it open before he reached the door.

They entered the corridor that contained the paintings, the paintings that Katie had admired so much on her first day at the club.

“Should we take a painting as well?” she whispered, smiling.

“Please, Katie, shut up, this is no time … ”

“Spoil sport,” she said, giggling.

The corridor was L-shaped. As they turned the corner leading to Demetrius’ office, they saw a light under the door and, as they neared, saw also that the door was slightly open.

“Shite!” muttered Katie. “Do you think there’s someone in there?”

As they approached the door, they could hear talking from inside. Whoever it was, was talking in Greek.

“That’s Demetrius,” whispered Pierre. “Let’s go back.”

“No, I want to hear what he’s saying or who he is talking to.” At that she pushed her way to the front and leaned forward with her ear to the door. Pierre’s head was leaning over her shoulder, listening.

Katie decided to let Pierre go back to the front, so that he could hear better, so she moved aside to let him get past. As she did so a shoe fell from her pocket on to the heavily carpeted floor. The voice stopped.

Pushing the safe cracker around she pointed back down the hallway. He needed no prompting, but started to run, his shoes banging on the side of his face. Pierre followed behind.

Demetrius heard the sound and told the person on the other end of the phone to hold, got up and went to the door. Opening it he peered outside and saw a figure disappear around the corner. “Who is there?” he shouted in Greek, then shouted again this time in English. He went back to the phone. “I think someone was listening but I do not know who. Better close off now, goodnight and remember what I said.” He hung up.

The three escapees threw caution to the wind and did not stop running until they lunged breathlessly into Katie’s room.

“What happened?” asked Rode in a voice trembling with fear.

Katie held one hand up and the other to her chest showing they were out of breath. Rode waited.

Pierre was the first to speak and he spoke to the safe cracker in Greek. The safe cracker nodded and sat on Rode's bed.

"What did you say to him, Pierre?"

"I told him to wait awhile here then I would take him to my room."

"Can someone please tell me what happened? Did you get them? Why were you running?"

"Whoa, girl," said Katie. "One question at a time please. No, we didn't get the passports. Demetrius was in his office."

Rode gasped and raised her hands to cover her mouth.

Katie turned to Pierre. "What was he saying? Was he on the phone, do you think?"

"Yes, he was. I could only hear a few words, but it sounded like this." He paused before continuing. "He was asking someone for a bigger share of the money. The fights earlier were not his fault, and he should not be blamed. If he was to take the blame then he required more money. At least, that's what it sounded like."

"Bastard." hissed Katie. "The fights not his fault, indeed. Bullshit they weren't."

"Let's forget it for tonight, Katie." broke in Rode. "We are all tired and the men want to get some sleep."

Pierre and the safe cracker rose and went to the door. Pierre turned and said in a voice with no true conviction, "We will have to think of another way, ladies."

As they left, Katie whispered to herself, "I know, but how? How do we get our passports back?"

CHAPTER EIGHTEEN

Nikki's mood matched the weather outside his spacious bedroom in the 'Turkish House'; dark foreboding clouds which threatened a thunderstorm. The humidity was way up high, as was his temper. Ever since he had overheard that Demetrius was using Rode as a Whisky Dolly he had brooded what he would do when he caught up with Demetrius.

The two guards, Vlascis and Tselios, had noticed the change in Nikki the past twenty-four hours, and had so informed Cicero Andreas. He had told them that Nikki was probably thinking about his girl friend and wishing they could meet and be together. They were not to worry unduly.

Nikki spent most of the time lying on his bed deep in thought. Thoughts of Rode were uppermost in his mind. Oh, how he loved that girl. He recalled the first time that they had made love. He had been with other women before, but with Rode it was like being with a china doll; something that he wanted so badly, yet was frightened of hurting. Every time he held her in his arms, he would try not to break her, so to speak. She seemed so delicate, not only in size but in her temperament as well. How tall was she? Five foot two, and he was over six feet. Surely not a good match. Then, he thought, love matches are made in heaven and not in department stores.

Those romantic loving thoughts were interspersed with plans of how to escape from this place. The two guards were always behind him, watching. How was he to escape? He could not move anywhere without one of them asking where he was headed and one would accompany him. The only break he seemed to have was when he went to the bathroom. The windowless bathroom!

So if he was to escape then he would have to escape when they were with him. Should he try to get their attention and lock them in a room somewhere in this house? No, one would follow him while the other remained at the small room which was the nerve centre. It had television screens of the grounds and from that room they could control the alarm systems.

Should he phone the club in Cyprus? He had tried that. Finding a phone in a small hallway at the back of the house, he had picked it up to speak. Tselios' voice had answered.

No, he thought, the only way was to get them both outside, and escape then. But how? He had wrestled with this problem for many hours and had come up with no answers. He had resigned himself to his captivity.

Lying on the bed on the hot thundery evening, with the television on, he was not really listening, his gaze fixed on the screen. There were highlights of a football game being shown. He loved football, so he got the remote and raised the volume. The sportscaster was giving the highlights of a match that had been played in Crete. He finished by saying that the next game in Athens was one of the local clubs, and Nikki's favourite team, Panathinaikos versus Kastoria.

An idea started to form in his head. He switched the television off to help his concentration. Yes, that was it! He would ask them both if he could go to see the game, which was due this coming Sunday. Two days hence. Surely they would both attend; after all there would be a large crowd and both would be required to look after him.

He would ask them, tomorrow at breakfast. They would phone his father to ask permission. No doubt he would be a bit sceptical, Nikki was sure, but if he agreed to some sort of disguise, then his father should have no objection, surely.

The next morning at breakfast, Nikki posed the question.

"Certainly not," Tselios had said adamantly. "Out of the question. Right, Vlascis?"

Vlascis had known Nikki since he was a lad, and knew Nikki's love of football. "I don't see why not, as long as he is supervised. Phone Mr. Andreas and ask his opinion. I would not mind seeing the game myself. It is not being televised."

Nikki breathed a sigh of relief. He had not thought about that. Most games are televised, but Kastoria were bottom of the league so the match was not too important.

Tselios smiled. He had been born in Kastoria, a small town in the remote northern region of Greece. It would be like old times to go to a game. "Will he be upset at being disturbed at breakfast, do you think?"

"I shouldn't think so," replied Nikki, his heart racing with excitement. It seemed to be going better than he had planned. Both of them seemed to be football fans first, and guards second.

"I'll speak to him myself," Vlascis said, taking the phone from Tselios.

Behind his back Nikki crossed his fingers. Ever since he was a young lad, whenever he wanted something, he would stand with his hands behind his back and cross his fingers. Most times it had worked. It never occurred to him that the things he wanted his father and mother could grant quite easily. He had always assumed it was his crossed fingers.

It was obvious that Cicero did not like the idea. What if they should be seen? While there was a pause in the conversation, Nikki said in a matter-of-fact voice, "I could wear a disguise, tell him."

Vlascis brightened up at this suggestion and relayed it to Mr. Andreas. "Yes sir, we will phone when we are about to leave and as soon as we get back from the game. Most definitely, sir. Thank you."

Nikki could have hugged Vlascis, but instead feigned lack of understanding of the phone call and said simply, "Did he agree?"

"Yes, he did. Said it would most likely do you some good. Get you out of brooding."

Nikki retired to his room to make preparations for the next day. He had no money on hand but in his personal things by his bed he found the credit cards given him by his father. The disguise was easy; a pair of very black sunglasses and a trilby hat pulled well down over his face. Vlascis had given him a child's false nose, but they both thought it looked stupid.

Athens was the home of the first Olympic Games where the Athenians gave vent to their sporting passion. Nowadays that passion is reserved for the football game. Between games the Greek is not as passionate as say, the Italians, but put them in a crowd at a game, then they go wild. This was what Nikki was hoping for. Unfortunately, however, this game was going to be one-sided, as Kastoria was a poor club in relation to Panathinaikos, one of the wealthiest clubs in Europe.

The match was to be held at the smaller of the two grounds Panathinaikos used as their home stadium. It only held about twenty-five thousand, well below the seventy-odd thousand that their other ground held, and which they shared with Olympiakos, another Athens' team.

The ground was old and was being eaten up by the downtown core spreading outwards. Perfect for Nikki's plan. When and if he was successful, he would be fleeing in heavy traffic.

The seating area was segregated from the playing field by a high fence with strong iron bars. The local joke was to say that the fence was there to keep the referees from attacking the fans.

As the Kastoria team entered the field, silence greeted them interspersed with a few whistles - the Athenians way of booing. Tselios appeared to be the lone spectator cheering as they entered. Dirty looks greeted him as he stood up to cheer.

Then all hell broke loose as the Panathinaikos team took the field. Flares were lit and pandemonium reigned. Nikki and Vlascis joined the crowd on their feet while Tselios sat silently.

The stadium went quiet as the game was about to get started. Nikki noticed a few spectators flipping through their worry beads. Each bead bore the picture of the local heroes. Not required, thought Nikki. It will be too easy for Panathinaikos.

He had not seen his team for about two years yet he still recalled a few of the players. He had decided to wait until the first goal scored by the home team. When the panic followed, he would slip away, hopefully unnoticed.

The first half produced no goals, nor indeed any exciting moments. It was dull boring football as Kastoria, who knew their limitations, decided to defend their goal with every player back defending. The Panathinaikos team, far superior in talent, could not find a way through to score.

Boredom had settled on the crowd. A number of them removed their shirts and decided to sunbathe, saying that it was more exciting. As the whistle blew for half time, the loudest cheer of the day was heard.

Nikki was getting anxious. He had counted on lots of goals and thrills to keep the crowd in a festive mood, especially his two guards. Instead, though, the three of them were as bored as everyone else.

In search of cold drinks and some nuts, they all trooped down to the concourse for refreshments. The crowd was really dense around the snack bar and both Tselios and Vlascis knew that it would be a good time if he had any notions of escaping, which they doubted.

Nevertheless, they stood one on either side of him as they ate their treats.

Tselios was the only one who was thrilled with what he had seen so far. His team was tied with the mighty team from Athens.

The second half started off the same way as the first had ended. The Panathinaikos team had apparently changed their strategy.

The part-timers from Kastoria were tiring noticeably. Then it happened …

Midway through the second half the Panathinaikos goalkeeper, in trying to kick a pass back from a defender, missed the ball altogether and it trickled harmlessly into the net. One nil for Kastoria.

Amid the boos and whistles from the crowd, Tselios jumped up and down and hugged his pal Vlascis. During this hugging, Panathinaikos forward Kaisariani sped down the wing and unleashed an unstoppable shot which sailed high into the net. The crowd went berserk. Flares were set off again and the firecrackers exploded all round the ground. People in the next seats were cheering and shouting. All of them were now enveloped in pink smoke from the flares. Tselios and Vlascis were still hugging. Tselios' joy had not yet abated when Vlascis joined him in the celebration. This was Nikki's chance. Pretending to hug the man in the seat behind, he stepped up and quickly left the row and disappeared into the pink haze. He made his way up the aisle. Glancing behind, he saw nobody coming after him, yet he still ran. He ran along the concourse amid the giant concrete columns, looking for an exit. He found a large double door marked Exit but it was locked. By this time he had run half way round the stadium. To his good fortune, Panathinaikos scored again, and now the sound was deafening as it reverberated from the concrete. He hid behind a pillar and waited for the noise to subside. He tried to hear if there were footsteps following, but could not, knowing that they would have discovered his disappearance by now. He was panting so fast his heart was exploding in his chest. Think Nikki, think. What would they do? They would split up and run around the concourse. "That means one of them will be coming toward me, and the other will be at my back." Looking left and right, he could see no doorway close by. What to do? Continue until he found a door open? No, he decided, the best thing would be to go back in the crowd and wait. The game could only last about another fifteen minutes or so, then he could get lost in the crowd exiting the ground. He went up a ramp and spotted a seat at the top of the terracing. Sitting down, he removed his glasses and hat, thinking that would be what they were looking for.

As the game ended with Panathinaikos winning, two goals to one, a fan had left a large team flag on the seats. Nikki picked it up and holding it aloft so as to hide his face, joined the crowd leaving the stadium. He made sure he was in the thickest part of the crowd. Bending slightly at the knees, he was swept out of the stadium in a wave of singing and chanting young fans. Most of them were shouting obscenities at the few Kastoria fans that were there.

Once outside he continued being a part of this rowdy group, which by this time was wondering who he was. They started to split and left him exposed. He began to jog easily, still carrying the flag which furled out behind him. Quickening his pace he soon left the area of the stadium and found himself running full tilt along Leofros Alexandras. This was a wide six-lane highway where the traffic, now that the game had ended, was extremely busy. Nikki had counted on this, yet still he ran, glancing back now and again to see if he could spot Vlascis or Tselios.

He felt sorry for them, as they would no doubt be in a lot of trouble from his father. Hopefully, when he had time, he would phone his father and tell him not to blame them.

By this time his chest was heaving from his running and he felt exhausted. Spotting a bus, he ran and just managed to get on by hanging onto the door. The bus was crammed. He breathed a sigh of relief. Now he would get away.

His heart stopped. The bus was going the wrong way, it was heading back to the stadium, and he was hanging on outside in full view. He started to force his way into the bus, discarding the flag as he did so. There were shouts and grunts of displeasure from his fellow passengers, but he managed to get inside before the stadium bus stop.

Luckily for him the bus did not stop to either pick up or let off any passengers. A few stops past the stadium some passengers got off and he made his way down the bus. After ten minutes he managed to get a seat. He asked the very attractive young lady beside him where the bus was headed.

She explained that it was going to Rafina, about another forty five-minute journey.

"Oh, thank God," he said. "I thought maybe I had got on the wrong bus. I was caught up in the football crowd and didn't notice which bus I got on."

The driver on the bus shouted that anyone not having paid on entry, would they please pay on the way out.

Nikki turned to the girl. She was tall and heavily tanned. Her oval shaped face was nicely framed by jet black hair, giving her not quite a beautiful look but more of a pleasant appearance.

"How much is it to Rafina? My wife has gone into labour with my first child and I ran out of the office without money."

"You have no money? No money at all?"

"No, just credit cards." He opened his wallet to show her. She was very impressed as she saw some that only the wealthy carry. He seemed respectable, well spoken and dressed in expensive clothes. She hesitated before saying anything. He was certainly good looking. "I could lend you the money, if you wish."

"No, I couldn't let you. Yet," he paused, "I may get in trouble with the driver and delay getting to my wife."

"Here," she said handing him a few notes from her bag. "I will write my name and address on a piece of paper and you can repay me later."

He took the money with genuine gratitude and the slip of paper.

"I promise," he looked at the paper, "Katrina, that I will repay you the money. My family is quite wealthy and I will repay with interest. I promise."

The bus trundled on until, after ten minutes, Katrina excused herself and got off. He gave her a wave and blew her a kiss, vowing that such kindness would not go unrewarded.

The urban sprawl of Athens was now behind them and the bus travelled through some of the many vineyards dotted all over Greece. Large commuter homes stood silently, like sentinels watching over the precious vines.

Since coming on board, he had simply taken each moment as it came, thinking nought of the future. Now, however, he had to make plans. How was he to get to Cyprus? He could not go to any airport, they would be watching for him.

His fears grew as the bus made its way to the coast. What had he done by escaping? He had put himself in double jeopardy. Not only was his father looking for him, but surely Janus would find out. It seemed he had spies everywhere, as nothing went unnoticed by Janus and his thugs.

So airports were out. By boat, perhaps? But he knew of no boat plying between Greece and Cyprus. If there was one it would surely leave from Piraeus, and that would mean returning to the city. No, there had to be another way.

The bus dropped its remaining passengers at the central Platia or square in the centre of the old town of Rafina, situated on a high cliff overlooking the beautiful blue Aegean Sea. The old town is in complete contrast to the waterfront down below. Being a mecca for Athenians who wish to sail among the islands, it has blossomed into a tourist trap, comprising large hotels and condominiums. A large naval base, jointly for the US and Greek navies, occupies most of the adjacent coastline.

Nikki was hungry, as all he had had since a late breakfast was the cold drink and nuts at the stadium. He found himself a small awning-shaded cafe and went into the cool inside and ordered a meal.

When the very fat lady appeared to take his order, he had to smile as she could only just move between the tables with fractions of an inch to spare. She must have been doing it for a long time as she missed those tables without looking.

He ordered a cold meal and asked if there was a phone that he could use. He also asked if she would put the cost of his call on the bill as he had no cash, and was paying by credit card. She agreed, asking what card he would be using. He showed her the most elite in his collection. She was suitably impressed.

Going behind the counter, he asked the operator to connect him to his home in Athens.

A servant's voice answered. "Is my father there? This is Nikki."

"No, sir, but your mother is home. Do you wish to speak with her?"

"Yes, please, put her on"

"Hello, Nikki why are you phoning? I thought that you were not allowed … "

"It's all right, Mama, I can explain. We went to the football game this afternoon, Vlascis, Tselios and me. It was all planned by me as a means to escape."

"Escape! You have escaped? But why, oh my, Nikki, the danger, what have you done?"

"I had to Mama. I overheard one of the men saying that Rode, the Mexican girl, was looking for me in Cyprus. Apparently she is working for that good-for-nothing Demetrius."

"I see, but why escape son?"

"Because I love her, and she loves me. I'm sure that is why she went to Cyprus to find me. Remember, I had to leave Mexico in unusual circumstances."

"Yes, yes, I see that but that does not … "

"Mama, she thinks I am dead. I have to go to her and tell her my feelings and get her out of that place. Lord knows what has happened since she arrived."

His mother's voice now softened as she asked, "You do love her then, Nikki? Are you sure?"

"Yes, very much. I would die for her, she means that much to me. I intend to marry her." Pausing, he added hurriedly, "With your blessing, of course."

"Well, I hope it never comes to that, but then, that is what your father said about me when we were young. We will see, we would have to meet her of course, before we could, well, you know. . ."

"I hope I can bring her to Athens to meet you, but in the meanwhile I am going to Cyprus, and just phoned to let you know that I am fine and you are not to worry."

"Do you have money and have you got some clothes?"

"Yes, don't fuss. Will you tell Papa?"

"No I will not tell him yet. He will be so angry. I must wait for the best time."

"I will be all right and will take good care of myself. I will keep a sharp lookout for any strange characters that may be some of Janus' thugs. Goodbye Mama. I send my love."

"Take care, my darling boy, take good care of yourself."

"Oh, and Mama, before you go, could you do me a favour? Could you send a hundred American dollars to a Katrina Patinkin?" He read the address from the paper she had given him on the bus.

"Why, Nikki?"

"Let's just say, that I am returning the favour. On the accompanying note say: 'from your friend on the bus'. Bye, Mama."

"Goodbye, Nikki, my son."

Vlascis and Tselios had not noticed Nikki leaving. When they did notice, they assumed he had gone to the washroom as he had at half time, so neither of them was too worried.

After a while, they began to get agitated. Standing up and looking around the immediate area, they saw no sign of him. Leaving their seats, they went to the stadium concourse, which was deserted except for a few people going to and from the toilets.

"Let's split up. You go that way around, and I'll go this way and we'll meet up." Vlascis gave Tselios a prod in the back as if to start him off.

They both began a slow search around the entire perimeter of the stadium, until they met up with each other again, both looking disconsolate as each had thought the other would find Nikki.

Tselios asked, "Has he escaped, do you think?"

"Why would he? He knew the dangers of doing such a thing. Let's go back to the seats. He may already be there. If not, perhaps he has met a friend."

Tselios looked dubiously at Vlascis. Both men knew that was not an option, and both knew that Nikki had indeed escaped their grasp.

They returned to their seats. Although the game was now exciting and very close, neither of them could enjoy it. Both men were fearful of Cicero Andreas' wrath, especially Vlascis.

He had been with Cicero for twenty-seven years and in all that time had never let his boss down.

They had met when Vlascis was sixteen years old and working the streets of Piraeus, selling matches, shoelaces or anything that would bring in a few drachmas. Of limited education and having no parents that he knew of, Vlascis resorted to doing anything for money. A big boy for his age and much older looking than his tender years, he was in fact a bully. The other boys were afraid of him. Even then, there were rumours that he had killed people. This was in fact true, but he only killed in self-defence. In the late sixties and early seventies Greece was a poor country, and Piraeus being a seaport town, it was every man for himself, and gangs of hoodlums were common sights around the docks.

Late one night Vlascis was roaming the dock area, looking for mischief or someone to steal from, when he came upon a black car parked in the middle of the road, its doors lying open. This was interesting; a car he could steal. He already knew how to hot-wire a car without the key. He approached and as he got nearer he heard moans from inside. A man lay on the floor with his head covered in blood. Vlascis bit his lip in disappointment. Someone had beaten him to this victim. This did not deter him from going through the man's pockets, just in case. As he reached into the inside jacket pocket, the man grasped him in a vicelike grip around the neck and started to squeeze the breath out of him.

"Stop it you punk, have you not done enough to me?" The man hissed through his blood-stained teeth. Vlascis tried to loosen the grip but the hands were strong.

"Fuck off, Mister. It wasn't me who did this to you. Have you got any money or have they taken the lot?"

The grasp relaxed and the man let out a low moan of defeat and visibly sagged. "You want money, eh? Well, if you get me home in one piece … " At this he tried to laugh, seeing the funny side of that statement, "I'll see you get your money. Can you drive, kid?"

"Are you a cop or something? Yes, I can drive, but no licence."

"No, I'm no cop or something as you say, but if you will get me home I will reward you. I don't care about your bloody licence, just get me home."

And so it was that Vlascis took Cicero Andreas to his home that night and, true to his word, Cicero rewarded him with not only some cash, but with a job as bodyguard. Since that time Vlascis had carried out many tasks, including killing, for his employer, and had been rewarded with a life-style that he could never have dreamed of. Vlascis had never married, his women were the kind that one paid for, but he was aware of the love that Janus felt for Kasta as both men had courted for her affection. Janus had the more money but Cicero had the debonair style that seemed to please Kasta.

Janus' operation had been centred on gambling and casinos.

When Cicero had started breaking the law he and Kasta had bitter fights. Being a devout Catholic, Kasta found it hard to reconcile her faith with the love she felt for Cicero and during their engagement, after one such row, Kasta had gone to Mass. While there, she was approached by a well-dressed man.

"I see you are deeply distressed," he said softly. "Is there anything I can do?"

"No thank you, sir," she muttered between her sobs.

Over the ensuing weeks, whenever Kasta went to Mass, this man, whose name was Janus, would also be there. She thought it a bit strange until one evening he told her that he followed her to church every evening.

Speaking very quietly, as the choir were having their practice, he told her that he had come to be very fond of her, and that the relationship with her boyfriend Cicero seemed to make her unhappy.

"Thank you for your concern, Janus, but Cicero and I will work it out."

"Do you love him? I'm not sure that you two are suited for each other."

"Ye--es I do," she replied without much conviction.

A few weeks later, as Cicero's income increased and their arguments diminished, Cicero popped the question. Kasta loved Cicero very much and had loved him since they were children so there was no hesitation as she answered, "Yes, Cicero, my love."

The news of her marriage had been a blow to Janus, and since that day there had existed a bitter rivalry, although not hatred; more of a mutual respect for each other. Each had, over the years, tried to outdo the other for money and position. Cicero had eventually moved to Cyprus, and set up operations there.

The death of Janus' son had been a blow to the Andreas family. They all knew that Janus would be only too eager to exact revenge and that Nikki was a prime target.

Kasta Andreas could hear her husband shouting over the telephone as she approached his study door. "No," she thought, "this is not a good time to tell him." But why was he shouting and who was he yelling at?

She knocked on the door and entered to see her husband, red

faced at his desk.

"Think man, think. Did either of you say anything to him? Go back, not necessarily today."

"Cicero, can I come in?"

He waved impatiently at her and by his actions ordered her to sit down.

He listened on the telephone then, putting a hand to the receiver, he whispered, "Nikki has apparently run away. Yes, who? Demetrius, yes, yes, I see, phoned Tselios, yes. " As he listened, his face began to go red again as if he was about to have apoplexy. "What! He overheard? If you don't find him, I will have your head on a platter. How could you, Vlascis? Tselios I can understand, but you … "

Again he covered the phone. "Vlacis thinks Nikki found out that the Mexican girl is in Cyprus. Yes, Vlascis, all right, but bear in mind I am most upset."

Should she tell him now that Nikki had phoned? Perhaps not. He already knew of the escape. So why trouble him more?

Cicero slammed down the phone. "That son of yours … He'll be the death of me."

"What happened?"

"Its all garbled right now, but it would appear that Tselios got a phone call from Demetrius. Tselios was told that the Mexican kid was there, in Cyprus I mean, looking for Nikki. Demetrius did not know what I would do, or how I would react, so he phoned Tselios to ask his opinion. Imagine, that asshole Tselios having an opinion, huh!"

"How did Nikki get to know?"

"We're not sure, but we think he must have overheard Tselios on the phone and made plans to escape. That outing to the football game was just an excuse, I'll bet. That's it. A perfect place to disappear. I have told Vlascis to go to Cyprus and watch out for him at the club. You do not seem to be too worried about this, my dear."

"No. I am worried of course, but I am also very proud of him."

"Proud of him? In God's name why?"

"Because he has escaped to go to this girl. He must be really in love to do that, knowing the dangers, not only from Janus, but from you, your anger with him."

"Romantic bunk! He has endangered his life, and placed untold worry on both of us. You will not call it romantic if he is found dead somewhere with a bullet in his back."

"I have faith in our son, Cicero. Think back to when we were young. You were aware of the dangers when we got married, yet you thought nothing of that when we walked down the aisle."

"That was different."

"Was it, my Cicero?" she leaned forward and kissed him.

"Go away, woman and let me think."

Smiling the smile she knew would melt him, she left the study.

Perhaps Kasta was right. Maybe I should be proud of him. That night after the operation when Nikki had told him about this girl, what was her name? Rode, yes, that was it, Rode. He lowered his head in prayer and stayed like that for several minutes.

CHAPTER NINETEEN

His first day of freedom dawned cloudy and overcast. Yet his spirits were high as hopefully it would not be too long before he would be with Rode.

The bank should be his first stop, as he needed cash to buy a change of clothing. But first he would have to find some way of getting across to Cyprus. He had come to the realization that the only way was by boat, if he was to have any chance of not being detected.

He walked down the steep hill that separated the two parts of Rafina leading to the dockside and waterfront. Here there were loads of boats being hired, as well as pleasure boats taking the visiting tourists out to some of the Greek Islands. There were boats of all shapes and sizes, from large schooners to the small Jet-skis which roared around the bay, sounding very angry. Their noise and large wash was a constant nuisance to the local residents.

He asked the way to the Harbourmaster's office and found it located in a back street off the main dock area.

Inquiring for ships that might be making for Cyprus, he was told that no ship left for that kind of voyage.

"Where would I get such a ship?"

The girl behind the counter explained, "You will have to go to Piraeus for a boat of that kind."

"Do you know of such a vessel leaving today?"

She punched into her computer and said, in a completely disinterested voice, "Yes, the IPSALACA sails at 20.15 hours tonight."

"Going to Cyprus?"

"Yes, well, at least it sails for Heraklion. That's on Crete," she said in a snooty voice. "Then Limassol and finally Beirut."

"How long will it take to get to Cyprus, do you know?"

"It should be about three or four days. If you wish to join that ship it sails tonight from Pier 23C."

"Thank you very much." He left the building in a dark mood. He would have to go to Piraeus after all and if, he could get on that ship, then four days! A lot could happen in four days. Alas, he did not have much choice. How to get to Piraeus, back into the city?

Wandering deep in thought along the front, he stopped in front of a sign which read MOTOR BOATS FOR HIRE, BY THE DAY / WEEK.

Why not? Nobody would be looking for him to enter the Athens area by boat, they would be expecting him to leave by boat!

He entered the small hut which served as an office. A young teenage lad was reading Penthouse Magazine. Nikki coughed to announce his arrival.

The boy looked up startled, hastily stuffing the magazine behind his back. Seeing a potential customer dressed in posh city clothes, he immediately sprang to life. “Yes sir, what can I do for you?”

“Is it possible for you to take me to Piraeus today?”

The boy’s face fell. Disconsolately he replied, “Piraeus, that’s a long way.”

“I know, but could your boat do that kind of journey, what is it, about forty miles, eh?”

“Yes, but it would have to carry extra gasoline for that trip. That would mean extra cash as well.”

Nikki threw down an American one hundred dollar bill. “That cover it, do you think?”

The boy stood up. “When do you want to go, sir?”

“I’ll be back here at twelve o’clock. See that everything is ready.”

“Aye aye, sir!” he shouted, beaming from ear to ear.

Nikki asked who would do the sailing and navigating and was told that the boy himself looked after the boat.

Leaving the harbour area Nikki again walked back up the hill to the old town, where the shops lay open yet sleeping, awaiting the sun which was trying so hard to break open the cloud cover. The shops looked as if they had not had a customer for years, especially the little clothing store he now entered. Dark and dingy inside, clothes were hanging everywhere. To get to the back of the shop to the counter was like walking through a backyard clothesline. The shop had a musty smell.

A wizened old lady, looking like a painting by Michelangelo, lined face and deeply tanned, watched him like a hawk as he fumbled through a table full of clothing. At last he found what he was looking for: a black polo-necked sweater, jeans and a black knitted hat favoured by the local fishermen. Not having shaved that morning, he definitely looked the part.

Asking the old lady if she wanted his city clothes, she spat on the floor before answering in a voice as cracked as her face, “You want to swap, eh? Take ’em off, then.”

Nikki looked around for somewhere to undress. The old lady cackled and her face broke into a toothless smile. “Shy little brat, aren't you? I've seen it all before, son." She cackled again.

Shrugging, he undressed in front of her.

"As I said, I seen it all before, but not seen as good before." Once more the toothless grin appeared.

"How do I look?"

"You look like a city boy dressed as a sailor." This brought about another spit on the floor and a hearty laugh.

He threw some coins down on the counter and left the premises, her guffawing echoing behind him, as he went down the street, Nikki continued his shopping spree, buying food for the journey, a change of underclothes and various toilet articles. All of these he stuffed into a camping bag which went around his shoulders. He had bought a razor but had no intention of shaving. Having a beard and a moustache, he thought, suited him. If he was lucky enough to get aboard the steamer he would, no doubt, merge in with the crew.

Just before noon he walked down to the small hut where the motor boat *Pepe* was moored. It looked quite seaworthy and had nice soft seating. It would hold about eight people, he figured. The name especially got his attention - a boat with a Mexican name, carrying him back to his Mexican love. He smiled a wry smile with a faraway look in his eyes.

He got into the boat, sat and waited for the boy to appear. The sun was now high in the sky and getting very hot. The large sweater he had purchased, or exchanged, was too warm for the heat of the day, so he removed it and instead put on a T-shirt.

Sitting there, his thoughts were focused on the journey ahead. Four or five hours for the trip to Piraeus would get him there about the supper hour. Enough time to locate the 'Ipsacala' and attempt to bribe the Captain to take him as a passenger.

Lost in his musings with the heat of the sun welcome on his lithe body he lost all sense of time. He looked at his watch, 12.30. The boy was late, or was he? He had given him the money. Had the boy run off with it and, indeed, was not coming at all?

Nikki left the boat and walked past the hut to the dockside, looking both left and right. There was no sign of the boy. But over there on his left in the shadows of a large warehouse two men were standing. Nikki did not waste a second, he darted into the hut and peered out of the tiny, oily smeared window. The men were still there. Were they watching for him? They obviously had not seen him or they would be walking this way. He remained watching them for about seven minutes until a car drove past the men and stopped. The men ran over to the car and got in. The car sped off at a great speed.

Had they been Janus' men, or his father's? Were they after him at all, or were they just waiting for that ride?

Where the hell could he be? It's nearly one o'clock. We have to get going to have any chance of getting on that freighter.

He sat in the darkness and cool stillness of the hut and listened to the sounds of the dockside traffic as it passed by. He could not relax, but instead his feet and hands fidgeted constantly. At last he heard a noise outside, and peering through the window spotted the boy unloading four cans of gasoline from the back of a truck.

Nikki went outside. "Where the hell have you been? I was worried."

"Not to worry, sir, I was delayed getting this extra gasoline."

"Do we need that much?"

"Yes, sir, we do, I … "

"Yes, yes, all right then. Here, let me give you a hand."

When the gasoline, the boy's tools, and food and other articles were all on board, Nikki asked. "How long do you think, it will take to get to Piraeus?"

"About six hours, sir."

"That long, are you sure?"

"Sure thing, sir. I have done this trip before." He held up two thin bony fingers. "Two times."

At last everything was ready and they cast off from the mooring. The boy seemed quite skilful at manoeuvring the boat through the traffic in the harbour. As soon as they were clear of the hundreds of moored vessels, he opened the throttle and they sped off.

Leaping and dancing over the small waves, they gradually lost the details of the land in the haze of the hot sun.

"My Greece is disappearing," lamented Nikki. "When will I ever see you again? Will I ever see my beloved country again?"

The boy sat at the back of the boat and waved a hand at Nikki, telling him to come to the rear of the boat beside him. Nikki started to ask why, but the noise of the motor and the wind thrashing at his face did not seem conducive to talking.

Gradually Nikki's body relaxed, and he began to sit lower in the boat as the waves, now that the were on the ocean proper, were getting larger by the minute. The boy cut the speed of the motor to compensate for the turbulent waves. This was exhilarating, racing over the blue Aegean Sea with some islands popping up on both sides. Nikki as a boy had been to some of those islands, he knew, but could not remember their names. Memories of he and his father fishing off the coasts of the islands came back to him. Happy days, when he and his father had been close. As Nikki had grown older, and finally left home, the closeness they had enjoyed diminished.

The boy leaned down to Nikki and shouted, "I could stay here all day, on the water, I mean. It is in my blood."

"I know what you mean. By the way, what's your name?" shouted Nikki.

The young boy pointed to the side of the boat. "Pepe?" asked Nikki. The lad nodded.

Once more they both lapsed into silence and let the swish of the sea, the rolling of the boat, the spray on their faces and the hot sun beating down envelop them and hold them in the beauty of the moment.

Nikki was brought back from his dreaming by the sound of the engine sputtering. He looked at the boy questioningly. "Gasoline?"

"Yes. Could you reach one of the cans, and open it, please, sir?"

Doing as he was told, Nikki stood up rather shakily as Pepe again cut the throttle back and came to a stop.

Taking the can from Nikki the boy poured it into the motor.

"Okay?" asked Nikki.

"Yes, fine, sir. Be away in a minute." At that he started up the motor and once more they were on their way, skipping over the swells of the whitecaps.

Nikki took from his bag a bottle of coke and offered it to the boy. Pepe smiled one of his ear to ear grins and taking the bottle took a large swig which consumed half the contents. He passed it back to Nikki.

Nikki was drinking his share when the engine crackled and grunted and went silent. They coasted for a little way then stopped, bobbing up and down in the eerie silence. The silence was deafening after the roar of the engine and spray that had been their companions all this time.

"What's wrong?"

"Don't know, sir. It's not gas this time." He switched the engine to the off and raised the outboard from the water. Bending over they both saw some fish net tangled in the blades. Pepe reached down and tried to clear the netting. He tugged and pulled and freed quite a bit of it, but he could not reach the lower end of the outboard.

He took off his shirt and pants and was taking his sandals off when Nikki asked, "What are you doing?"

"I am going overboard to untangle the rest. Hand me that rope. I will keep hold of that so that I will not float away."

As Nikki handed him the end of the rope the boy jumped into the water. Going to the rear, he disappeared under. He came up blowing hard, with a large piece of net in his hand, and with his great smile.

He leaped on board as if he was getting on a bicycle. The engine exploded into life at the first try and with a thankful look on their faces they continued their journey.

An hour or so later, after another gasoline stop, the motor stopped once more. Again the lonely silence of the ocean.

"My turn to go over the side," said Nikki, jokingly.

Pepe put out a hand to stop him. "No, Let's see what it is first. We are too far from the fishing grounds for it to be netting." He raised the outboard. Nothing seemed to be amiss. He tried to start the motor, nothing. Nikki looked at his watch. It was three o'clock.

Getting his tool box, the young lad opened up the outboard. It seemed to Nikki to be all screws; big ones that were long and hard to remove. Painstakingly he removed each one and laid them carefully on a rag. "Must remember," he said, "to put them back in the same order."

After ten minutes he had the cover of the motor off and with a screwdriver as a pointer, began to go over the whole engine, very carefully.

"See anything, son?"

"I'm not sure, yet. But wait, I need to get into the gear-case."

Once more there were screws to undo, and lay alongside the others. "Oh, my God!" the boy shouted.

"What is it? What do you see?"

"The gear-case has no lubricant left. The net when it was wrapped around the motor must have loosened the seals and seized the motor. We have been losing lubricant all this time."

"Do you have any spare?"

"You joking? No, we don't. We are stuck here, I'm afraid, until we are spotted and can be towed back to land."

"How far is the coast?"

"About ten miles, I would guess."

"What are our chances of being spotted out here?" Nikki voice was beginning to register panic.

Pepe, noticing the change in tone, said, "Pretty good, I should think. There are lots of tourist boats in these waters." He knew his lies would bring some sort of comfort to his city-type passenger.

They both remained silent for what seemed like an eternity, but was in fact about four minutes.

"What have you got in your bag, sir?"

"Nothing much; a bit of food, clothes, that sort of thing. Nothing that would be of any help."

"Let me look."

He took Nikki's bag and turned it upside down, emptying out its contents on the bottom of the boat. Clothes, bananas, wrapped sandwiches, another coke bottle and shaving cream and razor.

"Told you it would be of no help."

The boy went silent. Nikki did not like the silence. He needed to be reassured by this young boy. This lad was his only method of survival. Nikki had been on boats before, but knew absolutely nothing about how they worked. That had always been left to the hired hands his father had on board. Nikki knew how to drink and enjoy himself on boats. Even make love on them, but to sail or drive them, forget it!

"Ah hah! Just maybe. It might work."

"What? What will work?" Hopefully, thought Nikki, the boy genius would have an answer.

The boy rummaged around the boat and held aloft the bunch of bananas.

"Start peeling them. Peel them all and place them on the rag with the screws."

"Why? In heaven's name why?"

"Just do as I ask, please, sir."

Nikki started peeling and laid them on the rag. Pepe pulled the motor forward and, reaching over to the gear-case, asked Nikki to hand him a banana. Puzzled, Nikki did so. The boy started mulching the banana into a mash and stuffing it into the hole in the gear case. "Keep coming with the bananas."

The boy jumped into the water and continued from there.

"What are you doing?" asked Nikki, completely bewildered with this turn of events.

"I'm hoping to simulate the grease that's packed in here. It should work, I think. It will make a lubricant that will hopefully get us on our way. Cross your fingers."

After about four bananas the boy held up his hand. "That's enough, I think." He jumped back on board. Then began the slow task of putting everything back together. It had taken about fifteen minutes to undo the motor, but it was a much longer job to seal it back up.

Finally everything was back in its place, and the boy looked over at Nikki apprehensively. He took the key and turned the motor. Nothing. He tried again, a sputter. Once more, while closing his eyes and praying hard, the boy tried. The motor sparked into life. Nikki let out a yell that went around the boat and was lost out to sea in the wind.

"How long will it last like this?"

"Not sure. About three hours, I hope. That should see us in Piraeus."

The next three hours went past very slowly in the minds of the two men on board. Each of them took turns to stare at the outboard motor without letting the other know.

Pepe brought the boat into the lee of the coastline where the sea was not as rough. The passage was slower as they had several islands and rocky promontories to manoeuvre around.

At last they came in sight of the tall buildings of Piraeus. As they neared, they could see a great number of cargo vessels, cruise liners and a multitude of fishing and pleasure craft. From a distance it appeared that there was no way to get near to the shore. Nikki had not realised until now what a great port Piraeus was. Seeing it from the land side was one thing, but now, seeing it from the sea, it took his breath away.

He tapped Pepe on the leg to attract his attention, which like his own was riveted on the sight before them. "Do you know where Pier C23 is?"

"No, sir." He turned back to concentrate on getting them into shore. "I would imagine that it is in the commercial dock area and not the tourist area," Pepe said, staring straight ahead.

Nikki looked at his watch. It was seven-fifteen. One hour to sailing time. He would never make it. He had come all this way for nothing.

"Could you do me a favour, Pepe? Would it be possible for you to hug the dock area and look for the Ipsacala freighter or Pier C23?"

"It might be slower finding it that way, sir."

"I'll have to take that chance. At least if we find it I could hail it from here, before boarding."

Pepe steered the small craft away from the tourist area and the cruise ships and made for the large freighters that were further north.

They sailed right into the main dock area and started a systematic search for the Ipsacala. There were ships from almost every port in the Mediterranean, some with Hebrew names and others with Arabic lettering on their sides.

Pepe skirted around all of them but with only a couple left to try they found it. It was a container ship with its decks piled high with box containers. There appeared to be no room left on the deck. It was fairly large, although neither of them knew anything about tonnage. Dirty and rusty, it sat in the water quietly with no sign of activity anywhere.

It was now seven forty-five; still half an hour to go. "Let me off at the dockside, Pepe. At that steel ladder over there." He pointed to a permanent ladder leading up to the quay. Pepe cut his engine, wondering, as he did so, whether it would ever start again.

Nikki felt in his pocket and extracted two hundred dollar bills and handed them to Pepe. "Please," he said, "take these. You will need them for repairs." He offered his hand in friendship. Pepe shook his hand, and though he knew it would be proper to refuse the money, he did not have enough for those same repairs or for the gasoline for the journey home.

"Thank you very much, sir. It has indeed been a pleasure serving you. I hope you get your ship and Bon Voyage."

"Bon Voyage to you, Pepe."

Nikki watched as the little boat slowly made its way out of the dock area with Pepe waving until he disappeared around the hull of a tanker.

Making his way to the gangplank of the Ipsacala, he saw no one on deck, so he walked gingerly up, expecting to see someone to challenge him. As he reached the top, he shouted, "Hello, anyone on board?" No answer. He moved down the deck toward the bridge area, shouting as he went. Hearing a faint cry above him, he looked up and saw a sailor leaning over a railing shouting down at him. He was speaking in a foreign tongue.

"Do you speak Greek, or maybe English?" Nikki shouted.

The man waved for Nikki to stay where he was and disappeared. He reappeared a few minutes later coming down a metal staircase behind Nikki.

"I speak a leetle English," he said with what sounded like an Arabic accent. "I am the Capitaine, of thees sheep. Do you wish help?"

"Yes, please, Captain. My name is Nikki. Er. Nicholas Andrase, and I wish to buy passage to Cyprus." Nikki was proud of himself, for not giving his real name. Just in case. "I understand that you sail tonight for Heraklion and Limassol. Is that correct?"

The Captain looked Nikki up and down, seeing straight away that this young man, although dressed as a sailor, was not, and had never been, a sailor.

"Why you wish to go Limassol? You run from police, eh?" He laughed. He was short and stocky with the broadest shoulders Nikki had ever seen on a man. His face was tanned like leather but was covered in pockmarks. Scars were all over his head. No doubt from many fights, Nikki thought.

"No I live on Cyprus, in Nicosia. I am returning home."

The captain eyed him carefully before asking, "Why you not fly? Thees is slow way. Chug chug!" He moved his arms to imitate a train.

"I have my reasons."

"Aaaah! I see from your eyes, you are man in love, no? Run to or from girl? Never mind, ees no matter. Five hundred English pounds you can passage with me."

Nikki smiled. It had been much easier than he thought. He decided not to bargain with this man, or he might change his mind.

"Two hundred and fifty, now, the rest when I get to Limassol. O.K.?"

The captain laughed, and nodded his head, holding out a hand as large as a frying pan. Nikki turned his back and took out the bills from a waist pouch.

Putting his arm around Nikki's shoulders and squeezing the breath out of him, the captain led him down many stairs and along endless corridors to a small comfortable room with two bunk beds.

"No one else," he said waving an arm at the bunks. "Only you. You hear bell you come for supper." With that he left. Nikki fell exhausted onto the lower bunk.

He awoke with a bell ringing in the distance. It came from above his head. The supper bell, no doubt. He left his cabin and tried to remember the way back to the deck. He met no one on his way, but knew he would reach the deck if he continued upwards.

Nikki came out on deck just as the ship blew a blast on its mighty horn and slowly moved away from the dock. He looked at the quay and saw two men dressed in sombre clothes, standing by a black limousine, watching the ship leave.

Nikki darted back into shadow, hoping that they had not seen him.

He watched the two men until they were out of sight. Had they seen him? If they had, it was too bad. There was nothing he could do now.

A large sailor with an apron was approaching. "Friend, friend, come, supper here for you."

Nikki followed the man who took him past the galley to the mess, where a welcoming group of five sailors were waiting.

"Ah, Mr Andrase, we have special surprise for you. You very special guest for us. We make something special for you."

Nikki tried to smile but his heart sank. Something special? He had heard that people from their part of the world welcomed special guests with sheep's eyeballs, which was a delicacy.

He sat down to supper and enjoyed a lovely crab chowder, the best he had ever tasted.

CHAPTER TWENTY

Cicero entered the old world atmosphere of his favourite restaurant. The Coliseum was a distinctive place for Athenian businessmen. The walls were oak panelled from floor to ceiling and their dark richness glowed in the light from several chandeliers that hung from the ornate carved alabaster ceiling decorated with battle scenes from throughout Athenian history.

As he dined alone this evening, earlier than usual, his thoughts naturally turned to Nikki. What a strange boy he had developed into. From a childhood of having anything he wanted, spoilt in fact, he surprisingly had turned out to be very much like Cicero had been in his youth. This defiance of his father's authority and wishing to be with a girl he had obviously fallen in love with, had awakened in Cicero memories that he had thought long since vanished.

He was proud of his son, yet this was tempered with a sense of foreboding. It had been reckless, given the circumstances, but Cicero could not help wishing his son well. He would have done the same, had the positions been reversed.

Lost in thought, Cicero had not noticed Janus enter the dining room with one of his aides, as Janus liked to call his bodyguards.

Janus took a table across the room where he had a good view of Cicero. He liked Cicero although the two men, ever since the rejection by Kasta, had been bitter rivals, each determined to outdo the other with power, wealth and position in Athens society. Cicero might have Kasta but Janus had more power. It was poor consolation.

Janus' feelings for Kasta had changed over the years, from undying love to that of a friendly affection. He did not see her often, but each time, there was a slight stirring in his heart. She had remained beautiful over the years, and each time they met, her obvious affection for him came out with the warmest of smiles.

Dinner for Cicero was over and he ordered a glass of his favourite brandy. While waiting, he glanced around the room. Seeing Janus he gave him a nod of the head. He barely noticed the waiter silently place his brandy on the table.

Cicero had not seen Janus since the son, Leo's, death. Taking his glass of brandy, he got up and walked slowly over to where Janus was sitting.

"May I join you, gentlemen?"

Janus waved him to a chair. "I would like to offer my

condolences on your son's death." Cicero said. "It must have been very distressing for your family."

"Leave us," Janus ordered to his companion, who got up in the middle of eating and, looking very hurt, walked out of the dining room.

"Thank you for your concern, Cicero, but it was, I assure you, no great loss for my family. My son Leo was, how shall I put it? Well, he had not been a son of mine for a long time. I know that over the years I have not been an angel." He smiled at his choice of words. "But as for him, he was the devil himself. For most of his adult life he shamed us. Shamed us by cheating his mother and me, cheating my family and friends, but most of all, he cheated himself. I will not go into details, as he is dead after all, but his mother on more than one occasion has cried herself sick over him. I myself have had to pay enormous sums of money to get him out of scrapes."

"Sorry, I had no idea." Cicero cut in.

"No one had. I saw to that. It was poetic justice, I suppose. He died as he lived, in violence."

Cicero did not know what to say, so he kept silent. The silence between the two men lasted for several seconds, and Cicero noticed a change come over Janus' face. It changed from scorn and rage to deep disappointment and regret. It was obvious from the change that there had been some feeling for the boy.

Cicero felt that the silence should be broken and that he should show a bit of compassion. "I know how you feel, Janus. My son Nikki"Oh Cicero, come now. What do you take me for?"

"What do you mean?" Cicero sat up in his chair, trying to appear offended.

"You know perfectly well, you old trickster. Nikki has been seen. He's not dead."

Cicero did not know what to say. How could Janus know?

"My men have seen him. If you don't believe me, and you think your little scheme has succeeded. I will mention the football game between Panathinaikos and Kastoria, a few days ago."

Cicero could feel his face and neck go red. How should he react? For the first time in many years, he was at a loss for words. Instead he smiled.

"Aha, I knew it!" shouted Janus. "I caught you out. My sources had not been certain that it was Nikki they saw, that day, so I was feeling you out, so to speak."

Cicero visibly relaxed and was about to speak when Janus went on. "Why? Why did you go through that charade with the funeral and everything? Was he in some sort of trouble? Had he done something terrible in Mexico?"

"In Mexico? How did you … ?"

"How did I know he had gone to Mexico? Cicero, this is Janus you're talking to. You and I know everything that goes on with our families. You probably were aware of my son's indiscretions, right?"

Cicero started to reply, but was again cut off as Janus went on. "I don't know what Nikki did in Mexico but it must have been something really terrible. Did he kill someone, perhaps?"

Cicero was troubled. Janus had not mentioned the fact of Nikki being involved in the death of Leo. Something was wrong here. Janus was a sly old dog, could it be that he was fishing as to Nikki's whereabouts? Cicero, never one in the past to be afraid to speak his mind, decided to jump in feet first. "Enough of Nikki for now, do you know how Leo died, and who did it?"

"No, he was in a fight with Nikki … " He paused. "Oh Holy Mother of God, that's it! How could I have been so stupid?" He slapped his hand on his forehead.

Cicero knew at the same time what was coming, and he too was astonished.

Janus went on. "You thought Nikki had killed Leo and you sent him away, didn't you?" Cicero nodded. "Of course, and the funeral … yes, I see. It was to throw me off the scent." At that he started to laugh. He laughed so heartily and so loudly that everyone in the dining room turned to look at those two old enemies. Cicero began to laugh also, a nervous laugh at first, but soon the two of them were laughing and slapping each other on the back.

The headwaiter approached the table and whispering silently to the two of them asked them to please contain themselves, and to remember where they were.

The two men looked around the room sheepishly like two schoolboys caught with their fingers in places they ought not to be.

Sobering up quickly, Janus said in as serious a tone as he could muster. "Seriously, though Cicero, my friend, it is time that you and I became friends. This feud of ours has lasted too long."

"I agree it is time for us to be friends and not enemies. Well, we have not exactly been enemies, have we? More like rivals, in business."

"Yes, but those days are past. We are not getting any younger, Cicero. I do not know about you, but I am quite willing to let someone younger take over my business ventures."

"I have thought the same for some time now, but Nikki, now that he has met and fallen in love with a Mexican girl . . . "

"Has he indeed? Good for him. Go on please."

"He does not really want to be part of the family business. His mother, of course, is delighted, but me, I wonder what is to become of the, dare I say, empires that we have built up. Perhaps we could amalgamate in some way."

"Perhaps, but let us not be too hasty. In the near future I will have my lawyers contact your lawyers and we will go from there. Let's leave it at that, shall we?"

Cicero proffered his hand and Janus took it. In apparent friendship they clasped each other for a moment in silence. Cicero rose and left the table without looking back.

Cicero went to the lobby and used the phone there to call Kasta. He did not tell her too much except to say that he had met with Janus and that he had a lot to tell her. She asked question after question, but he told her all her questions would be answered when he got home.

Next he phoned the Turkish House. Tselios was there. "Is Vlascis there? This is Cicero"

"No sir, Vlascis has left for Cyprus. He flew out late this afternoon."

"Is he in the usual place there?"

"As far as I know, sir. By the way, I'm sorry for what happened."

"Right," said Cicero curtly, and hung up.

The usual place, as Cicero had called it, was a small discreet guest house, just outside Nicosia, very close to their former home on the island.

He decided to go home as Kasta would be anxious. Phoning from home seemed like a better idea than here in the lobby.

Vlascis had taken the first flight he could book out of Athens. As the plane flew across the blue Mediterranean, he never ceased to marvel at this part of the world. He had travelled to every continent but still the blueness of the sea and sky, which seemed to merge with the horizon into one large blue shell, kept him enchanted.

His thoughts were of Nikki, the boy he had known since birth and who he loved as the son he never had. Vlascis had devoted his life to the safety of Cicero, Kasta and Nikki and he would not have changed places with anyone.

Where had Nikki gone? Or, more to the point, how had Nikki gone? There were only three ways to travel from mainland Greece to Cyprus: overland to Turkey then by boat to the island. He dismissed that idea as it would take too long. Nikki would be anxious to get there as fast as possible. No, that way was out. The other methods were by air or by sea. By air was undoubtedly the fastest, but also the more dangerous. Unless Nikki was a master of disguise, which he doubted, Nikki was bound to be spotted at either airport.

No, Nikki would travel by sea. But from where? The obvious place was Piraeus, but would Nikki do the obvious? Probably not. So that was out. Also, what type of ship? Passenger cruise ships were on itineraries and fully booked anyway. The journey was too far for a small boat, however seaworthy it might be. So the answer had to be a freighter of some kind.

The normal port of call on Cyprus was Limassol, but would Nikki be stupid and adventurous enough to land on the Turkish side at Famagusta? He hoped not.

As Vlascis pondered these problems, there was one certainty. Nikki would make all haste, once on Cyprus, to get to the club to see Rode and sort out Demetrius.

Vlascis smiled a smile of satisfaction. He had never liked that weasel Demetrius. He thought of him as a slimy scumbag. He did not like what Demetrius had done to the club. When Cicero had run the club, it had been a place where the clientele could go for a good night out with female company. Female companionship, but not sexual relations in any way. If the customers wanted that sort of thing, they did it outside the club.

Now, since Demetrius had been given the manager's job, he had virtually turned it into a high-class bordello. Cicero knew of this, of course, but as it raised the profits substantially, nobody could care less how they were obtained.

Vlascis' plane sped over the ocean with its passenger thinking up ways to get even with Demetrius.

Kasta embraced Cicero as he entered their house, situated in an exclusive and private walled estate. The house was Kasta's pride and joy.

"Oh Cicero, how happy your phone call made me. To think that Janus did not like his son all those years. Poor man."

"Poor man, indeed! He has put us through hell, woman! But no matter, that is all in the past. Our thought must be to let Nikki know. As soon as possible. I will phone Vlascis in Nicosia and tell him the news. He will be as pleased as we are, I am sure."

"Do it right away, darling. I cannot wait to hear Nikki's reaction. Do you realise what this means?"

"What?"

"It means we will get to meet this wonder woman from Mexico that he is so enchanted with."

"Hmm!"

"Is that all you can say?"

"What else do you want me to say? Oh, that would be lovely dear or some such drivel?"

"Now, now. This is me remember? No, I simply want you to be prepared, that's all. Now go and make your phone call."

Cicero retired to his study. Wonder woman from Mexico indeed! How could she live in this environment, or indeed how could Nikki live in hers? No this feeling of his would pass in time, he was sure.

Reaching the Guest House in Nicosia, he was informed that Vlascis had not yet arrived. So he left a message for Vlascis to phone Athens on his arrival.

Replacing the phone, he pondered. Should he tell Kasta? Ever since his meeting with Janus, something had nagged at his brain. It did not surface until this moment when he tried to phone Vlascis. If Nikki had nothing to do with Leo's death and no blame was attached to him, then who had tried, twice, to kill him in Mexico?

CHAPTER TWENTY-ONE

Katie and Rode had stayed awake most of the night after the attempt to get the passports out of Demetrius' safe. Rode left the thinking to Katie, who seemed to have the more devious mind.

As she awoke in the morning, Katie realised that she had fallen asleep on top of the bed still clothed in her pseudo-burglar clothes.

Not having come to any decision on how to get the passports back from Demetrius, she decided that the best way was to confront him and ask him straight out for them.

She went down to his office taking the same route that they had taken the night before.

Knocking on his door, she entered to find him crouched down in front of his safe, where she felt sure the passports were hidden. Not only hers but those of all the other girls employed at the club.

Looking around and noticing Katie standing there, he hurriedly pushed the door half shut, stood up and said, "Yes, Katie, what can I do for you?"

"I was thinking about last night." Noticing the question in his face, she went on. "The fight, you know."

"Oh, that," he said, relieved. "It often happens I'm afraid, but not to worry."

"But I do worry, Demetrius. Not only for me but for Rode. She doesn't belong … "

"How do you … ?"

"Let me finish, please. No, Rode is not cut out for this life. I would like her to go home, and I am willing to pay her fare. Also …" She held up her hand as he was about to interrupt, "I want to leave as well. Last night's fight is not what I want to see again. No one was hurt, thank God, but someone could have been, and I don't want that someone to be me."

"Oh come now, Katie. Have you never seen a bar room brawl before? That's all that it was. These soldiers had a great time. They love these fights. Nobody gets hurt, because they are just letting off steam."

"That may be right, but I don't want to get caught in the middle. I came to this job thinking I was bettering myself with a career in management. You will remember our conversation at the outset."

He nodded. "But you told me you loved the island."

"Yes I do, but things changed when Rode came. Somehow, don't ask me why, I feel like an older sister to her and want to take care of her. She's grieving badly for that Greek boy she loved."

"Nikki."

"Yes, Nikki. I want her to leave and I would like to go with her. That's why I am here today. Could you return our passports to us, please?"

"You are over-reacting to the situation, Katie. I will see that you get more administrative duties to perform, I promise. As for Rode, she has only been here a couple of days. She's attractive, the customers seem to like her and I will keep a special eye on her. As for her grief, this is the perfect place for her to get over Nikki's death. If she went back home, the memories would return … "

"Perhaps, I'm not sure. Give me the passports anyway."

"I … er … do not have them at this precise moment. They are still with the Ministry of Labour. Tell you what. Take today off, the two of you and have a day on the island at my expense. You will see that I am right, that this is where you belong. Go to your room, stay there and I will send Pierre to chaperone you." He laughed at his own words.

Katie tried a weak smile. She realised that he had no intention of giving them their passports, at least not until he had made some money out of them. If only last night had succeeded, Rode and she would have been gone by now.

She had not mentioned the newspaper clipping to Demetrius. With both him and Marty being large club owners, they might even know of each other. In this day and age nothing surprised her.

When she had gone he got up and closed the safe. He was pleased with himself, the way he had handled a difficult situation.

He had not totally convinced her, he knew, but what he had done was to buy some time enabling him to cash in on the girls.

Rode was the core of the problem. If he could keep her happy then Katie would not think of leaving, and Katie was his prized possession.

He had lied when he had told her that the customers liked Rode. They did not even know her. But they knew Katie and liked her best. He had heard rumours that the soldiers held raffles, with an evening with Katie as the prize.

Picking up the phone, he called for Pierre.

Pierre was troubled. He had been summoned to Demetrius' office the morning after the attempt to open the safe. Had he been seen by Demetrius as they fled down the corridor?

If he had been seen, surely Demetrius would have stormed into his bedroom and demanded to know what was going on, so perhaps it was not about last night, but what?

"Ah good, you are here Pierre. Thank you for coming so promptly."

"Not a problem, Demetrius. How can I be of help?"

"Katie came to see me this morning, wanting to leave the club and return to the UK with Rode. I do not altogether believe her as, until Rode arrived, Katie seemed to like it here. Don't you agree?"

"I suppose so. Did she say what changed her mind?"

"Some crap about being a sister to Rode and looking after her. But enough of that. I told Katie that she was to take the day off at my expense, so that she could come to her senses. Here's where you come in." He flung a set of keys across the desk. "Take these, they are for the Mercedes. Take the girls away from here. Show them the island. Drive them to the beach. In other words give them a tour, so that they will appreciate what it is they will miss if they leave. Wine and dine them, but not too much. Try to make it look like you are spending a lot, but don't."

Pierre wondered how that was possible. He simply smiled and nodded.

"Good old faithful Pierre. I knew I could count on you. Off you go now, the girls are waiting in their room."

"Should I return at any special time tonight?"

"No, just get them back here for duty tomorrow night."

Pierre relished the thought of escorting the girls on an island tour. To him it would be a labour of love, not only for the island that he cared so much about, but also it would keep him close to Katie for a whole day.

As they drove away from Nicosia to the south west, Katie retold the story about her meeting with Demetrius.

"You are still determined, then, to go ahead with leaving?"

Katie thought about telling Pierre that she knew about the newspaper clipping, but thought better of it. "Yes, as I said before, this may be the only chance that I get. You heard Demetrius on the phone saying he wanted more money. So perhaps he is in trouble with his superiors. Who knows what may happen to the club and the staff in the near future."

Rode piped up, "Let us not think about that for a few hours. We have been told to enjoy ourselves at Demetrius' expense, so let us do just that. Lead on Pierre, show us a good time. What is it you English say Katie? Don't spare the horses!"

They all laughed, the tension of the moment broken.

Pierre drove them across the Troodos Mountains keeping to the smaller roads so that they would better understand his love for the people and places on this island gem in the Mediterranean. He kept going south until they reached Paphos.

He informed them that there were in fact two towns. The old Paphos, which was one of the original cities during Roman times, and the newer town built at the coast. The whole area around contained some of the most beautiful tombs and buildings found in Cyprus. Leaving the car, they walked extensively around a Roman Villa which had wonderful mosaic floors. Pierre had seen all this before, but the enthusiasm of the girls made him view it with fresh eyes.

Leaving Paphos, he followed the southern coast road and they marvelled at the countless beaches to be found there. They begged him to stop, but he said that they would go to a beach, but to a special one that he knew of. It would be late afternoon when they would get there. They would have to be patient.

They stopped for lunch at a roadside cafe on the outskirts of Limassol for a light lunch, as it was hot and the girls were not hungry.

Sitting under the gaily striped umbrella, the sounds of laughing made them turn around. Looking in that direction, they spotted three men at another table. They were apparently talking and laughing at them.

"Isn't that one of the men in the fight last night?" asked Rode.

"Yes," answered Pierre. "It is the Canadian they call Yukon." Pierre raised his arm and called across the room. "Hello there, Yukon, have you recovered from last night?"

"Invite them over, Pierre," whispered Katie.

"Would you like to join us?"

The three Canadians whispered amongst themselves and Yukon shouted, "Sure thing Pierre. Let's go, boys."

Rode whispered to Katie, "What did you do that for?"

"I dunno, but it might be fun. After all, we are on the loose today, aren't we?"

The soldiers had carried their chairs over with them and as they sat down Yukon introduced them. His companions were Frankie from Quebec and Andy from Chatham, Ontario. Yukon introduced himself only as Yukon who came from Whitehorse.

As everyone was seated and a stony silence descended, Rode broke the silence by saying, "Thank you ever so much for coming to my rescue last night. You were very brave. Were you scared at all?"

"Scared?" roared Yukon. "No little one, it would take more than a bully to scare me. Tell you what would scare me, though."

"What's that?" Rode asked shyly as the other two Canadians smiled knowingly.

"Why, trying to shove some barbed wire up the ass of a bear when it's in heat." He then roared with laughter, as Rode blushed to her roots. Katie laughed and as she did so she spluttered the mouthful of drink she had been taking over the tablecloth.

"That's enough Yukon. She is not used to guys like you."

"Don't mind him, Miss," said Andy. "He's always coming out with bits of hill-billy humour."

"Tell me something," said Frankie, "how come a girl like you is working in a place like the Britannia club? You are working there as a Whisky Dolly, aren't you?"

Katie answered for Rode by saying that Rode working there was a mistake, and that last night was her first night.

"I thought I hadn't seen you around. I know you Katie, I've seen you there, but even you have not been here long, have you?"

"No, and we are trying to get away from that place, but Demetrius wants to keep us."

Pierre looked at Katie and put a finger to his lips, telling her not to go on. Katie saw him, shook her head and went on, " No, Pierre. Perhaps these guys can help us."

Rode felt bad. She did not like Katie talking to strangers about their predicament. She placed a hand on Katie's arm and gave her a look that meant, 'no, Katie, don't say anymore.' As if to emphasize the point, she started to cry slightly.

Katie was moved and understood, but she was determined to go ahead. They did not know what was in her mind, and how it was scheming.

"What do you guys know about Demetrius?"

All three of them looked at each other, puzzled. "In what way, Katie?" asked Yukon.

"Has he got any weak points or do you know of any skeletons in his closet, so to speak? The reason I'm asking this, and I can see by your expressions you don't know what I'm talking about, is that we need help. Right?" She nodded at Pierre and Rode.

"Go on," said Andy.

"Well we wish to … Can we trust you fellas? I don't want this conversation to go any further than this table. Do I have your word that what I am about to say will not be repeated?"

"I do not think, Katie, that this is a good idea," said Rode.

"Nor do I," joined in Pierre.

Seeing the seriousness of the situation, and now realising that this was no joke, the three Canadians looked at each other and putting their hands in front of them and joining them together said in unison, "All for one and one for all!"

"Don't be flippant," said Pierre in a stern tone of voice.

"We're not," said Yukon. "This means that we have pledged our word and that we take this very seriously indeed."

Katie looked at Pierre and Rode. "Sorry guys, but we do need help." She then looked at Andy. "Rode arrived here two days ago looking for her boyfriend who is Greek but lived here on Cyprus."

She then related the events leading up to and including last night botched attempt at snatching the passports, then her meeting this morning with Demetrius. She finished by asking, "Does anyone here have a clue as to how we can get our passports back?" Katie sat back and waited.

Andy said, "You ask if Demetrius has any weak points? …"

"He's as greedy as hell," broke in Yukon. "All the bastard thinks about is lining his pockets."

"You also said that, didn't you, Pierre?"

Pierre nodded. "Yes, that's the language he understands."

"That's it!" shouted Andy excitedly. "He has already forked out quite a bit of dough on you girls, so why not repay him his money?"

Everyone was now staring at Andy as he added, "With some interest of course. Say perhaps 10 per cent. Could you afford that?"

Rode shook her head and turned to Katie. Katie hesitated trying to work out sums in her head. "I think so. I have some money in the bank here, but the bulk of it is still in London."

"What say you, Frankie?" asked Yukon slapping Frankie on the back. "You're the brains around here."

Frankie smiled weakly and turning to Katie. "You say you have enough money to repay your own and Rode's debt to Demetrius, even with 10 per cent added on. Is that right?"

Katie nodded nervously.

"Are you willing to pay that much for your freedom?"

Again she nodded but ever so slightly.

"Third question. The money here, is it enough for two fares to

London?"

"How much is that?" asked Rode.

"About three hundred pounds," Pierre said.

Katie nodded. "I can manage that."

Frankie was silent for a moment and they all waited for the result of these questions to Katie. Finally he said, "Good, now here's what I think you should do."

They all pulled their chairs closer to the table, and leaned forward expectantly like children listening to a ghost story.

"Tell Demetrius that you will repay him all his expenses. The airfare, the board and keep and any other expenses he has incurred. Tell him to add it up and give you a figure. You will know from this conversation if it is fair. Then add your 10 per cent if you wish. If he is as greedy as we think, and the cost has already gone into legitimate club expenses, then it means that the money is his to keep."

"This sounds good," said Pierre.

"Remember," went on Frankie, "that both of you must go and see Demetrius together. Rode, do you have money in a bank in Mexico?"

"Yes, I have plenty back home, enough to cover this and more."

"Why both of us?" asked Katie. "I already told Demetrius that I would pay for Rode."

"You both have to go to the bank. Two withdrawals, two passports. You need passports to either take money out or transfer from another country." He raised his eyebrows and waited.

"You sonofabitch, Frankie. You've done it again!" Yukon again slapped him on the back.

Katie looked around and all of them were smiling.

Frankie went on in a serious tone, "It should take about twenty-four to thirty-six hours to get the money from Mexico. At least that's what you tell Demetrius. If he bites, then we are in business."

Rode was silent then she asked, "If you mean what I think you mean, then, we only pretend to get the money, saying we will bring it back to him. But we don't, do we?"

"No. Yukon here has a cellular phone, the number he'll give you later. When Demetrius agrees, tell him that first thing the next day you will go to the bank and arrange for the money. We will await your call and will be at the bank waiting in a private, not a military car, to whisk you away." He sat back with a satisfied smirk on his face.

"Aha!" said Pierre, "I am beginning to see daylight. Two doors at the bank, aren't there? One at the front, the main entrance, and a side door."

Frankie continued, “Yes, the side or back door can only be opened from the inside. Later I will draw you a plan. You girls pretend to go to the bank to do your transactions, but instead you slip out the rear.”

“But I have to get money for the plane tickets,” said Katie. “Will there be enough time to do that?”

“Oops!” said Yukon. “Good thinking, Katie.”

Pierre coughed and, slightly blushing, said, “I will get the ticket money and give it to you before you set out for the bank. But wait, you cannot buy tickets any more at the airport. You have to go to a travel agency in Nicosia and get them.”

As Andy had not added anything to the conversation, he felt guilty. Plucking up courage, he blurted out as if to stop himself from changing his mind, “I will phone the agency and book the flights. The tickets and money to be picked up later.”

“Atta boy Andy!” said Yukon. “Now let’s go over the plan. First here is my cell phone number … ”

“And here is a rough drawing of how to get to the side door of the bank,” Frankie said, interrupting.

Yukon went on, “Pierre gets the money and gives it to Katie or Rode.” Pierre nodded. “The girls then face Demetrius and plead their case.”

“This is exciting,” said Rode. “Like those old black and white movies where the gang works out the heist and the getaway.”

All of them looked at Rode in utter amazement. She saw their looks and added quickly, “TV couch potato when I was young.”

“OK. Let’s get serious here.” Yukon tried to maintain some sort of control. “One of you phones me on my phone. You drive or whatever, to the bank. Get out at the front. We are waiting at the rear. The girls then run out and jump in the car. Andy, you will be driving as you will know where the travel agency is.”

Andy raised a finger in mock salute.

“Frankie, you will be in the back of the car. When they jump in, get them covered or out of sight somehow.”

“Oui, mon Capitaine.”

Yukon smiled as he said, “All for one etc.” Then getting to his feet, he announced, “All is ready, any questions?”

There was a silence, a long silence then Katie piped up. “What if Demetrius won’t give us our passports?”

“We will worry about that when the time comes,” said Yukon with a malicious leer that sent shivers through Rode. Not a man one should cross, she thought.

"So that's it," said Katie, getting up from the table. Holding a hand out in front of her, she intoned in a solemn voice, "All for one and one for all."

With great dignity they all rose and placing their hands on Katie's repeated: "All for one and one for all."

It was a quiet car that pulled away from the roadside cafe and drove east toward the beaches that stretched along the coast.

Pierre was excited, yet unhappy. His drab life had taken a complete about-face when Katie appeared. Yet he was sad that maybe, just having met this new and challenging life, he was about to lose it.

Katie was thrilled beyond her wildest dreams. She had always loved the unknown, the thrill of the unexpected. Now here she was about to experience the thrill of a lifetime. It was dangerous as well and could, she knew, mean her death.

Rode's excitement was not the same as Katie's. No, her excitement was in the knowledge that here were five people, strangers until two days ago, who were prepared, for whatever reason, to help her escape.

But this kind of commitment was beyond her comprehension. She was excited slightly, yes, but also fearful for her companion's safety. She also felt alone. What a cruel trick fate had dealt her. Falling in love for the very first time, only to have it snatched away so cruelly.

The phone rang in the empty study in Athens. As Vlascis replaced the receiver, he was perturbed about the message to call Athens. He had tried twice that day, unsuccessfully, to get in touch with Cicero.

Arriving that day in Nicosia, he had decided not to go looking for Nikki. If, as he guessed, Nikki would arrive by boat, then the best place to meet him was at the club. He would wait there; outside, not inside. He hated Demetrius with a passion, and now this affair with Rode, it was too much. Demetrius hired his girls with no knowledge of their background or who they were. That would be his downfall, Vlascis hoped.

If he'd sailed right away, it could be two or three days before he got here. Vlascis realised that all it would take was a look at the boat arrivals at the harbour, and he would be able to guess which ship he might arrive on. But Nikki was on the run. He would leave the ship secretly and probably in disguise. The chances of recognising him were remote. Here at the club there was a better chance of Nikki being recognised. He might even discard the disguise, as he would be at journey's end.

Vlascis showered and changed into his best suit. He wanted to look his best on this visit.

Leaving the building, he drove his rented car down to Limassol. He would visit 'The Family'. The 'Family' were three Greeks who ruled the crime scene in Limassol and throughout most of the island. They were feared by most people on Cyprus, especially those in similar types of business.

They had been known to Vlascis for many years and as he was no threat to them, he was received like a long-lost cousin.

Two of the brothers were not at home, but Konstantis met him with the usual Greek gusto. Many kisses and hugs, with glasses of wine appearing as if out of nowhere.

Konstantis was the elder of the three brothers and had the most dominant personality. It seemed strange that he was also the shortest of the three. Five foot three inches, almost balding with small piercing eyes and a nose like a bird. It dominated his whole face. Behind the eyes there seemed to be a look of cunning - or maybe it was hatred. A rather unpleasant fellow.

After the usual pleasantries and catching up with the ages and escapades of the children, Vlascis asked about news from the island.

"Bad goings on, Vlascis."

"How do you mean?"

Konstantis leaned back on the leather couch which seemed to have cushions all over it, before saying, "Your man Demetrius, there are rumours, my friend."

"Go on."

"If my sources are correct, then Demetrius is skimming money, no, stealing, from Cicero and his family."

Vlascis sat perfectly still.

"You do not seem surprised?"

"No, I am not."

"I see. You are not worried?"

"Surprised, no, but worried, yes. I think it is almost time for filth like him to leave us, no?"

"Are you asking … ?"

"Not really, at least, not yet. I may be in touch very soon."

"Should it come to pass, it would be a pleasure, believe me."

Konstantis gave a smile that would have wilted a flower.

Later that evening, the phone in Vlascis' room exploded, shattering the silence. It echoed shrilly almost impatiently, over and over. Then just as suddenly as it had started, it stopped. Silence enveloped the room returning it once more to its peaceful rest. Moonbeams entered silently and fell on the feet, then the body of Vlascis as he lay on the bed. His heart, which had been big enough for several men, had simply given out. He lay in peace, still dressed in his good suit, as if it had been an omen.

Pierre gave the girls their time at a beach as they had asked. Not having swim suits with them, and both Rode and Katie being sun worshippers, Katie asked if he would mind if they went topless.

This flustered him, which seemed to encourage Katie that much more. Without waiting for an answer she removed her dress and bra and lay down on the sand clad simply in her panties.

"How about you, Rode? If Frenchie here can bare his chest then why not us, eh?"

Rode looked around and as the nearest person was a fair bit off and topless, she too disrobed down to her panties, giggling like a silly schoolgirl. Her regret was that it was Pierre beside them and not Nikki.

Pierre stared at the two of them with their bare breasts swaying as they manoeuvred down onto the sand. Katie's were large, somewhat fat, and pure white surrounded by her pink and red body. Rode's were smaller and with their light brown shade merged evenly with the rest of her.

He turned his head away from these beautiful sights.

"You are allowed to look, you know," giggled Katie. "They won't bite you."

Rode turned over onto her front and buried her nipples deep into the warm sand.

Pierre kept stealing glances at Katie's body as his excitement grew. The sight of her beauty aroused his passion and thoughts of them together clouded his mind. He got up, not realising that his passion was there for all to see. He quickly made off away from the girls.

"Poor Pierre," sighed Katie. "Did you see the poor man?"

"No, what?"

"Seeing us like this has, I think, got him a bit steamed, so to speak. I'm sure he fancies me, as his pants gave him away. That's why he has wandered off."

Rode turned and stared at the receding Pierre. "Men cannot hide their … "

"No, and a bloody good thing too! It serves as a warning to us girls."

Both of them lay on the sand convulsed in laughter as Pierre's spirits sank lower and lower.

They dined that evening in a cliff-top restaurant which could only be reached by wet mossy steps leading from the beach. Climbing the slippery stone steps Katie got into a fit of giggling and the other two joined in, as their efforts to climb the steps deteriorated into scrambling up on all fours. Reaching the top, they were all wet and covered in patches of green slime. The other patrons, who had apparently come up by the road, stared from their clean shirts and gaily coloured dresses.

As the stars came out, they watched the distant lights of Limassol light up the sky, while out to sea the occasional pinpoint of light seemed to pulse in the inky blackness.

That night they stayed in a boarding house away from the beach and the noise of the highway. The house bordered on several small vineyards. A two-storey building, it was the original house of the vineyard's owner. As he had moved to larger premises inland, the house had been sold to the present owner, who had converted it into what it was today.

Katie lay awake, the anticipation of tomorrow's events preying on her mind. She could not relax. Rode beside her was sleeping the deep sleep of the pure of heart.

She crept out of the bed without disturbing either the bedclothes or Rode, and went next door to Pierre's room. Entering, she stood for a moment while her eyes became accustomed to the darkness. She then crossed the room and got into bed beside Pierre.

He did not awake at once, but with gentle hands fondling him, he awoke. "Katie?"

"Shush, don't say a word," she whispered, putting a finger to his lips. Turning him away from her she kissed his neck and shoulders while her hand started caressing the front of his body. Starting on his forehead she expertly caressed every inch of him, all the time her lips smothering kisses on his back and shoulders.

At last, her hands reached down to his hardness below. He tried to turn to face her. “Not yet, my love,” she whispered in his ear.

He put his hand round his back and felt a thigh. It was soft and warm. He tried to grope around but could not. She shifted her body slightly and his hand fell between her legs.

“You bastard,” she whispered. “I was prepared to wait you out, but not now.” So saying, she turned him around onto his back and mounting him expertly, made love to him with a passion born out of emotion stored over the weeks, as well as the anxiety of what the future might bring. Katie put her whole being into her lovemaking, as it might be the last time she and Pierre would be alone.

“I love you Katie. Have done since the moment I picked you up at the airport.”

“I figured you did.”

“Do you have any sort of affection for me, dearest Katie?”

“Yes. I think I love you, but I’m not sure. You see, I have been carrying around that newspaper cutting that dropped out of your pocket back at the club. The one about Marty.”

“I see. You still love him then? Is that why you are in a rush to get back to London? I knew there was a reason other than looking after Rode.”

“I don’t know if I love him, or if in fact I love you. That is why I have to go back. I know it sounds like a corny bit of dialogue from a cheap novel, but I love you both. I simply cannot make up my mind.”

“I know one thing, Katie. If you leave this island you will never return and I will have lost you forever.”

“We’ll see, you silly old thing. Now where were we? You haven’t lost me yet.”

CHAPTER TWENTY-TWO

Pierre, Katie and Rode got back to the club at lunchtime. The girls wanted to get the meeting with Demetrius over and done with.

Katie phoned him as soon as they returned, and asked to be seen right away.

"Certainly," he answered, putting down the phone. He was glad that they had come to their senses.

They knocked before entering. "Come in, ladies."

"Thank you for seeing us, and thanks for the lovely time off. Pierre showed us around this beautiful island of yours. You must be very proud."

"Thank you, yes, I am proud. It is beautiful. Now what can I do for you ladies?"

Rode looked nervously at Katie so Katie stepped forward. "Demetrius, you know we wished to leave the island and return to our respective countries?"

"Yes. Have you changed your mind?" he said smiling.

"No, I'm sorry, but our resolve is greater then ever … "

"Now, Katie … "

"Hear me out, please Demetrius. May we sit?"

He waved his hand. 'Oh dear,' he thought, 'I am going to have trouble with them. However I am much too clever for them so we will see.'

"You will recall," continued Katie, "that I was willing to pay Rode's fare and expenses to return her to Mexico? Well, Rode tells me that she has money in her bank in Mexico. More than enough to cover her fare and such."

Demetrius frowned ever so slightly. He realised that he was losing control and he was unaccustomed to that position. "What are you getting at, Katie?"

"As for me," she went on, ignoring what he had asked, "I have money both here and in London."

"So?"

"So, we have a proposition for you." She stopped, letting her words sink in.

"Go on," he said impatiently. The word proposition scared him. It was always 'either or something' and it usually turned out bad.

"The proposition is this. You have laid out quite a bit of money to bring me over here. I would guess about four hundred pounds. Then there are your costs while in London, say another 200 hundred pounds, and your expenses for me while here in Cyprus, that would be about two hundred as well."

He nodded slowly, his eyes piercing through hers and making her uncomfortable. Nevertheless, she continued. "I am willing to repay you that sum and give you, say, an extra 10 per cent for a grand total of eleven hundred pounds."

"How much is that in American dollars?" asked Rode.

"About two thousand dollars, I think." She turned again to Demetrius. "I will give you that sum if you will let me return to Britain."

"I too, will give you two thousand dollars, although I realise that you are not out of pocket with me."

Demetrius was dumbfounded. The gall of these women, offering what amounted to a bribe for their freedom. But what a wonderful idea. His heart was racing but he tried to hide his feelings. Four thousand dollars! All Katie's expenses had been entered properly in the accounts, so there was no need to show any payment. No one need know. The girls would know. No, they would be on their way to wherever, and not likely to return. Better pretend it hurts to accept. Not fair, never been done before and all that honest type of crap.

"I don't know, Katie. It is highly irregular. I would have to alter the company records, and such, also I would have to pass it through my accountant … to give you a receipt, I mean."

"I understand," Katie said apologetically, but inwardly smiling. Just what the army guys had said. Rode hid her face by pretending to cough, yet stifling a giggle.

"I am disappointed," he said in much louder excitable voice, "to think that you would bribe me. For that is what this is, you know, a bribe."

The girls remained silent.

Demetrius got up from the desk and paced across the room, as if in deep thought, and his conscience bothering him. But his thoughts were of all that money. It would go a long way to relieving some of his debts. The timing was right also, as only last night he was wondering how he could lay his hands on some money. He had already stolen some from the club and any more would surely be detected and give him away.

Straightening up, as if coming to a decision, he said, "All right, girls, I agree. But my expenses are more like five thousand dollars."

Rode and Katie looked at each other and both nodded.

"When can I expect the money?"

"Tomorrow morning as soon as the bank opens," answered Katie in as calm a voice as she could.

Rode coughed and they both turned to her. "I am sorry," she said, "I can get the money, that's not a problem, but it may take twenty-four hours. Would that be a problem?" she asked demurely.

Katie turned to Demetrius and without asking said, "I can't see that as a problem, right? I can give you mine tomorrow when we return from the bank."

"What? Oh yes, right, yes."

Speaking in her most innocent voice Rode went on, "Sorry to be a nuisance, but will I not need my passport to do the transfer, for identification purposes?"

"Shit, that's right," said Katie. "Mine as well I suppose. Do you think you could get them back from the Ministry before tomorrow morning?"

"I don't know," he said, casting a glance over to the safe. Good, the door was closed. "I think so."

"Great, that's settled then," said Katie. "Three thousand dollars or fifteen hundred pounds from me and two thousand from Rode. Will we meet here tomorrow morning, say, fifteen minutes before bank opening? Oh, and may we use the Mercedes again? It made us feel like VIP's. It would be nice to drive up to the bank in a car like that. Make us feel like royalty or something."

Demetrius ushered them out saying, "See you tomorrow morning, then. Oh, and don't bother showing up for work tonight. Take the night off."

"Oh, thank you so much," said Rode as she gave him a kiss on the cheek.

As the door closed behind them, Katie said, "Nice touch that; the kiss, I mean."

The steamship Ipsacala lay at anchor in the bustling port of Heraklion, on the north shore of the island of Crete. The island's chief port, it is noted for its Venetian fortifications which date from the 15th and 16th centuries.

Nikki leaned on the rail and watched as the dock hands unloaded the cargo with huge derricks. He watched fascinated. Although born in Athens, as a youngster he had messed about in his father's boats, but he had never seen this side of the shipping industry.

It had only been a few hours since they had left Piraeus but the journey had been slow as they wanted to land here at daybreak.

His thoughts all last night had been for Rode, wondering how she was coping with the new life that she had been thrust into. Was she missing him? It must have been a real blow to arrive on Cyprus only to find that the person you came to see had died. He could not imagine her grief, or what she must have gone through.

The ship gave a loud blast signalling that she was about to leave port. Only about two more days and he would be with her. It would be a long wait. He looked up at the sky as if in prayer and shouted to the wind, "I love you, Rode."

Cicero Andreas was worried, having phoned Vlascis several times and not been able to reach him. Also, Vlascis had not returned his calls.

He dialled the number one more time.

"Hello, who is there and how may I help?" He always smiled at this form of answering the phone. It was as if the person on the other end was scared of the thing. He was probably right in that assumption.

"This is Mr. Andreas from Athens. My friend Mr. Vlascis has not answered my calls. Would it be possible for you to go to his room and see if you can find out anything, for me, please? Give me a call back as soon as possible, my number here is 498 - 1234."

"Yes, certainly Mr. Andreas, sir. I will go and look and telephone you back. Thank you, sir."

"Goodbye."

A few minutes later the phone rang. The ring seemed to be more urgent than usual. It was a strange phenomenon, how phones seemed to register urgency or whatever the message was about to be.

"Hello, Andreas."

"Oh Mr. Andreas. Something dreadful has happened. He is cold on his bed and my wife and I do not know what to do. Will we … ?"

"Calm down man and tell me what is wrong. Who is cold? … "

"Oh sir, your friend Vlascis is on the bed, cold. He appears to be dead."

"Dead! Vlascis? Are you telling me that Vlascis is dead?"

"Yes, sir. Shall I ring for the police?"

Cicero thought for a moment before answering. "No I will send a doctor over to look at my friend. Do not do anything or touch anything until he arrives."

He dialled the number in Cyprus of his former family doctor. He was not home but he left a message about Vlascis.

Going upstairs, his feet dragged in sorrow for his oldest and dearest friend. They had been together for so many years. Never once had Vlascis ever complained about the tasks that Cicero had asked him to do. Right up to the end he had proven his loyalty, for it was to keep an eye out for Nikki that he had gone back to the island.

One question jumped in front of his eyes, repeatedly. How? How had he died? Had the unknown enemies who were out there got to him in retribution for what had happened in the last few months?

Reaching the sitting room, and seeing Kasta there by the unlit fireplace, he went down on his knees and told her what had happened. He then lay his head on her lap and cried.

She looked down at her husband's head and felt his pain and grief. 'This life has got to end. We cannot take anymore,' she thought.

As they were getting ready to retire for the night, the phone downstairs rang. "I'll get it, you stay here," Kasta said and left the room.

"Hello, oh, hello Doctor. No, he has gone to bed." She listened as the doctor told her that Vlascis had apparently lain down on his bed and had suffered a heart attack. There were no signs of a struggle or anything that looked suspicious.

"Thank you, Doctor. I will tell him."

Demetrius, knowing when to expect the girls, called for one of his bodyguards, Petros Hecatus, a man who had been loyal to him for a long time. Demetrius had made sure of that loyalty by giving generous handouts and bonuses whenever a nasty job had to be done.

Demetrius rushed Petros inside and locked the office door behind him. Petros was puzzled by this secretive behaviour so early in the morning. Both of them were men of the night, so eight o'clock in the morning was not his time at all.

"I have a job for you, Petros, my friend," he said quietly. "The two girls, Rode and Katie, you know them right?" Petros nodded doubtfully, as he was not sure.

"Well, I want you to drive them to the bank and get there when it opens. They are going to transact some business which is very important to me. Keep a sharp lookout as I am not sure I trust them."

Going over to the safe, he took out a shoebox full of passports of all different colours and nationalities. Picking through them he extracted two and handed them to Petros. "These are the girls' passports. Hand them over when you get to the bank, just before they enter. Not before, you understand?"

"Yes, boss. Do I bring them back here after the bank?"

"Yes, and come straight to my office here. I will be waiting."

"What about the girls, boss? Do I bring them back as well?"

Demetrius nodded, irritated by Petros' questions. "Yes, of course, you stupid … "

Just then there was a knock on the door. "That will be them. Go and bring the Mercedes around to the back door. I will escort the girls out to you."

Pierre had been to the girls' room and handed over some money for their plane tickets. He had tried to give a proper goodbye to Katie but Rode's presence prevented that. He was left to hold Katie's hand affectionately.

Rode, though, had seen his dilemma and made an excuse to leave the room.

Katie rushed into Pierre's arms and said, "I will contact you somehow, phone or letter, when I get back to London."

Pierre pleaded his love once more, but Katie was determined to leave.

"I do love you, Pierre, but I have to go. You can see that."

"No I cannot, but obviously it's of no use arguing with you. This is goodbye forever, my darling. I know I will never see you again."

"You're a silly old thing for loving me as you do, and I don't deserve the pure love that you offer." So saying, she took him in her arms. Their kiss was long and passionate, and ended by each withdrawing their lips in an act that they both knew was final.

Rode came back in. "All set?" Pierre hugged Rode and whispered in her ear, "Take care of her for me."

With one last glance at Katie, he left.

Sitting in the back of the big Mercedes, they really did feel like VIP's. The driver they did not recognise, nor did they want to. He looked like what he was, a bouncer and bodyguard. His shoulders went down at a forty-five-degree angle from his ears. There did not seem to be any neck area.

The bank was only about four minutes away, and as the big car left the back of the club, Katie leaned over and said softly to Rode, "Hope the boys are there."

"We have to trust them," answered Rode.

Katie leaned forward. "Driver, could you please drive up to the front door." Then she added: "Very slowly. We want to make an impression on the bank officials, so that we may get special attention when we're there."

"Right miss, slow and important it is." He knew how they felt. He, too, liked driving this car for the same reason.

They reached the bank at eight thirty-four, four minutes after opening. As they had guessed, the employees were idly staring out of the large plate glass windows. No customers had yet arrived. The slow arrival of the car had the desired effect. As Petros opened the door for them, chauffeur style, they could see the tellers scurrying back to their places.

"Here are your passports," the driver said as he handed them to the girls who took them gratefully.

"We won't be long," Katie shouted over her shoulder.

They did not go straight to one of the tellers but instead went to one of the tables at the back and pretended to be filling out forms. Petros opened the outside doors and peered in. Seeing the girls busy with papers, he crept slowly into the bank and watched them from just inside the door.

"What do we do?" asked Rode. "We can't run if he is watching us."

"Let's wait and see what happens."

Just then the doors opened and in walked Yukon. Katie nudged Rode and nodded her head towards Yukon.

As Yukon entered he saw the two of them with fear in their eyes. He also saw Petros standing inside the door watching the girls intently. He wondered how he could distract him.

As luck would have it, he noticed that Petros was standing relaxed with one foot crossed over the other and his arms folded across his chest. Better act quickly, thought Yukon. He lurched forward limping as if he had injured his leg, and fell heavily into Petros. Yukon said, "Sorry," ever so quietly as Petros, already slightly off balance, fell like a giant oak tree to the ground, with Yukon on top of him.

"What the hell … ?" Petros shouted as he fell.

Yukon was much taller than Petros. As they struggled on the ground, Yukon made no attempt to free himself from Petros. Instead, he signalled the girls by waving a hand behind his back.

The girls needed no second hint. They did not run, but went swiftly to the passage that led to the side door. Rode paused before leaving the main room and saw Yukon and Petros still fighting and arguing while a couple of female tellers stood close by watching helplessly.

The push-bar door was stiff, but with both of them heaving it opened. The bright hot sunlight was a surprise from the cool air-conditioned and slightly darkened bank interior. A pillar-box red car stood waiting at the kerbside with a back door open.

Petros caught a glimpse of Rode looking back from the rear exit. Realising that they were trying to escape, he put a foot into Yukon's groin. That was it, thought Yukon. Now he was for it. He rushed headlong into Petros but Petros had fought many men before and as Yukon reached him, Petros side-stepped and put a large fist into Yukon's midriff. Yukon dropped like a stone, as Petros went after the girls.

"Girls get in," shouted Frankie.

They needed no telling. They fell through the car door and were immediately covered by large blankets. "Stay put until we say it's safe."

"OK, Andy, let's go," shouted Frankie.

Petros came bursting out of the side door and emerged to see the car about fifty feet away gaining speed. He tried to see the licence plate, but another car obstructed his view. "Damn them," he cursed under his breath and ran back through the bank. His assailant from before was nowhere to be seen. 'No matter,' he thought. 'They won't get far in that car.'

The bank employees were shouting something at him but he ignored their cries and burst through the doors to the front street taking the car keys from his pocket as he did so.

Jumping in, he turned the ignition and the powerful engine sprang into life. Looking up he saw the red car emerging onto the main street about three blocks ahead.

"Got you, you little tarts!"

He checked his rear view mirror and pulled sharply away from the kerb.

HURUMPF! HURUMPF! HURUMPF! Was all he heard. He stopped the car. "What now?" he shouted as he got out and saw that both nearside tyres had been slashed. He saw the flat tyres, but did not see Yukon, hands in pockets, leaving the scene singing, under his breath, one of the dirty songs he was famous for.

Kasta got out of bed leaving Cicero sleeping. He had been restless and awake most of the night, having got out of bed two or three times.

As she dressed, he awoke and watched her. How long had he loved this woman? It seemed for all his life, but was in fact thirty-nine years.

If he looked closely, he would see the bags under her eyes, the spreading middle, and the veins in her legs getting worse. But he never looked closely at her, so all he saw was the young, beautiful, vibrant woman he had fallen in love with and married. Every day he fell in love all over again. Now in this moment of sadness at the death of Vlascis, he knew he would have to rely on her more than ever. She was strong …

"Which flight are you taking today to Cyprus?" she called over her shoulder, noticing that he was awake.

"What? Oh, yes." He sat up in bed and rubbed his eyes. "No, I cannot go today."

"Why not?"

"Today's the day I have a meeting with the men from Los Angeles. They have come over especially. They want another shipment of ivory."

"Oh Cicero, dear, can't you say no to them? Tell them you want to retire. We are getting on, and I would like to spend the last few years together … " she hesitated before continuing, "alive and not in prison."

He got out of bed and putting an arm around her said, "We'll see my love. We'll see." The thoughts that she voiced had passed through his mind lately also. 'But how would I get out, even if I wanted to?'

After showering and dressing he went to his study and phoned the doctor on Cyprus. He informed the doctor that he would fly out tomorrow. Could the good doctor look after things until he arrived?

Vlascis had no known relatives so there would be no need to put an obituary in the papers, either there or in Cyprus.

As he and Kasta sat down to breakfast, the sombre silence that surrounded them was disturbed by the phone again ringing in his study.

"Leave it," she said. "Let it ring. You're whole life revolves around that damned telephone."

He thought about what she had said, but rising said, "No, I don't like to leave phones unanswered. You should know me by now."

He went downstairs slowly, as if he was wishing the phone would stop ringing before he got to his study.

"Mr. Andreas, please? Cicero Andreas."

"This is he speaking."

"Cicero, my old friend, this is Konstantis, from Limassol."

Cicero tried hard to place the name of Konstantis, and what it meant to him.

"My brothers and I were talking about you last night."

At last Cicero placed the name. "Ah, yes, Konstantis. It has been a while. How are you and your family? Well, I hope."

"Yes, indeed, and yours? Oh sorry, Cicero, I apologise. I forgot about your son."

"That's all right. Why are you calling?"

"We think there should be a meeting between us. It is important. Can you come over?"

"If you say so, then yes. I will be in Cyprus tomorrow. I am not yet sure of my schedule but I will call you from there."

"Fine, see you tomorrow."

"Can you see anyone following us?" muttered Katie from under the blanket. "It is stifling under here, let us out, for Pete's sake."

"I think we are safe," said Frankie. "What kind of car was it you came in?"

"A black Mercedes, big thing."

He took the blankets off them and told them to sit up. "I don't see a car like that. We must be O.K. How far to the travel agency?"

"Round the next corner," said Andy. "I picked it especially as the building has an underground garage."

They all trouped into the travel agency and Katie produced the money for the tickets. However, they were informed that the first available seats were not until Friday afternoon. They had no alternative but to book them.

Back in the car Andy said, "What are we going to do with the girls for two and a half days?"

Frankie pondered before replying, "Let's take them to the Leave Centre and they can stay with us. Yukon will make straight for there anyway, then we will arrange something."

"That was very brave of him, back there," said Rode.

"Why, what did he do?"

Rode went on to explain the incident in the bank. They all laughed.

As they left the city and headed south for Limassol, Frankie explained about the Leave Centre. He told them that it was a large block of flats or flats that were used by the UN troops when they were given short leave passes. The three of them were now on a short leave, and that was how they had met in that cafe yesterday.

During the drive to Limassol, Rode told Andy and Frankie of her life in Mexico. Of how she had met and fallen in love with Nikki and why she had come to Cyprus.

Katie told a little of her story, but made no mention of Marty and his wife. She simply said that she had wanted to go somewhere warm and sunny and she saw the 'ad' for the job in the club.

Arriving at the Leave Centre, they all went straight to Frankie's room which he shared with Yukon. It had two beds. Andy had a single room down the hall.

"The girls can have the beds tonight, if that's all right with you?" Frankie said nodding at them. "Yukon and I can sleep on the floor. There are some extra blankets in that closet over there. That will do us."

Rode looked at Katie waiting for her reaction. "I don't mind," she said. "Eh, Katie?"

"Sure thing."

Later, that day Yukon arrived. He had hitched a ride in a truck that was coming to Limassol. He had gone to the travel agency expecting to find them, but he had missed them. He then related the tale of the tyres.

"Where are the girls going to sleep tonight?" asked Yukon.

"We'll bunk down on the floor," said Frankie, "and the girls can have our beds."

Petros reported back to Demetrius.

"Who were they?"

"Don't know, but the guy in the bank, I'm sure he was one of them. Looked like an UN soldier. Tall, straight back, a short haircut and talked like an American."

"Canadian, maybe?"

"Could be."

Demetrius picked up the phone and dialled Pierre's number. He was not there. "Find him and bring him to me."

When Petros had gone, he thought about what had happened.

Such an act they had put on. All to get their passports back. That money he was supposed to receive, now down the drain. What would they do now? Obviously they would fly out to London.

He dialled the operator and asked for the number of the airport at Larnaca.

"Any planes leaving for the UK today?"

"Yes, sir. This afternoon at four o'clock."

"Could I please book a seat on that flight?"

"Sorry sir, but the flights to London are booked solid for the next three days. There has been a large conference here which has just ended."

"Really? Well, thank you so much."

"Aha! They are not going to get away that easily. But how did they arrange this charade?"

Petros returned with Pierre.

"You wanted me?"

"Yes, Pierre. No, Petros, you stay," he called as he was leaving the room. "Where did you take the girls yesterday and did you meet anyone?"

Pierre hesitated just a fraction, but it was noticed by Demetrius. "Oh, I took them to Paphos, then along the coast to Limassol. We were on a beach for a bit, then stayed the night at an inn off the highway, why? What did you mean when you asked if we had met anyone?" Pierre asked but knew what was coming.

"Did you meet any soldiers, either in uniform or in civvies?"

"No, why do you ask?"

"It's nothing. You may go." He realised that if as he suspected Pierre was sweet on Katie then that would be all he would get out of him.

When Pierre had left Demetrius turned to Petros. "Go to the Leave Centre at Limassol. Take someone with you just in case. Find out what you can about the two girls, and the soldiers."

"Why the Leave Centre, boss?"

"If it was Canadians, then that will be where they have taken them. Now go!"

The next morning Demetrius was a very worried man. Petros had not come back from the Leave Centre. It had been a routine enquiry that he had sent him on. Why the delay in getting back to him? Had something happened to Petros? Maybe the Limassol Family had intercepted them. Oh my God, what if Petros or the other fellow talks? The Family will surely come after me.

He went down to the main room as he wanted to speak to the staff to ask if they had seen Petros. While crossing the floor he noticed two strangers talking to the staff. He approached to see if he could help.

"May I assist you in some way?" he asked in his business, butter-wouldn't-melt-in-his-mouth, voice. "I am the Manager of this club."

"We hope so, sir. Would you please look at this photograph and tell us if you recognise the man?"

Demetrius took the photograph and as he gazed at the picture a sweat came over his forehead and he started to breathe heavily. He felt the blood rush from his face and knew that it was going white. He asked to sit down. "Been overworking I think," he blurted out as he sank into a nearby chair.

Pulling himself together with difficulty, he asked, "Why do you want to know?"

"Never mind that. Do you know this man or not?"

"I think so, what is his name?"

"Niklos Andreas. You obviously know him."

"Of course, that's Nikki." He kept trying to restore some calm within his body. "He was the son of the owner of this establishment."

"Where could we find him? You said, 'was' … correct?"

"Yes. Sorry, but I did not catch your names."

"Names don't matter. Go on."

"Well, sirs, Nikki is dead. I am sorry to say that he died about three or four weeks ago … "

"No, he's not," blurted out the second man. "He's alive and we want to find him bad. We think he's here in Cyprus."

Demetrius sank back in the chair and passed out.

Demetrius 'came to' in his office, having been helped there by some staff members, along with the two strangers who had refused to give their names, except to say they were Johnny and Mike.

"Sorry about that little episode in the main room. I cannot ever remember doing that before. As I said, I have been under a lot of pressure lately, and when you told me that our beloved Nikki was alive, well! Are you certain of your facts?"

"Yes. He was seen about three days ago."

"Where?" interrupted Demetrius.

The man called Mike who had been doing the talking, looked at his friend.

The man calling himself Johnny said, "In Piraeus."

"What was he doing?" asked Demetrius.

"That's enough for now," broke in Mike. "No more questions from you, but we have some to ask."

"Go ahead."

"We understand," went on Mike, "that he may arrive on this island any time now. Where would he go when he gets here?"

"Not sure. His family used to have a home here but it is all closed up awaiting a sale." Demetrius did not like these two. He was an expert at smelling trouble and he could smell it from them. But how do I get rid of them? They obviously want to do harm to Nikki, and much as I don't like Cicero, I do like Nikki. He has never done me any harm.

He then had what he thought was a brainwave. 'If Nikki is coming here then he'll make straight for the club. If he does then I could warn him of these two hoodlums.'

He went on: "I'm not really sure where he would go, but one thing I can tell you. Nothing happens on this island that a certain 'party' does not know about. If Nikki does arrive on Cyprus then this 'party' would know immediately. They also know Nikki by sight."

"Who is this so-called 'party'? Where can we find him?"

"In Limassol. The 'party' is the Limassol Family. Here, I will write down their address for you. But be careful, they run most of the illegal goings on here, er hmm … or so I am told. I myself have never had any dealings with that sort of riff-raff. If you go there please do not tell them I sent you. I try to be a respectable citizen running a respectable club."

Johnny and Mike left Demetrius' office, without a word.

'Nice guys,' thought Demetrius, glad that he had a stroke of genius. Telling them about the Family would get rid of them for sure. Might even get rid of some of the Family members too!

Outside Mike said to Johnny, "I don't trust that snake. As we are going to Limassol anyway to see this 'Family' as he called them, let's go to the docks and see if any ships have arrived from Piraeus today. If the ship we saw him on is coming here then it should be here by now, don't you think?"

"Maybe. Let's go." Mike was a man of very few words, but certainly a man on a mission and his face attested to that fact.

Reaching the docks at Limassol they enquired of some sailors where could they find out about ship arrivals. They were directed to the Harbourmaster's office, and informed that the Ipsacala from Piraeus via Heraklion was due tomorrow morning at first tide, which was about 7.42 am.

Petros and his friend Victor drove up to the flat complex known throughout the island as the Leave Centre. He was not very sure how to go about getting information as there was no one about. He decided to wait in the car and question anyone who came out or entered.

As luck would have it, a man walked over to the entrance. Petros leapt from the car and approached him.

Asking if the man knew of any girls inside the building, he was greeted by laughter. “Girls in here, you’ve got to be joking. We don’t do that kind of thing here, you know.” The man entered laughing heartily.

“It’s no use here, they are not going to tell us anything. Let’s try the Yankee club. Lots of soldiers go there for a drink.”

At the Yankee club they asked various people and were greeted in somewhat the same manner as before. They decided to leave when a man who had had too many drinks told them that yes, there were two girls he had seen go into the Centre.

“Were they a Mexican and a girl from Scotland?”

“Don’t know, never heard them speak, but they went in with some guys this morning.”

“Do you know the room number?”

“No, but they went to the second floor.”

“Let’s go, Victor.”

Back at the Leave Centre they went inside and up to the second floor. Knocking on the first door they came to, they were answered by a young man still in his pyjamas. Petros asked the man if he was sheltering two girls as Victor pushed open the door and went inside.

“Hey what’s going on?” the man shouted at which Victor pushed him roughly onto the bed. Petros went round the flat and, satisfied that it was empty, left, with Victor following closely behind.

This scene was repeated several times, and each time the exchange seemed to get a bit more heated. Petros by this time was angry as he thought he might have been set up, back at the Yankee club.

When they were two flats away from his room, Frankie heard the commotion and looked out. Listening to the conversation he heard only the words: “Two girls in here.” He did not hesitate but shut the door fast and locked it.

The girls and Yukon asked what was the matter?

"I think its Demetrius' men looking for Katie and Rode. What are we going to do?"

Yukon took charge. "Girls, get into the bathroom and lie down in the tub as flat as you can. Don't make a sound. We'll try to fend them off and stop them from coming in."

The girls needed no more persuasion but went through to the bathroom and lay down as best they could so as not to be seen. Yukon pulled the shower curtain and said, "Remember, not a word until you hear either mine or Frankie's voice."

Yukon went back into the room and they could hear the thugs next door. They could also hear some voices down the corridor. Some were shouting, "What's going on? Who are these guys?"

Suddenly there was a knock on the door. "You go, Frankie, they don't know you. Try to stem them off. I'll be behind the door."

"No, let's pretend there is no one here. Keep quiet."

Petros and Victor arrived at their door and as before, knocked. This time however there was no answer. A voice shouted, "Perhaps there is no one home."

Victor knocked. No answer. "No one home, Petros, let's go."

"No damn way!" shouted Petros and charged at the door which gave way slightly.

"Hey, what are you doing? You can't do that," said someone outside.

Once more Petros heaved at the door and it gave way, crashing into Yukon who was hiding behind it knocking the air clean out of his body. Frankie stood there and gaped. Then he realised what was happening so he went after Petros. He took a swing at Petros' chin and landed a glancing blow. Petros smiled and hit Frankie right in the gut and Frankie fell to the ground moaning.

"That's it," shouted Yukon coming form behind the door. "I've had enough of you today. You want some more, then here I am." So saying he launched himself at Petros' stomach headfirst and sent Petros flying across the room where he crashed into the far wall. Victor then grabbed Yukon from behind in a bear hug and started to squeeze as hard as he could.

Frankie shouted, "You guys out there, give us a hand!" as once more Frankie tackled Petros. Following Yukon's example, he too flew headfirst into Petros who once again went down. Meanwhile help arrived as three others entered the fray. It took two of them to free Yukon from the grasp of Victor while Frankie and the third guy pummelled Petros as he was trying to rise up against the wall.

When Yukon was free and Victor was being bloodied by severe blows to his face and head from the two helpers, he went over to Petros and, waving Frankie and his pal to one side, waited for Petros to get up. Petros rose with fire in his eyes. "You are the bastard from the bank."

"Yes, I am, asshole, and I'm about to finish what we started there." With that he took careful aim, and lifting his leg he took a hefty kick at Petros' crotch. He hit it square on, his toes meeting soft flesh and sinking in deep. "Bullseye!" he shouted lifting his hands in the air as if his team had scored the winning points. Petros let out a terrible cry and fell to the ground unconscious.

Yukon turned to see how the others were doing with Victor, but he need not have worried. Victor was a sorry sight as he had been kicked around the head while on the ground.

"Let's get them out of here. Frankie, you stay here."

"Right. What are you going to do with them?"

"Don't know yet but I'll think of something."

Yukon and the three other men half carried, half-dragged Petros and Victor downstairs to the Mercedes. While they were bundling them inside the car, two men approached. One of them had a gun pointed at Yukon's stomach as he asked, "These Demetrius' men, by any chance?"

"Yeah, who wants to know?"

"We do, friends. You have done quite a job on them. It will save us some trouble, thank you. We will take over from here." The speaker turned to his friend. "Get the van over here."

"So who the hell are you?" shouted Yukon.

"Let's just say we are no friends of Demetrius, enough?"

The two strangers bundled Petros and Victor into the back of the van and with a screeching of tyres and a cloud of dust the van sped off.

As he looked at the retreating van in shock, Yukon could not know that Petros and friend were in the hands of the mighty Limassol Family, who were about to have some fun.

Half an hour later the Mercedes was driven away.

All of them, the girls and the soldiers, realised that they had to move to another location.

"I know of a nice clean hotel near Penrolia, called The Flamingo," said Andy.

"Penrolia, where's that?" asked Frankie.

"Along the coast toward Larnaca. If you like I'll phone ahead and book two rooms."

"Nothing wrong in that," cut in Yukon. "Count me out, though. I'll stay here and settle up with the leave sergeant about the damages. Give me the number of the hotel. If anything develops at this end, I need to be able to contact you."

"Do you think anything might happen?" asked Rode, giving Yukon a look that said 'even if you think it, do not speak it'.

"No, I don't think so."

During this conversation Andy was phoning. "Thanks, okay, by eleven o'clock, that's fine. Name? Oh the name is Lacroix. Goodbye." He hung up the phone. "That's settled. Two rooms for two nights. Pack up your things, girls, and we'll get out of here."

"Yukon, what do you think will happen to the two men who broke in?" asked Katie.

"Don't know. Perhaps … " He drew a flat hand across his neck. There was an eerie silence in the room.

It was getting dark when the four of them arrived at the Flamingo Hotel.

Cicero's meeting with the Los Angeles group had gone better than he expected.

They had been rather anxious to receive another shipment of ivory, in the same manner as the previous one. It had been a great success and their customer base was growing larger.

Cicero had informed them of his desire to leave the business, citing personal reasons which he did not elaborate upon.

They were sympathetic but resolute in their desire for more ivory.

The meeting broke up amicably with Cicero asking for twenty-four hours, at which time he would have made arrangements for a further shipment. They seemed well satisfied.

He told them that he had urgent business to attend to in Cyprus and if they felt like a short holiday then he would be pleased to offer them a seat on his private plane, while telling them of the beaches and the beautiful hotels along the coast. "Probably not up to Californian standards, but nevertheless very high class resorts."

There were four in the group but as one of them had to return home to Los Angeles urgently, three accompanied Cicero on his private Cessna. Of all the things his wealth had brought him, Cicero was most proud of his plane. It had given him and Kasta countless hours of pleasure as they winged their way around the Mediterranean.

That same morning Cicero and his guests flew out to Cyprus. On arrival a few hours later Cicero saw his guests settled in at one of the large resort hotels that line the beaches near Limassol.

He bade them farewell, saying that he would be in touch sometime tomorrow or the day after.

Leaving them happy, he rented a car and drove fast to Nicosia and went straight to the doctor's surgery.

The doctor confirmed that Vlascis had apparently died of a heart attack while taking a rest or nap on the bed. He had informed the police but there was no reason to suspect foul play.

Cicero asked where the coffin was and was told that it lay at a funeral home not far from the surgery.

"Is it open?"

"No, I am afraid not. It has been too long for it to be, shall we say, decent."

Cicero drove to the Funeral Home and asked to see the coffin. It lay in a room at the back, together with five or six others, all sealed. A simple small plaque on it said 'Vlascis Bagdaddis' and the date of death.

Taking a chair and setting it beside the coffin, Cicero said a silent prayer. When finished the prayer, and with tears running down his cheeks he said in a whisper, "We had a good life together, you and me, dear beloved friend. Sleep well. You have deserved your rest. I hope the Lord above will not treat you too harshly for your deeds. I am sure that by now He has discovered what a nice man you are and how loyal you can be. Kasta sends her love and prayers." So saying he leaned forward and kissed the small brass plaque. "Goodbye, old friend, I don't suppose it will be too long before you and I will be together again."

He went through to the office and, leaving a substantial amount of money, asked the funeral director to attend to the burial. He left instructions that Vlascis was to be buried beside or as near as possible to the plot of Cicero's father and mother.

"The inscription should read 'Here lies a true friend'. A simple plaque in the ground will be sufficient."

Next he drove past the club but decided not to go in. There would be time later to look it over.

He drove back to Limassol, arriving there quite tired after his flight and long car trips.

The large grey European-looking home was out of character with the usual white or pink buildings found on the island. The home of the Limassol family was impressive, enhanced by the large wrought iron gates, which opened noiselessly allowing just sufficient room for his rented car to enter.

The driveway leading up to the mansion was dead straight, which Cicero realised was rare but with similar business dealings to his own he could understand. A circular driveway allowed visitors a chance to be out of sight from the house, however briefly. The straight driveway allowed full view of whoever was arriving.

As his car pulled up at the imposing front, several men materialised from behind bushes, statues and pillars that graced the steps leading up the front door.

Silently they watched him until he disappeared into the home.

Inside, the statutes continued up a wide, burgundy coloured, marble staircase. Cicero smiled at the irony of the situation. He had over the years used such statues in his business as decoys. Whether these were the real thing or not he could not tell.

He was led to a small drawing room done in simple modern furniture in stark contrast to the entrance and staircase.

Konstantis was there with his two brothers, Georgiou and Paulo.

"Welcome Cicero, please take a seat. You know my brothers, of course?"

Cicero nodded and looked around for a seat. The only one available was a moulded iron thing that appeared to have been made from one long iron bar and twisted into the shape of a chair. Metal slats were all that he could sit on. If this was intended to intimidate a guest, then it succeeded.

"How is your family, Cicero? Well, I hope," said Georgiou. Unlike his brother Konstantis, Georgiou was tall, six feet four with a neck like a wrestler.

"Yes, fine, and yours also, I trust."

"Enough of this," said Konstantis abruptly. "Let's get on with the business in hand. As I told you over the phone, there is a matter of some importance we have to discuss."

"I am listening. Go on."

"Our sources tell us that your manager Demetrius, who I may say is no friend of this family, has - according to what we hear - been stealing money from you." He paused letting that sink in. As there was no response or indeed a gesture from Cicero, he continued, "I should also tell you that in one of his not too bright moments, my brother Paulo actually lent Demetrius money. At enormous interest, I may add, but sad to say that, in paying off this loan, it appears that you and the club have suffered badly."

"I know you want me to be surprised but in fact I have suspected all along that Demetrius has been raking money off the top. He is a slimy weasel of a man, and I cannot for the life of me think how I could have employed him. But I did, and now it seems this is how I get repaid. But anyway, why have you told me this story? It surely can be no surprise to you either. Also it cannot be why you asked me to come here today."

"No, Cicero, it is not. Demetrius and his small Nicosia group have for some time now been infringing on our interests in Larnaca and especially in Ayia Napa. It is our intention to build a massive Las Vegas type hotel at Ayia Napa and we do not want Demetrius ... Well you know … In light of these circumstances we wish to put a delicate question to you and would appreciate an honest answer."

"If I can, I will, but what is the question?" asked Cicero, now feeling a little bit threatened. He had told no one of this visit, so nobody knew where he was.

Konstantis and Paulo looked over at Georgiou, who cleared his throat before saying, "We do not like Demetrius and would like to see him eliminated. We wondered if you had any objection, as he is, after all, your employee."

The phone rang and Konstantis, obviously irritated, said, "Paulo, get that. Keep it short or take a message."

Paulo, who seemed the most ordinary-looking of the three brothers, and looked like an accountant, listened intently on the phone for several minutes, his face not registering any expression.

"Who is it and why is it taking so long?" Konstantis hissed at Paulo.

Paulo held up his hand for silence. Konstantis, now thoroughly disgusted, went over and tried to wrestle the phone from Paulo. Paulo turned away saying, "Thanks," then a pause. "No, no orders yet."

"This'd better be good, Paulo. We do have a guest here, and our business is not yet concluded."

"Sorry about that, but that was Theo. It seems that two of Demetrius' men went to the Canadian Leave Centre, burst into the place demanding to know where two girls were. One was a Scottish girl and the other a Mexican called … "

"Rode Benetino," interrupted Cicero.

"Yes, that's right," said Paulo, surprised.

"Why is Demetrius looking for them?" Cicero asked before Paulo could say anything else.

Paulo, now addressing himself to Cicero, said, "It seems that they cheated Demetrius out of some money and they were escaping. They had help from some Canadian soldiers. I'm not sure, but there was also trouble with passports in some way."

Konstantis, having lost control of the situation, tried to regain it by asking, "Do you know this Benetino woman, Cicero?"

"No, but she is, or was, in love with Nikki." He stopped abruptly. Nikki's life was still in danger. The Limassol family might be that danger.

"And Demetrius' men?" asked Georgiou.

They all turned to Paulo whose wide grin was accompanied by a glint in his impish eyes.

"Good, now let's all calm down." Konstantis returned to his seat, followed by Paulo. As they sat down, Cicero stood up. His bottom, he was sure, had the imprints of the metal slats on it. The others watched as he rubbed the tender spot.

Cicero's rear end now sufficiently recovered, he said, "As for Demetrius, I have no love for the man. I have no love for killing either, unless it is deemed absolutely necessary. If you consider it so, then so be it."

Paulo clapped his hands and quietly said, "Good."

Konstantis stood up. "Thank you, Cicero. May we offer you some refreshment before you go?"

"No thank you, but gentlemen, please remain seated. I have a proposition for you."

The three brothers looked anxiously at each other and sat down like obedient schoolchildren.

"I have, for some time now, been thinking of retiring. To this end I have slowly divested myself of most of the various enterprises that I used to control. I only have a few left. It would please me if your group would consider taking one of them off my hands. No strings, no conditions. Call it a gift from me."

As the brothers listened in enraptured silence, Cicero explained the ivory business, telling them that the Los Angeles men were already here on Cyprus. "Would you gentlemen be interested in taking over?"

All three of them began talking at once, but with a glare at the other two, Konstantis spoke up.

"I am sure I speak for my brothers when I say it would be a pleasure to accept, and may I say thank you. It is a very generous offer."

"Not at all." Cicero waved his hand.

There followed hand shaking all around.

"May I use your phone? I will call the LA people and set up an appointment for you to meet them tomorrow."

"Would you like to stay for dinner? A room will be prepared for you. You will stay the night here as our guest?" Cicero nodded. "Good, then welcome to the family, Cicero. If ever you have need of us, we are at your disposal." With that Konstantis put his arm around Cicero's shoulders and led him into the dining room.

As they walked Cicero said, "A funny thought came to me as I walked up your magnificent staircase. Those statues that look old and priceless are identical to the ones we use for transporting the ivory."

After dinner Cicero phoned asking Pierre to meet him at the club tomorrow morning around ten o'clock.

He went to bed that night more bewildered than ever about who was trying to harm Nikki.

"Would the defendant please rise?" ordered the Judge.

The defendant rose together with his lawyer.

"Martin Arthur Charles, having been charged with the wilful murder of Theresa May Charles on the seventeenth day of this month, and having pleaded guilty to this charge, it is the sentence of this court that you be taken from this place and incarcerated for a term of not less than twenty-five years. Parole will not be considered until the expiration of one third of the sentence. Do you wish to address this court?"

Marty hung his head as he slowly and deliberately answered, "No, sir, thank you."

The newspaper reporters at the back of the courtroom rushed outside to the telephones arrayed in the hallway. They hoped to reach the evening editions.

Others sat and punched furiously at their laptop computers as Marty was led away through a door behind the jury seats.

CHAPTER TWENTY-THREE

The sea was smooth and the moonlight cast a long white path across the dark rippling water. As little scudding clouds wisped across the face of the moon, it appeared to be racing fast across the night sky.

The Ipsacala drove through the dark waters, her engines throbbing rhythmically.

Nikki had been listening to that throbbing ever since they had left Piraeus. Not being a sailor, they had throbbed in his brain constantly, the only respite being when the ship had docked at Heraklion.

Not much longer to endure this noise, he thought to himself as he sat on the bunk in his tiny cabin. The Captain had told him that they would dock at Limassol in the morning, but would arrive offshore and wait until the tide was favourable before moving in to dock.

He had tried to sleep, but the excitement of finally getting to Cyprus and of seeing Rode was too much. He sat on his bunk in his vest and shorts, the sweat glistening on his body. Being below decks and close to the engine room, his room was stuffy and hot, with very little air coming through the tiny vent high above the wash hand basin.

The cabin reminded him of the sleeping compartments that he had encountered on his many train travels through Europe.

He lay back on the sweaty sheets and tried to sleep. If he could sleep then the morning would come that much faster, and the rendezvous with Rode would come more quickly.

His heart ached for that meeting. He had rehearsed what he would say over and over in his mind. How he would speak of his love and the heartache that his family had caused them both. He did not blame his father for what had transpired. After all, his father had only been thinking of him. Had his father known of his love for Rode then things might have gone differently.

Each night in bed, ever since he had escaped from that Turkish house in Athens, he had fantasized about being with Rode. He had thought about her smooth skin, her small firm breasts and her lips caressing his. He had dropped off to sleep each night locked in the memory of her embrace.

As he lay on the rumpled sheets picturing the two of them together, he was unaware that the engines had stopped. The silence slowly entered his brain and he sat up in surprise.

"We must be there, off the island," he murmured to himself. Getting off the bed he hurriedly put on his money belt and dressed in jeans and that sailor-like sweater he had purchased in Rafina.

He left the cabin and walked down the passage toward the stairs leading to the upper decks. He made no noise, as he was bare- footed.

After he had climbed a few rungs of the stairway, he heard voices coming down the passageway. Surprised to hear voices at this time he crouched and waited to see who was coming.

As the voices approached, he recognised one of the voices as the captain. The other, he thought, sounded like the cook. He tucked his feet up under him and sat still. Two bodies appeared underneath him, and as he had guessed, they were the cook and the captain.

They were speaking in their native Arabic. During this voyage he had not tried to pick up this language. Most of the conversations between himself and the captain had been in English. As he sat there and watched the two men he heard his name, Andriase, mentioned.

They continued down the passage and stopped outside his cabin. The cook put his ear to the door and listened. He turned to the captain and shook his head.

Nikki crept up a few more steps. If the cook turned around he would be in his line of sight. They knocked on his door, calling out faintly, "Meester Andrase, are you asleep?" Getting no reply, they went into his cabin.

What did they want, wondered Nikki, at this time of night? He stole a glance at his watch as he continued up the stairway. 4.20 am. He was still at a loss to understand when he at last came up on deck.

The coolness of the night air met his hot sticky skin and made his flesh cold and clammy. He regretted putting on his large sweater. He walked over to the guard rail and looked down at the still dark water. Looking up he could see no shore lights. He padded silently through the maze of wires and lines that were strewn over the deck and made his way to the other side of the ship.

The sight that greeted him made him gasp with longing and desire. There, about two miles away he figured, were the lights of Limassol. At least, he hoped it was Limassol. The mountains behind the city stood out stark against the moonlit sky.

He heard the voices of the captain and cook at the head of the stairway. The captain said something to the cook and he heard footsteps on the metal deck drift away to the bow of the ship.

Thinking that both of the men had moved away, he started toward the stairway, then he heard it- the unmistakable sound of a shotgun being primed. It came from behind him on the other side of the deck. Then footsteps started coming round to his side.

He dropped back from the rail into the shadows, and tripped clumsily over a pile of rope. He fell backwards and grunted as he did so. The footsteps stopped.

Why were they after him? It seemed that they were, but why? 'Oh, the money I owe them,' he thought. 'I owe them the remaining two hundred and fifty. But why the gun and the apparent secrecy at this time of the morning? They want it all, that's it! They want to steal my money belt.' He had noticed during the voyage some shifty glances between the crew but had thought nothing of it. Now he understood.

The footsteps started up again and approached his hiding place. If the man came close, he would be spotted. He had to find another hiding place, one that would hide him until daylight. They would surely not confront him with the rest of the crew up and about.

Rising to his feet he padded quietly down the deck, then stopped abruptly. The other man! Where was he? He had gone down to the far end, why? They were coming at him from both sides so that he could not escape! That must be it.

Where to hide? Tarpaulins lay scattered over the deck. He could lie under one of them. Maybe not; they might be moved in the morning so he would be quickly discovered.

He went on down the deck then he spotted an old iron bench seat, like those found in city parks. Grabbing one of the tarpaulins, he squirmed under the bench, pulling the tarpaulin around him. He tried to make it appear that the tarpaulin was randomly lying beneath the seat. The deck was wet and slippery and the tarp smelled of musty salt water. Oh, how he wished he had put something on his feet. He would have to endure this position for about four hours, he figured. Not a pleasant thought.

The footsteps of the gun carrier approached, then stopped a few feet away from his hiding place. Had he been spotted? 'Lord, please do not let them see me. If they find me,' he thought, 'then not only will they take my money but will surely kill me, making some excuse to the other crew members that I have gone ashore early or some other reason.'

As he waited, hoping that he had not been spotted, the gun carrier called in a loud whisper. There was an answering voice from the far end. The man with the gun walked toward the other voice. They met a few yards from Nikki's spot, and were engaged in heated conversation.

As the voices seemed to get louder, as if they were arguing, he recognised the captain as the gun carrier. After some heated exchanges they moved off and left him in silence.

His body ached, as he had not changed his position from the one that he had first gone into. It was not a good choice of position, as one of the legs of the bench was pressing into his back. He knew that if he tried to change position then the tarpaulin might come away from his body and expose him, so he lay there and endured the ever-increasing pain from the chair leg.

After what he thought was twenty minutes, and having heard no sound from the deck, he decided to get up and find a better hiding place. From the movies he had seen, most stowaways made for the lifeboats and hid there. Perhaps that would be his best bet.

He gingerly got up, the pain in his back stopping momentarily. Looking both right and left and seeing no one, he trotted to midships where the lifeboats were hanging. Reaching them he realised that the lifeboat was quite high above his head. He would have to stand on the rail and get up that way. The rail was wet and slimy under his bare feet and it was all he could do to keep from slipping. He reached up. The top edge of the boat was still too far to reach. It would require him to jump up and try to grab the edge of the lifeboat.

As he was gathering strength for the dangerous leap, he heard a shout and looking behind him he saw the captain running down the deck toward him, the shotgun held out in front of him ready for firing. He knew he was spotted. It was then he heard the cook's voice coming at him from the other side and as he turned to look in that direction he lost his footing and fell between the lifeboat and the rail.

Letting out a yell of horror he dropped to the ocean below. Just before he hit the water, he thought that he was going to die. Images from his past and the face of Rode appeared as he hit the water hard. Just before going under he had the presence of mind to take a large breath and close his mouth and eyes.

He sank down and down, so far down that he was frightened that he would hit the bottom. Instinct now took over his brain. *Have to get to the surface, cannot keep going down!* His body was flat so he turned so that he was erect. He placed his hands above his head and slowly the downward motion stopped and he began to rise to the surface. *Cannot open my mouth, have to keep it shut, but how?* He knew that he had not taken much of a breath before going under. Would it be sufficient to get him to the surface? He kept his hands over his head and opened his eyes. The darkness of the water put fear and panic into his head. *Shut your eyes, you fool!* He waited as his lungs tried to hold his breath inside his body. He wanted so desperately to stop the pain and open his mouth.

He could hold out no longer. *If I don't take a breath then . . .* He burst out of the water into the cold night air. He opened his mouth taking large gulps of salt water. Gasping for air and spluttering, with the salt water making him cough he bobbed on the surface. Instinctively he started to swim. After a few strokes he stopped. Treading water, he looked around. He could barely see the lights of Limassol in the distance. Turning, he saw the hull of the ship a few feet away from him. It towered above him, dark and rusty.

I have to move away from the ship. He started to swim, then he saw it! A searchlight was waving across the water in front of him. It came from the deck above. They were looking for him. He went back to the shadow of the hull and waited.

Finally the light went out and he was left once more in darkness. He again started to swim away from the ship. He swam slowly as he knew he would have to conserve strength for the swim ashore. He swam with slow deliberate strokes putting some distance between himself and the ship. He stopped to rest. He had come about two hundred yards, he guessed. As he lay on his back, the thick sweater, now full of water, felt like a lead weight. So did his trousers.

Have to get rid of them. He removed his sweater, then struggled to get his trousers off. He kept going under the water and each time he did he seemed to take a mouthful of salt water. At last he removed his trousers and watched them and the sweater slowly float off. He watched them carefully as they might give him an idea as to the direction of the current.

Making sure that his money belt was secure around his waist, looking up for the shore lights, he set off at a steady pace. The water was cold and he felt it getting colder. He wore only his underpants and vest. It meant that he was not hindered in his swimming but they offered no protection from the coldness of the black sea.

He started off with short strokes to save his energy, but as the minutes went by he knew he was losing control to the current. He lengthened his stroke and kicked out more with his legs. The stronger the stroke, the warmer his body felt.

After every fifty strokes he floated on his back to rest, then getting his bearings again, would set off. After two such intervals, he looked for the lights of Limassol, but to his dismay he could no longer see them. He must have come further with the current than he thought.

Think man, what should I do? He lay on his back gathering his strength, then as best he could he lifted himself out of the water to peer at the shoreline which had not got any closer. The sky by this time was becoming clearer as the rising sun started its long journey across the skies. Either the lights were going out or he was way off course. He had to change his direction.

He fixed a spot on the shoreline that looked like a clump of trees which lay slightly to his left. Shifting his position so this clump was directly in front of him he started off again.

His arms went in and out of the water as if they had been put on automatic pilot. Not long after, he started to feel the weight of tiredness spread across his body and his mind start to play tricks. He was getting delirious but did not know it.

His eyes would stay closed for long moments as the tiredness was taking over his conscious mind. He tried to shake it off. *Have to think about something. I know, the swimming pool back home in the garden outside Athens How far have I come?* He looked at his watch. Through half closed eyes dripping with water, he thought it said five o'clock. *Forty-five minutes I've been in the water. How far is that? Let's see.The pool back home is ten metres long. How many feet is that? Forty feet, no is it thirty? Yes it's thirty.* His eyes shut tight and he stopped swimming. A piece of seaweed attached itself to his legs. The wet clammy feeling roused him from the sleep.

Mustn't fall asleep. Where was I? Oh yes thirty feet. How many strokes did I take to cover the pool? Eight I think. So if I took eight to cover 30 feet then its four feet to every stroke. Once more he fell asleep but this time he started to sink under the water. Spluttering and coughing he stopped swimming and lay on his back to rest.

Two miles from ship to shore. How many feet in a mile? Five thousand something. So at four feet to a stroke then one thousand strokes to cover the distance. His meanderings were cut short as his head came crashing into a large piece of wood. It cut him above the eye and he felt blood pour down his face. *Blood, that's what sharks like, isn't it? Are there sharks in this water? Stop these thoughts.*

He took off his vest clumsily and tied it around his head to stop the blood reaching the sharks. The sudden cold against his chest made him shiver. It was the first shiver. The body seemed to like shivering as it started doing it non-stop. He grasped hold of the piece of wood, which he thought looked like a piece of a window frame, and hung on tightly. *Must keep moving. Must move my legs toward the shore. Where is the shore? Keep moving, can't lie still. So tired, oh so tired. I will have a short rest and try again in a few minutes. No keep my legs moving, must keep ...* He laid his head on the window frame and fell asleep.

His face slid under the water and once more he took a gulp of salt water. Looking around he saw the piece of wood drifting away from him. "No wait," he shouted. "Come back here, I need you." *No use, the wood is too far away to hear.* But he saw it from afar. He looked up at the sky and sure enough the sun was up. He held an arm above his head and felt the warmth penetrate the cold blue skin.

Must start swimming again. Where is that clump of trees? Must swim, must get to shore. I have four thousand strokes to go. One, two, three. He could feel little fish biting and gnawing at his ankles but was unable to do anything about them. *One, two, three must not stop moving ... Stop biting my legs, leave me alone.* He could feel the rough cuts on his skin and was sure they were bleeding. *Have to stop the bleeding. Sharks will get me. Four thousand more swims to get to Athens. Did I leave my towel in the water, or is it over the window frame? Must scratch my leg, the blood is pouring out.*

He bent down to scratch his leg and felt something hot. *Hot blood, I am bleeding, must wake up I am bleeding cannot let the sharks have me. Why are there sharks in my swimming pool?* He awoke and looked down at his leg. It was not moving. It was covered in sand. *Covered in sand? Where am I?*

He lay on the shore, the vest still around his head like a turban. The hot sun was making that and his underpants steam. He rose up on his elbows and saw that he was on a beach. Away to one end of the beach he saw children and adults playing in the water.

I made it! I am alive. Rode, where are you?

I must have slept longer than I thought. The current has washed me ashore.

CHAPTER TWENTY-FOUR

Demetrius' day had been long and distressful, and now at the end of the day he was scared; more scared than he had ever been in his life.

The absence from the club of Katie and Rode had got around, and a few of the other girls, local Cypriots, had handed in their notice, the fight at the club the other night being the main cause of their concern. There were but a handful of Whisky Dollies left, but he still held their passports.

If they tried anything funny, then he would be prepared. No more would he be taken in by a soft voice and pretty smile.

He had sent Petros off to ask about the girls. Petros had apparently taken Victor with him as no one had seen Victor all day.

Where were they? Petros had not only been an employee, but a friend, the only friend that Demetrius had. Now that Petros was gone, he was alone, and afraid.

Then there had been the two men calling themselves Mike and Johnny. He could smell killers a mile off and these two were definitely killers. Why would they want to kill Nikki?

He hoped he had seen the last of those two. The Family would take good care of them, for sure. That had been a masterstroke, sending them there.

All these events preyed on his mind but what had actually scared him had been the news that Stavros had given him.

He had phoned Stavros, in Limassol, a manager at one of Demetrius' legitimate businesses, to discreetly ask around for any news that might be of interest.

Stavros had called back at the supper hour to say that he personally had seen Cicero Andreas drive into the Family's large mansion. He had most certainly been expected as the gates were opened for the car almost immediately.

Demetrius closed down his office, after clearing up some odds and ends, and left for his flat. It was a bachelor flat adjoining the main club but with a separate entrance.

It was late when he finally got to bed and tried to sleep. His body ached with tiredness but his brain would not stop sending him pictures. Pictures of Petros dead at the hands of the Family. Nikki lying dead at the club shot by Mike and Johnny. Cicero and Konstantis standing over Demetrius' cold dead form in the club office.

He tossed and turned. The night was hot and as he slept only in undershorts, his body was clammy with sweat.

Getting up he went into the bathroom and sat in the dark, on the toilet seat. However much he tried he could not get those pictures out of his head. Finishing his pee he opened the mirror cabinet and took out a bottle of sleeping pills. Putting two in his mouth and swallowing them without water, he returned to bed. 'They should help me sleep,' he thought.

Once more he tossed in the crumpled sheets, his brain still hammering out the picture of his own death. He started to cry. He had no Will as he had no one to leave his ill-gotten gains to. All that money stashed in the safe, and if he died who would it go to? No doubt to Cicero.

He had married when he was young, at the age of twenty, but now as he lay in the dark he could not remember her name. It had only lasted a short time as she had left him for another man. From that moment he had developed a 'thing' about women. It was not hatred but more contempt.

With all these thoughts churning over in his mind, he at last fell asleep.

He awoke and lay in the dark listening. Something had disturbed his already disturbed sleep. He looked at the clock by his bed, three fifteen in the morning. He had only been asleep an hour.

Hearing nothing, he turned over and tried to go back to sleep. There it was. A low hum, followed by a light on his bedroom ceiling.

Getting up and going to the window, he looked out to see two cars pulling up at the front entrance to the club. As he looked, the lights on one of the cars were extinguished. He could now see some shadowy figures go to the front door.

Perhaps it was someone calling for a member of the staff working late. He turned away from the window. Then he heard the voices. He looked again and saw a couple of figures go from the front of the club around to the back.

"Mike and Johnny! They have come back for me!" He started to grind his teeth, which he always did when he was frightened. Hurriedly putting on some clothes and remaining barefoot, he grabbed his keys and let himself out of the house. Keeping to the shadows of the building, he made his way around to the front of the club.

Peering around the side wall he saw no one in the cars or at the front door. He crept silently along the wall, stopping every few yards to listen. Arriving at the door he tried the large doorknob. It did not turn. Good, they had not got in that way.

Fishing in his pocket for the keys, he opened the door and let himself into the dark interior. There was a foyer, with a hat-check counter. The wide doors to the main hall were still open. He went in and, standing just a few feet inside, stopped and listened. He heard nothing so ventured further into the main room. All seemed in order.

"My office! If they are not after me, then they will be burglars after my money or the passports. Those damnable passports!"

He rubbed his forehead as he had a headache, trying desperately to stop grinding his teeth. He crept over to the far wall and leaned against it as he was feeling dizzy. Must be tired, only an hour's sleep, no wonder! He opened the door which led to the stairs up to the first floor. He walked up the stairs and kept falling against the wall. "What is wrong with me? What is happening? Must be the sleeping pills that I took."

He wobbled along to his office and listened at the door. All seemed in order. The door was still locked so he opened it with his key and went inside, falling on the floor as he did so. "Boy, I must be more tired than I thought."

Then the pictures started again. No not that! He pressed his hands to his head which by this time was throbbing with pain. The pictures would not go away. "Got to make it to the safe, get my money, and those damned passports!"

Falling on his knees he crawled over to the safe, opened it and with his head splitting and the pictures dancing in his mind, he took out the shoebox that held the passports and also his money, wrapped in elastic bands.

He rose unsteadily to his feet clutching the box. Then he heard it! A shuffling noise above the office. In his haste to get out of the office, he crashed into the open safe door which was metal and several inches thick. His left knee hit the door with a sickening smack. He fell to the floor, with a loud moan, trying to touch his injured knee which was rapidly swelling, yet keeping a firm grip on the box. Then he heard the noises above again, but this time they seemed louder.

"Oh my God! They are coming for me. They are going to kill me!" Then the picture of him lying dead in his office, with Cicero looking down at him, came to the front of his brain. "No! No!" he cried out. "Not here, not Cicero."

"Got to get out, cannot stay here." He looked at his leg as he painstakingly rose to his feet. The swelling was large, the pain unbearable. Just to feel his knee made him want to faint with nausea.

Dragging his leg behind him, he left the office, still clasping the shoebox tightly in his arm.

Reaching the corridor he felt sure that he heard voices muttering on the back staircase. They would be on his floor any moment.

He went the opposite way, back down to the main room. He felt himself passing out with the pain and every now and then some vomit would come into his mouth and he would spit it out.

"Got to keep going, got to hide." Slowly he made his way behind the counter of the bar and slid down on the floor with his left leg straight out behind him. He crawled down to the end of the bar into the dark shadows and lay there as best he could. It was then he heard the voices in the room. In his haste to move his leg further into the dark shadows, the pain mercifully took over his brain and he passed out.

"He must be in the building somewhere. He would not leave his office door open."

"Perhaps he heard or saw us and has run outside."

"I'm going to enjoy seeing the bastard suffer before we . . . "

"Keep your bloody voice down and start looking. There are girls upstairs, remember."

"Perhaps after we dispose of Demetrius we can enjoy ourselves upstairs, eh?"

"Keep your lecherous thoughts out of this."

"No, he isn't here. The bastard must have got away. Not to worry we'll get him again. Let's find the girls, yes?"

As he said that his partner gave him a hefty fist into the shoulder. "Cut that out, imbecile. That's not what we are here for. Let's get out of this place."

Both men were arguing as they left by the front door.

It was still dark when Demetrius regained consciousness. Immediately the pain sent messages to his brain and his body responded by going into convulsions. He let out a horrific cry of anguish at the intense pain his body was inflicting on his mind. He thrust his hands against his mouth to stifle his cries. The tears that now dripped from his eyes were falling on his hands which also started to tremble.

"I'm going to die. I'm dying. Oh, dear God in heaven, help me!"

The image of Cicero standing over his dead body now came through clearly, but now Cicero was joined by Petros and Katie. All were looking down at the dead body and laughing.

"Stop!" he shouted. "Stop it, please!" Once more his hands went to the sides of his head and he squeezed. He was being told by something that the pain would cease if he squeezed it out of his head, and the pictures would go away.

It was all Katie's fault, and Cicero. Demetrius ran this club, not them. It was he who had made it what it was today; large, profitable and popular with the troops. Not Katie, and definitely not Cicero. The club should be his by rights. What has he ever put into this club?

His body stopped shaking, his head cleared somewhat and his hands stopped trembling. He took a deep breath, tried not to think of the pain, and rose to his feet.

The answer now came to him. No one would have the club. It was his and his alone to do what he liked. It was his to, to … dispose of. Yes that was it! His to dispose of, but how?

He fumbled through his pockets for some matches. Finding none he limped around the end of the bar. Taking the weight off his bad leg by leaning heavily on the counter, his eyes went slowly round the room looking for some clue as to how to set a fire.

His ghostlike eyes came back to the bar. "Of course. That will do the trick."

Reaching down behind the bar he groped around and found the box of large wooden matches that were kept there. He then hopped over to the mirrored wall behind the bar and took a full bottle of Ouzo.

With his shoebox under one arm and the bottle and matches in the other hand he hopped and jumped over to the far wall of the room, where the booths were situated.

Laying his shoebox down on a table nearby, he uncorked the bottle and, striking a match, he ignited the bottle of Ouzo. This was a popular drink in the bar. The bartenders usually blew out the flames before they got too high, then served up the drink in glasses.

Slowly the flames started and as he tipped the bottle slightly the flames would get longer. Soon he had a flaming torch in his hand which he held to the long drapes which hung on either side of the booth. They lit immediately and he staggered back slightly against the table and surveyed the burning drape. He was exhilarated. Taking his shoebox he proceeded to the next drape and so on down the length of the room. Soon the noise of the roaring got louder, the sprinklers came on in the ceiling while the fire alarms went off in order as if by command. Laughing, giggling and soaking wet, he then went over to the other side, hopping past the tables in the centre.

He went too near one table, and his foot got caught in the table leg. Turning to see what had happened, the pain, which had temporarily left him, shot up through his body and he let out a fiendish scream and fell to the floor.

As he fell, the flaming torch flew out of his hand and crashed to the floor, spilling its contents. Still clutching his shoebox which had fallen under his body, Demetrius could not help but notice that the wine had spilled out, and like a lit fuse on a bomb, the spillage was on fire and the pool of wine led right to his eyes.

His tortured screams were lost in the roar of the flames.

CHAPTER TWENTY-FIVE

The sun was getting hot as Nikki came out of his deep sleep upon the beach. His head was still wrapped in his vest and, as he removed it, a large bruise on his forehead started throbbing.

He took stock of himself. He was cut and bruised over most of his legs and arms, no doubt from stones while being washed ashore. His underpants were torn and dirty, and they did not hide enough of his anatomy. He rectified this position by tearing his vest so that it could be tied around his waist.

His money belt was still fastened around his middle. On opening it he discovered his money and credit cards still intact.

The sun was relatively high, so he had spent most of the morning hours asleep. The beach area was empty, which surprised him, but as his gaze went further afield he could understand. Behind the beach was a sheer cliff, not of rocks, but open hillside which had apparently been washed away over the centuries.

Unsteadily he made it to his feet and took a few tiny steps. Nothing seemed to be broken, but he was very weak.

Where was he? He looked around, but was unable to make out any landmark that was familiar to him. If, as he thought, the current had carried him eastward, and the position of the sun confirmed that, he would be somewhere east of Limassol.

At least he was on Cyprus and closer to Rode. Oh, how she must have suffered the past weeks. He knew only too well that the last few days could not have been endured by him had it not been for the love he knew he had for Rode. Her love, the love that he remembered, the love that seemed so very distant now, the love that he hoped that she still had for him, made his resolve that much greater.

But she thought he was dead. Was her love strong enough to remember him? He hoped so, and through all the trials he had undergone he had counted on that love.

Every night he had gone to sleep with her name on his lips, praying that one day they would be together. If that happened and if this was that day, then he would surely ask her to marry him so that they would never again be parted.

First things first, though. He had to find a way to leave the beach, but which way? If he was east of Limassol, then how far east? If he went further to the east, then he was in danger of running out of shoreline and meeting the Turkish side of the island. No, he had to go back westward toward the populated areas.

He set off along the beach, his eyes searching the cliff face for a cleft or track up to the top. After ten minutes he saw something. It looked strange and out of place here on the sand. As he came closer, he saw that it was a pile of rocks, definitely man-made, and about four feet high. What purpose did it serve, he wondered? Then he saw the reason. Just a few feet away was the start of a pathway.

It led to a cleft in the cliff face hidden from the beach area. Had it not been for the cairn then he would never have found the path. The cairn had been someone's brainchild, goodness knows how many years ago.

He took off along the path which gently took him up the face of the cliff by many twists and turns until at last, exhausted from the effort, he emerged onto a grassy field. Resting, he saw that the path continued to a patch of trees about a hundred yards away.

The trees were cool and a welcome relief from the bright sun. He rested in the trees, but only for a moment. Following the path through the trees led him to a clearing in which was a castle or fortress-like structure.

He had seen many castles and coastal fortresses on Cyprus, but never one like this. It appeared to be a square, with the side facing him about a hundred feet wide. It looked deserted and probably had been for hundreds of years. Yet the path was not overgrown and looked well used. It took him to a wooden door reinforced by metal straps.

The door stood recessed from the outside wall. On closer examination he found on looking up, a niche or large slit, and in that space he saw several spikes. No doubt this was a form of portcullis or trap for unwanted guests.

In a recess at the side of the door was a long metal rod which hung down from the niche. The bottom end had been turned to look like a walking stick handle while the top end disappeared into a large bucket like contraption. It had a use, but what? Was it used to lower the spikes? He doubted that. The rod was meant for pulling so he pulled on it, but nevertheless he jumped back from the spikes, just in case. Nothing happened.

Maybe I should shake it, he thought. Grasping the handle once more he shook it from side to side, and again jumped back. A loud clanging sound, like the ringing of a cracked bell, came from the bucket.

Here he was in the middle of nowhere, almost naked, ringing an unused bell that had probably lain dormant for who knows how long?

He smiled at the ludicrous position he was in.

He heard a noise above his head. Stepping back from the doorway, he saw a face peering over the wall.

"Hello there!" he shouted in Greek. Still the face peered down at him. "Hello, up there." This time he tried in English. The face disappeared.

"Don't you understand?" he shouted after the face but his shouts came echoing back from the wall.

Picking up a rock from the ground, a good sized one, he banged it hard against the door. "Is anyone there? Please let me in."

There were sounds of locks creaking and wood grinding as the door opened about three inches.

"Yes?" a voice asked in Greek. "What do you want?"

"Oh thank you, thank you. I need clothes and food as you can see. Also a telephone, if you have one, please?"

The door opened further with more weird noises until he was face to face with a person in a monk's habit. He could see no face so he crouched down to look into the dark space where the face should be.

"Excuse me, I am sorry to trouble you, but as you can see I am badly in need of some clothes." He held his hands out to his side as if he was modelling. As he took a step ahead, he slipped on a piece of rock and fell awkwardly against the heavy wooden door, dazing himself as his already sore head hit the door.

In his half-conscious condition he felt himself being carried by several hands, and was aware of the drastic change of temperature from outside to inside the building. The heat of the sun gave way to a cool dank and musty atmosphere with a definite peculiar odour.

He struggled a bit as he became more aware of his situation and the hands let him down gently to the floor in a standing position.

"What is this place?" he enquired, adjusting his eyes to the darkness. There were four men, all dressed alike, and they ushered him down a stone flagged corridor, stopping at a room with a grilled gate like a prison cell. For a moment he thought he was being imprisoned, but one of the group whispered to him, "Rest - clothes will be brought."

"Do you have a phone I could use? I am most anxious to speak to someone. It is very urgent."

They turned and walked away, closing the gate after them.

As soon as they were out of sight, he tried the gate. It opened at the slightest touch.

He did not have to wait too long. He heard a cough and a monk appeared, like an apparition, at the gate, holding out an armful of clothes for Nikki to take.

"Thank you," Nikki said, lowering his head in a deferential manner.

As the monk turned to leave, Nikki put his hand on the monk's sleeve. "Please," he said quietly, almost a whisper. The monk turned back and faced Nikki, removing the cowl from his head and revealing a completely bald pate. He gave Nikki a wide smile and raised his eyebrows in question.

"I have many questions, as you can appreciate."

The monk stood motionless, watching him.

"Where am I, for one? Do you have a telephone? It is extremely urgent that I get in touch with someone, to let them know I am alive and well."

The monk smiled benignly and once more turned to leave.

"No – please - don't go. Do you understand what I am saying?"

The monk nodded and as he did, he came up close to Nikki and whispered. "This is the Monastery of Cilicia. We are about twenty miles east of Limassol. We are an Order that has a code of silence. We cannot speak to each other, but may speak to others not of the Order in whispers only." He bowed, raised his hands in prayer fashion and made to go out.

"What about a phone? May I be allowed to use one?"

As the monk was now halfway down the corridor, he turned and, smiling, nodded his head in agreement. He then disappeared, his brown habit merging with the gloom and shadows at the far end of the stone corridor.

Nikki looked over the clothes that had been brought. A pair of trousers, a plain white T shirt, socks and a pair of open-toed sandals.

He dressed, then lay on the metal cot that one sees in prison movies. It was half of the furniture in the room. The other half was a simple wooden kitchen chair.

Nikki dozed a little, thinking about the predicament now facing him, until he was alerted by a scraping sound. He then saw a plate lying on the floor with bread, cheese and a piece of currant cake. A mug of wine stood at the side.

He leapt to the door, only to see his monk again disappearing in the shadows.

Nikki was very hungry, and ate the food ravenously, drinking down the wine in one gulp.

They were very kind and very shy. They also seemed distant but this was probably because they did not meet many outsiders, at least not his kind - half naked, smelling of salt water and other unmentionables, and a filthy, dirty body.

He was engrossed in these thoughts, when his monk again appeared out of nowhere, ushering Nikki to follow.

Nikki was led down that stone corridor into the darkness. The gloom was intensified as the corridor merged in to a tunnel hewed out of the stone. The tunnel was dark, but thankfully not long.

It emerged into a large dining hall which had wooden tables and benches that could seat about fifty men. The monk did not stop but continued through a door at the far end of the hall which led to a carpeted hallway with the walls covered in ornate panelling.

Stopping outside a door, he beckoned Nikki to enter. He did so and found himself in an office. There was a large desk, with a telephone, several filing cabinets and chairs galore.

He turned to say "Thank you", but the door was closed with no sign of the monk.

Finally he would find out about Rode, but more importantly she would discover that he was alive! He dialled the number of the club, letting it ring several times. There was no answer. "That's strange," he quietly murmured. He hung up and tried again, this time letting it ring many times. Still, no answer.

"I have to get there as soon as possible, but how?"

He left the room and stood in the hallway wondering which way he should go. Should he try to find the monk or should he return to his room? Thinking of their kindness to him, he went back.

Seconds after returning, there he was, his monk at the door, watching him.

"Ah good," said Nikki relieved to see his friend again. "Thank you for the use of the phone. Unfortunately I could not get an answer. It was to a number in Nicosia, the number was a club … " Nikki realised he was rambling on, with the monk probably not the least bit interested. "It is more important than ever that I leave here. Also, I have intruded too much on your generous hospitality. Do you have a car that I could buy? I do have cash on me."

The monk stood looking at Nikki intently, then stepping back, and darting his head from right to left, he fumbled in a pocket and produced a small pad of memo paper and a pencil, like those given out on golf courses.

He began to write, and as he did, another monk slid silently past the doorway. His monk had seen the other one coming so he could not speak.

Nikki took the note and read: 'Can you ride a motor cycle?' His spirits rose. "Yes, I can," he whispered.

The monk held both hands out in front of him, indicating that Nikki was to stay here, then left.

Nikki laughed at this ludicrous situation. Ask a question, he leaves, then returns. Ask another and again he leaves and returns. Nikki smiled as he thought this was probably the busiest day this monk has had for years.

True to form, the monk appeared and waved for Nikki to follow. This time, however, they turned away from the gloom. Through a maze of corridors and countless doors, they finally emerged outside in the hot sun.

There, sitting on the gravel driveway, was the oldest, shabbiest and most forlorn motor bike Nikki had ever seen. His face registered disappointment.

Seeing the expression, the monk sat side-saddle on the bike and kick started the motor, which purred sweetly immediately.

Nikki's eyes lit up and he fumbled in his belt and extracted several notes. The monk shook his head but Nikki said, "No, I insist. If nothing else, use it to further God's work among the poor."

It was accepted and Nikki offered his hand in friendship. They both stood there, gripping hands and looking into each other's eyes. Their eyes mirrored the brief comradeship they had experienced.

Nikki raced off to Nicosia, his heart singing. He shouted to the wind. "Rode! Here I come!"

Mike had waited for this moment for a while. He wanted Nikki Andreas dead, but he did not want to do the deed himself, which is why Johnny was here.

Johnny was a hired killer who thought nothing of taking a life. Life to him was meaningless. His own life had been that way, so every life had to be also. Strange logic, thought Mike, but it was a strange world.

Here was Johnny, who had those weird mind games with no conscience, but an extremely wealthy man. Hiring himself as a killer was very lucrative. It was indeed a topsy turvy world!

Sitting in their hired car waiting for the Ipsacala to dock, they watched as the dirty black vessel with orange trim came alongside the wharf.

"Ships fascinate me," Mike said, poking Johnny in the ribs with an elbow. "Especially when they dock. It always seems that the ship is too large for the space it's going into, but somehow it always makes it."

"Hmm," grunted Johnny, not happy about the nudge in the ribs.

They both watched the delicate manoeuvre, until the Ipsacala was moored.

"Let's go," said Mike getting out of the car, "before anyone gets off."

They approached the large vessel and Johnny shouted the age-old greeting, "Ahoy there, anyone home?" The stupidity of his call of home made him turn to Mike and hunch his shoulders.

A voice, with a heavy accent, shouted down, "What do you want?"

"To speak to the captain, please."

"Come aboard, please. Enter there," he pointed, "at the stern."

Once aboard they were greeted with a few members of the crew who stood around and stared at them. Then a man with a hat fit for a captain, pushed his way through, roughly scattering the men unceremoniously.

"What ees the matter eer?"

Johnny asked rudely, "You the captain of this piece of junk?"

"Of the Ipsacala? Yes I am." The captain felt the hair on his neck tingle. They did not look like very good men. He was a little scared.

Johnny was about to say something else when Mike stood in front of him and said, "Don't mind my friend. We are looking for Niklos Andreas, who we understand is a passenger aboard this ship."

"No passenger with theese name on my sheep." As he said that, one of the crew members nudged the captain who turned and let the man whisper into his ear. "Oh yes, maybe, that ees right. We did have a Mr Andrease as a passenger, but he no eer now. He went." With that he moved both his hands in a sweeping motion toward the water.

Mike looked at Johnny, not quite comprehending. "You mean overboard into the sea?"

"Yes, that ees correct, he goes over in the night. He now dead perhaps?"

"What did he look like?" asked Johnny. "Was he a Greek? Tall black hair, young?"

The crew members all nodded vigorously.

Johnny took Mike aside. "Something fishy going on here, Mike. I don't like it. I think they're lying. Ask to see the cabin he had."

"Why should they lie to us?" Then, turning to the seamen. "May we see his cabin or where he spent his time on board? Did he have a cabin?"

"Yes he did, follow me, please. But ees true he fell overboard last night. We searched with big lamp but no could find. I show you." He called to a man at the back, and spoke in a curious language, with much pointing and waving of arms. "Follow him, please."

When Mike and Johnny had gone below the captain spoke to his cook. "I do not like this, should we . . .you know?"

The cook nodded. "They know he was here. Knowing that makes them dangerous. What if he is alive? He will tell the authorities. I will make the arrangements." He left the captain with a worried look on his face, and fear in his belly.

Mike and Johnny had looked at Nikki's cabin, saw nothing that could prove it was Nikki who had stayed there and started up the succession of ladders back to the main deck.

Reaching the deck, two men with knives jumped them, and a fierce struggle ensued. First Mike got cut on his shoulder and before he fell he lashed out with a foot and caught something soft. The man he hit moaned a little but came after him again with a knife which looked like a kitchen carver. Johnny had taken out his gun and shot his assailant in the leg. The man fell across the deck and was about to fall overboard when he grabbed the rail and dangled above the water his eyes staring in utter terror. Mike had gone behind Johnny's back as he was unarmed, when the captain and rest of the crew came running.

"Let's get out of here Johnny, before something ugly happens. We don't want any killing here."

"Right, boss."

They walked slowly toward the metal steps which led to the dock, followed by the crew looking menacing, but unable to attack for fear of the gun. Mike started down the steps but Johnny remained at the top until Mike was safely down. He then turned and pointing his gun at the ground, fired a warning shot, scaring the crew into retreating. Unfortunately, he hit the captain in the foot who screamed and hopped around. The crew went to his aid allowing Johnny to scamper down the steps and join Mike. They then ran to the car.

"What did you do back there? I heard an almighty yell."

"I shot the captain in the foot. Let's get the hell out of here. Where to, Mike?"

"Back to the club. We have to talk with that weasel Demetrius."

"Not long now Rode," Katie said in an excited voice as she emerged from the tiny bathroom in the hotel. "A few more hours and we'll be on our way to London. Do you know anyone there at all?"

"No, nobody. I do not wish to sound rude, Katie but the sooner I am home in Mexico the better. You have my address, so as soon as you are settled, write and let me know. I do not wish to lose contact with you, ever."

"Wow, Rode! That's the most you have ever said since we met. I can't wait to see you in your own environment."

Rode turned away blushing, pretending to be fussing with her meagre belongings.

There was a knock on the door. "Come in," Rode said moving toward the door, pleased that the moment had passed. She opened it to find Frankie and Andy.

"You girls ready? We have to be at the airport an hour ahead, remember. They say two hours but … "

"Yes, all done," piped up Katie. "We have packed our three things each. A brown carrier bag would have done just as well as these," she said, pointing to a small suitcase and a holdall.

They all left the Flamingo Hotel in a light-hearted mood. That mood had been brought about by the previous day. They had spent it on the beaches around Cape Kiti and exploring the lighthouse and generally beachcombing and having a lazy day. After the turmoil of the past couple of days it was time well spent.

Katie was not as anxious as she thought she would be at the prospect of returning to the UK. Pierre had called and told her about Marty. The British papers had reached the club, and he had heard the soldiers talking about the case. She wished that she had Rode's enthusiasm for the flight home.

They drove leisurely into Larnaca with lots of time to spare for the flight to London. Andy suggested a coffee in the small cafeteria at the end of the concourse.

The boys were a bit sad at the departure of the girls. It had been a very exciting three-day leave. One that they would remember always.

All four of them were quiet with their own thoughts as they killed time drinking coffee. Now and again one of them would start off some small talk, but it would fizzle out quickly. There did not seem to be anything to be said.

A TV set in a corner was on and there was a small crowd huddled around it. There were gasps of excitement, but as it was all in Greek, they paid little attention. In one of their frequent silences the name Pierre Gauthier sounded from the TV set.

"What was that?" snapped Katie, getting up from the table. "Did I hear Pierre's name spoken on the TV?"

"I'm not sure," said Andy. "I wasn't really listening."

Katie did not hear him as she was halfway across the room making for the small knot of people huddled around the TV set. She brushed aside a couple of teenagers who were standing hugging and kissing, to get nearer.

"What's got into her?" Rode stood up and moved away from the table. She made her way across the room and heard Katie moan. "Oh my God, it's Pierre!"

Rode ran the last few steps. "Katie, what's the matter? What about Pierre?" It was then that Rode saw the screen. The Club Britannia was on fire, and had been for several hours, according to the reporter. The fire was dwindling at this moment and was in the background of the picture. The reporter was talking to one of the fire chiefs.

"What is he saying Katie, can you understand?"

"No, but I heard him say Pierre's name, several times."

"Have you seen Pierre at all, has he been on the screen?"

"Not yet. Oh, I wish I could understand what is being said."

A small woman carrying a baby in her arms, turned to the girls and said in a soft spoken voice. "There has been a fire in Nicosia, early this morning. It is a night club, called The Britannia. The police have found some bodies. They think they belong to two men and three girls. One of the men has been identified as the manager, but they do not know who the others are at this time."

"Thank you so much," Rode replied. "How did the fire start, do they … ?" Her question was cut short when she heard Katie start to cry.

"They mentioned Pierre's name. I heard it," Katie stuttered between sobs. "He was probably the other man they found. Oh Pierre, my love. Why did I leave you?"

Rode put an arm around Katie and tried to comfort her, but Katie brushed it aside and strode purposefully back to the table.

"I hope your friend will be all right," said the small woman with genuine concern on her face.

"I hope so," answered Rode laying her hand on the baby. "Thank you again."

"Can you boys drive me to Nicosia?" spat out Katie. " I have to get back and see if Pierre has indeed been ... "

"Certainly, Katie no trouble." Andy said rising to comfort her. We don't have to go back until this evening."

"Katie, what about our flight?" asked Rode. But the question was lost as Katie was already walking toward the door into the concourse, with Andy following her.

Frankie looked at Rode with sympathy, then, shrugging his shoulders, followed them out.

Rode wondered what to do. She had to make her mind up soon or they would leave her behind. She had to go with Katie, she thought. Katie was now the one in need. She had received comfort from Katie. It was her turn to give it back. Picking up her small suitcase and Katie's holdall, she ran after the others.

She caught up with them in the car park and they hurriedly bundled into the car and sped off towards Nicosia.

Cicero had slept in rather late. The anxiety of the past few days had finally taken its toll. The death of Vlascis, the pursuit of Nikki and the disposal of the final cog in his business empire to the Limassol Family - that exchange had been achieved more amicably and peacefully than he had expected.

There was a knock on his bedroom door and a servant of the Family poked his head around the door. "Sorry, sir, but Mr. Konstantis sends his compliments. He hoped you had a good night's sleep and would you please turn on the TV set over by the fireplace. Turn to channel six. It is most urgent." With that he left closing the door gently.

"Strange behaviour," muttered Cicero, getting out of bed and crossing the floor to the TV. It stood beside a large open-hearth fireplace with two or three sofas around, for viewing, no doubt. The room was comfortably appointed; the only thing out of place was the four-poster bed that he had slept on. It seemed to be a hundred years out of date with the other modern pieces of furniture.

He turned to channel six on the set. A reporter was telling of a fire that had taken place last night. The street behind the reporter's back looked a little familiar. He turned up the volume.

"To bring new viewers up to date. The fire is almost extinguished but there is still no trace of the owner." The reporter looked at his

notes: *"A Mr. Andreas who lives in Athens. The body that has been identified is that of Demetrius Thermopoulos the manager. The other bodies, one man and two women, are believed to be staff members who slept on the top floor of the club."*

Cicero fell back onto one of the sofas, in a state of shock. He shook his head, trying to clear his mind.

He rose and went hurriedly to where his clothes had been neatly arranged at the foot of the bed. Dressing in haste and without a thought of washing or shaving he left the room and hurried downstairs.

Hearing voices coming from an open door at the end of the hallway, he knocked. A voice inside called out to enter.

"Ah, Cicero, you got my message? What a distressing state of affairs. I don't know how much you heard … "

"Not much. As soon as I heard it was the club, I came down."

Konstantis went over to a bell-pull to summon a servant. "Please, sit down and have a coffee. You cannot go out without some coffee, first."

A servant entered. "Will you bring the Fiat around? Mr Andreas will be using it shortly. Thank you."

Cicero really did not want the coffee but as his host was being more than kind, he took the cup offered.

"How did it start? The fire, I mean."

"No one is telling yet, their investigations seemingly are still ongoing. Don't you like the terminology they use at times like this? Now drink up, I know you are anxious to get going. Besides, the authorities are looking for you. Probably want to see if you can identify any of the bodies. Are you all right to drive? If not, I can send a driver with you."

"No I will be fine. But I must go now!" With that he rose and made his way out. Konstantis followed and putting an arm around Cicero, quietly said, "I'm sorry about the fire."

Cicero drove the Fiat to Nicosia wondering what had happened, and would he be able to identify the bodies. It was then he realised that he had arranged to meet Pierre this morning so that they could go to the club together. Too late now, he would have to catch up with Pierre later. Or would he? Was Pierre the unidentified male in the ruins of the club?

CHAPTER TWENTY-SIX

As Cicero approached Nicosia, he could see the pall of smoke that hovered like a ghastly apparition over the site of the club.

Turning the corner that led to the building, the sight that confronted him made him brake sharply to a halt.

Where the club had been was now a pile of rubble. Cement blocks encased in mounds of white and black ash were piled like pieces of toy lego, mingled with the charred remains of tables, chairs and beds. From this mountain of destruction sparks still flew into the air, while wisps of smoke emanated from lingering smouldering embers. Above, the pall of smoke hung over the whole area, blotting out the morning sunshine.

In the parking lot, ambulances, fire trucks and police cars were packing up and leaving the scene. Pools of water lay everywhere, covered in endless lengths of hosepipe that were being folded and put away. The whole place had that aura of death.

Cicero parked his car facing the ruined building, as the memories came flooding back.

He had bought the club from a man who, when the deal was completed, had committed a horrible suicide by hanging himself with a scarf in the office that Demetrius had used.

At the time Kasta had warned Cicero: "No good will come from that purchase. Mark my words." She, like most women, had that uncanny 'feel' of something pending. Usually something bad.

He, of course, had scoffed at her doom and gloom prediction. Over the years, however, she had been proved right. His association with the club had not been a happy one. He had made money from the club, lots of it. He was aware, however, of the unhappiness within the club and over the years had tried to distance himself.

Now it lay in ruins, a fitting end to its troubled past. Even in its own death, the club had caused more death.

"Mr Andreas."

He came out of his black thoughts, aware that Pierre was standing watching him through the car window.

"Are you all right, sir?"

"What? Oh yes, Pierre, yes, I am. I'm so glad to see you're alright!"

Pierre smiled and motioned with his hand for Cicero to open the door.

"Oh yes, right." Cicero realised that Pierre could not hear him. He opened the door. "Sorry, Pierre. I am so glad to see you. When I saw the TV this morning and heard that bodies … "

"No, I'm fine. I slept at home, fortunately, but there were four others. Demetrius is dead, together with two girls who lived upstairs and an unknown man. He must have been with one of the girls." At this he gave Cicero a knowing smile.

"I see, but tell me. What started the fire?"

"Let's walk over there." Pierre took Cicero's arm and propelled him toward a couple of gentlemen. "These men wish to speak with you. One is a police officer. The other is a fire inspector."

They walked in silence over to the remains of what had been, until last night, one of the more fashionable clubs in the eastern Mediterranean.

"Officer - please - a minute," Pierre called to the two men who were sifting about in the ashes with sticks.

The men looked up and slowly approached Cicero and Pierre. They wore long rubber boots, like fishermen's waders.

"I'd like to introduce Mr Andreas, the owner of the club."

Both officers shook hands with Cicero. When the pleasantries had been exchanged, the policeman put on his 'Funeral Face' as he called it. He wrongly assumed that Cicero would be most upset at the damage the fire had caused.

"I am sorry, sir, to meet you under these sad circumstances. I am sure … "

"How did the fire start? Do you know yet?" interrupted Cicero, who thought that this was no time for small talk.

The policeman nodded to the fire inspector who coughed awkwardly before replying, "It seems to have been deliberately set, Mr Andreas. Your manager a Mr … er … Demetrius Thermopoulos … Is that correct?"

Cicero nodded. "Yes, he was my manager."

"Well, sir, it would appear that it was he who set the building on fire. A liquor bottle was found close to his body. It had contained Ouzo, which I am sure you are aware is a highly flammable liquid. Also, the remains of a box of matches was also discovered, more or less intact, under his charred body."

"Any ideas or clues as to why?" asked Cicero.

The police officer again took over. "Possibly. We were hoping that you could throw some light on that matter, sir. Did he have a grudge against you or anyone else?"

"Not that I am aware of. Pierre, what do you know?"

Pierre had been dreading this moment. How much should he disclose at this time? "Not much I'm afraid, Mr. Andreas." However, as he said it, his eyes were darting among the three men apprehensively.

Cicero noticed the look and turned to the policeman, saying, "I do not wish to speak ill of the dead, but I must tell you that Demetrius was not one of my trusted employees. He was a good manager, but I had doubts about some of his dealings."

"What dealings?"

"I never asked."

"Thank you, gentlemen. That simply confirms our suspicions. You see … " He paused as a red sedan drew up a little way off with two men in it. "You see," he continued, "he was clutching a large sum of money in his hands when he died. It is our belief that he intended to start the fire and then escape with the money."

As he and the Fire Inspector turned to leave, he asked, "What do you know about passports?"

"Why do you ask?" Cicero asked, puzzled.

"Oh, it may be nothing. It can wait. By the way, do you either of you recognise that red car over there?" He pointed to the car in which sat Mike and Johnny.

"No," said Cicero.

"Never seen it before, but judging by the plates it's a rental," said Pierre.

The two officers turned and went back into the rubble and once more started prodding with their sticks.

"Thank you, Mr. Andreas," said Pierre. "I was not sure what to tell them. You see, it had been suspected for some time that Demetrius was stealing from you. Cooking the books, so to speak."

"Yes, I had heard that. In fact I believe it to be true. I am sure he had put away a substantial sum."

"Oh my God!" said Johnny. "To think that only yesterday we were speaking to that creep Demetrius. I wonder what happened to him?"

"Shut up and let's get out of here, but slowly as if we were not supposed to be here. These four men are looking our way, no doubt wondering what we are up to. There is a police car, so one of them must belong to that."

Johnny started the car and they moved off at a leisurely pace.

"The fire truck is leaving," said Mike. "Keep it between us and those men until we are safely out of sight."

"That car is moving off," said Pierre, tapping Cicero on the shoulder. "Probably just busybodies."

Cicero glanced briefly over his shoulder, then moved closer to the remains of the fire. Inwardly he felt quite elated. He had wanted to rid himself of the club for some time now, but, knowing Demetrius could not afford to buy, he had wondered what to do. Still, it was sad to see the club in this state and he felt really sorry for the people who had died. He made a promise to himself to find out their names and to write letters of condolence to their families.

Inside the car Mike laid a hand on Johnny's arm. "That's fine. We're out of sight, let the fire truck get ahead of us. We are in no hurry. We should try to find a place close by to stay tonight, and make further enquiries about Niklos tomorrow."

"Do you think he's alive, then?"

"Not sure, but if he is, he will try to reach the club. If not, then his body will wash up on shore, somewhere."

Johnny was listening so intently to Mike he was unaware of the motor cyclist bearing down on them.

"Watch out!" shouted Mike.

Johnny swerved the car, narrowly missing the cyclist who turned and waved his arm angrily at them, while shouting curses.

"Stop the car, quick!" shouted Mike as he swivelled around to look out the back of the car. "Johnny, do you hear me? Stop the bloody car!"

Johnny did not like to be shouted at, but nevertheless did as he was told.

Mike fished in his inside jacket pocket, and extracted the worn photograph that he had been carrying for several weeks. "That's him! That's Niklos Andreas."

"Who's him?" asked Johnny, puzzled by Mike's behaviour.

"That cyclist we almost hit. I'm sure of it. Turn the car around quickly. Follow him, he's headed for the club."

Johnny executed a neat U-turn and sped after the cyclist who was by now out of sight. "How could you tell it was him?" he asked, his heart pounding at the thought of not only the chase but of what was to come. He was like a bloodhound with the scent of blood in his nostrils.

"When he turned to shout at us, I got a good look at his face. It all fits. He must have stolen a bike when he came ashore. He would have no money to rent a car. Who else would be travelling at high speed towards the club?"

"Please hurry, Andy." Katie was sitting on the edge of her seat behind his shoulder.

"Sorry, girl, but I daren't go too much faster. All these fire trucks and police cars that are coming at us are a bit unnerving. We don't want to get picked up for speeding, do we?"

"No, I suppose not. At least we're not far away. Just two more streets and we'll be there."

"Don't worry, Katie. I am sure Pierre will be all right." Rode tried to sound convincing, but was aware that she was making a hash of it.

"Slow down, Andy," said Katie anxiously. "It's around this corner."

"You want me to slow down now? A minute ago you were all for breaking the speed limit." He then realised what she meant. The thought of what she might see, either real or imagined, was getting to her. He obeyed and went around the last corner slowly and cautiously.

Nikki squealed around the bend, expecting to see the club as he had remembered it. Instead the sight that confronted him almost made him fall off his bike. Where once had stood a beautiful building, one of the landmarks of Nicosia, there was now a pile of smoking rubble. It took him only a few seconds to take in the scene, then he saw his father with Pierre.

"Father – Father - Pierre!" he shouted as he leapt from the bike and ran to where they stood.

"Nikki, my boy." Cicero ran to embrace his son with tears streaming down his face. The two men fell into each other's arms kissing and embracing. A long fervent embrace full of pent up emotion that only a father and son can experience.

Pierre stood mesmerised, his limbs becoming heavy, seemingly rooted to the spot. His stomach felt as if it was coming up into his throat. He mouthed the words, "Can it be true?"

He watched father and son embrace, Cicero with his back to him and Nikki facing him. He walked to them, staring, his legs so wobbly that he stumbled crazily, like a man drunk with alcohol.

"Can it be true?" he cried out excitedly.

Nikki released his hold on Cicero and held his arms out in greeting. Pierre hugged Nikki still stammering, “Can it be true? Is it really you? We were told you were dead.” He looked at Cicero who still had tears in his eyes. “Did you know?”

Cicero nodded and he and Nikki put their arms around Pierre’s shoulders. The three of them stood lost in that embrace, each with loving thoughts for each other.

The touching moment was broken as the red sedan suddenly came in to view.

“Isn’t that the car that was here earlier?” said Cicero, letting go of Pierre and Nikki. “It has come back, and in a rush too. What are they up to, I wonder?”

As the sedan pulled up and parked, a second car appeared. It had several people inside.

“How come we were told you had died in Mexico?” asked Pierre, still holding tightly to Nikki, afraid to let go for fear that he might disappear again.

“It’s a long story. What are these cars doing here? Come to gloat on our misfortune, no doubt.”

The first car had taken up a position about two hundred feet away and was just sitting there. No one had got out. It was eerie the way the car sat facing them, the occupants doing nothing.

The second car drove up to where the three men were standing. Before it had come to a stop, a back door was flung open and there was a shout.

“Pierre! Pierre! Are you all right?” Katie jumped from the car and raced the few feet to Pierre’s side and fell into his arms, laughing and crying with joy.

“Yes, I am fine, Katie, but what are you doing here? You’re supposed to be on your way to London.”

Rode, visibly trembling, emerged from the car her face ashen. She stared across at Nikki. “Is that him? Is it really Nikki I see standing there?”

“Rode,” whispered Nikki as he slowly made his way to the car. Could it be? Was it her? Realisation dawned on him and he cried out, “Rode - it **is** you!”

Rode took one or two steps towards him, but before they could grasp each other, she fainted. Nikki caught her before she fell to the ground. Laying her gently down he tried to revive her by calling her name and slapping her cheeks gently.

As Katie and Pierre reached Rode and Nikki, there was a loud crack, like a gunshot, and Katie fell in a heap.

Pierre turned to look in the direction of the sound, and did not immediately notice that Katie had been shot. "Why is someone shooting at us?" he asked of no one in particular.

"Katie's been shot," shouted Andy getting out of the car and rushing over, followed by Frankie.

Pierre turned. "Katie, Katie, my love you're hurt," spluttered Pierre. It was then he saw the pool of blood coming from underneath her crumpled body.

"Frankie, give me a hand here," shouted Andy, gently pushing Pierre aside while turning Katie's body ever so carefully, to see the damage.

Nikki turned from the unconscious Rode and got up to help the others with Katie. As he did, another bullet whistled past his ear, narrowly missing Cicero, and went boring through the burnt-out rubble raising clouds of ash as it went.

Cicero threw himself to the ground in a reflex action and landed next to the still body of Katie.

Meanwhile, the two inspectors had come running, the policeman holding a gun ahead of him, at the ready. He fired at the sedan but missed. The red car started up, backed up fiercely and turning sharply, sped out of the parking lot.

Cicero, on the ground beside Katie, saw his clothes soaking up some of her blood. "Someone get an ambulance, for God's sake."

The fire inspector ran to his car and radioed for help. The policeman jumped in his car and set off after the sedan.

Nikki said breathlessly, "That must be them, father. They killed this woman, instead of me. Take care of Rode, she has only fainted. I am going after them." Turning while running he shouted, "I'll get the bastards for you I promise, Pierre." He hopped on his bike and sped away.

"That must be who?" asked Pierre, but his words were drowned in the noise of the motor cycle and cars leaving.

The red sedan, from where the shots had come, had a good head start on Nikki. The police car, however, was not far behind the sedan.

Even although the bike was old, it still had good power and by cutting corners quite recklessly he was able to make up the ground between himself and the police car until he eventually passed it.

As the bike beneath him responded to his request for more power, and the air whistled through his hair, he felt exhilarated. This exhilaration brought back the thrill of seeing Rode. She was more beautiful than he had remembered her. All those weeks apart had dimmed his memory of her face.

He caught a glimpse of the red sedan about three hundred yards ahead. Where were they going? Judging by the haphazard way they drove, they themselves did not seem to know. Their indecision at various road junctions gave Nikki a chance to catch up.

They had left the rather quiet area around the club and were headed for the centre of Nicosia, and the mid morning traffic.

Who was that other woman, the one that got shot? Pierre seemed most upset. Nikki felt a little guilty about running off and leaving them, like he did. Was his father all right too? The blare of the police siren behind him was muddling his thoughts.

The traffic was definitely much heavier now and the pedestrians were leaping out of his way, no doubt thinking that the police car was chasing him.

Ahead of him he saw the red car swerve as a bus pulled away from the kerb. They had only seen the bus at the last second. The bus came to an abrupt halt as the sedan manoeuvred around it. When Nikki came up to the bus, he decided not to go around but to overtake on the inside to save a little time. An elderly man decided at that moment to leave the sidewalk and try to get on the bus. Nikki shouted at the top of his voice but the man did not hear him. However, the man must have heard the siren and looked up. He saw Nikki bearing down on him, and, like a rabbit caught in a headlight, froze not knowing which way to run. Nikki hoped that he would run back towards the kerb and so he drove the bike through the gap between the man and the bus. Too late. The man thought Nikki was going behind him, so stepped forward towards the bus. Nikki caught a glimpse of a heavy bearded and pockmarked face, almost white with terror, as he swept past, missing the man by inches.

With the traffic now much heavier, the car ahead slowed down and Nikki, shaking with fear, was relieved. He had almost killed an innocent pedestrian in his frenzy to get at the men who were trying to kill him.

He was definitely gaining on them. His bike was much more manoeuvrable around the corners. It was then that he saw the rear window of the sedan being smashed, with glass flying in all directions. An arm was extended out towards Nikki. "My God! They are going to shoot me! Shoot me here in the streets!"

Nikki began to swerve the bike, as cars do around pylons on a test site. The police car, meanwhile, was gaining on both him and the sedan, as the traffic parted before it.

"Go down a side street, Johnny," Mike shouted from the back seat.

"Let me do the shooting Mike, you drive."

"In God's name, how?" ranted Mike.

"Lean over and grab the steering wheel. I'll slide under your arms and climb over to the back."

"You're mad, Johnny, I can't do that."

"Yes, you can. I'll slow down enough to help you, and I'll keep the car straight."

"But they'll catch up to us. At least, the Andreas chap will."

"Isn't that what we want?"

Mike leaned over and put one hand on the wheel, as Johnny slid down to allow him to get his other hand there also.

"Can't do it, Johnny. I'll crash the car at this speed. I know I will."

"All right then," said Johnny, sliding back behind the wheel. "But if you want him dead, make your bullets count. Leave one for the cop as we don't want witnesses."

"Kill a cop?" shouted Mike frantically. "No way."

"Do as I say Mike, it's the only way we are going to get out of this alive. You have got to kill them both and be quick about it."

By this time the chase had reached the outskirts of Nicosia, the traffic was much quieter and there were no people around.

Mike went back to the rear window and pointed the gun at Nikki. "He's swerving too much for me to get a shot."

Johnny, in the front was frustrated. This was what he loved to do. Just him, his weapon, and the enemy in a battle of wits. The ending was always the same, Johnny killing his enemy. Johnny enjoying the feeling.

As Mike was waving his arm back and forward he heard Johnny mutter, "Jesus, another police car."

Mike turned his head to the front and sure enough there was a police car bearing down on them. "Get off this road quick, Johnny! Make a turn. Here, turn here!"

The car jolted around the corner as both men were flung around inside, Johnny just managing to keep control of the car to avoid rolling it over.

Nikki checked his fuel gauge. It was perilously close to empty. The journey had seemed an eternity, but was probably only a few minutes in duration.

The car ahead swerved suddenly and disappeared around a corner. Why are they going down there? Then he saw the police car heading from the other direction.

'Now I know they don't know the city,' he thought to himself.

His tyres squealed as he rounded the corner. He braked hard, and he was glad that he did. Not fifty feet away was the red sedan halted at a curious angle, obviously from braking too hard. They were in a dead end street. Down both sides were bricked and boarded up houses and shops which, judging by their condition, had been like that for many years. At the far end there was a high fence with a large vacant lot behind. Nikki sat frozen with panic as his bike slid and slid almost crashing into the red car.

Realising he was a sitting target he purposefully fell off his bike and as it came to a grinding scraping halt, he crawled on all fours and crouched down behind it to shield himself from possible attack. Nikki looked closely, there was no one to be seen inside the car. Just then the two men leapt from the back seat and ran around to the rear of the car.

Nikki lay there, wondering what to do, as both police cars came screaming round the corner with sirens blaring and lights flashing.

Nikki was relieved and turned to motion the policemen nearer. It was then he heard the shot and felt the searing pain. For an instant Nikki saw his blood spurting from his left leg. Feeling suddenly cold, blackness descended.

A shot was fired from behind him as the police had returned the fire. The bullet disappeared harmlessly somewhere, as both of the men had the car shielding them.

A policeman crawled from his car over to where Nikki lay. Turning Nikki over, he called back to his partner, "He's badly wounded, but alive." As he said it, one of the men from the red sedan surprisingly ran over to a boarded up door, and tried to kick it open, without success. His partner called out to him, "Don't be a fool, Johnny. It's no use, there's no escape."

The other one waved the gun in his hand, fired one shot down the street aimlessly, and leapt for the fence at the end of the street.

The policeman still at the car was radioing for 'back up', while the one at Nikki's body called out to Johnny to stop or he would shoot, but the man seemed crazed and dropped over the fence nimbly, and ran across the field.

A mighty explosion rent the air as the man was blown up into the sky. Legs and arms went sailing skyward before being lost in the cloud of smoke. The explosion was followed by another moments later. The street was enveloped in the dense pall of smoke. Pieces of wood, rocks and assorted debris showered down on Nikki's body and the policemen. Nikki saw Rode walk towards him and he pushed out an arm to touch her. She opened her mouth to say something to him but all that came out was a deafening roar. The noise roared into his ears and he cried out her name. She turned and smiled and said to him, '*Wake up darling it's time.*' Nikki awoke but instead of seeing Rode, he saw the ground a few inches in front of his eyes. As reality returned to his brain, he looked around. The motor bike was lying across his chest with bits of weeds and grass entwined in the spokes of the wheels. Coughing and choking he waited for the smoke to clear.

Moaning sounds came from behind him, but Nikki was unable to turn around.

When the smoke finally dispersed, a scene of devastation greeted him. Some of the buildings had their front walls caved in. The red sedan was a huge pile of scrap and had been moved several feet. There was no sign of the two occupants.

Nikki struggled to lift himself up, but the pain shot up his leg. Thinking he was the only one alive in the devastated street he rose carefully to his feet, using a piece of wood that had fallen close by him for support. Looking over beyond the red car, he saw that the fence and buildings that had stood there were completely gone. Turning to where the police car had been, he was relieved to see it still standing, badly damaged but still serviceable. Both policemen, although badly shaken and bruised, were alive.

Nikki struggled over to where they stood leaning on their car. "What happened? Did I black out?"

"Yes, you did," one of them said. "You missed the big explosions."

"Explosions?" said Nikki puzzled. "What explosions?"

"Land mines," the policeman said, shaking his head.

"Yes," said the other man. "This is a border street. It's full of land mines and booby traps, left by the warring factions here in Cyprus."

"Are the two who were in the car dead?"

"One is, the guy who leaped the fence. The other one, I don't know, but there is a body lying close to where you fell."

Helped by one of the policemen he asked to be taken down to find that man. They found him, barely alive, with the handlebars from Nikki's bike protruding from his side. He was covered in dust and had several beams lying across his chest. He was moaning and muttering something in a foreign tongue.

"What is he saying? What language is that?"

"Spanish," said Nikki, then realising what he had said, shouted out. "What the … ? Who is ... ?" Nikki knelt down beside the dying man and speaking in English, asked slowly and deliberately, "Who are you? Why are you trying to kill me? Did you try to kill me in Mexico? Was it you?" He started to shake the man to make him open his eyes.

The man opened his eyes, and it was then that Nikki saw the hatred behind those eyes. "Yes, Mr. Andreas—I have been trying…" He closed his eyes and seemed about to sleep. Nikki shook him again. "Who the hell ARE you? Why me?"

"My name is Miguel, or Mike."

Nikki turned to the policemen. "That means nothing."

Mike looked up at Nikki and with a fiendish smile hissed, "I am Miguel de Valaras Santiago."

Nikki's heart missed a beat. Where had he heard that name before?

The man continued. "You caused the death of my … of my brother Julio and … " He coughed, bringing blood into his mouth. "In my country a death has to be … "

"But how did you know I was here and alive?"

Mike did not answer, but it was obvious from the pain in his eyes that he was struggling to get the words out. "We have a friend … a doctor … clinic … Athens. He … called us." Once again Mike drifted into unconsciousness. Mike's eyes opened slightly and Nikki could see the blood appearing behind them. There was the sound of air escaping from the mouth and the head lolled to one side, and fell at an awkward angle.

CHAPTER TWENTY-SEVEN

Nikki was taken by ambulance to Nicosia Hospital. During the trip he could not get the words of Miguel out of his brain. 'You caused the death of my brother Julio.'

He recalled that night, when he and Rode had met. Seeing that beautiful girl with her clothes torn and in acute distress had touched a nerve. He had been brought up to respect women, and the thought that some man had lured Rode up to his room had been like a red rag to a bull.

That night, late, he had gone to Julio's room, not to harm him, but merely to scare him, hoping in some way to stop him from doing it to some other unsuspecting girl.

He had found Julio lying naked on top of his bed, playing with himself, his eyes closed. Opening a small penknife that he kept in his pocket, Nikki had scratched the hand that was playing. The blade was cold and Julio had opened his eyes and started twitching in utter fear. He was about to shout, but Nikki had put a hand over his mouth, which only made the situation worse. It was then that Julio had started wetting himself and the bed.

Nikki had been surprised at this reaction and all he could think of saying was something like: "Don't mess with women, or else."

Nikki had then left the room with Julio whimpering like a tiny baby.

The following day the news of the death had been quite a shock.

The more Nikki thought about it, the more he came to realise that if, indeed, Julio and Miguel belonged to a noble Mexican family, then the manner of his death could not be revealed publicly. There had to be a scapegoat. There had to be a vendetta.

At the hospital, having the bullet removed from his leg, he asked a nurse about the young lady who had been brought in earlier with a gunshot wound. Had she been admitted? Was she dead?

He was told that she had been, was not, and that her condition was stable. He then asked if a message could be sent to the friends of that young lady, telling them of his arrival in the hospital.

A few minutes later, a breathless Rode burst into his room and rushed over to his bedside, and sat on the bed.

"Oh, I am so sorry," she said jumping off. "I forgot about your leg. How is it?"

"Oh, it's fine, but you can sit on this side," he said, patting the bedcover.

She came around, sat down and leaned forward and kissed him on the forehead.

"I know it's been a while," he said. "But we are surely not just good friends." So saying he pulled her to him and, holding her in his arms, gave her a long lingering passionate kiss. "I've waited so long to do that," he whispered. "Every minute of every day I have thought about nothing else, except holding you once more like this. I love you Rode. Love you with all my heart."

"I love you too, Nikki. I never want you to leave me again. My world was turned upside down when I heard that you had died. I was going to return to Mexico and … "

"Will you marry me, Rode?"

"Yes, of course."

As they kissed, they did not notice the door open. Cicero stood there with a smile on his face, but saying nothing.

Nikki had travelled thousands of miles to be with this young lady. She, also, had come more than halfway across the world to find him. He knew their love for each other was strong, and would survive. At that moment, he was as happy as he had ever been. His son Nikki was in love and was loved. During the little time that he had known Rode, he knew that he could love her as well. Oh, why wasn't Kasta here to share in this glorious moment?

Cicero cleared his throat gently. The two of them turned and started laughing in embarrassment.

Rode got off the bed and straightened her clothing.

"Father, I am glad you are here. Rode … " As he said her name, he took her hand. "Rode has done me the honour of accepting my proposal of marriage." Nikki looked at his father anxiously, not sure what his reaction would be.

Cicero moved forward, stood beside Rode. Taking her hand in his, he raised it to his lips and kissed it gently. "Welcome to the Andreas family, my daughter. My son has chosen well. I am extremely happy for you both and I know that I speak also for your mother, Nikki."

Rode went to give Cicero a hug, but stopped. "May I?" she asked.

"Please do." Cicero took her in his arms. "I will leave you two alone now. I have to get back to Pierre."

Nikki asked. "How is the young lady?" He hesitated. "I'm afraid I don't know her name."

"Katie, Katie Docherty," Rode answered. "She is fine. The bullet entered her flank, here." She pointed just above her hip. "It went right through her body, but it did not touch any organs. She was very lucky indeed."

"Before I go," said Cicero, "what about those men who shot her?"

"Not now, Father," Nikki said, winking at him while nodding at Rode.

"What? … Oh yes, I see … Silly of me." Feigning embarrassment, he left the room as Nikki and Rode started giggling.

The last thing Cicero saw was Rode climbing onto the bed beside Nikki. He walked down that hospital corridor, a very happy man.

CHAPTER TWENTY-EIGHT

The late afternoon sun had mercifully cooled down as Nikki and Rode, with the cathedral bells pealing joyously, emerged outside as man and wife.

Cameras clicked and video recorders whirred as the couple stood at the top of the ornate staircase that led to the massive wooden doors of the cathedral. At their rear stood the matron of honour and best man, Katie and Pierre.

In the months leading up to this day Cicero had admitted to the Press that Nikki had not died. But believing his life to be in danger, the family had staged the mock funeral.

Kasta had insisted on having a lavish wedding at the cathedral. "To show our fellow Athenians that we are celebrating both the wedding and Nikki's return."

Asked if she had any relatives or friends she might wish to invite to the wedding, Rode had said, "No, I have no relatives, but if possible I would like my priest, Father Acquilienta, to assist at the service."

"Certainly, that will not be a problem."

Father Acquilienta had sent his best wishes but had declined the invitation.

As most of the guests could not speak English, Rode asked Nikki if they could leave the reception early. Also, they had a long flight ahead of them to the cottage in Cuernavaca, where they wished to honeymoon.

As the happy couple said their goodbyes, Rode whispered to Katie, "See you in a month, in Cyprus, for your wedding to Pierre."

They gave each other a lengthy embrace, both of them happy in the knowledge that they had found the sister both of them had yearned for.

Nikki and Rode arrived at the Hotel Krystal tired, weary, yet still full of that honeymoon excitement. This was the hotel where they had met, and Nikki had gone to great lengths to get the same room booked.

"Room 1139 please. The name is Andreas. I have a booking."

The hotel clerk checked his computer. "Sorry sir, but that room has been taken. It appears that my colleague before me must have given it out to someone else."

"How can that be?" asked Nikki. "I booked it weeks ago."

"Do not make a fuss, Nikki. We will take another room," said Rode, looking around to see if anyone was listening.

"No, I'm sorry Rode, but you know the sentimental value that room has for us."

The clerk left the counter area and went into a back room. He emerged a few minutes later with another clerk. "This is the clerk who booked your room to someone else. Perhaps he can explain why."

Nikki glared at this new person. "Go ahead then, explain."

"Our hotel is fully booked because of a conference, sir, and as you were quite a bit late getting here to confirm the booking, I gave your room out to someone else. I am so sorry, sir. However, we do have a room for you and your wife. If you would like to sign … "

"May I be of assistance?" A gentleman approached the desk.

Nikki turned and glared at this intruder.

The second hotel clerk stammered, "This is the gentleman I gave the room to."

The stranger looked at the clerk. "Is there a problem with my room?"

"Yes sir, this couple booked the room … "

"Yes," interrupted Nikki, "it has sentimental attachment for us. This is the room where we met."

"Ah, I see, honeymooners, eh?" said the stranger.

Rode blushed as Nikki said, "Yes, we are."

The stranger went over to the desk. "Let them have my room. I will take something else."

"Certainly, sir," said the clerk, thankful that this nasty situation would not get as far as the manager.

Nikki offered his hand to the stranger. "Allow me to introduce myself. My name is Niklos Andreas and this is my wife, Rode."

The stranger took the hand offered. "Congratulations, sir, your wife is very beautiful. May your life together be all that you wish. So sorry, I am forgetting my manners. My name is Felipe, Felipe de Valaras Santiago. Delighted to meet you, Mr. Andreas."

ACKNOWLEDGEMENTS

Grateful thanks to Don Barry for not only suggesting the idea, but for his valuable help.

To Greg Aldrich from Harper's Marine in Calgary for his expert knowledge and suggestions.

To Dr. Tom Lay for his help in keeping me right about the medical technicalities.

To D.A. and B.G. for their invaluable help.

To my wife Vera who keeps me on the right path to better grammar and for suffering endless readings and ideas.